THE HAUNTING OF BORDEN HOUSE

KIM POOVEY

THE HAUNTING OF BORDEN HOUSE

Dickens Ghost Publishing, LLC

Cover design by Rena Violet

Author photo by Jasmina Kimova

ISBN: 978-0-9996219-6-7

❀ Created with Vellum

To God, my rock and my redeemer

CHAPTER 1

Lizzie Borden took an ax and gave her mother forty whacks...

Three children, one boy and two girls, held hands as they moved in a circular motion chanting the century old rhyme. Sunlight filtered through their golden locks as they repeated the lines again and again. The area was unfamiliar to Sarah and she noticed the children's clothing was that of the mid-nineteenth century. Smiling, she watched as the kids turned in a circle, their tiny feet stomping the grass and a rosy glow tinting their cheeks. Then it hit her. The ax murders of Andrew and Abby Borden took place in the 1890s so why were these children dressed in mid-Victorian style?

From the corner of her eye, Sarah caught a glimpse of something moving along the edge of the property near a copse of trees. Her mind screamed for her to stay where she was, but curiosity nudged her forward. Walking towards the shadowy figure, Sarah felt her pulse quicken. By the time she reached the wooded area, the mysterious form was gone. The breeze picked up, carrying the children's chant which grew louder and louder until Sarah's ears rang like she was standing next to the speakers at a rock concert.

Her head pounded as she cupped her ears in an effort to block the thunderous sound of the chanting. Turning slowly, she noticed the three children now stood behind her, their blank stares slicing through her fortitude. The two smaller children morphed into bloated, ashen images; an expression of terror etched into their tiny faces. Panic burned Sarah's chest. She started to back away when she thumped against something. Spinning around, she screamed. A petite woman stood there, her throat slashed and blood staining the front of her bodice. Unable to move, Sarah screamed again, this time jarring herself from the dream.

Gasping for air, Sarah sat up in bed, her body trembling. These were the perils of being a dreamist, a woman who can communicate with the dead in her dreams to help them resolve the manner of their death. She took a deep breath, held it for a count of five, and released. She and Danni were set to leave for Fall River, Massachusetts in a couple of hours. Garrett, Sarah's boyfriend, had asked her to accompany his ghost hunting team to the infamous Lizzie Borden House for a one week stay.

Garrett had been an unexpected addition to her existence after a lifetime of being alone. Over the summer, Danni had been hired by one of her college buddies, Brady, to help with his cousin's trial in Edgefield. Sarah handled the estate sale to help defray legal expenses. During her time there, she met Garrett Duncan and his ghost sensing dog, Dallas. While she and Dallas hit it off immediately, it took some time for Sarah to relax around Garrett. He was a good-looking man who worked construction by day and hunted ghosts by night. An unforeseen bonus was his knowledge of dreamists. His grandmother, Ola, had been a dreamist, just like Sarah, and taught him about it should he ever have daughters with the gift. In essence, he was the perfect match.

Fortunately for Sarah, he not only accepted her strange abilities but was all too willing to help her develop them. Although Sarah had spent her life isolated because of her haunted proclivities, she now had her best friend and boyfriend to help her interpret and cultivate her unconventional skills.

Harry and Ralph were Garrett's partners in the ghost hunting endeavor. The group filmed at various haunted locations, occasionally capturing misty figures and glowing orbs on video. Months before, the team had been selected to do a paranormal investigation after entering a contest. If all went well, and they were successful in filming anything of significance, they'd be given a contract with the Ghost TV network.

Of course, Harry and Ralph were unaware of Sarah's unusual abilities to communicate with the dead through her dreams, a gift she'd inherited from her biological mother, Edie Monroe. It had been a stressful time clearing out the Monroe Manse estate over a year ago when Sarah discovered what had haunted her throughout life wasn't a mental deficiency but an actual skill passed through the females in the family line.

As Sarah's heartrate resumed a slower pace, her mind drifted back to the gruesome scene in her dreamscape. She hadn't even left for Massachusetts yet and already the ghosts were finding their way into her nocturnal visions. But the people in her dream hadn't been killed by an ax and none of them resembled Andrew and Abby Borden. So, who were they and what connection did they have with the heinous murders? Sarah's shoulders slumped as she exhaled. Something told her this endeavor wouldn't be as easy as she'd hoped.

Slipping from bed, Sarah padded across the heart pine floors to the master bathroom and flipped on the light. She stared in the mirror at the shadows eclipsing her eyes. This was usually a sign she'd tossed and turned during the night. Sarah pulled back the shower curtain and leaned over to turn the knobs when the shower scene from *Psycho* skirted through her mind. All of a sudden, a bath seemed like a much better idea.

Sarah rotated the nickel-plated knobs and watched steam rise as water gushed from the tub spigot. Plugging the drain, she added some bubble bath, and slipped into the warm embrace of sudsy water. No *Psycho* shower scenes today, she thought, resting her head against the curve of the old iron tub.

Twenty minutes later, Sarah was dressed and refreshed. Her muscles felt like melted butter as she grabbed her suitcase and started for the stairs. She jumped when her cell phone barked, the ringtone she'd programmed for Garrett. It seemed apropos since his Jack Russell, Dallas, was always at his side.

"Hey Garrett," she said, trying to sound chipper as she descended the steps. He'd gotten pretty good at picking up on her tone when she'd had a ghostly encounter.

"How are you?" His baritone voice rippled across her flesh, sending a flush to her cheeks.

"A bit tired," she replied with a yawn, plunking the suitcase on the floor in the entryway.

"Haunted dreams?"

"More like a nightmare," Sarah said, her shoulders beginning to tighten as she walked to the kitchen. Putting the phone on speaker, she filled the kettle, and set it on the stove for tea. "I was reading the book you gave me about Lizzie Borden before bed. It probably led to the bad dreams."

"Are you sure?" he asked, concern accenting his words.

"Pretty much. I took a hot bath and feel much better."

"Good. I wanted to let you know we'll be heading out soon."

"Danni and I will be leaving in an hour, if she pulls herself out of bed by then."

"How's she doing?" Garrett asked.

"As well as can be expected. I think this trip will help take her mind off of Brady."

"We're all still stunned by it. He'd always been arrogant growing up but none of us suspected he was a serial killer."

"I think that's what's bothering Danni the most. She's upset she didn't see it sooner. I keep telling her he was a charmer and there wasn't anything she could have done differently." Sarah wasn't about to let Garrett, or anyone else, know the extent of Danni and Brady's relationship. Deep down, Sarah knew the greatest struggle for her best friend was accepting she'd allowed herself to be seduced by a homicidal maniac. For someone as controlled as Danni, it was a devastating occurrence.

"True. We've known him a lifetime and didn't suspect anything. I know she's a great attorney but there's no way she could have known. Brady was good at fooling people."

"Like I said, this trip will give her a chance to get away from it all. Hopefully, she'll be so busy helping me interpret my dreams, she'll forget about Brady."

Steam erupted from the kettle as Sarah poured water over a tea bag.

"Let's hope so." Garrett paused. "Can't wait to see you."

"I can't wait to see Dallas."

Laughter erupted from the other end. "He misses you too."

"I'll text you when we leave. And Garrett…."

"Yeah?"

"I'm looking forward to seeing you too," she said.

Sarah hung up the phone, her palms sweating. Closing her eyes, she thought back to the soft brush of his lips against hers the last time they'd seen each other. She'd never had a boyfriend growing up so this was unchartered territory. In the depths of her soul, she felt a strong connection to Garrett and suspected he felt the same for her. Nevertheless, she was guarding her feelings. She'd suffered enough distress and alienation throughout her life. She needed time to adjust to her romantic inclinations before she let down the wall she'd spent a lifetime constructing.

Dealing with the dead had been complicated enough, yet the living seemed much more difficult. At least she had a handbook, despite its convoluted nature, to guide her with the haunted dreams. She'd found it in her biological mother's library when cleaning out the estate. Up until that point, Sarah had no idea her haunted dreams and ghostly visions were part of her DNA. As for love, she'd have to take her chances and hope for the best.

Sunlight streamed through tree branches as Sarah and Danni traveled along the back roads of the Lowcountry toward the highway. Fall was taking hold, tinting the leaves in orange, red, and gold. Sarah loved autumn with its colorful splendor and pumpkin flavored everything. As a child, fall was marked by the arrival of the pumpkin sale at the Methodist church on Carteret Street. Hundreds of orangey gourds filled the church yard in various shapes and sizes. She and her parents would spend an afternoon searching for the perfect one to carve. Her mother would roast the seeds, and they'd place the newly carved Jack-o-lantern on the front porch. Halloween night, a candle would sputter from within the fleshy orange walls, casting shadows across the porch stairs.

Despite her haunted dreams, Sarah actually loved Halloween with its ghoulish themes and buckets of candy. Once again, her ghostly propensities showed through in some of her fondest memories, making her realize the spirited visions of her youth were part of her identity. The latest revelation from the *Dreamist* book, with Garrett's help interpreting, was that each dreamist held a skill specific to them. Generally, they entered an occupation related to their particular ability without realizing it. In Sarah's case, it was dealing with antiques and estates. Garrett's grandmother, a fellow dreamist, had been a librarian, who was able to interpret messages from the dead using books. Tara, one of the women who had been murdered by Brady, deciphered messages through her genealogical research. Relieved to know she wasn't alone, Sarah was beginning to enjoy learning more about her abilities. However, she still had difficulty accepting her dreamist skills as a gift. Most times it felt more like a curse with all of the morbid visions.

"Explain to me again how this works?" Danni asked, speeding toward the highway.

Danni and Sarah had been best friends since high school when Danni's father was stationed at the Marine Corps air base in Beaufort. They'd survived some crazy antics in their years as friends to include protesting unnecessary development in town, pranks, and most recently, Sarah's ghostly endeavors. Danni was the bold outspoken one while Sarah was more reserved. Regardless, they were inseparable and supported each other in every way.

"Garrett and the crew will spend a week filming at Borden House. During the day, they'll research Lizzie's life to use as background for the final product. Once they finish, the footage will be submitted to the network for editing and then it will air. With any luck, the ratings will be good and they'll get picked up for more episodes."

"Sounds creepy," Danni said. "I mean, spending a week researching one of history's most notorious killers and then trying to capture it on film? I've never understood people's fascination with this particular case or its outcome. It was pretty cut and dry."

"Ugh, that was in poor taste," Sarah moaned.

Danni snorted. "Maybe so, but the facts showed Lizzie butchered her parents with an ax and got away with it."

"First of all, Lizzie was acquitted, thus innocent."

"She was found not guilty; doesn't mean she was innocent," Danni corrected.

"Aren't we skeptical. From everything I've read so far, the evidence was sketchy at best."

"Only reason she was acquitted was because she was a lovely young lady. Very few men would believe a pretty woman of social standing could commit such a heinous act," Danni said. "She probably turned on the charm and fooled every juror."

"Or she didn't do it," Sarah replied.

"Unlikely. They never arrested or suspected anyone else. In a town that small, people would have known things, especially if someone had hacked two prominent citizens to death."

"Nevertheless, I'm going to give Lizzie the benefit of the doubt and see what's revealed when we get to the house."

Danni shuddered.

"What's wrong?" Sarah asked.

"Can't believe you talked me into staying at the location of a double ax murder. Do you know if we'll be sharing a room like we did in Edgefield?"

"Afraid of a little spiritual activity?" Sarah teased.

"With you? Absolutely! Based on your track record we're likely to be dodging hatchets as we sleep."

Sarah shoved Danni's shoulder. "We'll be fine. If you're too scared, I'll ask Garrett if Dallas can stay with you. You couldn't get a better alarm."

"Just what I need. A canine emergency broadcast system alerting me to an incoming ax attack."

Sarah chuckled. Despite nursing a broken heart, her friend still maintained her satirical perspective on life.

"After last night's dream, I'd like to have his canine sensitivity to keep my wits about me," Sarah said.

"What did you dream? And why didn't you tell me about it?"

"It was so bizarre and horrific I didn't feel like discussing it."

"Now that you've brought it up, we're going to talk about it," Danni said with a sideways glance.

"It didn't make any sense. None of the people in the dream were the Bordens. There were three children and a woman. Oddly, the children were dressed in mid-nineteenth century attire but they were reciting the Lizzie Borden chant which didn't come about for another forty years. Everything started innocent enough and then two of the children's appearances shifted. They were bloated and gray like Thomas looked in my dreams in Edgefield." Sarah winced at the memory.

"So, the kids drowned?" Danni queried.

"Looked that way, except the third child didn't change at all. The woman was even worse. Her throat was slit and her bodice was covered in blood."

"Bodice?"

"The upper portion of 19th century dresses. Nevertheless, the scene had nothing to do with Lizzie Borden which makes me question the meaning behind it."

"That is strange. Maybe your next dream will explain it."

"Kinda hope I don't dream about this again. It was pretty disturbing."

"With any luck, your dreams will reveal the truth behind the Borden crimes. Wouldn't it be amazing if you were able to figure out the mystery after all these years?"

"I suppose. Even if my dreams do lead us to the killer, we'd never be able to prove it. I'm not about to go public with this. I think there's a good reason dreamists have kept this skill a secret, and I'm not about to break the tradition."

Sarah stared out the window as they sped down the highway. A shudder rankled her body and her hair stood on end when she noticed a hitchhiker up ahead. As they drew closer, Sarah sucked in a breath. The man's face was shattered, blood oozing from the wounds, and his right leg was bent unnaturally to the left. At the moment they passed him, his hand smacked against Sarah's passenger side window causing her to jump. The words, *didn't want to die* resonated in her brain.

"You alright?" Danni asked.

"Not really," Sarah muttered, rubbing her upper arms as the

handprint evaporated from the glass. "Thought I saw something."

"In that case, keep it to yourself. I'd rather avoid any otherworldly prequels to the creepy stuff we're going to encounter in Fall River."

CHAPTER 2

After two days of travel with an overnight stay at a questionable hotel, Danni and Sarah were relieved to cross the border of Fall River, home of Lizzie Borden. Fall River was an hour south of Boston and a mere eighteen miles from Providence, Rhode Island. The town was the epitome of a Hallmark movie, a northeastern community with old timey brick store fronts, church spires, and autumn hued trees. The scenery was almost cliché. Sarah half expected to see a tall, gorgeous man in a flannel shirt embracing a dark-haired beauty amidst Christmas trees and snow laden sidewalks.

They followed the GPS through town to a two-story sage green house trimmed in black. A chill rankled Sarah's frame as she gazed at the famous structure, making her question her willingness to engage in this endeavor.

Sarah's phone barked. "Hey Garrett," she answered, excitement tinting her words.

"Where are you guys?"

"Parked in front of the Borden House. Where are you?"

"We stopped at the television station to meet with the executives for the project. We'll be there in about an hour," he said as Dallas yipped in the background.

"Sounds good," Sarah replied. "Give Dallas a kiss for me."

"I'll let you do that when you see him," Garrett chuckled.

They disconnected and Sarah looked at Danni. She was trying not to flaunt her burgeoning relationship with Garrett. The last thing she wanted to do was make Danni uncomfortable after the disastrous end to her fling with Brady.

"What did lover-boy have to say?" Danni asked.

Sarah shifted in her seat. "Garrett said they'd be here in about an hour."

Danni's expression altered. "You don't have to shield me from your relationship. I'm happy about you and Garrett."

Classic Danni. She could read Sarah like a book. Grasping her hand, Sarah smiled.

"Thank you. The last thing I want to do is make you uncomfortable."

Danni sat up straighter.

"Don't you dare hide your happiness on account of my foolishness. You've endured a lot in your life and foregone things most people take for granted, including having a boyfriend. No one deserves this more than you."

"Thanks, Danni." Sarah's eyes misted. Even though she and Danni were close, they generally didn't venture into the sappy, sentimental stuff.

"Any good restaurants around here?" Danni asked. "I'm famished."

And just like that, the Danni Sarah knew and loved was back.

AFTER EATING LUNCH AT MONKS, a nearby restaurant, Sarah and Danni returned to Borden House to check in. The site of the gruesome murders was now a B&B, popular with those who enjoyed haunted places. As they parked in the back, Sarah's heart skipped when she saw Garrett's truck. The guys were here.

Sarah and Danni grabbed their bags from the trunk of the Mercedes and headed along the side of the house to the front door. Stepping inside, Sarah drew in a breath as she scanned the space with its period Victorian décor. The childhood chant, *Lizzie Borden took an ax and gave her mother forty whacks*, circulated through her mind, sending a shiver skittering down her neck and across her shoulders. Although the home was beautiful, there was something eerily suffocating about the atmosphere. Sarah jumped when Danni grasped her shoulder.

"This place gives me the creeps. How about I stay at a hotel in town and meet up with you for meals?" Danni said, arching her eyebrows.

"Don't be silly," Sarah huffed. "You're staying here."

With a heavy sigh, Danni wrinkled her nose. "Sounds like we might need to make a trip to the grocery store. I'm gonna need several cloves of garlic if you expect me to sleep in this place."

Sarah shook her head and smiled. "Let's get checked in. We'll string garlic later."

The innkeeper appeared with a broad smile and sparkling eyes. Her gray hair was swept into a bun and she wore black pants and a crisp white shirt. Her appearance was professional yet welcoming.

"Good afternoon, I'm Mrs. Pearson and I'll be taking care of you during your stay. The men are in the kitchen sorting through equipment. Do you need to join them or would you rather unpack first?"

"Unpack," Sarah said.

"Follow me and I'll show you to your rooms."

"We have our own quarters?" Danni asked, seemingly pleased she had a room to herself.

"I can put you in the same one if you'd like, but you'd have to share a bed."

"No," they chimed in unison.

"Separate quarters will be fine," Sarah said with a sideways glance at her friend.

They followed the innkeeper up the narrow staircase to the second-floor landing, an open area resembling a small informal parlor. Velvet covered chairs filled the space along with two small tables and a camel back trunk.

Mrs. Pearson showed them through a door that opened to adjoining rooms.

"These rooms belonged to Lizzie and her older sister, Emma."

"I definitely don't want Lizzie's room," Danni blurted.

"Then you'll have Emma's quarters right through here. It's a bit smaller but cozy," she said, walking through Lizzie's room and opening the door to a tiny space with a burled walnut dresser and double bed.

"I have to go through Sarah's room to get out?"

"It is an odd layout, but the owners of the house wanted to keep everything as authentic as possible," Mrs. Pearson said with a proud smile. "There aren't any hallways on this floor, only the central area at the top of the staircase. All the rooms interconnect with doors, although Mr. and Mrs. Borden's room can also be accessed by a staircase at the back of the house."

"Wonderful," Danni replied, plastering a smile on her face as she headed to her room to unpack. Sarah could tell her friend was uncomfortable with the sleeping arrangements. However, it was a relief to know Danni would be close in case she needed her. The Borden House's haunted reputation was inducing a bit of anxiety in Sarah.

"Is your friend alright?" Mrs. Pearson asked.

"She's just tired from the trip," Sarah replied. "Do you stay on the premises?"

"No, dear. I have a cottage a few blocks away. Not to worry, if there are any issues, I can be here in less than five minutes."

Mrs. Pearson proceeded to share instructions about breakfast the next morning and then left Sarah to unpack.

Plopping her bags on the bed, Sarah walked across the room and peered out one of the two windows, wondering how things had looked when the Bordens lived here. She gazed at the yellow house next door. Something about it was discomforting. A flash of heat warmed her neck as the word, *cursed* echoed in her ear. At the same moment, she noticed a flicker of movement near the back corner of the neighboring home.

Swallowing the fear lodged in her throat, Sarah closed the blinds and scanned the room she'd be staying in for the next week. A lovely maple bed was centered on the wall with a matching marble topped dresser across from it. Built in shelves to the right of the bed housed books and bits of Lizzie Borden memorabilia.

Sarah gasped when a swirling mist wavered near the doorway. Seconds later, it vanished. She'd not been here an hour and already the ghosts were closing in on her. Her pulse quickened at the thought of sleeping alone even though Danni would be in the next room. Maybe Garrett would let Dallas stay with her since Danni slept like the dead and would likely slumber through any spectral activity.

Unpacking her clothes, Sarah set her *Dreamist* book on the bed. While in Edgefield, she'd learned she needed to bring it with her when traveling since ghostly encounters were probable no matter where she went. Exhausted from days of travel, Sarah longed to take a nap but thought better of it. No sense entering into haunted escapades any sooner than need be. Hopefully, her dreams would help the guys with their quest to gain the attention of network executives and land a contract for a ghost hunting series. While Sarah was excited about their opportunity, the idea of Garrett having to relocate was disconcerting.

The long-distance relationship they were already navigating was difficult and that was only three hours. What would happen if he had to move farther away? She couldn't bear the thought of leaving her home but finding another match as cohesive as theirs was unlikely.

Moments later, Danni came back into the room interrupting Sarah's ruminations.

"You unpacked yet?" she asked.

"Pretty much. And you?"

"Everything's put away."

Danni looked around. "This room is nice, even if it did belong to an ax wielding murderer. I like the wallpaper."

"She was acquitted," Sarah said, cocking her head. "It is a lovely room, although I don't think I'll get much sleep."

"You're already seeing ghosts?" Danni asked, her brows arching.

"Not so much seeing them. I heard the word cursed and caught a glimpse of something."

"Like what?"

"A misty form near the door a few minutes ago."

"I did not need to know that," Danni whined. "How did I let you talk me into this?"

Sarah laughed at her friend's reaction. Even after a year and a half of helping Sarah with her haunted dreams, Danni was still freaked out by the idea of ghosts.

"Don't worry. Your room should be free from specters. The Bordens were murdered in other rooms and Emma was out of town in Fairhaven when it happened. I doubt she's an active spirit in the house."

"Not helping," Danni retorted. "Ghosts can move throughout a house, right?"

"True, but I doubt they'd pay you a visit," Sarah said, trying to soothe her friend's nerves.

"I wouldn't count on that," Mrs. Pearson called from the staircase landing making Sarah and Danni jump.

"Sorry, didn't mean to interrupt," she said, holding a stack of towels as she peeked in Sarah's door. "Many of our guests have reported sightings in all the rooms at various times of the day and night."

"Great," Danni mumbled.

"However, your ghost hunting crew will probably want to set up cameras in the most active rooms."

"Which ones are those?" Danni asked, her eyes wide.

"The guest room where Mrs. Borden was found, the sitting room downstairs where Mr. Borden was killed, the master bedroom attached to this one, and the third-floor rooms. The one directly above us is haunted by children."

"Children?" Sarah asked.

"Many believe it's the ghosts of the children who were murdered next door."

"Ghosts from another house haunt this one?" Danni's voice raised an octave.

"The property where this home now sits belonged to the family next door forty years ago when the murder-suicide took place."

"Murder-suicide?" Sarah asked, her nerves prickling.

"It's a tragic story. The woman who lived in that yellow house killed two of her children and then committed suicide."

"Great, wayfaring ghosts," Danni grumbled.

"I assure you the children's ghosts are harmless and generally stay in the third-floor room. A toy box has been placed up there to occupy them."

Sarah gently gripped her friend's arm. "You'll be fine," she whispered, even though her own heart was racing. Surely, these weren't the same specters from her dream. Couldn't be, she reassured herself, since there'd been three children in her dreamscape.

"I'll leave you two alone. Here are some towels. The bathroom is the door between this suite and the guest room," Mrs. Pearson said.

"Is that the only one on this floor?" Danni queried.

"The master suite has a private bath," she replied with a smile. "Let me know if you need anything else."

"Thank you," they responded as the innkeeper descended the stairs.

"Sounds like this place is ripe for ghost hunting. The guys are gonna go nuts with all the spectral activity, especially with your insight to guide them," Danni said once they were certain Mrs. Pearson was out of earshot.

"Let's hope," Sarah said. "Considering the house's reputation, they're bound to capture something on film."

"With your skillset, there's a good chance they'll discover more than a few shadowy figures. They're likely to learn the truth behind the deaths that have baffled this town for more than a century."

Danni was right. The only problem would be proving anything revealed in her dreams without exposing her special abilities, not to mention deciphering which ghosts were haunting the place. It seemed this endeavor was getting more complicated by the minute.

"I need to check my email," Danni said, returning to her room.

Unsure what to do, Sarah decided to see what the men were up to. Unbeknownst to her, a shadowy hand grabbed at her neck as she left the room.

CHAPTER 3

Sarah made her way downstairs where she found Garrett, Harry, and Ralph setting up equipment. Dallas ran to Sarah as she entered the main parlor of the house, resting his paws on her leg as he let out a spirited *yap*. Reaching down, she patted his head.

Sarah hadn't seen Garrett in two weeks although it felt more like two months. His gaze met hers making her heart skip like a stone over water. The whole dating thing was still new to her. Should she give him a hug? A kiss? She wasn't sure what the protocol was when others were around.

"How'd it go at the studio?" Sarah asked. Ugh, that's the best you can do? she thought as her cheeks warmed.

"It was intense. There's a lot we have to do to prove our abilities as well as providing an entertaining episode."

The curve of his jawline and the stray auburn lock brushing his forehead stilled her breath. If Ralph and Harry hadn't been there, she would've wrapped her arms around him and kissed him in a way he'd not soon forget. The longing in his eyes conveyed similar thoughts on his part. As it was, they had an audience and would have to steal away later.

"The studio loaned us some pretty amazing equipment," Ralph announced, his eyes glinting with excitement as he fiddled with a camera. "This is the kind of stuff that can capture a speck of dust on film."

"With our secret weapon for ghost detecting, I have full confidence we'll get everything we need," Harry said, with a nod in her direction.

Sarah's heart skipped. Surely, Garrett hadn't shared anything about her abilities.

"Secret weapon?" Sarah queried, bracing for the response.

"Dallas, our ghost sensing dog," he replied.

Sarah released the breath stuck in her chest. Dallas stared up at her with his soulful brown eyes as if to say, *I'm going to make these guys stars.*

At least with Dallas at her side, she'd have a warning signal if anything supernatural materialized. Sarah had discovered the Jack Russell had a keen sense for the spiritual world, often growling or barking when a ghost was nearby. Of course, others only suspected the dog possessed these skills but Sarah knew them to be true since she could see the specters he barked at.

Even though Ralph and Harry were unaware of her dreamist abilities, they had noticed her proclivity for seeing the dead. On several occasions, while she was in Edgefield over the summer, Sarah had seen some of the more notable ghosts in town to include half-headed Howard and the dueling cannoneers. Only Garrett and Danni knew the extent of her true abilities.

"The network is in favor of Dallas being a part of the show?" Sarah asked.

"She loved the idea," Ralph said. "Not many of the ghost hunting crews have a canine sidekick with skills."

"She?" Sarah asked, arching her brows.

"Valerie," Ralph replied with a sly smile.

"Me thinks, he's in love," Harry snickered.

"Oh my," Sarah said. "What has she done to capture your heart?"

"She breathes," Ralph sighed.

Sarah glanced at Harry and Garrett, puzzlement scrunching her forehead.

"Let's just say she's gorgeous," Harry added.

"You'll meet her when she comes by," Ralph said, starry-eyed.

"I look forward to it," Sarah replied, scratching Dallas's head. Maybe this wouldn't be as scary as she thought. The fervor radiating from the men was contagious, making Sarah feel more confident in her ability to withstand any haunted encounters.

Garrett caught Sarah's gaze with a sideways nod, indicating he needed to speak with her.

"Be right back," she said, following Garrett from the room.

He grasped her hand and led her up the stairs to the second-floor landing. Once they were away from the others, Garrett pulled Sarah close, kissing her lightly on the lips.

"Been waiting two weeks to do that," he smiled.

"I know you guys are going to be busy but maybe we can sneak away for a little alone time," she replied. "Two weeks was entirely too long."

Their lips met once again, this time lingering a bit longer. Taking a step back, he brushed a strand of hair from her cheek.

"Sure you're OK with all this?" he asked. "You know I'll help any way I can."

"I know," she answered. "This place is scary but I'll manage. By the way, would it be possible for me to have some company tonight?"

Garrett's eyebrows quirked. "Company?"

"I was thinking maybe Dallas could stay with me."

"Of course," Garrett stuttered. "He'd probably like that."

"Thanks."

Sarah grinned. She enjoyed toying with Garrett like this. Their little flirtations were fun with Dallas at the center of it.

"Where are you staying?" she asked.

"I'm in Mr. and Mrs. Borden's room."

"Next to mine, according to what Mrs. Pearson said."

"If you're in Lizzie's room, then yes," he said, waggling his brows. "That could be convenient."

"Stop it," she replied, shoving his arm. "Danni's in the connecting room to mine. The floorplan of this place is bizarre. I've never seen a second-floor layout where all the rooms interconnect without hallways. Definitely had to put a damper on the Borden's privacy."

"Maybe that's what drove Lizzie to kill her parents. She needed her own space," he chuckled."

Sarah rolled her eyes. "Where are Ralph and Harry staying?"

"Third floor rooms."

"I'm surprised no one is sleeping in the second-floor guest room where Abby Borden was murdered."

"We need to do a lot of filming in there so it was easier to leave it vacant for this job," Garrett said, kissing Sarah once more. "I need to take Dallas out and finish helping with the equipment."

"Do you need my help?"

"Not yet. You should probably get some rest. It's probably going to be a busy few days."

"I'll be back down in a little while," she replied, watching him descend the stairs with Dallas on his heels.

Popping into her room, Sarah took in the floral wallcoverings, polished antique furniture, and carpeted floors. From what she'd seen on the website, most everything in the house was period correct even though most of the original pieces were gone. The piano in the front parlor had belonged to the Bordens, and the settee in the sitting room where Mr. Borden was murdered was an exact replica of the original. Sarah shivered. It was a horrific crime that had haunted and intrigued Americans for generations.

By all accounts, the murders seemed pretty straightforward. Abby Borden had been cleaning the upstairs guest room when someone attacked her from behind with an ax. Several whacks later, she lay prostrate on the floor in a pool of blood. More than an hour later, Andrew Borden returned home, reclined on the sitting room settee, and was butchered in the same manner while he napped. Reportedly, Lizzie and Bridget were on the property at the time of both murders yet didn't hear or see anything, making their presence suspect. It was this bizarre twist that fueled much of the speculation surrounding the crime. The improbable nature of two women being in the home during vicious attacks that occurred an hour apart had led people to believe the worst. After Sarah's recent exposure to Brady's killing spree in Edgefield and beyond, she'd learned even the strangest of circumstances were plausible when it came to murder mysteries.

Cars drove by on the street below, splashing shimmers of light across the walls. Sarah glanced in the mirror when something shifted behind her, sending her heart racing. Closing her eyes, she took in a deep breath, held it for a count of five, and released. Something told her, she'd be using this technique a lot over the next few days. When she looked in the mirror again, nothing was there. Probably just a shadow, she thought. A rap on the door broke through Sarah's ruminations.

"Come in," she called.

Harry peeked his head inside. "There's a ghost tour starting downstairs in thirty minutes. Wanna come?"

"A ghost tour of the house?" Sarah asked.

"Yup. This place has its own staff of tour guides."

"I assume you guys are going?"

"Heck yeah. We want to learn everything we can about the hot spots in this place. Hopefully, it will help us capture some good stuff on film."

"Count me in," Sarah smiled. "Are you going to ask Danni?"

"Getting ready to go there next," he replied.

"I'll go with you," Sarah offered. "She might need some nudging."

They walked to the adjoining door and knocked. Danni appeared; her dollar store spectacles perched on her nose.

"What's going on? Don't tell me the ghosts have already started up," Danni said, scrunching her forehead.

"Not yet," Harry snickered. "Would you like to take a ghost tour of the house with us?"

"Don't think so," she replied. "I've been reading one of the books about this place. I'm going to need a pound of garlic and a wooden stake before I go to sleep tonight."

"Wooden stakes are for vampires," Sarah huffed. "Blood wasn't sucked here, it was spilled."

"Then what do I need to ward off ax murderers?"

"There aren't any ax murderers in this house, just the ghost of one, or so we've been told for a hundred years," Harry said.

"Not helping," Danni replied.

"You don't have to go with us," Sarah added.

"Us? You're going?"

"Yup. But I wouldn't worry about being up here by yourself. I'm sure you'll be safe from any shadowy figures, strange noises, or things that scurry about in tight spaces."

"You're mean," Danni grumbled, glaring at her friend. "What time does it start and where do we meet?"

Harry looked at his watch. "Half an hour in the foyer."

"I'll be there," she said, closing her door.

Thirty minutes later, they gathered in the entryway of Borden House for a ghost tour. Everyone seemed eager except for Danni whose sullen demeanor stood out like a brightly colored dress at a funeral.

The tour guide, Cynthia, was clad in a high collared frilly blouse and long black skirt with her hair piled on her head in an 1890s coiffure. With a broad smile, she started her dramatic rendition of the events of August 4, 1892. Luckily, the entire house had been reserved for the week of filming so they were getting a private tour, including areas of the home not usually open to the general public.

As a child, Sarah had sung the Lizzie Borden song about forty whacks with an ax but never imagined she'd be staying at the actual house or sleeping in Lizzie's room. Two years ago, she wouldn't have even considered doing something like this with her spirit-filled dreams and periodic daytime glimpses of the undead. But now, touring a haunted house where two people were brutally murdered wasn't as intimidating. She attributed her newfound confidence to her best friend and Garrett. With their help, she was beginning to embrace her special skillset.

Dallas stayed with Sarah while Danni trailed behind. Watching Danni's expressions was almost as entertaining as the tour. She scanned each room as they made their way through the house as if she expected a monster to jump from under a chair or out from a closet.

Cynthia explained the purpose of each room and how the family would have lived in it during the 1890s. Sarah's skin began to crawl upon entering the sitting room where a camelback settee was nestled against the wall.

"This is where Mr. Borden's body was found," Cynthia explained in a dramatic tone. "He'd reclined on the settee for an afternoon nap having no idea what awaited him. Of course, this isn't the actual settee but it is an exact replica."

Cynthia went on to describe the violent nature of the attack and the condition of the body when it was discovered. Sarah rolled her shoulders as unease bumped across her skin and the hair at the nape of her neck bristled. A low grumble emanated from Dallas, letting her know this wasn't a mental reaction to the story but something ethereal. Taking in a deep breath, Sarah looked about the room. Dallas's growl grew louder until his lips curled into a snarl. Garrett's gaze met Sarah's. Something was here.

Out of the corner of her eye, Sarah noticed a dark mist forming in the doorway where Dallas was looking.

"Is he OK?" Cynthia asked.

"Sorry, sometimes he gets a little excited in new places. He's probably reacting to the scent of another dog."

"We normally don't allow pets at Borden House," she said, furrowing her brows. "The owners made an exception this time at the network's request."

As if concerned the owners might change their minds, Garrett scooped up his dog. Dallas struggled against him but eventually quieted.

Great, Sarah thought. Her alarm system had been disarmed. She swallowed the trepidation clogging her throat. She was on her own now. Looking around, Sarah was relieved when nothing materialized and the tour guide led them to the dining room.

Garrett stayed back with Sarah as Ralph, Harry, and Danni walked ahead of them with the tour guide.

"What's going on?" he whispered in Sarah's ear.

"Don't know. I sensed something at the same time Dallas started growling. Caught a glimpse of a dark mist in the doorway but nothing manifested."

"Looks like that'll be an active room," he replied as they rejoined the others.

The dining room was cozy with a large table, six chairs, and a china cabinet at the far end of the room.

"This is where the initial autopsies were performed," Cynthia said, sweeping her hand through the air like a game show hostess.

Danni's eyes widened as her jaw dropped. "On the dining room table?"

Cynthia chuckled. "No, they used an autopsy board," she

replied, walking across the room. Pointing to a folding table with a wooden frame and open caned surface, Cynthia continued. "This is a replica of what would have been used at the time."

"Looks like a morbid massage table," Danni groaned, her upper lip curling into a sneer. "Why did they autopsy them in here?"

"It was only a partial autopsy to determine if any poison was present in their systems."

"Seriously?" Danni griped. "They couldn't tell what the cause of death was by the missing parts of their skulls?"

"There was speculation about poisoning based upon a purchase Lizzie had made the day before the murders." Cynthia smiled as she opened the china cabinet door and pointed at two skulls with chunks missing from the craniums. "These are copies of the Borden's skulls to show where the hatchet made contact."

"And just when you thought it couldn't get any creepier," Danni groaned.

"Most people believe the murders were committed with an ax but it was actually a hatchet," Cynthia said enthusiastically. Despite the homicidal basis of the tour, Cynthia seemed to enjoy sharing facts about the home's macabre history.

"What's the difference?" Ralph asked.

"Hatchets are smaller," Cynthia replied, before continuing with her script. "The items on the other shelves also relate to the day's events."

Swallowing hard, Sarah glanced at the collection of crime scene photos, autopsy implements, and a few apothecary jars. Unease slithered down her spine as a vision of a postmortem body splayed on the autopsy table flashed across her mind. Sarah inhaled slowly and released in an effort to settle her nerves. The last thing she wanted to do was appear squeamish in front of the group.

"Makes for a lovely dinner conversation," Danni scoffed.

Sarah elbowed her friend and gave her a stern look before whispering in her ear. "Cut it out. Let the woman talk."

"What? I'm just pointing out the obvious," Danni shrugged.

"Like anything would hinder your appetite."

"Couple of corpses and a bloody ax would do the trick."

"Hatchet," Sarah retorted.

Cynthia grinned and led them to the kitchen.

"A great deal happened in the kitchen three days after the murders. Lizzie burned one of her dresses in the wood stove claiming it was worn out and had paint on it. The prosecution argued it was probably stained with blood and Lizzie was destroying evidence," Cynthia said, pointing at the stove. "However, witnesses upheld Lizzie's story about paint splatter adding reasonable doubt to the prosecutor's claims."

From the kitchen they made their way to the basement.

"The alleged murder weapon was found hidden in this area. A hatchet with a broken handle was discovered with a hair on it.

Danni gave Sarah a sly look as if to say, *Lizzie did this.*

Cynthia continued. "The police believed the hair on the hatchet might have belonged to Andrew or Abby, so locks of hair were taken from their bodies for comparison."

"I assume by the outcome of the trial it wasn't a match," Danni said sarcastically.

"You're correct," Cynthia replied. "The hair on the hatchet turned out to be animal not human."

Once Cynthia finished the stories about the basement, they climbed the stairs to the second floor to tour the bedrooms. The spare bedroom was the first stop.

"Mrs. Borden's body was found face down between the bed and the dresser. The time between her death and Mr. Borden's is one of the most mysterious aspects of the case. She was reportedly killed between 9:00 and 10:00 a.m. that morning while Lizzie was in her room and Bridget was washing windows downstairs. Mr. Borden was murdered around 11:00. The likelihood of someone outside of the house killing one and then returning later to kill the other was extremely unlikely. This led prosecutors to surmise the murderer had to have been someone in the residence. This included Lizzie and the housekeeper, Bridget. Of course, this is one of the most active rooms in the house for spectral activity."

Cynthia escorted them to Lizzie's room and from there to Emma's bed chambers with dialogue about how Emma was out of town when the murders occurred and her stalwart support of her sister's innocence.

"Believe it or not, there's very little activity in these two rooms."

Leading them into Mr. and Mrs. Borden's suite, Cynthia stood on the far side of the room near the door to the back staircase.

"Mr. Borden was known to be a frugal man who made his fortune through strict business practices. It was these practices that led many in town to dislike him. As you can see, most of the second-floor rooms are connected by doors; however, when the Bordens lived here, the door adjoining Lizzie's room would have been bolted for privacy. Many guests report a great deal of spectral activity in this room, especially those who handle the pennies on the bureau," she said, pointing at a few coins scattered across the top of the dresser.

"What's the purpose of the coins?" Garrett asked.

"To keep Mr. Borden content. Some guests have been brazen enough to swipe one only to find themselves physically ill until the pennies were returned."

"Sounds like Mr. Borden doesn't like thieves in his residence," Danni chuckled.

"He was tight with his money when alive and continues to be after death," Cynthia said with a simper.

From there they made their way to the third floor where

Bridget's room abutted a small chamber. Both rooms were modestly decorated much as it would have been during the time period since servants were not generally allotted extravagant quarters.

In the cramped room next to the housekeeper's where Ralph would be staying, was a double bed, a small rocker, and a toy chest.

"Is this a play room?" Harry asked, puzzlement masking his expression. "I don't recall any record of small children at this residence."

Cynthia grinned. "The toy chest is to appease the children who haunt this room."

"Whose children are they?" Ralph queried.

"It's suspected they're the two little ones who were drowned in the house next door."

Sarah swallowed hard. The two children in her dream were bloated and dripping wet. Could they be the same ones? And why would she dream about them? She knew nothing about their deaths.

Danni shuddered as she glanced around. "Are they active?" she asked.

"Harmless is more like it. Several guests have heard them giggling at night, but nothing more."

Sarah's skin tingled as they followed Cynthia from the room. Glancing over her shoulder, she noticed a flash of something near the curtains at the same time the small rocker swayed ever so slightly. Rubbing her upper arms, Sarah forced herself to ignore it. The last thing she needed to do was expose her discomfort and stir up suspicions about the depth of her ghost skills. Whoever was haunting the third floor would make itself known soon enough.

Feeling overwhelmed, Sarah contemplated the potential ghosts she might encounter. There were the two children from next door, Abby and Andrew Borden, and probably

Lizzie. Five spirits in one place. This was going to be a long week.

Once the tour was over, Garrett and the guys began discussing the logistics of setting up cameras and recording devices. They decided to start filming at nine o'clock, giving plenty of time for darkness to take hold.

Sarah would stay with Garrett. Danni decided to lock herself in her room. She was willing to walk about the house in the daylight, but after dark was off limits. Sarah managed to find a clove of garlic in the kitchen and left it on Danni's night table.

At six o'clock the group went to dinner at Riverside Grill. They garnered a great deal of attention at the restaurant since most people in town had heard about the filming. Although ghost hunters were a common occurrence in Fall River, the idea of a television network backing their efforts seemed even more appealing to the locals. If it increased the number of tourists while providing an entertaining series for viewers, it was a win-win situation for everyone involved.

Over dinner, the group discussed the ghost tour and how to incorporate the information into their filming.

"With any luck, we'll get enough footage to please the producers and make a spellbinding and informative segment," Ralph said, taking a swig of his beer. "Walter is on stand-by to help with editing. Even if we don't capture anything clearly, he's got some new software that filters out static and sharpens fuzzy images."

"I'm thinking we need at least two cameras in the room where Abby was killed, two in the sitting room, and one in the room connected to Bridget's on the third floor," Harry added.

"Let's add one in Mr. and Mrs. Borden's room. We might capture something based on what the tour guide mentioned about the coins," Garrett said.

"Agreed," Harry replied.

After dinner, they returned to the house. Sarah and Danni

stayed with Dallas in the front parlor while the men set up equipment.

"Are you ready for this?" Danni asked.

"As ready as I can be. I only hope I'm an asset and not a hindrance. Last thing I want to do is mess up their chances."

"I don't think you'll mess up anything. If nothing else, your presence will stir up the spirits."

Sarah shuddered. "As long as they're unarmed, I can handle it."

Voices echoed from the back of the house as the sound of a door closing shook the floor. Moments later, Garrett escorted a shapely woman into the room. Her eyes were the deep blue of fake contact lenses and her hair was the glimmering shade of boxed blond. Bright red lipstick made her full lips look like a blow fish. Basically, she resembled an overdone Barbie doll, her body-hugging dress stopping several inches above her knees as she tottered on four-inch heels. Despite the apparent need for attention, and the extreme lengths she'd obviously gone through to achieve it, she was a fairly attractive woman by modern-day standards. This had to be the woman Ralph had spoken of earlier.

"This is Valerie Jenkins, producer of *Haunted History and Homes*," Garrett said. "Valerie, this is Sarah Holden and Danni Cook. They're helping us with the filming."

Sarah's heart plummeted. She was *helping with the filming*? What happened to being his girlfriend? A broad smile spread across Valerie's lips revealing perfectly white teeth.

"Nice to meet you ladies. I look forward to seeing what the men are able to capture on tape." Turning her gaze toward Garrett, she beamed. "Garrett, why don't you show me where *you'll* be filming."

With a grin, he motioned for her to follow as he climbed the stairs.

Sarah's heart felt like it was being crushed in a vice. "What was that?" she muttered.

"A seriously insecure woman who's got very little of her original body left," Danni snorted.

Tears stung the back of Sarah's eyes, threatening to fall. Valerie was the type to turn any man's head. Even worse, she resembled some of the pretty blonds Sarah had met in Edgefield whom Garrett had dated before they got together.

"I was talking about the introductions. Why didn't he introduce me as his girlfriend?"

"He was probably trying to look professional. These guys are hoping to land a network contract. Bringing the girlfriend and her best friend along sounds a bit lame."

Sarah sighed. "You're right. I'm probably overreacting."

"Exactly," Danni replied. "You two are in an exclusive relationship and I don't think Garrett would violate that."

Sara's breath caught. "I'm assuming we're in an exclusive relationship. We've never actually discussed it."

Danni quirked a brow. "You've never talked about *not* dating other people?"

"Didn't know I was supposed to. Everything has been going so well, it never occurred to me we could see other people."

Danni squeezed Sarah's shoulder. "I'm sure he feels the same way. He's a great guy and I can tell he cares about you."

"Cared enough to introduce me as a helper," Sarah grumbled.

Footfalls on the staircase alerted Sarah of their return. Valerie was giggling at something Garrett had said, her hand resting on his upper arm as she cocked her head coquettishly.

Rage pulsed through Sarah's limbs. How could this woman be so brazen? For all she knew, he could be married or engaged. As they walked past, Garrett gave Sarah a quick glimpse, his emerald gaze melting her resolve. She was being silly. Their relationship was strong. Like Danni said, he was probably being professional in his dealings with the network executives.

Relieved when Garrett returned without the boxed blond, Sarah stood. "Need help with anything?" she asked.

"Nope," he replied. "You ready?"

"Ready as I can be." Sarah glanced at Danni. "Are you going to your room?"

"Think I'll sit here for a bit," she replied, apprehension in her eyes.

Sarah and Dallas followed Garrett upstairs, her gut doing somersaults. The relationship thing was still new to her. She'd isolated herself from boyfriends until she met Garrett. They'd dated over the summer and she'd felt secure, until now. With little experience, she wasn't sure if this was typical behavior or something she should be concerned about. She was probably feeling insecure with all the ghost stuff, at least that's what she told herself. Regardless, she needed to maintain her focus and not get caught up in dating drama.

Darkness shrouded the house in a blanket of dread. Both murder sites were heavily equipped with cameras. Garrett manned the cameras in the guest room while Harry covered the ones in the sitting room. Danni changed her mind about staying alone in her quarters, instead sitting in the kitchen with Ralph. They'd designated that room as headquarters since all of the monitoring equipment was located there. Thankfully, Valerie had to leave for a meeting.

Sarah lingered in the guest room with Garrett and Dallas. No matter how hard she tried, she couldn't shake the apprehension filtering through her veins. Whether her discomfort was legitimate because of nearby entities or the idea of what had occurred in the house, remained to be seen. Knowing Valerie would be part of this endeavor wasn't helping. Why couldn't the network have assigned a crotchety old man to the team? Either way, Sarah's muscles were as tight as a noose and her nerves as sharp as an ax blade.

Every creak and groan of the old house set Sarah on edge. Although perfectly quiet, Dallas seemed to be on high alert too, his back stiff and his eyes darting about the space. The energy in the room was electric, making Sarah's skin prickle and her heart race. In spite of the spirit charged atmosphere, Sarah's thoughts continued to drift back to Valerie and her flirtatious nature. Sitting for long periods without conversation left too much time for her mind to wander. She needed to let it go, yet it stuck in her head like a bur under a saddle.

Sarah startled when the cell phone in her back pocket buzzed. She let it go to voice mail. Probably her parents. A wave of longing crashed over her. Whether it was the stress of her current situation or wanting reassurance about her relationship with Garrett, she suddenly missed her mom and dad. Normally, they were galivanting around the globe. However, her mother needed dental surgery, grounding them in Beaufort for a while. Even if she did want to talk to them, she couldn't discuss anything about hauntings since her mother didn't believe in such things.

After three hours, her back was beginning to ache. She reached to the floor and touched her toes, stretching her lower spine when something brushed against her hand. Shooting upright, Sarah bit her lower lip to prevent a scream from materializing. Probably just a bug. Dallas continued to stare at the doorway while Garrett watched the camera. Even in the dark, he was handsome, she thought.

Another hour passed without so much as a murmur or flash of light when Ralph's voice echoed from the walkie talkie.

"Ready to call it a night? Nothing's showing up and my eyes are beginning to blur."

Garrett exhaled. "Yeah, let's turn in."

"I'm with you guys," Harry's voice crackled over the speaker.

Relieved the evening's attempts at capturing ghosts had come to a close, Sarah yawned. Garrett flipped on the overhead light and checked the camera.

"Sorry you didn't get anything," she said, resting her hand on his shoulder.

"It happens sometimes," he shrugged. "It's only the first night. We still have a week left to get something."

The disappointment accenting his words tugged at her heart. Sarah squeezed his hand and smiled. "I'm sure you'll have better luck tomorrow."

She knew how much this opportunity meant to him and the guys. Yet as important as it was to him, she was equally thankful nothing had shown up. However, Sarah knew she'd not be so lucky in her dreams.

CHAPTER 4

*A*fter the camera batteries were placed on chargers and the other equipment put away, everyone gathered in the front parlor.

Danni plunked onto the settee near the window and leaned her head against the plush velvet back. "Don't know about you guys, but I'm tired. Waiting for no-show ghosts takes a lot out of you."

"That's the truth," Ralph said with a yawn. "My eyes are still blurry from staring at the monitors."

"Who would have thought sitting around could be so draining?" Danni added. "Almost makes me want to take up exercise."

"Careful what you wish for. I'll be glad to take you for an early run," Sarah said.

Danni squinted. "Don't even think about it. There are axes in this house and I'm not afraid to tell the ghosts to use them."

"Don't you mean hatchets?" Sarah replied.

Laughter erupted, alleviating some of the tension in the room. Everyone was exhausted from the disappointment of a ghost free night.

"Don't know about you all, but I can't hold my eyes open any longer. I'm going to bed," Danni said, standing.

"I'm with her," Ralph declared, trudging to the doorway.

"Me too," Harry added, following suit.

"Goodnight," Garrett and Sarah called out.

Sarah slumped back in the chair and sighed.

"Forgive me for saying this, but there's a small part of me that's relieved nothing happened tonight."

"I know this is hard on you. I really appreciate your coming along. Even though nothing happened this evening, I suspect your dreams will reveal something. We can always adjust our filming depending upon anything you discover."

Sarah rubbed her eyes. "That's what I'm afraid of. Something tells me I'm not going to get much sleep while I'm here."

Garrett reached over and grasped her hand. "Dallas will be with you."

With a half-smile, she stood. "Then I better get to bed. My legs feel like lead weights."

Garrett got up and took Sarah in his arms. "If things get too intense, you can text me and I'll be right there."

"Pfft," Sarah chortled. "The things you'll do to get into my room."

Garrett gave her a sly look. "You know what I meant."

"Too bad you can't film me while I sleep. Chances are, something would show up."

"Now who's being brazen?" Garrett's eyes twinkled. "Then again...."

"What?"

"Why not set up one of the cameras in your room?"

"Are you serious?"

"Yes. We know you'll probably dream about something. Maybe we can capture the spectral activity on tape."

"I suppose it wouldn't do any harm," she replied hesitantly.

"Unless you're shy about being filmed in your sleep."

"It doesn't matter to me. Might be interesting to see what things look like when I'm dreaming about ghosts," she said. "What if you do capture something? How do we explain it to Harry and Ralph?"

"I could tell them you saw something in your room and we wanted to record anything otherworldly that might show up."

"Nothing about my being a dreamist?" she asked.

"That's your secret. Only you have a right to disclose that," he said.

She kissed him gently on the lips. "You're a good man."

He deepened the kiss, leaving her knees quavering.

"I'll grab one of the cameras and meet you in your room."

Twenty minutes later, Garrett had the camera positioned in the far corner, pointed at the bed. Sarah sat on the edge of the bed with Dallas at her side as Garrett made the final adjustments.

"You OK with just Dallas? I can stay if you want," he offered.

Sarah's eyebrows arched. "That would be a difficult thing to explain in the morning if anyone saw you leaving."

His cheeks colored. "I only wanted to make you comfortable. The spirits in this house are probably intense. Besides, with the crazy layout of this place no one would see anything. All I have to do is walk through the adjoining door," he said, pointing at it.

His attempts at explaining away his offer warmed Sarah's heart. They were taking their time getting to know each other and had agreed to go slowly. This was unchartered territory for her. Her reclusive ways due to her unusual ghost sensing abilities had prevented her from indulging in the typical life experiences, including relationships. Thankfully, Garrett was not only understanding of her circumstances, but patient as well. Despite her original trepidation, she was adjusting to the aspects of dating. Garrett was easy to be around and always made her feel comfortable, even when spectral activity was prevalent.

"Everything is running. If anything shows up, the camera should capture it."

"Good to know," she said, cuddling the dog. "Thanks for letting Dallas stay with me."

"Any time. Text if you need anything, or just knock."

"I will," Sarah replied.

Garrett leaned over and kissed her before leaving the room.

"Well Dallas, looks like it's just me and you, unless any spirits decide to join us."

He let out a spirited *yip* before curling up on the pillow.

Sarah went to the bathroom, changed into her night clothes, brushed her teeth, and washed her face. After her evening ablutions were complete, she slipped beneath the covers, feeling a bit subconscious about a camera recording her while she slept. She switched off the lamp, patted Dallas on the head, and closed her eyes. Taking several deep breaths, Sarah tried to settle her overactive mind. In the quietude of night, every little noise and creak seemed amplified. As she lay there, her mind skittered about, pondering if she'd have any spectral activity in her dreams and if so, would it be from the victims or Lizzie Borden herself? Only sleep would tell.

LIZZIE CLOSED HER BEDROOM DOOR, turning the knob slowly so the latch didn't make a noise. The last thing she wanted was to let anyone know where she was. Leaning against the door, she licked her lips as her heart thudded and perspiration moistened her brow. She couldn't stand the thought of him any longer. He was a horrid man and she wanted him gone forever. If she had her way, she'd be rid of him. As it was, there was little she could do, unless....

Lizzie stepped away from the door, her light brown hair falling in strands about her porcelain face and her grayish eyes deepening to the shade of her blue dress. That's when Sarah noticed something spotting the edge of her skirt. Was that blood at the hemline? Lizzie turned to Sarah, her eyes blazing as she mouthed *not as it seems* before vanishing. Seconds later, a black swirling mist formed near the door.

Terror compressed Sarah's chest at the same time the fetid taste of iron saturated her tongue. There was something ominous about this apparition, making her want to sprint from the room. Despite her need to flee, Sarah's legs remained cemented to the spot where she stood. The mysterious fog moved toward her, spinning like a nightmarish cyclone before shooting straight through her, a wicked laugh echoing in her ears as it evaporated. At that moment, Sarah's lungs filled with air and her limbs quivered. What just happened?

Relieved the dark entity was gone, Sarah glanced around the dreamscape. Oddly, this dream was different than the ones she'd had prior to coming here. The spirits seeking her assistance generally appeared in a grisly manner until their mystery was solved. Lizzie hadn't been in a state of decay. In fact, Lizzie was nowhere to be seen. She'd appeared and then disappeared, leading Sarah to question who she'd be helping to move on. The Borden House was purportedly haunted by several ghosts, including Mr. and Mrs. Borden, Lizzie, Bridget the house-keeper, and possibly the children from next door. So far, she'd only witnessed Lizzie in her room, the dark mist, and the family from the neighboring house. Would Abby and Andrew be making an appearance and if so, would they be like the macabre images Sarah had glimpsed from the crime scene photos? Or was the dark mist one of them?

A low rumble vibrated against Sarah's arm, shaking her from the dream. Dallas was growling. Her eyes darted around the darkened space, taking in the unfamiliar surroundings. As her mind's fog dissipated, she remembered she was in Lizzie Borden's room. A clicking sound emanated from the far corner. Dallas's eyes were fixed on the camera, his lips curled in a snarl.

The hair on Sarah's arms stood on end as her breath caught. Staring, she braced herself for something gruesome to materialize. The only other sounds were Dallas and the ticking of the mantel clock keeping time with the beating of Sarah's heart.

Without warning, the overhead light flashed several times, a moaning sound accompanying each burst. How could the light flash when it was turned off? Gulping down the fear rising in her throat, Sarah swung her legs over the edge of the bed and padded toward the camera, her eyes scanning the room for any signs of movement.

Fear squeezed her chest. From the corner of her eye, she saw something move. Shifting her gaze, she exhaled when she realized it was only her silhouette reflecting in the dresser mirror. Dallas stopped growling. Whatever had been in the room was gone now. Sarah's shoulders slumped. Both relieved and disappointed, she climbed back into bed, rested her head on the pillow, patted her canine companion, and returned to dreamland where a host of entities waiting to reveal the secrets to a hundred-year-old murder mystery dwelled.

MORNING PEEKED THROUGH THE CURTAINS, tickling Sarah's eyelids. Dawn's light was a welcome relief after a surprisingly mild night of dreams. Daytime was generally a more comfortable atmosphere for Sarah, even with the haunted visions that plagued her waking hours. Somehow, the ghosts weren't as frightening in the light of day. Sarah hopped from bed and walked to the dresser as Dallas stirred with a full body stretch and an eager expression as if to say, *I'm well rested and ready for a busy day ahead, but first a visit outside for my morning constitution.*

A soft knock startled Sarah. Dallas leapt from the bed; his nose trained to the bottom of the door.

"Come in," she called.

Garrett entered. Dressed in a black t-shirt with the emblem

of a ghost on the front, he was every bit as handsome in jeans as he was when donning 1930s attire for their dance excursions to Fitzgerald's, a Jazz Age themed club in Edgefield.

"Good morning," she said, as Dallas scooted out of the room and stood at the top of the stairs, waiting for Garrett to take him outside.

"How'd you sleep?" he asked, anticipation glimmering in his eyes. Obviously, he was hoping something of significance had shown up in her dreams.

"Actually, I slept rather soundly," Sarah chuckled, pulling a shirt and jeans from the top drawer. "Might need to keep Dallas with me from now on."

"Any good dreams?" he asked.

"Bizarre, but nothing of significance."

Dallas let out an ear-shattering bark that echoed from the stairwell.

"We can talk about it later," he said, planting a kiss on her cheek. "Better get him outside. I'll check the camera after breakfast."

"See you in the dining room."

Once Garrett and Dallas were out of sight, Sarah grabbed her clothes and headed for the bathroom. After a hot shower, she slid her hair into a ponytail and dressed in jeans and a neon pink t-shirt with the phrase, "I'm haunted! What's your excuse?" printed in black. Danni's idea of a little joke. Nevertheless, she thought it would be fun to wear on this trip. For the first time in her introverted existence, Sarah was beginning to relax a bit. It was kind of nice being with people who considered the idea of seeing spirits amusing instead of freakish.

As she was putting her night clothes away, Danni emerged from her suite.

"Good morning," Sarah chirped.

"Mornin'," Danni grumbled.

Surprisingly, her friend was already dressed which was quite a feat for Danni at this early hour. The only time Sarah knew Danni to be up before noon was when she'd been researching the case in Edgefield or she had to be in court. Sarah had touted this trip as a mini getaway for Danni. No doubt, Danni would expect that to include sleeping late.

"I'm surprised to see you up this early," Sarah said.

"Me too," she replied with a scowl. "I smelled coffee and figured I better get some before everyone drinks it all."

"Let's get you a cup and wipe that grimace off your face," Sarah said, draping her arm around Danni's shoulders.

As they started down the stairs, Danni noticed Sarah's shirt.

"Hey, you're wearing the t-shirt I gave you. Didn't think you'd wear it in public," she said, her eyes brightening.

"Thought it was apropos for this excursion."

The sound of voices resonated from the dining room where Garrett, Harry, and Ralph sat around a long table sipping coffee. Dallas ran from Garrett's side, plunking at Sarah's feet as she sat down. Danni walked over to the sideboard and poured a cup of coffee from the carafe as Mrs. Pearson placed a small teapot and mug on the table in front of Sarah.

Sarah grasped the teapot, tipping it over the cup. As the steam swirled, an image of Andrew Borden's body formed. His dismembered visage turned slowly toward her, droplets of blood falling from his faded lips to the tablecloth as he mouthed, *not what you think.*

"Will you want sugar with that?" Mrs. Pearson asked, jolting Sarah from her trance.

"No thanks," Sarah replied as she set the pot back on the table and buried her trembling hands in her lap. Inhaling deeply, she closed her eyes and let the scent of tea leaves wash over her. Nothing was more soothing than that first cup of tea in the morning. If only the tea leaves could scrub the memory of Mr. Borden's butchered face from her mind.

Danni sat beside her, drinking her coffee in blissful oblivion.

Sarah did her best to hide her distress. If her friend knew ghosts were recreating autopsy scenes during breakfast, she'd run from the house and never return. At this hour of the morning, Sarah also knew better than to engage Danni in conversation until she'd finished at least two cups of java. Danni's brain ran on caffeine and without it she was an irritable curmudgeon.

The innkeeper returned with plates of eggs, bacon, pancakes, and fruit. Once everyone was served, they started discussing the lack of footage from the night before as well as plans to do some filming during the day. Sarah honed her gaze on the men sitting around the table hoping to avoid any further visions, her appetite suppressed by Mr. Borden's appearance.

"Supposedly, the spectral activity during the day is as prevalent as it is at night," Harry said, taking a bite of his eggs. "We might have to do some daytime filming if we don't get anything substantial after dark."

"Is there anything Danni and I can do to help?" Sarah offered.

"Actually, we could use your research skills. Any possibility you could go to the library and the museum? We have most of the commonly known history but could use something more in-depth," Ralph said.

"We can do that," Sarah replied before Danni could refuse.

When the breakfast dishes were cleared, Harry stood in a stretch. "We've got a long day, and night, ahead of us. Better get to work."

Harry and Ralph walked into the kitchen to boot up the computers. Sarah and Garrett headed to the hallway while Danni poured another cup of coffee.

"Let me know if you find anything on the camera in my room," Sarah whispered, gazing up at Garrett.

"I will. You okay doing research?"

"It's a much safer choice than staying in a house with a hatchet wielding ghost," she chuckled.

Garrett leaned down, planting a kiss on Sarah's lips. She returned the kiss, lingering for a moment as she took in his scent of lavender and sandalwood when Danni walked up.

"Oops, sorry," she mumbled, turning back to the dining room.

Garrett straightened, his cheeks coloring slightly. "Stay," he said. "I've got to help the guys."

With a wink, he started from the room when his cell phone rang.

"Hey Valerie," he said, his voice fading as he walked away.

At the sound of Valerie's name, Sarah tensed. Get a grip, she thought. As the network executive, Valerie would be interacting with the men for the next few days. There was nothing to worry about.

"Didn't mean to break up your little tryst." Danni grinned. "I'd tell you to get a hotel room but we're standing in a B&B which is a bit more romantic, even if it is the scene of one of the most notorious murders in the country."

"I'm sorry, Danni. We should be more careful," Sarah replied as she started up the stairs, her shoulders knotted knowing Garrett was on the phone with Valerie.

Danni grabbed her arm and stopped her. "I've already told you once, don't apologize for having someone in your life!"

"Sorry, I forgot," Sarah said.

An hour later, Sarah and Danni were at the library researching newspaper records from August 4, 1892 through the end of the trial when Lizzie was acquitted. Danni made use of her technological prowess while Sarah searched periodicals the old-fashioned way. Although she'd gotten fairly proficient with her cell phone, Sarah still struggled with anything that had chips, megabytes, or hard drives. In a library, the Dewey decimal system was as technological as she got.

After copying several articles and making notations for additional resources, Sarah found Danni at the computer.

"Find anything useful?" Sarah asked, leaning over Danni's shoulder.

"Actually, yes. It seems Maplecroft, the house Lizzie moved to after the trial, is also quite haunted. It's only a mile from where we're staying. Wanna check it out?"

"Is it open to the public?"

"Private residence. Maybe one of the show's producers could get us access," Danni suggested.

"Let me text Garrett and see if he can make the arrangements."

Sarah sent a quick text. Moments later, her phone dinged.

"He'll check into it when he gets back to the house. I wonder where he is?"

"Ask him. Maybe he'll want to join us for lunch," Danni offered.

"You're already thinking about lunch?"

Danni arched her brows. "How long have you known me?"

"Good point."

Sarah sent another message to Garrett. His response was instantaneous, wiping the enthusiasm from her face.

"What's the matter?" Danni asked.

"He can't join us. He's having lunch with Valerie."

"Poor Ralph. That'll break his heart. I think he's in love with her."

Sarah exhaled. "The guys are probably going with Garrett. After all, they are a team."

"Then Ralph will be a nervous wreck and probably blather on like a teenager."

"True," Sarah replied. "What should we do next?"

"Check out the museum."

"Sounds like a plan."

They drove less than a mile to a stunning architectural gem

that housed the Fall River Historical Society. The stone façade of a French Second Empire mansion loomed before them, its arched windows and delicate ironwork making Sarah's heart flutter.

"Wow, this place is pretty grand for a museum," Danni said, stepping from the car.

"It's stunning," Sarah muttered, taking in every detail of the magnificent old structure.

They walked along the manicured landscape past a wrought iron gazebo when a slight breeze ruffled Sarah's hair. She smiled when she noticed a lovely young woman in a bustle gown standing by the front door. Her hair was swept into a period correct chignon and she held a lacey parasol above her head.

"I love it when museum staff dress the part," Sarah said to Danni.

"Huh?"

"The woman by the front door," Sarah pointed, but no one was there. "She must have gone back inside."

Danni stopped and stared at Sarah. "I don't know what you're talking about. Nobody was there."

Gulping down the lump forming in her throat, Sarah grimaced. "Looks like this is going to be an interesting visit."

"Maybe so, but I'd appreciate it if you kept your translucent friends to yourself. I don't mind hearing about your escapades with Mr. Dreamy, but you can keep the ghostly encounters secret."

"Agreed," Sarah replied as they stepped into the museum.

The interior took Sarah's breath away. Original architectural details, period furnishings, and exquisite decor made the place one of the most beautiful Sarah had visited. Despite the stunning surroundings, she felt as if several spirits were crowding around her, making it difficult to catch her breath.

An older woman in a plain black skirt and simple button-down shirt approached them.

"Welcome to the Fall River Historical Society. I'm Millie. How can I help you today?"

Her twinkling blue eyes and warm smile put Sarah at ease.

"We need to do some research on Lizzie Borden. We're here with —"

"The ghost hunters filming at the Borden House," she said, finishing Sarah's sentence.

"You know about that?"

"Everyone does," she smiled. "This is a tightknit community."

"Sounds like our town," Danni snorted.

"Where are you from?"

"Beaufort, South Carolina," Danni and Sarah said in unison.

"I hear it's a lovely place."

"It is," Sarah replied, joy filling her chest at the thought of home.

"What exactly are you looking for?" Millie asked.

"Information regarding the trial and any notable facts about the Borden family."

"We have a room dedicated to Lizzie," she said, leading them down the hall. "The archives in the basement house everything about her life including trial transcripts."

Danni and Sarah followed Millie into a room filled with an array of Lizzie Borden memorabilia. Photos of Lizzie in her youth along with images of her older years covered the walls. Mementos and personal items cluttered glass cases. Danni spoke with Millie while Sarah scanned all of the displays. Without warning, the air cooled as an icy breath whispered, *not what you think.*

CHAPTER 5

Sarah and Danni walked around the room studying artifacts and reading the snippets beneath each photo.

"Check this out," Sarah said, pointing to one of the display cases.

Danni walked over and scowled. "Is that hair?"

"Yup. It's locks of Andrew and Abby's hair as well as a microscope slide with the hair found on the hatchet recovered from the basement of Borden House."

"This is seriously creepy," Danni said. "Think I'd rather peruse court documents."

Sarah chuckled. Danni's squeamish nature about the physical evidence of a murder was laughable, especially since she was a trial lawyer. Granted, she'd never defended anyone who'd committed such a gruesome murder, although Brady's case came close.

Once they finished looking through the Lizzie Borden room, they descended the stairs to the basement. The archives room was well lit with a couple of small desks and chairs snuggled amongst numerous metal file cabinets.

They poured through files about Borden House, Fall River,

and the murder trial of Lizzie Borden. Much to her surprise, Sarah found documents alluding to other local grisly events long before the hatchet murders of Andrew and Abby Borden.

"Listen to this," Sarah said. "Sixty years prior to the Borden murders, a Fall River resident, Sarah Cornell, was found hanging in a haystack yard. At first, it was believed to be a suicide but further investigation led authorities to believe it was murder. An autopsy showed the young, unmarried woman was four months pregnant. On December 20th, she'd left a note stating *'If I should go missing, inquire of the Reverend Mr. Avery of Bristol. He will know where I am.'*

"Things got worse for the Methodist minister when Miss Cornell's doctor disclosed she'd named Mr. Avery as the father of her child. He was charged with her murder but eventually, went free after the defense attorney sullied Sarah Cornell's reputation. The judge in the case was also a Methodist, purportedly helping ensure the acquittal in an effort to avoid further shame for the church."

"Wow, that's pretty scandalous. Can't believe the world hasn't heard about that," Danni said as Sarah continued reading.

"Another shocking crime occurred several years prior to the Borden's deaths on the property adjacent to their home," Sarah muttered, her mouth going dry. "This article is about the murder-suicide that happened next door to the Borden House."

"The one the tour guide mentioned with the kids haunting the third-floor room?"

"Looks like it," Sarah replied. Skimming the document, Sarah read about the 1848 tragedy where a mother tossed her two younger children into the cistern in the cellar of her house before slipping behind the chimney and slitting her throat with a straight razor.

Closing her eyes, Sarah tried to calm the roiling of her stomach as images of the deceased children with their mother filtered through her mind.

"Are you OK?" Danni asked, touching Sarah's arm. "You look pale."

"I knew we'd eventually hear the story about the woman and her children next to Borden House, but I wasn't expecting it to be so…gory."

"What happened?" Danni asked.

"It's pretty bad," Sarah replied, relaying the horrid tale. "These are the ghosts from my dreams."

"You're freaking me out," Danni declared, her face drawn. "Are you suggesting these spirits have been actively seeking your help?"

"Apparently so. But what do they have to do with the Borden's deaths? This murder-suicide happened forty-four years before Andrew and Abby Borden were killed."

Danni shrugged her shoulders and shook her head. Sarah read a few more lines and drew in a sharp breath.

"What?" Danni asked, leaning in.

"The woman's name was Eliza Darling Borden, the second wife of Lizzie Borden's great-uncle."

Danni threw her hands in the air. "This is getting crazier by the minute. What the heck is going on with this family?"

"The article states Eliza gave birth to three children close together. She drowned the two younger children, sparing her oldest daughter, before killing herself. At the time she was deemed insane; however, many today believe her actions were the result of post-partum depression."

"I suppose it's possible, although it's a stretch," Danni replied. "Everyone wants to give a reason for bad behavior. Maybe the woman was just a lunatic."

"You're so cynical," Sarah declared, rubbing the back of her neck. Her spine felt like a tension rod ready to pop at any moment. She'd witnessed some frightful images in her dreams connected to some monstrous events, but nothing this bizarre.

"It's hard to believe there have been so many horrific crimes in this town. It seems so quaint and picturesque."

"I need a break," Danni grumbled, running her hands across her face. "My eyes are blurring and my stomach is screaming for something to eat."

"I could use a break too."

"Let's ask Millie for lunch recommendations," Danni said, rising from the chair.

After speaking with Millie, Sarah and Danni decided on the Tipsy Tailor for lunch. Housed in an old brick building where a tailor's shop had been located a hundred years prior, the place was dripping with period atmosphere. The original sign from the tailor's shop hung on one of the exposed brick walls above an antique piano. Across the room was a massive brick hearth illuminated by a chandelier constructed of antlers.

A young woman with dark hair and deep brown eyes escorted them to a table and gave them menus.

"Hi, I'm Holly. I'll be your server today. What can I get you ladies to drink?" she asked, her smile dimpling rosy cheeks.

"Coke," Danni replied.

"Same," Sarah said.

"I'll be right back with your drinks," she grinned, scooting to the kitchen.

The menu was filled with everything from heavy appetizers to gourmet pizzas to burgers.

Moments later, Holly placed drinks on the table and took their orders. Danni decided on the hot honey chicken sandwich with fries while Sarah chose the burger with cheddar cheese on a brioche bun. Once the waitress was gone, they discussed their discoveries at the museum.

"I'm still trying to process all of the savage murders in this town," Danni said, sipping her soda.

"It's the stuff nightmares are made of and I don't look

forward to them," Sarah replied. She took a long sip of her drink and slumped back in the chair.

"What's wrong, aside from being haunted by a half dozen ghosts at once?"

"What if I'm not able to make sense of the Borden murders with all of these spirits clamoring for my help? I don't want to let the men down. This is so important to them."

"You mean *him*."

"Well, mostly him," Sarah blushed. "But I care about Harry and Ralph too. Since Garrett is the only one who knows about my ability to connect with spirits, he's counting on my help."

"Don't let it bother you. Anything you do will be an asset but ultimately, it's their ability to capture ghosts on film and their chemistry with each other that will land a contract with the network."

Holly slid two plates on the table.

"Let me know if you need anything else," she offered before hurrying off. Apparently, this was a popular place as tables were filling up quickly. Danni and Sarah continued their discussion while eating every bite of their meals. Once the dishes were cleared from the table and the bill was paid, they headed for the door when Sarah's hair bristled.

Glancing over her shoulder, she inhaled sharply. A slender gentleman in a tattered white cotton shirt, striped pants, and silk waistcoat stood by the table they'd just left. His eyes were sunken and his pallor a pasty gray. He held a large pair of scissors in his skeletal hand with a tape measure draped about his neck. With a shudder, Sarah scooted out the door into the cool autumn air, releasing the breath she'd been holding. The last thing she needed was to pick up another ghost. There were enough specters in this town to keep her busy for a while.

When they arrived at Borden House, Sarah and Danni found Garrett sitting in the dining room. He was perusing a notebook filled with newspaper clippings about the Borden murders and Lizzie's trial. Looking up, he smiled as they entered the room.

"Where are Harry and Ralph?" Sarah asked.

"Filming in the shed out back," he replied. His emerald gaze locked onto Sarah's, causing her stomach to flop. "Any luck at the library or the museum?"

"If stumbling across several other horrendous murders in the town's history counts, then yes, we were successful," Sarah replied, sitting in the chair next to him.

Dallas rambled over, plopped at her feet, and stared up at her. She reached down and scratched behind his silky ears.

"How about you? Any ghostly sightings?" Sarah asked.

"Sadly, no. I can't believe we haven't caught anything on camera yet. Not even the one from your room last night. This place is purported to be crawling with ghosts."

"Give it time. The house is bound to give up its specters and their secrets," Sarah said. "How did the lunch meeting go?"

"Pretty well," he replied.

"How did Ralph do?" she asked.

"Ralph wasn't there. It was only me and Valerie."

"Oh. I assumed...." Sarah said, shifting in her chair away from him.

Garrett reached over and grasped her hand. "For some reason Valerie seems to view me as the leader of the group. Besides, it gave Ralph and Harry time to set up the cameras out back and get some footage. I hope they capture something significant. This is a once in a lifetime opportunity and we don't want to blow it. Valerie is a bit intense about our deadline."

"You'll be successful," Sarah replied, her gut twisting. Something about Valerie wasn't sitting right with her. Despite her unease, Sarah plastered a smile on her face. "I'm sure there's plenty of ghostly activity around here to fill a dozen television slots."

"On that note, I'm going to my room," Danni said, walking to the doorway. "I might place an order with the local grocery store for a bushel of garlic. Think they'll deliver for one item?"

"Don't think it's going to help," Sarah called after her friend. "Besides, I left a clove on your nightstand."

"One won't be enough in this place," Danni smirked as she walked away.

"Does she realize garlic is for vampires?" Garrett asked.

"Wouldn't matter," Sarah chuckled. "She's looking for ways to ward off her fears. If garlic is the answer, then so be it."

Garrett leaned toward Sarah, his lips meeting hers. "Finally, some alone time," he said, kissing her again.

Sarah pulled back, a yawn escaping her lips. "Sorry, I'm a bit sleepy after lunch."

"You know how to make a guy feel good," he chuckled.

"It's not you," she replied, brushing her hand against his cheek. "It's all these ghosts."

"Fill me in," he said.

Sarah shared everything they'd learned at the museum and the connections to her dreams. "I feel like a revolving door for whatever entity is in closest proximity. It's stressing me out and definitely interfering with any decent sleep."

"Maybe you should take a nap," Garrett suggested, running his thumb across her knuckles.

"Actually, a nap sounds good except for the haunted part."

"Take Dallas with you," Garrett said.

"Thanks."

She kissed him once more before trudging up the stairs with Dallas at her heels. Her legs felt like cement blocks. Once in the room, Sarah closed the door, kicked off her shoes, and rubbed her eyes. Dallas hopped up beside her and curled into a little ball, his big brown eyes giving her a 'come hither' stare.

Resting her head on the pillow, she ruminated on the information they'd gathered at the museum. There was so much to consider, especially since she'd already dreamed about Eliza

Darling Borden and her children. That case seemed pretty open and shut so why were they appearing in Sarah's sleep? If Eliza was able to infiltrate her dreams, would Sarah Cornell be able to do the same? Perhaps this would be a haunting of past victims in the township instead of just the house.

And what about Andrew and Abby Borden? If she did dream about the person who killed them, would it matter? It's not as if she could prove anything. Sarah rolled over and closed her eyes. Dallas's comforting presence was helpful. Her muscles relaxed as her consciousness succumbed to sleep.

ANDREW BORDEN WALKED through the front door of his home, hung his hat on the hall tree, and made his way to the sitting room. Lowering himself onto the settee, he leaned his head against the upholstered arm, closed his eyes, and drifted off.

The words, *not what you think,* echoed through the room when the shimmering blade of a hatchet descended on the sleeping man's head. Blood splatter sprayed as the weapon landed blow after blow. Sarah tried desperately to hone in on the person wielding the hatchet but the scene was too ghastly causing her to shield her eyes. The only thing she could make out was the outline of a medium sized form.

When the sound of blade meeting bone ceased, Sarah lowered her hand from her eyes and looked around. Repulsed by Andrew's butchered head and face, she looked away, swallowing the bile creeping up her throat. Sadly, she hadn't noticed what direction the murderer had escaped. Logic dictated the person had left through the back door of the sitting room and not the front. She scanned the floor for footprints but the busy pattern of the carpeting revealed nothing. Sarah hurried from the lurid scene to the kitchen.

A sizable woodburning stove anchored the space along with shelves of cooking utensils and a large porcelain sink on the opposite wall. According to reports, Lizzie and Bridget had been in their rooms when Andrew's murder occurred. Surely, they would have heard the footsteps of the killer or a door slam at his, or her, departure. Concentrating, Sarah tried to recall what she'd observed. Was the shadowy figure wearing a dress? She couldn't remember.

A scream echoed through the house as the phrase *not what you think* tickled Sarah's ear. Running toward the sound, Sarah re-entered the sitting room. Her gaze rested on a young Lizzie Borden who stood over Andrew Borden's mutilated body. Horror distorted her expression as she watched blood and brain matter ooze from her father's skull.

Gasping, Sarah sat up in bed, her breath coming in short puffs and her limbs quivering. Watching the murders in a television movie was one thing, but seeing them firsthand was disconcerting. Instantly, Dallas was at Sarah's side, licking her cheek.

The graphic nature of the dream left Sarah feeling nauseated. These were only visions of the past, she told herself, pulling her knees to her chest. The idea she'd just witnessed the murder without seeing who committed it was frustrating.

Sliding from bed, Sarah padded across the room and rapped on Danni's door.

"Come in!"

Sarah entered. Danni sat on the bed wearing EarPods while reading through one of the many books about the Lizzie Borden trial.

"OK if I join you?"

"Of course," Danni replied, pulling the EarPods out and placing the book on the bed. "Have any good dreams?"

"Had a dream but I wouldn't call it good," she said, plunking on the bed next to her friend. Dallas hopped up beside her, resting his head on his paws.

"Sounds like you dreamed about something important. Let's hear it."

"I dreamt about Andrew Borden returning home and reclining on the settee in the sitting room. He fell asleep and then I saw the hatchet splitting his head." Sarah shivered at the memory.

"Eww," Danni glowered. "Don't suppose you happened to see who was wielding the murder weapon?"

"Unfortunately, no."

"So, the identity of the killer remains a mystery," Danni said, shrugging her shoulders. "Maybe you need to take a nap in the same room where he was killed. As we've learned, location can play a significant role in what you dream."

"Do you really believe I'll be able to dream about who actually killed Andrew and Abby Borden by staying in the rooms where they were butchered?"

"Hard to say. In the past, your dreams revealed a century old murder and the victims of a serial killer. The information came more clearly when you slept in the same location the murders took place. I'd say the odds are in your favor of a likely identification of the hatchet wielding psychopath if you slept where the bodies were found."

"I know you're right, yet somehow I was hoping to avoid it." Sarah blew out a breath. "Maybe if I studied the trial in more depth, I could get an inside clue as to whether Lizzie did it or not. That would be easier than having to relive two ax murders."

"Hatchet," Danni said with a crooked smile.

"Very funny," Sarah replied, rolling her eyes.

"If you're so nervous about this, why did you agree to come here?"

"Seriously? You have to ask that question?"

"Got it, Mr. Dreamy." Shaking her head, Danni stood. "Looks like you're in for some creepy nightmares all in the name of love."

"Why can't I be like other women and just seduce a man with my charm? Lucky me, I get to catch a guy with my ability to commune with the dead."

"Ha! That's a good one." Danni walked to the door. "Come on, let's give you a break from your ghoulish dreamscapes and see what Garrett and the guys are doing."

CHAPTER 6

$\mathcal{D}$anni and Sarah found the men downstairs staring at a laptop.

"What are you looking at?" Sarah asked, peering over their shoulders.

"Going through last night's footage hoping to find something," Ralph sighed. "This is aggravating."

"It's only been one night," Sarah said, trying to be optimistic.

"Normally that wouldn't be such a big deal," Harry replied, the right side of his mouth wrinkling. "But we only have five nights to capture spectral activity."

"And we don't want to let Valerie down," Ralph added, his eyes gleaming like a lovesick schoolboy.

Poor Ralph, Sarah thought. He had it bad. She only hoped he'd recover from the heartbreak which was inevitable. Valerie had only shown a professional interest in him and no doubt, wouldn't reciprocate his feelings.

"What about the shed out back? Anything show up there?" she asked.

"Nada," Harry sighed.

Sarah rested her hand on Garrett's shoulder. He glanced at

her expectantly, obviously hoping she had something to share from her nap. She gave a slight nod.

"I'm going to take Dallas out," he said, walking toward the back door with his dog on his heels. Sarah followed them outside as Dallas scampered about the yard sniffing around. When she was certain they were alone, she spoke in a hushed tone, rubbing her arms in the nippy air.

"I had a dream although I can't say it was significant."

Gazing down at her, his eyes glimmered as he wrapped his arm around her and pulled her close. The warmth of his body filtered through hers, melting the chill from her skin. "Tell me what happened. There might be more to it than you realize."

"All I saw was Andrew Borden reclining on the settee and the hatchet slamming into his head. The person brandishing it was a shadow but appeared to be of medium build. I went to the kitchen thinking that was the most logical escape route but no one was there. Then I heard a scream and found Lizzie standing over her father's body. Her expression was one of horror, not of a person who had just butchered someone. I also heard the phrase *not what you think* but didn't see who said it."

With his free hand, Garrett smoothed his beard as he stared at the ground.

"How would you feel about sleeping on the settee in the sitting room tonight?"

Sarah gulped. "Danni suggested the same thing."

"Perhaps the ghost is trying to lead you to an area in the house where he or she is better able to communicate. Can't hurt to try."

"Says the man who doesn't have to sleep at a bloody murder scene and interact with the dead."

"I'll leave Dallas with you," he said, squeezing her shoulder. His confidence in her abilities mixed with the warmth of his body against hers gave her the courage to face the upcoming horror scenes.

"How are you going to explain this to Harry and Ralph? Won't they be suspicious of me sleeping in the sitting room while cameras are running?"

"Good point," he replied, hesitating. "I've got an idea. There's a technique where someone sits in the room with the cameras. We've had some luck catching ghostly images that way. Kinda like a moth drawn to a light."

"You're saying I'd be the light drawing the ghosts to me."

"Trust me, they won't question it."

"I suppose it's worth a try," she mumbled, looking at the row of houses peeking over the six-foot privacy fence behind the inn.

Garrett kissed the top of her head. "I know this isn't easy and I'd completely understand if you'd rather not do it."

Sarah gazed into his pleading stare. "I can't say I'm excited about it but I want to help you with this project. The worst thing I'm facing is some exceptionally gory visions. Can't be any worse than the *Halloween* movies."

Garrett's eyebrows arched. "You actually watched those?"

"Not exactly. I hid my eyes through most of them."

With a laugh, Garrett hugged her tightly. "I appreciate what you're doing for us."

Looking up, she planted a kiss on his lips. "Glad to hear it because you're going to owe me."

Dallas ran over to them and flopped on his back. Sarah leaned over and scratched his mottled belly.

"Looks like you and I are going to be bunking together again," Sarah said.

Dallas leapt to his feet and let out a loud bark.

Hand in hand, Garrett and Sarah walked across the yard with Dallas toddling ahead of them, the sun's rays glimmering against the wavy window panes of Borden House. It was easy to agree to this arrangement in the daylight, yet somehow Sarah knew she'd regret it after the sun went down.

. . .

DARKNESS ENVELOPED the room as Sarah curled up on the velvet settee, wrapped in a blanket with Dallas at her feet. Two cameras were positioned in the room, one trained on her and the other on the doorway, green lights blinking. Thankfully, Ralph and Harry accepted Garrett's reason for having her sleep in the room. Even though Danni had suggested the same thing, she thought Sarah was nuts to agree, good-looking guy or not.

Sarah took some comfort in Dallas's presence as well as knowing the men were close by. One scream and they'd be there instantly. Nevertheless, she'd taken a few shots of bourbon in an effort to slow her racing pulse and weight her eyelids.

Leaning her head against the plush velvety pillow, she took in a deep breath and released. She did this several more times until sleep escorted her to visions of hatchet wielding killers.

WARM AIR RUFFLED Sarah's hair as she stood in the front parlor of Borden House. Curtains billowed in the suffocating breeze as she scanned the space. *Why was she in the front parlor when she'd fallen asleep in the sitting room?*

The front door opened and a tall gentleman in a dark suit entered. Sarah recognized the man as Andrew Borden. He had a rolled paper beneath his arm as he settled his hat on the hall tree and walked toward the sitting room. Sarah followed close behind, wondering if he could see her. When he didn't turn around or acknowledge her presence, she exhaled. The last thing she wanted was to be confronted by this man, especially if his appearance changed to the butchered image from the crime scene photos.

He folded his long frame onto the settee, the very one where she had fallen asleep, and rested his head against the curved arm. Swallowing hard, Sarah looked around the space. In just a few moments, Andrew Borden would be massacred with a hatchet. Sarah braced herself for the shocking occurrence when an icy chill scurried across her scalp and down her spine. Instinctively, she glanced over her shoulder but nothing was there.

Turning back, Sarah found herself in a dank basement. A massive stone cistern took center stage. Her heart pounded against her ribcage with the force of a sledge hammer. She stepped closer and rested her hand on the cold stone, the thumping of her pulse resonating against the hard surface.

Sarah jumped when an ear-shattering scream pierced the silence and a woman appeared, her throat gaping open as blood seeped from the wound. It would seem she was in the basement of Eliza Darling Borden's house. Sarah's lungs tightened as she ran for the narrow stairway. This had nothing to do with the Lizzie Borden case, so why was it appearing in her dreamscape?

As Sarah reached the top of the steps, she wriggled the doorknob. It was stuck. Glancing over her shoulder, she saw Eliza's gory image materialize behind her, the two children on either side, their cloudy eyes and puffy faces staring.

"Cursed!" Eliza screeched before vanishing with her children.

Suddenly, the door opened, its hinges crying out in protest. Without hesitation, Sarah dashed through the house and out the back door into the fresh air where she gulped in breaths. Eliza reappeared, her bloodied hand reaching for Sarah. Paralyzed by fear, Sarah closed her eyes, preparing for what would come next. Something warm and wet touched her face, jerking her from the dream.

Her lids flitted open to find Dallas sitting on her chest, his velvety tongue lapping at her chin. Chasing the cobwebs from her mind, Sarah stroked the dog's soft fur. The lights on both cameras glowed red. Not a good sign. Then again, maybe Garrett had come in and turned them off. Sarah leaned up on one elbow, sending Dallas scurrying to the other end of the settee.

She scanned the darkened space. Nothing. Sarah exhaled when Garrett crept in.

"Are we done for the night?" she croaked, rubbing her eyes.

"Not quite. I needed a break and decided to check on you," he said in a hushed tone.

He sat down and wrapped his arm around her, drawing her close. She rested her head against his shoulder, letting the thrumming of his heartbeat sooth her trembling limbs.

"Everything alright?" he whispered into her hair.

"Strange is more like it," she replied. "Did you turn off the cameras?"

His head dropped to his chest. "No."

Standing, Garrett strode over to each of the cameras and fiddled with the controls.

"The batteries appear to be dead."

"Sorry about that," Sarah muttered. "I thought you guys kept everything charged. Are they old?"

"Brand new. We bought new ones for this trip. We didn't want to worry about this sort of thing happening."

"Could the batteries be faulty?" Sarah asked.

"I'll have Ralph check but I don't think that's the case. We tested everything before setting up. Hopefully, we caught something before the batteries died."

Garrett went back over to Sarah, offering his hand to help her up.

"Anything happen in your dreams?" he asked.

"Yeah, but they didn't make any sense." Sarah yawned as Ralph's voice crackled over the radio.

"Garrett?"

Pulling the radio from his waist band, Garrett answered. "What's up?"

"Not getting any feed from the sitting room cameras. You might want to check on those."

"Already did. They're dead," Garrett replied.

"Darn it!" Ralph declared. "Bring them to the kitchen and I'll take a look at them."

"Got it," he said, clipping the radio back onto his belt.

"Go back to work," Sarah said with another yawn. "We can talk about this later."

With a nod and a quick kiss, he started disconnecting the cameras. Sarah headed upstairs thinking about the visions of Andrew Borden returning home, Eliza's ghastly image, and the phrases, *not what you think* and *cursed*. What did it all mean?

Sarah felt as if she hadn't slept in weeks. Exhaustion kneaded her limbs and weighted her shoulders. If only she could figure this out.

After washing up and changing into her pajamas, Sarah padded to her room, slipped beneath the blankets, and rested her head on the pillow. Moments later, there was a soft knock at the door. Garrett poked his head inside as Dallas bolted in and leapt onto the bed. Sarah ruffled the little dog's fur.

"Did you want Dallas to stay with you?" Garrett asked.

"Of course. Now that I've got my sleeping buddy, I'm ready to call it a night."

"Pretty bad when I envy my dog," Garrett yawned. "Sorry about that, I'm beat."

"You need to get some sleep."

"Have to help Harry and Ralph first. See you in the morning," Garrett replied, closing the door behind him.

Turning off the night table lamp, Sarah snuggled with Dallas. Within minutes she floated into dreamland.

CHAPTER 7

Andrew Borden sat at the dining room table, worry etching the lines of his face as he made notations in his financial ledger. His precious Lizzie was suffering from those trances again and he was determined to find someone who could help her. The family physician, Dr. Bowen, had done all he could. There was a traveling doctor who'd recently arrived in town with impeccable credentials, including training overseas. He'd touted his remedies when Mr. Borden had met with him, and guaranteed he could heal Lizzie. His fee was substantial but it seemed the only hope to squelch the episodes and notable changes in Lizzie's demeanor as of late. He lifted his pen from the ledger and thought for a minute, then nodded. Yes, he would employ this man to help his daughter where local physicians had failed.

The dream shifted. Lizzie meandered through the house in a daze. Walking up the back stairs to her stepmother's dressing room, she rummaged through her jewelry casket and removed a pocket watch and several inexpensive trinkets. Lizzie started for the door when her head slumped to her chest. She stood in silence for a few moments before her head popped back up.

Looking around the room, her eyes dropped to the items in her hands. It was happening again. Every time her menstrual cycle arrived, she'd have these episodes. Lizzie started to return the pieces to their rightful place when she heard her stepmother's voice in the hall downstairs. Panic gripped her chest as she shoved the watch and baubles into her pocket and slipped out the door, through her parent's room, and down the back steps before anyone noticed her.

Moments later, a scream echoed through the house accelerating Lizzie's heartrate. Obviously, Abby had discovered the missing items. Panic fogged Lizzie's brain as she tried to figure out what to do. She couldn't afford to be caught again. If she could slip out the back and hide the things in the barn, perhaps she could find a way to replace them later. Thank goodness, her father loved her enough to seek alternative medical interventions for these episodes, otherwise she'd be deemed crazy and locked away in an asylum.

Things escalated when the police arrived, searched the premises, and interviewed the family. Too afraid to admit her actions, Lizzie answered as best she could while hiding the truth. Lying had never come easily to her; however, to have her theft discovered was unconscionable and would only lead to ruination. Her stomach churned. Why did she steal when she had everything she could possibly want?

The scene altered to another day where Andrew Borden sat across the dining room table from a gentleman whose image was obscured. How odd, Sarah thought. She'd never experienced anything like this before. It was like one of those TV filters that blocked out a person's identity with a whitish dot, except this one was black.

"Doctor," Mr. Borden said, his hands steepled as he rested his elbows on the table. "Do you truly believe you can help my daughter, Lizzie?"

"Indeed. I've had great success throughout Europe which is

why I have come to this country. I want to help others with this unfortunate condition," he said, his words tinged in a British accent.

"And your price is nonnegotiable?"

"I'm afraid so." His voice took on a more serious tone. "I've heard of your frugal ways, Mr. Borden. I will not adapt my fees to suit your thriftiness."

"Very well," he replied, sitting straighter. "My daughter's health is worth it." Reaching into his pocket he handed the man a bundle of cash. The doctor placed a vial on the table.

"This is a special calming remedy created specifically for women. Lizzie needs to take it when she feels the least bit anxious," he instructed, walking to the door. "I'll return tomorrow to begin the hypnotic therapy."

SARAH STIRRED, her arm brushing against Dallas as she stretched. Daylight poured through the lacey curtains and spilled across the carpeted floor. Much to her surprise, she felt rested despite a night filled with dreams and several changes of location. After a shower, Sarah dressed and headed downstairs with Dallas at her side. She took the little dog outside for his morning business before going to the dining room. Garrett, Harry, and Ralph sat at the table, their eyes shadowed and their shoulders slouched. They looked as if they'd been on an all-night bender.

"Good morning," Sarah said, taking a seat at the table next to Garrett.

"Mornin'," Harry muttered as he sipped his coffee.

Garrett started to get up when Sarah grasped his hand. "Already took him out."

Smiling, he leaned over and kissed her cheek. "Thanks."

Mrs. Pearson appeared and placed a small teapot and cup in front of Sarah.

"Thank you," Sarah said with a smile.

"Breakfast will be ready in about ten minutes," Mrs. Pearson announced, leaving the room.

The scent of ham and eggs wafted through the space, making Sarah's stomach grumble.

"Where's Danni?" Ralph asked.

"She's not much of a morning person so we probably won't see her until the aroma of ham makes its way upstairs. The only thing that overrides her need to sleep is her need to eat, and maybe drink," Sarah chuckled.

"Sounds like my brother Walter, except he's an early riser," Ralph said. "Food is his kryptonite. He'll walk away from a video game for a good meal."

"Did you guys have any luck last night?" Sarah asked, pouring her tea.

"Won't know until we go back through the footage," Harry responded. "A few blips showed up but nothing earth shattering."

"Have you figured out what happened with the camera batteries in the sitting room?" Sarah asked, bringing the tea cup to her lips.

"Possibly drained by the strength of the entities," Ralph said. "I've read about this sort of thing happening in high energy locations. Never experienced it before now."

"You didn't see anything specific before the batteries went dead?"

"Nope. We'll check again later."

Mrs. Pearson arranged trays of eggs, ham, biscuits, and fresh fruit on the sideboard. After filling their plates, the group sat around the table debating the guilt or innocence of Lizzie Borden. Sarah wanted desperately to share what she'd dreamed but knew she'd have to wait until she could get Danni and Garrett alone before disclosing anything.

Once their plates were cleared, they continued talking about the aspects of the Borden murders when Danni entered the room. She sported her favorite USC sweatshirt and jeans with her hair in a messy bun.

"G'morning," she grumbled, sitting down and pouring a cup of coffee from the carafe on the table.

"Sleep well?" Garrett asked.

"Like the dead," she replied with a sly grin. "How about y'all? Find any proof about whether or not Lizzie butchered her parents?"

"Not yet," Garrett responded.

"Don't mean to abandon you," Ralph said, standing, "but we need to get some sleep."

"Definitely time for some shut-eye," Harry groaned, following Ralph from the room.

"You're going to sleep now?" Danni asked Garrett.

"Decided it was easier to work through the night and sleep after breakfast until noon," Garrett replied. He planted a kiss on the top of Sarah's head and squeezed her shoulder.

"See you two later," he said, exiting through the kitchen where the back staircase led to his quarters with Dallas toddling along.

Danni glanced across the table at her friend. "You've already eaten?"

"Yup, we all have. There's plenty left on the buffet. Help yourself," Sarah responded.

Danni walked to the spread of food on the sideboard and fixed a plate.

"Any good dreams?" she asked, scooping a forkful of eggs to her lips.

"Several," Sarah replied, refilling her cup.

"Let's hear it." Danni's eyes sparkled with anticipation.

"Why don't we wait until Garrett is with us?"

"Seriously? You're going to make me wait until lover-boy is available?" Danni said with a scowl. "That's not until lunch."

"Fine, I'll fill you in," Sarah huffed.

Sarah started with the dream in the sitting room followed by Mr. Borden in the dining room, the vision of Lizzie with her stepmother's jewelry, and finally Mr. Borden's transaction with the doctor.

"What was wrong with Lizzie?" Danni asked, her brows furrowed.

"Not sure. I don't recall any accounts of her suffering from a medical condition."

"This definitely warrants further investigation," Danni said, swigging down the rest of her coffee and standing. "Let me grab my keys and we'll go back to the museum. If Lizzie suffered from any sort of disorders there's bound to be a record of it somewhere."

"Agreed," Sarah replied, thankful to have Danni's support and her research skills.

MILLIE WASN'T at the museum. Instead, they were greeted by a lovely young woman, her sandy blond hair tied in a ponytail with a nametag that read 'Jenny.'

"How can I help you ladies today?" she asked.

"We're looking for anything addressing Lizzie Borden's health," Sarah stated.

"Interesting," she said, arching her brows. "We rarely have requests of this nature even though there is information pertaining to her mental and physical health at the time preceding the murders."

"Wonderful," Sarah replied, relieved there might be documentation related to what she'd dreamt.

Jenny escorted them to the archives in the basement. Opening a file cabinet drawer, she removed a large manila folder and placed it on the table.

"This file contains all of Lizzie's health information. Let me know if you need my assistance for anything else," she said, leaving the room.

Danni opened the file and started sorting through the pages. She gave some to Sarah as she read through the rest.

"Says here, Lizzie was prone to temporal seizures and brownouts," Danni said.

"What are brownouts?" Sarah asked.

"Apparently, it's similar to a blackout except you have some recollection of what happened. Sounds like a daytime sleep-walking episode."

"What would cause such a thing?" Sarah queried.

"According to this, it's a form of temporal epilepsy."

"Lizzie Borden was epileptic?"

"That's what it says. She'd have these 'peculiar spells' three to four times a year during that time of the month."

"Weird. Never heard of anything like this before," Sarah said.

"Me either. Of course, modern science has explained so many things that were viewed as odd or crazy back then. I'm surprised they knew as much as they did. Interesting how researchers have been able to give insight on something that occurred more than a hundred years ago.

"How do these episodes relate to the murders?" Sarah asked.

"It says brownouts allow a person to commit certain acts while being unaware at the time. The article goes on to state that Lizzie was known to take things during these spells."

"Would it be possible to hack someone to death while in a brownout?" Sarah asked, her stomach churning at the thought. Could the mystery behind the murders be this straightforward? If that were the case, this would be the shortest amount of time she'd spent solving a mystery with the visions from her dreams.

Danni's eyes grew wider. "This article says it is."

A chill raced up Sarah's spine. "We need to get back to the house and share this with the guys. If they were able to capture any ghostly images, perhaps the clips will correlate with what we've found."

"I'll get Jenny to make copies of this stuff."

Sarah's heart leapt. If Garrett and his friends were able to solve a murder mystery that had intrigued the country for more than a hundred years, they were bound to land the network contract. The idea sent a rush of joy circulating through Sarah's veins, until Valerie's image intruded and dammed up the good vibes. Stop it, Sarah thought. She's a network executive, nothing more. She probably flirts with men all the time.

* * *

AFTER GRABBING A BITE TO EAT, they returned to the house where they found Harry and Ralph working on the previous night's video.

"Hey guys," Sarah said, stepping in the back door of the kitchen. "How's it going? Any ghost sightings yet?"

"We captured a few strange images but nothing we can connect to Lizzie Borden," Harry said, still staring at the monitor.

"I sent the footage to Walter to see what he could make of it," Ralph added, moving the mouse around on the fold-out table holding all the equipment.

"Where's Garrett?" Sarah asked.

"Dining room doing research," Ralph replied, still focused on the computer screen.

Danni and Sarah leaned over Ralph's shoulder watching clips that had been captured on the infrared cameras in different areas of the house.

"Actually, one of the most significant sightings was in the sitting room while you were asleep. Go back to that segment," Harry said to Ralph.

Ralph tapped the computer keys and the footage popped up on the screen.

Sarah's skin prickled as she watched herself sleeping on the settee with Dallas snoozing at her feet. This was when she'd dreamt about Andrew Borden coming home followed by the horrific basement episode of the murder-suicide next door. She'd had dreams jump from scene to scene before but never with two completely different scenarios.

"Focus on the end of the settee where Dallas is sleeping," Ralph said, pointing to the screen.

Sarah's back tensed as she watched a dark misty aura form at her feet, its shape wavering as it floated toward her head. It stopped and gazed down at her as if it knew her. The silence was pierced by a low growl as Dallas stood on all fours, his lips parted in a snarl as he stared in the direction of the entity. The spirit turned toward the small dog and dissipated into the darkness.

"That was eerie," Danni muttered, furrowing her brow as she straightened up.

Sarah gulped down the bile burning her throat. There was actually something there. It appeared Dallas had seen it too and possibly scared it off. What would the ghost have done if Dallas hadn't been there? More importantly, who was it? Andrew Borden, Lizzie, or Eliza? She'd dreamed about all of them.

"At least you were able to capture something on tape. Looks like your idea of having someone sleep in a high energy location worked," Sarah said, even though she knew the ghosts were drawn to her as a dreamist not because of her location when slumbering.

"Sadly, the batteries died so this was all we got."

"Did you figure out what caused that to happen?" Sarah asked.

Harry scrunched his face. "Looks like the energy levels from the ghost were pretty intense. Probably drained the power."

"This is freaking me out," Danni said with a shudder, her eyes bulging. "If these spirits can drain fully charged batteries, how do you know they won't cross the threshold into the living world and hurt someone?"

Harry smiled. "Depends on the entity. There are several different types. Granted, there's no scientific proof of these things but most ghost hunters accept them as fact."

"Great," Danni groused. "How am I supposed to know what kind of ghost I'm dealing with?"

"It's not complicated," Harry said. "First, we have ectoplasm. This is generally viewed as a swirling mist. It's usually white, gray, and sometimes black. These entities can hover or zip around."

Danni wrinkled her upper lip as Harry continued.

"Next, we have orbs. This is what most people capture in photographs. They're mostly transparent balls of light that pop up in various places and can move rather quickly. They're completely harmless."

"So, what you're saying is, ghosts can't hurt you," Danni muttered.

"In these instances, no. However, poltergeists can cause harm. It's believed these entities are able to cross over into the physical realm and interact with the environment."

"This isn't helping," Danni said, her gaze shifting around the room. "Maybe I'll get a hotel room and you can pick me up on your way out of town.

"There's nothing to fear," Harry continued. "Most hauntings are ectoplasmic or orbs. Basically, the ghosts who linger are curious about something or connected to the place being haunted."

Sarah shook her head, amused by her friend's reaction to the ghost definitions. It would seem the additional information was doing more harm than good. In order to keep Danni from fleeing the scene, Sarah redirected the conversation to the previous night's video. "Were you able to catch anything of significance in the other rooms?"

"Several orbs and flashes of light. We sent those to Walter too. He'll be able to manipulate the images and determine if there's anything remarkable about the orbs and lights or if they're just natural occurrences."

"Thanks for making the house creepier than it was," Danni said. "I'm going upstairs to check my email. I need a break from the haunted stuff."

"We'll text if we notice any spirits following you," Ralph said with a chuckle.

"Not funny!" Danni called out as she scooted from the room, leaving Sarah with the guys.

"Do you want to see more?" Harry asked.

"Not right now. I need to do some research of my own," she said. "Do you really believe poltergeists can do harm?" Sarah asked.

"Not sure," Harry responded. "That's one of the reasons we don't utilize artificial means like Ouija boards or séances to stir up spirits."

"We like old-fashioned hauntings," Ralph added. "Most people enjoy a little scare and the idea of loved ones lingering about. It's all harmless fun."

With a nod, Sarah grinned. Now that she'd gotten a lesson on the different types of ghosts and witnessed the entity from the sitting room the night before, she wanted to talk to Garrett about what she and Danni had learned at the museum. She'd let him find a way to share the information with Harry and Ralph without exposing her dreamist abilities.

Garrett sat at the dining room table with a laptop in front of him and a stack of books to his right. As Sarah entered, Dallas ran over to her, apparently alerting Garrett of her arrival. A smile creased his eyes as he leaned back in the chair, his gaze penetrating her soul.

Sarah placed a kiss on his lips.

"How's it going?" she asked, sitting beside him. Dallas leapt onto her lap and nuzzled her chin.

"I'm getting some good stuff but nothing directly connected to what we've filmed so far. Did Harry and Ralph show you the footage?"

Sarah shuddered. "They did."

"I assume Danni's speedy exit was connected to the video."

"In a sense," Sarah chuckled.

Reaching over, he gave her hand a gentle squeeze. "I know it's probably a bit overwhelming seeing things happen while you're asleep. By any chance, did you recognize the misty figure?"

"That's what I wanted to talk about."

"Tell me," he said, his eyes blazing with anticipation.

"The sitting room dreams were bizarre." Sarah filled him in on watching Mr. Borden recline on the settee and then being in the basement next door with Eliza and her children. "After I went to bed, I dreamt about Mr. Borden at the dining room table contemplating medical treatments for Lizzie. Next thing I know, I'm watching Lizzie in some sort of trance stealing jewelry from her stepmother's dressing room. Then, I saw Mr. Borden meeting with a doctor about Lizzie's medical condition."

"Do you think the image on the tape is Mr. Borden?"

"I watched the segment but couldn't make out the identity. Maybe it'll be clearer once Walter works with it."

"In other words, we have no idea who the misty figure is," he said, running his hand through his hair.

"Exactly," she replied.

"Did Mr. Borden say what sort of medical treatments he was seeking for Lizzie?"

"Not specifically, but the doctor he hired mentioned

hypnosis and gave him some sort of remedy to help Lizzie with her trance-like episodes."

"That was a pretty controversial thing back then. Most people would have believed she was possessed and called in a priest, not sought medical help from a physician."

"Which is why Danni and I went back to the museum to research Lizzie's health."

"What did you find?"

"We found information suggesting Lizzie suffered from temporal epilepsy which came in the form of brownouts. These generally occurred at the time of her menstrual cycle."

"Brownouts?"

"It's when a person loses consciousness but still functions, kind of like sleepwalking during the day."

"How does this impact her possible involvement with the crimes?" he asked.

"She was known to steal on occasion, including her step-mother's jewelry like I saw in my dream. According to what we read, a person in a brownout state could also commit a murder with a hatchet."

"Wonder why we've never heard about this stuff before now," he said, arching his brows.

"Doesn't make for good storytelling. When the world wants to see things a certain way, they choose facts that support their personal views or opinions. Like politics."

"Good analogy," he said, standing. "Let's share what you guys discovered about Lizzie's health and her father hiring an out-of-town doctor with Ralph and Harry."

"Nothing about the dreamist stuff, right?"

Leaning over, he kissed the top of her head. "Your secret is safe with me."

Sarah tilted her head back for a better kiss which he gave her. Grasping her hand, he led her to the kitchen where they sat with Harry and Ralph.

"Sarah and Danni unearthed some pretty interesting things at the museum today," Garrett said.

Both men stopped what they were doing.

"What did you find?" Harry queried.

Sarah filled them in on Lizzie's medical issues, the thefts, and the traveling doctor.

"Will this help with what you filmed last night?" she asked.

Ralph scratched his head. "Depends on how much Walter is able to process from the clips we sent him earlier."

All of a sudden, a scream ripped through the atmosphere.

"Danni!" Sarah gasped. Jumping to her feet, she ran for the stairs with Dallas and the guys close behind.

Sarah burst into Danni's room to find her standing on the bed, her eyes wild.

"What happened?" Sarah asked.

Danni grasped her chest as her head slumped forward, her cheeks coloring.

"Spider," she moaned.

"Seriously? You scared us half to death because you saw a spider?"

Folding her knees, Danni plunked onto the bed. "Yeah." Remorse stewed in her stare as she looked at the group standing in the doorway of her room. "Can't help it if I have a healthy fear of the eight-legged creatures."

"Unhealthy phobia," Sarah retorted. "Do you need me to remove it?"

"Didn't see which direction it went," she scowled, peering over the edge of the bed. "Don't know if I'll be able to sleep in here tonight."

"You can always sit with me and help monitor any activity," Ralph said with a grin.

Danni sucked her front teeth. "That sounds like a reasonable alternative."

"You're choosing to spend the night watching for ghosts in

order to avoid a spider in your room?" Sarah asked, hands on her hips.

"Pretty much," Danni stated, pursing her lips.

"At some point you'll have to sleep," Sarah said.

Danni stuck out her tongue.

"Since all is well, we're going back downstairs. Care to join us, or would you rather do battle with the spider?" Sarah asked.

"Coming with you," Danni replied, hopping from the bed and scurrying past the men into the hallway.

Garrett smiled at Sarah as they walked down the stairs side by side.

"That's a serious phobia," he said with a chuckle.

"You think that's bad, wait until she sees a mouse."

THE GROUP GATHERED around the dining room table planning what to do for the evening filming when Ralph's phone rang. Everyone sat in silence.

"It's Walter," he announced before answering. "Hey, Walter. Get anything? Yeah? Really? Incredible! Thanks!"

Ralph hung up and smiled.

"Looks like there are some details in the orbs and the misty figure appears to be a man."

"That's great!" Harry declared.

Sarah glanced around the table. All eyes had shifted to her.

"What does this mean?" she asked, almost afraid to hear the answer.

"Seems like your presence helped us capture something notable. Would you be willing to let us film you again tonight?" Harry asked.

"You want me to sleep in the sitting room again?" she asked with a shiver.

"There, or maybe the guest room where Abby was killed. If

she shows up, we can probably conclude the man in the sitting room is Andrew Borden."

After Harry's lesson about ghosts and the close encounters with a few aggressive entities she'd experienced over the past year and a half, Sarah was a bit nervous. Would this situation be different? And were the ghosts at Borden House the type to do her harm? There was no time to think or discuss anything.

"I'll do it," she said.

Dallas barked.

"Sounds like Dallas approves," Garrett chuckled, rubbing the dog's head.

"You're like some sort of ghost magnet," Ralph chortled.

"Just what I always wanted," she mumbled. "To be a lure for the undead."

Everyone laughed, easing the tension gripping the atmosphere. One thing was certain, Sarah was in for another spirit filled night whether she liked it or not.

* * *

DRESSED IN A SWEATSHIRT AND LEGGINGS, Sarah curled up on the bed in the guest room with Dallas nestled beside her. Garrett adjusted the cameras, double-checked the batteries, and walked over to her.

"Everything's set," he said, sitting on the edge of the bed. "I'll be watching from down the hall. We set up an extra monitor for these two cameras."

Sarah sighed as her eyes swept the room, nuggets of dread rattling around in her gut.

Apparently sensing her unease, Garrett grasped her hand and squeezed. "I'm a little worried about you."

"I'll be fine. Hopefully, we'll get something more than a shadowy form," she whispered, her lips brushing his.

He returned the kiss until the radio crackled and Ralph's

voice blared, "Don't have time for romance folks. Do your canoodling later."

"Guess this wasn't a good idea with the cameras trained on us," he muttered.

"Maybe we can sneak away for a few minutes tomorrow," Sarah whispered, kissing him once more. "Now get out of here and find some ghosts," she said, shoving his arm.

Reaching over, Garrett tousled Dallas's head. "Take good care of her, buddy."

Yip!

They giggled at the dog's spirited response. Once Garrett left the room, an icy chill embraced Sarah's body as she lay back and closed her eyes. Her mind drifted to the previous night's dream with Eliza's fearsome appearance as she uttered the word *cursed*. What curse? And who was she referring to? Women in general or the family?

Sarah's heartrate increased and her fingertips numbed, making her wonder what was happening. Through squinted eyes, she surveyed the room but saw nothing. Dallas was snoring by her side. If anything were around, he'd have picked up on it. She was probably overthinking. Pulling a throw over her shoulders, Sarah concentrated on her breathing until it reached a steady rhythm and her mind wandered to a land of dreams.

Glancing around, Sarah realized she was standing in the guest room where she slept. A woman in a white dress lay prostrate on the floor between the bed and the dresser, a crimson puddle forming a halo about her shattered head. Sarah gulped down the repulsion sticking in her throat. This was Abby Borden's body. She took a step backwards when a shadow raced through the doorway into the hall. The killer?

Sarah scurried into the hallway, her eyes darting around. Nothing. She went to Lizzie's room, her blood pulsing with the force of white-water rapids. Turning the knob, she pushed the door open and peeked inside. The bed was made and everything looked to be in place. There was no sign of Lizzie. Where was she? If Lizzie wasn't in her room but elsewhere in the house, could she have been the one who killed her stepmother? Was she burning her dress in the wood stove downstairs? And if so, what did she do with the dress she wore when her father was killed? Theories about the lack of bloodied clothing had suggested Lizzie committed the murders in the nude, a theory Sarah didn't buy into.

Sarah started down the stairs when frigid nails bit into the back of her neck. Closing her eyes, she fought back the urge to scream. Instead, she gathered all her courage and turned around. Eliza's soulless stare bore through Sarah's fortitude, her pale lips mouthing *cursed*.

The dreamscape altered. Andrew Borden strode along the dirt road to his house on 2nd Street. The sun was blazing in the sky, sending beads of sweat trickling from beneath his hat. Jaunting up the front stairs of his house, he unlocked the door and stepped into the entryway.

He placed his hat on the hall tree and walked to the sitting room, his mind still racing from the meeting with the doctor the day before. This had been the fourth appointment since hiring him and Mr. Borden was completely discouraged. He'd been certain the man would be able to help Lizzie. Turns out he was just another wayfaring swindler preaching nonsense to make an extra buck. Well, no more. From here on out, Mr. Borden would only rely on their family physician, Dr. Bowen. Whatever it took to keep his dear Lizzie safe and at home.

He glanced at the ring on his pinky. The very one Lizzie had slipped on his finger the day of her graduation from high school. All the other girls had exchanged rings with each other but not his Lizzie. She wanted to give it to her father. And he had treasured the gift and the sentiment accompanying it.

Mr. Borden reclined on the settee and closed his eyes. He was a fortunate man. He had a good family, a home, several properties, and money tucked away. If only he could take care of Lizzie's episodes, he'd be able to concentrate on business instead of worrying about what might happen should outsiders discover his daughter's malady. A sharp pain radiated through Sarah's head.

Bark, bark, bark!

Sarah jarred from her slumber. Leaning up on one arm, she looked around the darkened room, her head pounding. Massaging her temples, she startled when Garrett rushed in.

"You OK?" he asked.

Sarah nodded as Dallas licked her cheek.

His radio buzzed. "Everything alright up there?" Ralph whispered.

"Yeah," Garrett responded. He turned to Sarah and spoke in a hushed tone. "What happened? I heard Dallas bark."

"Dream activity," she mumbled.

"I want to hear about it later," he whispered.

Nodding, she cuddled Dallas as Garrett left. Things were getting more complicated. With a sigh, Sarah rested her head on the pillow as her mind tried to decipher the cryptic messages. This time she'd witnessed Mrs. Borden's body and a shadow running from the scene. Had it been the killer? And what did Eliza's repeated phrase of *cursed* have to do with Mrs. Borden's murder? The two incidents couldn't be related since they'd occurred forty years apart, or could they? Mr. Borden reclining on the settee in the sitting room was the only recurring vision thus far. Was he the shadowy mist they'd caught on tape? With only a few more days at Borden House, Sarah worried she'd run out of time before making sense of the messages in her dreams and how they were related.

CHAPTER 8

$\mathcal{R}$ain pattered against the window frames, nudging Sarah from her sleep. Sitting up, she glanced about the darkened space. Dallas was gone, no doubt with Garrett. She switched on the night table lamp, climbed from bed, and trudged to the window. Sheets of water clung to the panes, obscuring the view. A chill rankled her body as she stared at blurred images of cars driving by on the street below. Sarah took in a few deep breaths until she felt the tension in her shoulders dissolve. It had been a busy night of dreams.

As she peered out the window, her breath fogged the glass in front of her and a form took shape in the reflection. Turning, Sarah gasped when she saw Lizzie standing there, her eyes fixed on Sarah's.

"What do you want to tell me?" Sarah mumbled, hoping Lizzie would respond. Instead, the ghost shook her head before dissolving into the shadows.

It was obvious she'd seen Sarah so why not answer the question? And why were there so many entities haunting her at one time? During her stay in Edgefield, Tara had been the primary ghost along with Ola. The other ghosts hadn't shown themselves until Tara's murderer had been revealed.

Sarah pondered some of the facts she and Danni had uncovered. Following her acquittal, Lizzie lived at Maplecroft, a stunning Queen Anne Victorian a few blocks away, until she died of pneumonia decades later. Her sister, Emma, died of chronic nephritis nine days after that. Oddly, the sisters had parted ways years before. Emma moved to New Hampshire while Lizzie remained at Maplecroft.

It was rumored Lizzie haunted both houses, leading Sarah to wonder what would happen if she spent the night in the house where Lizzie took her last breath. If Lizzie wasn't willing to communicate in this house perhaps, she'd be willing to at Maplecroft.

She needed to remind Garrett to contact the current owners instead of going through the network. The less Valerie was involved, the better.

After a hot shower, Sarah dressed, pulled her hair into a bun, and dabbed on some concealer before heading downstairs. Much to her surprise, Danni was sitting at the table with the guys discussing the facts of the trial.

"Good morning," Sarah said, taking a seat at the table across from Garrett. "Have I missed anything?"

"Wanted to let you get some rest since...." Danni's words tapered off before mentioning the dreams. Everyone was staring in her direction. "Since you rarely get the opportunity to sleep late," Danni said.

"Thanks, I appreciate it," Sarah responded, exhaling. Thank goodness Danni caught herself before saying too much. Explaining away comments about her dreams would be difficult with Harry and Ralph. Mrs. Pearson entered the room and placed a teapot and cup in front of Sarah.

"Thank you, Mrs. Pearson."

"Be right back with your breakfast," she said with a smile.

"You guys already ate?" Sarah asked the group.

"Yup," Ralph answered.

Sarah looked at the wall clock which read 9:05 a.m. Wow, she had slept late.

"Did you have any luck last night?" Sarah asked as Mrs. Pearson placed a plate of eggs, bacon, and an English muffin in front of her.

"Actually, we did. The room you were in was the most active. You definitely seem to draw out the ghosts," Harry said enthusiastically. "We'll show you the video after you finish eating."

"We were discussing the trial before you came in," Garrett said.

"What exactly?" Sarah asked, taking a bite of bacon.

"The inconsistencies, mostly," Danni replied.

"Such as?"

"Lizzie's testimony contained a multitude of contradictions regarding her accounts of that day. Add the mountain of evidence against her and there's no doubt in my mind she got away with both murders," Danni said. "The acquittal was most likely the result of societal views toward women at the time, specifically that they were too delicate and weak to commit such heinous acts."

"I thought we read something about the family physician, Dr. Bowen, saying the morphine he'd prescribed could result in confusion, explaining the discrepancies in Lizzie's testimony."

"Still, much of what she said seemed farfetched. Her report about being in the barn searching for lead sinkers on the day of the murders was peculiar. When investigators searched the barn, they found no evidence of anyone having been in there. No footprints in the dirt and nothing rifled with. When questioned why she thought someone would want her father dead, Lizzie attributed it to the troubles Mr. Borden was having with disgruntled tenants," Danni added. "Lots of people have difficulties with their landlords, doesn't mean they butcher them."

"Then there are the housekeeper's statements about the Bordens having stomach aches the day before the murders," Ralph said. "There's evidence of Lizzie purchasing prussic acid days prior, and thus the appearance of guilt is clinched."

"Why would she try to poison them and then decide to hatchet them to death instead?" Sarah asked. "Violent acts are rarely attributed to women."

"Maybe the poison wasn't working fast enough," Harry chimed in.

"Or maybe she didn't do it," Sarah remarked. "What about the brownouts? Perhaps she was unaware of what she was doing."

"Lame excuse for killing your parents," Danni retorted. "If she was unaware of her actions, then where are the bloody clothes? You can't butcher someone and not get blood on your body which means she destroyed or hid the evidence. That's not a brownout, that's calculated. No sorrow there."

"Except Lizzie did feel remorse when she stole Abby's jewelry," Sarah added.

"How do you know that?" Harry asked.

Sarah gulped down the bite of English muffin she'd been chewing as everyone stared at her. Stupid, she thought. She knew that from her dreams. She'd felt the remorse in Lizzie and the panic when she wasn't able to return the stolen items immediately. Composing herself, Sarah mumbled, "I'm pretty sure I read it somewhere."

"You really believe she was innocent?" Garrett asked.

"She *was* acquitted," Sarah replied, glad they'd accepted her excuse about the jewelry without further inquiry.

"By a jury who no doubt saw a pretty, well-mannered lady. Most men couldn't conceive a prominent citizen, especially one of the female persuasion, could commit such a brutal crime," Danni stated. "In my opinion, the outcome of the case was based upon the defendant's gender."

"What's your take on this?" Harry asked Ralph.

"Not sure. For more than a hundred years the world has believed in her guilt. It's hard to shift that train of thought to her innocence."

"Don't forget about Lizzie's friend, Alice Russell, who said Lizzie was at her house the night before the murders where she expressed a foreboding feeling. She told Alice she was afraid to go to sleep for fear something terrible might happen," Harry said.

"The entire trial seemed inconsistent. One moment Lizzie acted as if she was making up stories regarding her whereabouts during the murders and the next minute witnesses were disputing her ability to commit the crimes," Danni said. "Needless to say, her attorneys, Jennings and Robinson, handled the case brilliantly and landed an acquittal."

Sarah finished her breakfast. She needed to find a way to get Garrett and Danni alone so she could share her dreams with them.

Fortunately, Danni appeared to pick up on her thoughts.

"Sarah, could you help me with something upstairs?" Danni asked.

"Sure," Sarah replied, relieved for the opportunity to speak with her friend in private. Now she needed to get Garrett up there without raising suspicion. Turning to him, she smiled. "By the way, Garrett, when you get a chance, could you check the light in my room? It was flashing again this morning."

"I can help," Harry offered. "I'm pretty good with electrical stuff."

Sarah tensed. She really needed to speak with Danni and Garrett alone.

"I've got it," Garrett said. "You stay and help Ralph."

"We'll look through the footage once more and see if there's anything else we need to forward to Walter," Ralph added.

"I'll be back down in a few minutes," Garrett replied, following Sarah and Danni from the room.

The three of them climbed the stairs to Danni's chambers with Dallas toddling behind. Once in the room, Garrett sat in the chair while Danni and Sarah perched on the side of the bed.

"Let's hear about the dreams," Danni said.

"In the first one, I found Abby's body." Sarah shivered at the gruesome memory. "I saw a shadow in the hallway and remembered something about Lizzie burning a dress in the stove so I decided to check the kitchen."

"So, you do think she's guilty, at least your subconscious does," Danni said.

"At this point, I'm trying to keep an open mind," Sarah replied. "Lizzie seems almost timid in my dreams which makes it hard for me to believe she hacked her parents to death. Anyway, when I was going down the stairs, Eliza grabbed my neck and said, *cursed.*"

Danni cringed. "Seriously creepy."

"The dreamscape shifted and Mr. Borden was walking down the street toward the house. He was pondering dismissing the traveling doctor because he felt he wasn't helping Lizzie. He stared at the ring on his pinky which Lizzie had given him after she graduated. A sharp pain stabbed at my head and then Dallas barked and woke me up."

"Do you think Dallas was sensing something?" Danni queried.

"He barked at the same time the pain ripped through my head so I'd say it's probable. What do you think, Garrett?"

"He doesn't usually wake up unless something notable prompts him."

"Now what?" Sarah asked.

"I'll talk with Harry and Ralph and see if there are any connections between what we've learned about Lizzie's case and the images on the tapes," Garrett said, rubbing the back of his neck. "It sounds like you were dreaming about Mr. Borden's murder when Dallas woke you. Too bad you couldn't have lingered a few seconds longer. You might have seen the killer."

"I was thinking the same thing," Sarah replied.

"Which reiterates Lizzie's guilt," Danni added. "She was at the house for both murders."

"So was Bridget and possibly someone else who we know nothing about," Sarah retorted. "It seems the more we learn about this case, the more convoluted it becomes."

"Your need to exonerate her is admirable but likely misplaced," Danni said to her friend.

"I just don't get a murderous vibe from her," Sarah replied.

"We can discuss this later." Garrett stood up and walked to the door with Dallas at his side. "In the meantime, I'll try to find a way to introduce what you've shared from your dreams with Harry and Ralph without exposing your abilities."

"You look tired," Sarah said, staring at the dark circles eclipsing his eyes. "You should get some rest."

"I will after I take a look at the footage from last night," Garrett yawned. "Then Valerie is coming by to meet with me."

"Thought you guys were going to start sleeping after breakfast until noon," Sarah said, annoyance poking her heart at the sound of Valerie's name.

"That was the plan but Valerie was insistent about seeing me so I'm kinda stuck. I'll get some rest after she leaves."

Sarah chewed her lower lip in an effort to prevent a nasty response from materializing. The best thing to do was support Garrett and keep her mind from wandering through the land of innuendos.

"Danni and I will go back to town and see if we can find any more information about the trial and Lizzie's life afterwards," Sarah said. "Oh, I almost forgot. Do you think there's any way we could get access to Maplecroft?"

"The place where Lizzie lived after her acquittal?"

"Yes," she replied.

"I'll ask Valerie about it. I think she's friends with the owners."

"OK," she huffed. Sarah's blood pressure ticked up another notch. Why did everything revolve around Valerie?

"I'd better get back downstairs. Thanks for all your help with this," he said with a wink, leaving the room.

"Do you think visiting Maplecroft will reveal anything of significance?" Danni asked after Garrett left.

"Who knows?" Sarah moaned, her shoulders slumping.

"What's wrong now?"

"Nothing," she replied, looking away.

Danni pursed her lips. "Your eyes are turning green."

"Can't help it," Sarah whined. "That woman makes me crazy. Why couldn't he ask Mrs. Pearson about Maplecroft? She seems to know everyone in town."

"Because she's the innkeeper and Valerie is his network connection."

"Please don't use the words, Valerie and connection in the same sentence when we're talking about Garrett."

"If you're going to be in a relationship, you need to toughen up. Garrett is a good-looking guy. Lots of women are going to find him attractive. It's a delicate balance between self-doubt and trusting him. Don't let Valerie make you appear needy."

"I suppose," Sarah replied. She knew Danni was right yet it was difficult to ignore the blond bombshell and her flirtatious manner.

"Come on," Danni said, nudging Sarah's arm. "Let's do some investigating. It'll take your mind off the floozy."

"Can't hurt to try," she replied, getting up. "Let's go to the museum and look through the records again. Maybe last night's dream will shed new light on the information."

"Sounds like a plan," Danni said, walking to her room to grab her purse.

They walked to the car in silence, Sarah still stewing over the situation. The last thing she wanted to do was seem clingy and drive Garrett into Valerie's arms. Danni was right. If she immersed herself in the research, it would take her mind off of her romantic worries, or so she hoped.

The rain had subsided, leaving gray skies in its wake. Water splashed against the sides of Danni's Mercedes as they drove across puddled streets and parked in front of the Victorian mansion housing the museum, its dampened façade appearing more ominous beneath the canopy of clouds. They walked into the well-lit interior where Millie was refilling one of the plastic holders with brochures about the museum.

"Hello, ladies," she said. "Nice to see you back so soon. How can I help you today?"

"We'd like to look through more of the Lizzie Borden records," Danni said.

"Is there something specific you need?"

Danni and Sarah looked at each other.

"We need to see the trial transcripts again," Danni said.

"You know where everything is," she smiled. "Let me know if you need my assistance."

Sarah and Danni went to the basement, removed files from the metal cabinet, and piled them on the table.

"We've already been through all this," Sarah sighed as she sat behind a stack of manilla folders bursting with papers.

"That was before your dreams. Things we dismissed as irrelevant before might have meaning now. I'll go back through these and you look through the post-trial records."

Sarah skimmed through the contents of a bulging file, when photos of Lizzie Borden at Maplecroft along with articles about her charitable work caught her attention. She appeared to be a lovely woman with a kind countenance about her. It seemed unlikely she could have brutally killed anyone, especially with a hatchet. By all accounts, Lizzie loved her father and he adored her. The only documented animosity was between Lizzie and Abby. Supposedly, Lizzie stopped referring to her stepmother as 'Mother' after a disagreement. From that point forward, she called her Abby. But lots of kids have fallouts with stepparents. Doesn't mean they kill them.

Sarah found another document reporting Lizzie left her estate to a local animal rescue, another indication of a good heart. With a bit more reading, Sarah discovered articles about themed parties at Maplecroft and other events. Nothing suggested criminal activity or sociopathic tendencies. Sarah gathered the contents, replaced it within the folder, and reached for the next file.

This one contained more photos of Maplecroft. An amazing example of Victorian architecture, the interior was a smorgasbord of period furnishings and artwork. Sarah exhaled. She'd love to see the house in person. Reportedly, the current owners had renovated everything to its period beginnings, every old house lover's delight.

"Find anything of interest?" Danni asked, paging through another stack of papers.

"Mostly stuff about her life after the trial. She loved animals and was fairly social. Sounds like a nice person."

"If chopping up your parents is an indication of being a nice person, then she was the nicest person ever."

Sarah looked at her friend. "She was cleared of those charges."

"Found not guilty. Doesn't mean she didn't do it and get away with it."

"Why are you so skeptical about this?" Sarah asked. "Not everybody is a homicidal maniac."

Danni folded her arms across her chest, her eyes glistening. "As we both know, the kindest, friendliest person in the world can turn out to be a lunatic."

Chewing her lower lip, Sarah chose her words carefully. She hadn't meant to upset Danni.

"Sorry, I didn't mean to be insensitive," Sarah said softly.

Danni unfolded her arms and brushed a strand of hair from her forehead. "Don't apologize. I need to get over Brady and all the memories I have of him."

"Don't let his depravity bitter you. Then he wins."

"Pfft. You sound like a therapist."

"I'll send you my bill," Sarah said, raising one eyebrow.

Danni shook her head, wiping a stray tear from her cheek. Sarah made a mental note to tread carefully when discussing mass murderers, at least until Danni's heart had time to heal.

Sarah put the file on the stack and stood.

"I'm going upstairs to the Lizzie Borden room and see if there's anything in the display cabinets that might add to what we've found so far."

"Sounds good," Danni muttered as she continued reading through the court transcripts.

The house in which the museum was located was almost more intriguing to Sarah than the contents. The high Victorian style with wallpaper friezes, period furnishings, vibrantly hued rugs, and original elements made the place a time capsule for the late 19th century lifestyle.

Sarah paused in the entryway to admire the elaborate details of the staircase with its intricate carvings and sweeping balustrade. Running her hand across the newel post, a corpselike image flashed through Sarah's head causing her to stumble backwards.

"Everything alright?" Millie's voice called from the doorway of the front room.

Grabbing her chest, Sarah spoke. "Just lost my balance," she replied, trying to steady her racing heart from the unexpected interruption.

"I've got some bottled water if you'd like some."

"No, thank you. I'm fine," she replied.

The kindly woman gave a quick smile and returned to her work. Sarah glanced up the staircase, her shoulders tightening. A translucent figure in a flowing gown of plum fabric, hovered at the top of the stairs. Her gaunt expression and skeletal form stole the air from Sarah's lungs. Frozen in place, Sarah watched as the image wavered in and out. Suddenly, the entity flew down the stairs, her mouth gaping open as the words, *I know what you are!* roared through Sarah's head.

Stunned by the angry feel of the spirit, Sarah hurried back down to the basement where she found Danni refiling folders.

"Decided not to investigate the Lizzie Borden room after all. You ready to go?" Sarah asked, her words falling from her lips in a jumble.

"What's the matter?" Danni asked.

"Strange encounter with an angry spirit."

"Anyone of the ghosts we're trying to garner information from?"

"Not that I'm aware of," Sarah huffed.

"Was it that bad? You haven't looked this frightened since you were dealing with the ghosts at Edgefield Manor."

"This one flew down the stairs at me and roared, *I know what you are.* I nearly fell over."

"I thought all dead people knew you were a dreamist. Like a bat signal to the spiritual world."

"That's what the book said. But I've never had one so angry about it."

"Maybe she's a dreamist too and doesn't want you invading her territory."

"If that's the case, I'm ready to skedaddle. The last thing I need is a territorial ghost messing around with me. Things at the Borden place are intense enough."

"Alright. I think we've gotten everything we came for anyway," Danni chuckled. She draped her arm around Sarah's shoulders and squeezed. "How about we look for a place to eat? I'm starved from all this research. Hauntings really do ramp up the appetite."

Shaking her head, Sarah grinned. She could always count on Danni to lighten the mood, even one inundated by ghosts.

They bid goodbye to Millie and stepped into the crisp autumn air. Relieved to be out of the house, Sarah took in a deep breath, relishing in the delightful smells of fall. Although she loved her hometown, she'd always enjoyed the multicolored display of autumnal bliss cloaking the trees in the mountainous regions and northern states, something Beaufort lacked. She'd been fortunate enough to attend a few auctions in the northeast during fall and had loved every moment. October in Fall River was the epitome of autumn splendor with its beautifully hued trees, front stoops laden with orangey pumpkins, and fireplace smoke filtering through the air.

Glad to be away from the angry entity, Sarah searched her phone for a place to eat.

"How about Willa's Grill?"

"Sounds good to me," Danni said.

Sarah hit the GPS button and they followed the computerized voice to the restaurant. The aroma of burgers and fries greeted them as they walked in.

"I'm going to text the guys and see if they want anything," Sarah said as they sat at a table.

Moments later, her phone dinged with their order.

"Hello ladies," the waitress said, her broad smile punctuated by dimples. "What'll you have to drink?"

"Sweet tea," Sarah said.

The woman cocked her head. "You want what?"

"Sweet tea?" Sarah responded hesitantly.

"What's that?"

Sarah glanced at Danni. She'd heard there were places like this but it was her first encounter with one.

"It's iced-tea that's sweetened."

"All of our tea is unsweetened but there's sugar on the table," the waitress said, before looking at Danni. "You want the same?"

"Do you have beer?" Danni asked.

The waitress almost seemed relieved Danni was requesting a drink with which she was familiar. "We do. What'll you have?"

"Whatever is on tap."

"Be right back."

Danni snorted. "We're definitely not in the South anymore."

"No, we are not," Sarah laughed.

The waitress returned with their drinks and watched with a puzzled expression as Sarah grabbed several sugar packets and dumped them in the glass.

"That's a lot of sweetener," she said, arching her brows.

"We're from South Carolina where you get tea with your sugar."

"I can add sugar next time, if you'd like," the waitress said, apparently feeling guilty about not offering to do so before.

"It's not achieved by *adding* sugar," Danni said. "You have to mix the sugar while the tea is still hot. It's more like a syrupy drink. Seriously, there's more sugar than tea."

"Oh," she replied politely.

They glanced over the menu and placed their orders. Sarah took a sip of her tea and crinkled her nose. "Ick, not even close."

She dumped more sugar in the glass, stirred, and sipped again. "I think this is as good as I'm going to get without going into a sugar coma. How is it we're able to achieve sweet tea in the south without making us all diabetics?"

"One of our many southern secrets," Danni grinned.

Over plates of burgers and seasoned fries, they discussed everything Danni had gleaned about the trial while at the historical society. When the waitress came back to check on them, Sarah put in the order for the guys. After a filling meal, they paid the bill, grabbed the bags of food, and drove back to Borden House.

Garrett, Harry, and Ralph were in the kitchen huddled around the computer watching clips from the previous night. The men looked up as Sarah and Danni entered, their eyes glinting at the bags of food. They followed the two women into the dining room like zombies after fresh brains, and dug into their meals. Garrett put a few chunks of his burger on a plate and set it on the floor for Dallas who scarfed it down.

"Anything worthwhile on the tapes?" Sarah asked.

"Actually, yes," Harry replied. "I'll show you after we eat."

Once the to-go containers were cleared, Danni and Sarah followed Harry into the kitchen and watched as he cued the tape.

The infrared light cast a green aura over the grainy scene. In the far corner of the room, a shadowy form waffled and wavered before collapsing.

"Is that Abby Borden?" Sarah asked.

"That's what we were thinking. She's in the right location."

Sarah shuddered. The form had been upright and then crumpled to the floor. Were they watching her murder? And if so, where was the image of the killer?

"No offense, but this is creeping me out," Danni grimaced. "I'll let you guys get back to it. I'm going upstairs to do a little research."

Sarah and Harry looked at each other and grinned.

"I take it she can only handle so much of the great beyond," Harry said.

"She's a good sport but yeah, she has her limits when it comes to the spirit world."

"Were you able to learn anything at the museum?"

"Danni got more details from the trial transcripts which I'll let her share. I went through some of the post-trial aspects of Lizzie's existence."

"Anything interesting?"

"Other than loving animals and actively advocating for a local animal rescue, she seemed to live a rather simple life. There were a few parties and social gatherings mentioned but nothing extraordinary."

"She loved animals?" Harry asked, his brows furrowed.

"Yes. She left a hefty part of her estate to the local rescue."

"Doesn't sound like a person who would butcher her parents."

"That's what I said," Sarah declared, thankful someone else had come to the same conclusion. "Usually, monstrous killers lack empathy and treat animals with the same contempt."

"Definitely puts a different slant on the idea of her innocence."

Garrett's eyes met Sarah's when he and Ralph entered the kitchen. She could tell by his expression he wanted to speak with her. Dallas parked at Sarah's feet, his tongue lolling to one side.

"Wanna go for a walk, little fella?" Sarah asked, patting the dog's head.

Bark!

"I'll go with you," Garrett offered.

Ralph and Harry exchanged knowing glances.

"What?" Sarah asked.

"Using the dog as an excuse for some alone time. Shameful," Ralph chortled.

"Come on," Garrett said with a sheepish grin as he escorted Sarah and Dallas to the back yard.

"Sorry about that," Garrett said once they were outside.

"Don't be," she replied with a smile. "We shouldn't be so cryptic around them. It's not like they don't know about us."

Staring down at her, Garrett wrapped his arm around Sarah's waist and pulled her closer.

"Then I suppose we should take advantage of our time

alone," he whispered, his lips meeting hers.

For a moment, the world around them with its silly friends and hair-raising apparitions disappeared. Soaking in the comfort of his essence, Sarah's lips lingered against his. She adored everything about him, especially his ghost-sensing dog who was gamboling about the yard. The breeze picked up, sending goosebumps skittering across her skin at the same time Dallas started growling. Instinctively, Sarah broke away from the kiss and looked around.

"What's the matter?" Garrett asked.

Sarah shook her head. Something was in the air; she could feel it in her bones.

Dallas ran toward Sarah, stopped at her feet, and snarled in the direction of the adjoining property. Biting her lower lip, Sarah suppressed a scream when the woman with the slit across her throat materialized. The cadaver's mouth wrinkled as the word, *cursed,* wafted on the breeze.

"Do you see something?" he whispered.

The ghastly vision dissolved when Garrett rested his hand on Sarah's shoulder.

"It was Eliza from the cottage next door."

"Did she say anything?" His words were gentle, calming Sarah while she recounted what had happened.

"She said 'cursed' and then disappeared."

"What curse?"

"Hard to say. Let's face it, between the deaths of Eliza and her children and the murders of Andrew and Abby Borden, the family seems to have something of a tumultuous history."

"But Eliza's murder-suicide took place more than forty years before the Borden's deaths. What's the connection?"

"That my dear Watson, is the million-dollar question. Answer it and perhaps we'll be able to solve both hauntings."

Garrett rubbed the back of his neck. "You brought your *Dreamist* book, right?"

"Yes."

"Let's look through the chapter about your specific skill set. Maybe it will help us piece together this multi-spirit mystery."

Garrett and Dallas followed Sarah to her room where she retrieved her copy of the *Dreamist* book. Dallas hopped onto the bed and curled up on the pillow. Garrett sat next to Sarah on the edge of the bed as she opened the small leather-bound tome.

"Any idea which chapter we should start with?"

He smiled. "Chapter nineteen covers your personal skillset. At least, that was the chapter in Grams's and Tara's books so I assume it will be the same with yours."

Sarah remembered this discussion when they were in Edgefield right after learning about Garrett's affiliation with dreamists. He was the one who disclosed that while each dreamist shared abilities, she also possessed her own skillset. Paging to chapter nineteen, Sarah started reading.

You're unique in your ability,
    To handle things of fragility,
    Let the items of the past,
    Guide you to the truth,
    Of those who hold fast,
    To the essence of their youth.

"Youth? Is this referring to young people who have died?"

"Not exactly. Grams told me that some who linger after death view their earthly bodies as young. That could be the meaning behind the phrase. From what I understand not all entities get assistance immediately."

"Tara hadn't been dead for long when she started haunting my dreams," Sarah said.

"Tara was a dreamist which may have expedited the process.

Didn't you tell me your biological mother had been haunted but unable to decipher the messages from the dead?"

"From what I can tell, yes. One of her friends told me Edie felt as if she was losing her mind because of the dreams and visions. Sadly, I never knew Edie when she was alive so I don't know the extent of her knowledge or abilities."

"Didn't you find the *Dreamist* book in her house?"

"Yes. It was buried behind a bunch of books covered in decades worth of dust. For all I know, the book had been hidden since Nora's death," Sarah said.

"Let's keep reading."

Behind them, Dallas started snoring, bringing a grin to Sarah's face.

LAY BUT A HAND ON ANTIQUITIES,
   To unlock your special abilities.
   Visions will appear,
   And lips whisper in your ear,
   The secrets of the past,
   Of which you must grasp.

BEWARE *of the groups that send you in loops,*
   Hiding the truth that leads to the proof,
   Which you must unlock,
   To remove the block,
   Holding them to earth,
   And concealing their worth.

SARAH RUBBED her eyes with the palms of her hands. "This sounds like a bunch of mumbo jumbo."

"Actually, it makes sense. You're looking at it too literally. It reads like poetry. There's a lot of inuendo and symbolism."

"Two things I stink at," Sarah grumbled.

"The first stanza talks about you handling old items and the whispers that reveal what the entity is trying to convey. The second one is a bit convoluted. If I'm understanding it correctly, I think it's saying there will be groups of ghosts who try to hinder your ability to see the truth clearly thus preventing you from assisting those seeking your help."

Sarah pursed her lips as she reread the stanzas. "That actually makes sense."

"Don't act so surprised," he grunted.

"Sorry," she replied, squeezing his hand. "I wasn't inferring you aren't smart. Danni and I have been struggling with all of this for well over a year. To have someone decipher it immediately is a bit shocking."

"I had a great teacher," he said, sorrow shadowing his expression.

"Wish I could have known Ola in person. At least I'm getting to know her through my dreams. I like having her around."

Garrett leaned over and kissed her.

"What was that for?" she asked, a flush warming her cheeks.

"For understanding how special Grams was, and for being pretty amazing yourself."

How had she been so lucky to find a man who not only understood her unusual talents but accepted her as well?

"So," she said, trying to get back to the task at hand, "the other ghosts are a ploy to distract me from finding the truth about the Borden murders."

"Sounds that way to me. It also reiterates your ability to touch something belonging to the deceased in order to make a connection."

"One of the early chapters actually covered that. It was one of the first things Danni helped me with."

"Makes sense since that seems to be the crux of your

skillset."

"Let's see if we can find a way to sever the connections with the other entities so I can get to the truth."

As they read on, they were able to determine Sarah must have touched something that had also been handled by Eliza at some point in her life. Since she was the second wife to Lizzie's great-uncle there was always the possibility a piece of furniture or some other family memento had made its way into the Borden House. Since the piano in the front parlor had been in the family, perhaps Eliza had played it. Sarah didn't remember touching it although she could have brushed against it when walking through the room.

"I haven't really handled much in this house. What are the odds that the few things I have touched would have belonged to Lizzie's great-uncle and his wife, Eliza?"

"Hard to say, but there must be something here. We could always ask Mrs. Pearson."

"What about this?" Sarah asked, pointing to the verse at the bottom of the page.

BEWARE OF WHERE YOU WALK,
For the ground on which you stalk,
Holds the power of those who existed
And whose souls have yet persisted.

"ELIZA'S HOUSE borders this property. Do you think I've connected with her because I've walked where she once did?"

A broad smile curled Garrett's lips. "For someone who claims to have no ability for understanding brainteasers, I think you nailed it. Perhaps you've connected with Eliza Darling Borden via the property and now her thoughts are intermingling with all the others vying for your attention."

"Great, just what I needed. A ghostly fan club," Sarah said, exhaling.

"Now we need to figure out how to break the connection so Lizzie can have your full attention."

"What chapter explains that?" Sarah asked.

Garrett's hopeful expression faded. "Not sure, but we need to find it so we can get to the truth behind the Borden murders."

"Want me to get Danni to help us?"

"Sounds good."

Sarah knocked on the door to Danni's room.

"Yeah," Danni called out.

Cracking the door open, Sarah peered inside. "You busy?"

"Depends on what you're going to ask me to do," Danni replied with a suspicious squint of her eyes. She was leaning against the headboard of her bed with her computer in her lap.

"Garrett and I are reading through the *Dreamist* book and may have figured out why I'm being haunted by so many different spirits at the same time."

"Seriously? she said, setting her laptop on the bed. "That's it?"

"Huh?" Sarah responded.

"You're alone with Mr. Hunky in your room and all you were doing was reading through a book?"

Sarah's head dropped to her chest. "Yes, we were alone, reading a book."

"Tsk, tsk, tsk, what a waste."

"Not really since we're making headway about what's happening in my dreams. We need to find the chapter that explains how to break the connection with these other ghosts. Are you up for a little light reading?"

"Humph. That book is far from light reading. But yes, I'm willing to help."

Danni climbed from bed and stopped at the door. "He's dressed, right? You weren't reading in the nude?"

Sarah smacked Danni's upper arm. "Get your mind outta the gutter. You can see I'm fully clothed."

Danni passed by Sarah, shaking her head. "Like I said, such a waste."

For the next hour, the three of them skimmed through the book hoping to find the answers they were seeking, but to no avail. The more they analyzed different chapters, the more confused they became.

"I don't get it," Garrett said, blowing a long breath across his lips. "It was so much easier with Grams's book."

A knock at the door made them all jump. Quickly, Sarah stuffed the book under her pillow, rousing a bleary-eyed Dallas. Somehow, he'd managed to snooze through their in-depth discussion of the riddles.

"Come in," Sarah hollered.

Harry stepped through the door. "We were wondering where you guys disappeared to."

"We were going over some of the information we gleaned from the museum and how it relates to the images on the tape," Sarah said smoothly, surprised at how well the lie flowed from her lips. It wasn't exactly untrue; they had been talking about her dreamist skills in relation to the Borden case.

"Were you able to make any connections?" he asked, hope brewing in his eyes.

"A little," Garrett replied. "I think we need to get some more equipment from the studio and set up cameras in the back yard."

"Why the yard? The only thing we're likely to catch out there are raccoons or possums."

"Whoever killed the Bordens most likely escaped through the back door. There would have been too many people on the street to risk going out the front, especially since the killer was probably covered in blood," Garrett said.

"Except Bridget was washing the back windows when Mrs.

Borden was killed. She would've seen a stranger leaving through the back, that is if you believe Lizzie isn't the guilty party," Danni said, giving Sarah a knowing look.

"The person responsible could have been in the house for both murders," Sarah suggested.

"And no one noticed a stranger lingering about with blood-soaked clothes?" Danni retorted.

"Maybe they knew the person and were too afraid to identify him or her," Sarah said.

"Then why not mention it to the police when they investigated?" Harry asked. "They could have made the arrest and eliminated any retaliation."

Garrett scrunched his lips. "Don't know. Perhaps they were trying to protect him or her."

"Again, you're assuming it was an outsider," Danni added.

Harry folded his arms across his chest. "Let's consider the possibility. Why would Bridget and Lizzie, the only ones reportedly at the house at the time of the crimes, be willing to protect this person after he butchered two people?"

"That's the mystery we have to solve," Garrett stated.

"Unless Lizzie is guilty," Danni said. "Which is the most likely conclusion."

"Well, we're not getting anywhere with suppositions. Let's get back to work," Harry replied.

They went downstairs to plan for the evening's filming. Garrett and Ralph went to the studio to get more equipment while Harry continued working on the previous night's footage. Sarah and Danni compiled everything they'd learned at the museum and possible connections to what had been captured on tape. With any luck, the pieces would begin to fall in place, revealing the culprit behind one of the most notorious crimes in history.

CHAPTER 9

Garrett and Ralph returned unexpectedly with Valerie. Apparently, she wanted to witness the ghost hunt firsthand and convinced the guys to let her come along. Ralph seemed to stand straighter as he followed her around like a puppy, too love-struck to notice she was focused on Garrett. Her presence grated on Sarah's nerves, sending a pulsing fury through her already tense muscles. More than ever, Sarah wanted to slap the coquettish grin from her face.

Dusk shrouded the interior of Borden House in hues of orange and gold as Garrett, Harry, and Ralph positioned cameras in strategic locations throughout the rooms and back yard. Meanwhile, Valerie stuck to Garrett like duct tape.

Sarah sat in the guest room where Abby was murdered watching Garrett adjust equipment. Valerie rested her hand on his upper arm, and leaned in so her shirt gaped revealing her cleavage.

"Explain why you chose this angle for the camera," she trilled, her eyelashes fluttering shamelessly.

Without looking up, Garrett explained the purpose for the placement.

"With infrared lighting, we need to avoid any extraneous light so we can be certain the images we capture are actually ghosts and not shadows."

"How clever," she replied with a seductive jiggle of her chest.

Sarah rolled her eyes. Valerie's motives were obvious, especially since she ran a network catering to paranormal occurrences and would have known about camera placement. Her ridiculous behavior suggested she'd never been around a ghost hunting crew.

Poor Ralph kept fumbling with cords and tripping while Valerie acted as if Garrett was the only one who mattered. Dallas sat on the floor at Sarah's feet, his expression suggesting he was just as disgusted by the bimbo's presence.

Much to Sarah's relief, Valerie's phone rang and she left the room to take the call. In a love-sick zombie-like trance, Ralph followed her while Harry went to double check the wiring for the monitors. Garrett sat on the edge of the bed next to Sarah.

"Are you ready for tonight?" he asked, gripping her hand.

"Ready as I can be," she shrugged.

"Has Grams shown up in any of your recent dreams?"

"Not since we've been here, then again, I haven't been trying to connect with her either. I've been so wrapped up in understanding the purpose of all the supplementary ghosts, I completely forgot to call on her."

"Since she's been a comforting presence in the past and we need you to stay calm, consider trying again."

"I will," Sarah said.

He leaned in to kiss her when footsteps from the staircase separated them.

"We need to find some time alone," Garrett whispered.

"Agreed," Sarah replied with a smile, resting her forehead against his.

"Woof!" Dallas added.

They both started laughing as Danni entered the room.

"You ready for tonight's ghost-a-rama?" she asked.

"I think so," Sarah replied.

"I'm gonna hang with Ralph again tonight. I figure since he's watching the monitors in the kitchen, it's the least likely place to be haunted," Danni grinned.

"The kitchen is where Lizzie supposedly burned the dress in question, so it's apt to be filled with supernatural energy too," Sarah teased.

"Not as much as the murder rooms," Danni retorted, tilting her chin.

"I need to help Harry," Garrett said. "I'm going to take Dallas outside before we start filming." He walked out of the room with Dallas at his heels.

"You look tired," Danni said, sitting next to her friend on the bed.

"I'm beat," Sarah replied, her shoulders slouching. "Garrett suggested I call on Ola in my dreams tonight for help."

"Makes sense."

"I feel silly for not thinking of it before now."

"Your mind has been on other things." Danni winked.

"Stop it," Sarah grumbled. "He's been so busy we haven't had any time to ourselves, except when he set up the camera in my bedroom the first night we were here."

"That's sick," Danni said with a grimace.

Sarah huffed. "It was to film the ghosts."

"That's what makes it so sick."

"You're impossible."

"And that's what makes me special," she chuckled. "Want a drink before we dive into the world of specters and ghouls?"

"Yes."

Danni produced a flask from her jeans pocket and handed it to Sarah. Unscrewing the cap, she took a long draw before giving it back to her friend.

After taking a swig herself, Danni put the cap on and shoved the flask in her back pocket.

"Have you got a plan for tonight's scare fest?" Danni asked.

"Try to keep my wits about me and concentrate on all the things we've discussed over the past few days. If I encounter any ghosts outside of those directly related to the Borden case, dismiss them. If I get scared, I'll call on Ola. Most importantly, I need to find a way to communicate with Lizzie. Since her parents likely never saw who killed them, Lizzie is our best hope of getting answers."

"What about Bridget?" Danni asked.

"What about her?"

"If she shows up you can ask her questions too. She was at the house when the murders took place. Maybe she saw something that didn't make sense at the time but might make sense to us now."

"Good point. I'll try to keep that in mind," Sarah said, rubbing the back of her neck.

"What's the matter?" Danni asked, arching her brows.

"Dallas will be with me and Garrett will be in the hall with *Valerie*." Sarah sneered when she said the woman's name.

"Let's hope you find answers, the guys get some footage, and the ghosts take Valerie with them," Danni chortled.

"Agreed!" Sarah said with a sly smile.

"I'm going to check my email once more before I join Ralph."

"The poor guy looks like a lost sheep. Sadly, I think he's smitten with Valerie. Too bad she couldn't be attracted to him instead."

"Don't wish that bimbo on someone as sweet as Ralph. He deserves better," Danni chuckled. She stood up, patted Sarah's shoulder, and left the room.

Leaning against the headboard, Sarah closed her eyes, going over everything she needed to do in her dreams. In an effort to calm her racing pulse, her mind drifted to the feel of Garrett's lips against hers and the warmth of his arms around her waist. The tension in her muscles melted away as a peacefulness enveloped her leading her to a land of dreams.

Sarah stood in the back yard of Borden House looking over the gardens. Bridget sloshed sudsy water with a rag onto the windows as birds chirped from nearby trees. The warmth of the sun massaged Sarah's neck as she scanned the area for any signs of otherworldly activity. A scream echoed from within the house, startling Sarah from her stupor. Instantly, her back tensed and her breath caught as she prepared for something gruesome to materialize when she remembered Ola.

Closing her eyes, she concentrated on Ola's welcoming demeanor and soothing gaze. A weathered hand rested on her shoulder chasing the fear from her body. Sarah turned to see Ola standing behind her with a broad smile.

"You're doing better," she said.

Determined to make Ola proud and accomplish her goal of communicating with Lizzie, Sarah straightened her stature.

"I'm trying," she replied.

Sarah started for the house when a shadow at the edge of the property accompanied by a sinister laugh caught her attention. Turning that direction, she moved toward it. A breeze whispered through the tree branches forming the words, *catch me if you can.*

Sarah chewed her lower lip and braced herself for something horrid to appear. Much to her surprise, nothing happened. Pleased with her fortitude, Sarah walked on. As she neared the wooded area, the temperature began to drop, sending a chill down her back. She glanced over her shoulder to see if Ola was still there. She was; however, she was a good distance back, like a parent letting a child take its first steps.

Advancing into the grove of trees, Sarah looked around,

jumping when a squirrel skittered past. She gripped her chest as she took in a deep breath. That's when she saw it. The shadowy figure hovered several feet away. Its dark essence immediately set her teeth on edge. This entity exuded a discomforting feeling, more than any of the others she'd encountered in her dreams.

With all the courage she could muster, Sarah forced her feet to move forward at the same moment the figure bolted from behind the tree, its wicked laugh resonating through the woods. A sharp pain stabbed at her skull when something grabbed her shoulder and shook, wrenching a shriek from her lips.

DANNI JUMPED BACK; her complexion as white as flour. Leaning forward, Sarah blew out a breath.

"You scared me," she managed to say, her voice raspy.

"Not as badly as you scared me!" Danni chided.

"You should know by now I startle easily when I'm dreaming."

Planting her hands on her hips, Danni arched her brows. "How do you expect me to wake you up? Besides, I've only been gone for a few minutes. I didn't think you'd be in a dream state so quickly."

"Sorry, I didn't mean to snap at you." Rubbing her eyes, Sarah straightened up. "What do you want?"

"To let you know the guys are ready to start filming."

"Got it," she replied, adrenaline pumping through her veins, making her lightheaded.

"Were you dreaming about something important?" Danni asked.

Sarah looked at her friend in the dim light of the room. "Now that I think about it, yes. I was able to contact Ola. She gave me the courage to pursue someone I saw at the back of the property. I assume it was the day of the murders because I saw Bridget washing windows and then heard a scream from inside. That's when a shadowy form appeared near the woods and I went after him."

"It was a man?" Danni asked, anticipation lighting her expression.

"I didn't see the person clearly but for some reason I get the feeling it was male."

"It's a good start. Go back to sleep. Maybe you'll pick up where you left off."

"Let's hope so," Sarah replied, as Danni left the room and Dallas came bounding in.

Garrett walked in behind his dog and grinned. "You ready?"

Sarah nodded. "Come on Dallas," she called, patting the bed. "Let's find some ghosts."

"Garrett," Valerie's annoyingly shrill voice called from the hall. "I think you need to adjust the wires on the monitor."

"Coming," he said, leaving the room.

"Adjust the wires yourself," Sarah muttered, her jaw clenched. Why didn't Garrett tell her to get Harry or Ralph to do it?

Dallas groaned as he rested his head on his paws. The atmosphere was heavy with doom. Something told her this could be the most intense night yet. Whether that was due to Valerie's presence or the spectral activity, remained to be seen.

Sarah turned off the light on the nightstand and curled up on the bed with Dallas at her side. Closing her eyes, she tried to concentrate on Ola but images of Valerie sitting with Garrett infiltrated her thoughts. The woman was infuriating even though she'd never done anything cruel to Sarah. Still, her obnoxious presence made everything seem convoluted.

Sarah tried thinking about the kiss she and Garrett had shared earlier. It was affectionate although now she questioned whether it held the same warmth as prior interludes. Was he changing toward her or was this nothing more than the green-eyes of jealousy? And what about poor Ralph? He was obviously smitten with Valerie. Surely, Garrett wouldn't betray his friend by hooking up with that conniving floozy.

Stop it, she thought, scolding herself for being insecure and petty. Garrett cared about her, of that she was certain, or was she? The idea they'd never cemented the relationship with an exclusive agreement nibbled at her subconscious. The emotional upheaval of the situation tugged at her eyelids like window blinds lowering until she entered dreamland where secrets skulked in the shadows.

THE DANK ODOR of mildew permeated Sarah's senses as she stood in a basement. Her shoulders tensed and her heart palpitated. Something was amiss. Closing her eyes, Sarah concentrated on Ola's image. Suddenly, a hand rested on her shoulder sending a wave of calm through her body. Sarah turned to see Ola standing behind her, a smile wrinkling her eyes.

Ola's presence gave Sarah the courage to look around the space with its exposed beams and dirt floor. The cistern stood before her, its smooth stone surface sucking the confidence from her lungs. *Cursed* echoed through Sarah's mind as Eliza's grisly image appeared. Inhaling, Sarah closed her eyes and focused on Lizzie Borden. Eliza's image faded at the same time a four-legged critter scurried across Sarah's foot into the shadows, jolting her from the dream.

Squinting, she noticed the green light blinking on the camera that was trained on her. Not wanting to alert anyone she was awake, she pretended to sleep. Her mind wandered to images from previous dreamscapes where the screams of drowning children echoed from the cistern and the image of

Eliza Darling Borden's slit throat hovered. *What on earth could drive a person to commit such a heinous act?*

Sarah concentrated on clearing her head. She didn't need to be distracted by other entities harboring their own messages. Although glad to be learning more about her abilities, some of them would require more study before they could be applied. Fixing her attention on a specific ghost was one of those skills. Understanding the message of one ghost was difficult enough, but blocking out multiple spirits while trying to focus on one was complicated.

Sarah centered her thoughts on Lizzie. Within minutes, she'd reentered the dream world. A warmth materialized beside her, letting her know Ola was there. Sarah gave her a smile. This time she was in the basement of Borden House. On the far wall was a crumpled pile of newspapers by a water closet. Something about the area drew her closer, specifically the stack of papers. She started sifting through the pile when a brooch rolled from within.

Picking it up, she studied it. Why was a piece of jewelry stashed in a stack of newspapers? She started to put it in her pocket but stopped. This was a dream; she couldn't take items with her. Or could she? When she was in Edgefield, the ghost of Brady's mother, Mrs. Anderson, was able to roll a poison bottle to her from the great beyond. Could she bring the brooch back with her to wakefulness? It was worth a try. She shoved it into her pocket and continued her search through the dank space.

The creaking of steps alerted Sarah that someone was approaching. Bracing herself, she watched as Lizzie entered the cellar, her eyes darting about. She ran to the water closet and moments later emerged, seemingly calmer. Sarah recalled reading about investigators finding something notable hidden in the water closet that was used by the prosecuting attorney.

Smoothing her dress, Lizzie climbed the staircase and disappeared. The sound of giggling tugged Sarah back to consciousness.

Darkness shrouded the room as Sarah's eyes fluttered open. She felt as if she'd run a marathon. Her back was stiff and her head felt fuzzy. Another giggle echoed from down the hall. For a moment, Sarah wasn't sure she was actually awake until she heard Valerie's whispers. Anger burned in Sarah's chest, bringing her to full consciousness. Honing in on the sound, she sat up, trying to decipher what Valerie was saying when she heard Garrett chuckle. The nerve of this woman to be flirting with her boyfriend!

She'd had enough. Sliding from bed, Sarah started for the door, determined to confront the floozy but stopped. As far as Valerie was concerned, Garrett was open game. He'd introduced Sarah as a colleague, not his girlfriend. The anger subsided, flowing down her cheeks in tears. What exactly was going on? Had she misread Garrett's signals? Were they an exclusive couple or not? With no prior experience in the romance department, Sarah was overwhelmed.

But Danni would have noticed if Garrett had been playing her. Not to mention, Garrett's grandmother seemed to be encouraging the match. Or was Ola's presence only connected to her dreamist skills? Either way, she was befuddled by the entire situation. Her mind wondered to dark places. Maybe Garrett was tired of always discussing her dreamist abilities, or lack thereof, and was bored with her. Valerie definitely seemed like the exciting type with her bubbly personality, executive position at the network, and her stunning good looks, even if they were fake.

Sarah took in a deep breath and released it. The giggling had stopped. Unsure whether that was a good thing or not, she decided to find out. Starting for the door, she stopped when something on the other side of the room moved. Squinting, she focused on the movement and took a step toward it. Amazed at her fortitude, she walked to the window. Apparently, romantic distrust stifled fear, something she'd have to keep in mind for future endeavors.

Without warning, the curtain rod fell from the wall in a clatter, dissolving her courage like sugar in a tea cup. She scurried across the room and out the door where she promptly ran into Garrett.

His hands caught her upper arms, sending a tingle across her skin. His gaze was filled with concern. Wide-eyed, Valerie stood behind him, her proximity a bit too close for Sarah.

"Are you alright?" Garrett asked.

"Fine," Sarah replied curtly.

He cocked his head. "Are you sure? You seem upset."

"Not at all. Something was in the room and I decided to check it out."

"We saw that," he said. "Then the curtains fell so we came to check on you."

The word, *we*, stuck in her heart like an ice pick.

"It's an old house, things fall. Maybe you caught something on tape," Sarah responded.

"I'm sure he did," Valerie purred, placing her manicured hand on Garrett's shoulder. When he didn't shrug it off, Sarah decided she'd had enough of Tootsie and her games.

"I'm going to the kitchen," Sarah announced, heading for the staircase with Dallas at her heels.

As she trudged to the landing, Sarah waited for Garrett to follow or at least ask why she was going but he didn't say a word. Without looking back, she hurried down the steps, through the house, toward the kitchen. At that moment, she didn't care if she was caught on tape or if it ruined the filming. She wanted to scream and cry all at the same time.

Before stepping into the kitchen, Sarah thought about her dream. Eliza had appeared and whispered 'cursed' yet Sarah had managed to block her out. This was a major accomplishment and she wanted to share it with the two people who'd helped her get this far. For now, she'd only be able to talk to Danni since Garrett was otherwise engaged.

Sarah remembered the brooch from her dream and checked her jeans pocket. Empty. Ugh, she thought. How stupid could a person be? Of course, she wasn't able to bring back something she'd dreamt about. Tears threatened to fall as she entered the kitchen and looked at her friend. Between her efforts at strengthening her dreamist skills and putting up with Valerie's nonsense, Sarah felt defeated. Danni seemed to read her mood. She whispered something to Ralph and nodded Sarah toward the back door.

Grabbing Sarah's arm, Danni led her to the back yard. The crispness of the night air bit at Sarah's skin, instantaneously chilling her to the core. Once she was certain they were out of earshot, Sarah broke down.

Danni pulled her close as Sarah sobbed into her friend's shoulder.

"My gosh, what did you dream?" she whispered, stepping back.

"It's more of a nightmare and her name is Valerie," Sarah croaked, wiping her eyes with the sleeve of her shirt.

"What on earth are you talking about?"

"She's constantly flirting with Garrett. The worst part is, I think he likes it," she sniffled.

Danni shook her head. "I don't think you have anything to worry about. First, Garrett adores you, everybody knows it. Second, he's probably being friendly with her to avoid messing up this contract."

"Then why not introduce me as his girlfriend?"

"Are you still hung up on that? I told you; he was probably trying to look professional," Danni scolded. "We know the real reason why you're here but Garrett can't disclose that to anyone else. Presenting you as part of the team sounds more professional."

Sarah had grown very fond of Garrett over the summer; however, this turn of events seemed to illuminate the depth of her feelings. There was no longer any question in her mind, she was in love with him. Just what she needed, one more thing to complicate her already muddled existence. Things in their relationship had been so comfortable and easy-going, she'd not questioned anything until the blond nemesis showed up.

Dallas bolted out the back door and plunked down at Sarah's feet, his adoring gaze locking onto Sarah's puffy eyes. She reached down to pet him as Garrett and Valerie emerged. Sarah glanced at Danni whose stare was burrowing holes through Valerie.

Garrett smiled at Sarah, melting her resolve. How could she question his intentions? He was one of the most loyal and steadfast people she'd ever known yet here she was flustered about where she stood in his life.

"Valerie has an early morning," he said. "She's going home."

Sarah's heart leapt. Tootsie was leaving!

"Walk me to my car?" Valerie asked, batting her fake eyelashes like an idiotic fool.

"Glad to," he replied, walking beside her.

Clenching her fists, Sarah gulped down the scream hovering at her lips.

"Danni, I might have to deck that woman," she growled.

"Calm down," she said quietly. "He's only walking her to the car. It's what gentlemen do. It's not like he could've said no. That would have been rude."

"Whatever," Sarah grumbled.

The car lights flashed to life, illuminating Garrett's tall stature as he watched Valerie pull down the drive onto the street.

As he started toward them, Danni whispered to Sarah, "Don't say anything about Valerie."

She shot her friend an angry look when Garrett joined them.

"Everything OK?" he asked.

"Just discussing the evening's events," Sarah said, forcing a smile.

"Any good dreams?"

"Actually, yes," she replied.

"Great. Let's talk about it later. I need to get back inside."

He walked away leaving Sarah's heart in shreds.

"He didn't give me a kiss."

"I think you're reading too much into this," Danni said. "Trust me, it's easy to misinterpret situations when you care about someone."

"You'd definitely know," Sarah huffed.

As soon as the words left her lips, she regretted them. The pain she was feeling now reflected on her friend's face.

"Danni, I'm so sorry," she declared. "I didn't mean it."

Rolling her lips, Danni glanced at the sky. "I get that you're upset and this romance thing is new to you." Then her eyes met Sarah's. "I also know you'd never hurt me on purpose so there's no need for an apology."

Sarah nodded as fresh tears streamed across her face.

"I'm going inside. It's cold out here," Danni said, returning to the kitchen.

Sarah stood beneath the twinkling canopy of stars, her heart in pieces and her mind in turmoil. She'd come to help with the haunting of Borden House but had managed to hatchet her own relationships. She was tired of all the drama and Valerie's seductive advances toward Garrett. Now more than ever, she longed to go home and forget she'd ever come to Fall River.

Entering the house, Sarah trudged up the stairs to her room, and reclined on the bed with Dallas next to her. She stared at the ceiling pondering the images from her dreams and how she might improve her ability to interpret what she'd witnessed. However, she couldn't concentrate. The idea she'd inadvertently hurt Danni weighted her soul. What had possessed her to respond so cruelly to her best friend? Add the agony of watching a voluptuous woman manipulate Garrett, and Sarah's entire existence had gone off track like a runaway train. More than anything, she wanted to talk to Garrett and determine the depth of their relationship.

Danni popped her head in the door interrupting Sarah's thoughts. "You up for a visit?"

"For you, always," Sarah said, sitting up.

Danni padded across the floor and perched on the edge of the bed next to Sarah.

"I'm so sorry about earlier," Sarah sniffled. "You know I'd never do anything to hurt you."

Danni wrapped her arm around Sarah's shoulders and squeezed. "I told you all is forgiven. You're under a lot of pressure right now with the ghost stuff and Garrett."

"Is this what happens when you give your heart to someone?" Sarah queried.

"Afraid so. Love can be brutal sometimes."

"I don't know how to handle this kind of thing," Sarah said with a sigh. "Dealing with ghosts is bad enough, but mending a broken heart is excruciating."

"You're causing yourself a lot a grief for nothing," Danni said, holding her friend's hand. "You need to talk to Garrett and get his side of the story before letting self-doubt torture you."

"I know you're right but I feel so foolish admitting my doubts to him."

Danni smiled. "Foolishness and love are best friends. You can't have one without the other."

"Great," she said. "Any other words of wisdom?"

"Get some sleep. And remember everything you dream so we can interpret it in the morning."

Sarah squeezed her friend's hand. "Thanks."

"For what?"

"Always being there for me."

"It's my purpose in life," she chuckled.

Danni got up and left the room. Sarah went to the bathroom, washed up, and changed into her nightclothes. Returning to her room, she flopped onto the bed, patted Dallas on the head, closed her eyes, and drifted off to a land of bizarre dreams devoid of voluptuous blonds and tormented hearts.

CHAPTER 10

Sarah stared through the front window of Borden House, watching people parade past. Ladies in flowing skirts beneath parasols walked arm in arm with gents in bowler hats and sack coats. Nostalgia swept over the scene, drawing a smile across Sarah's lips. There was a romance to the past that had always captured her heart. It was one of the few things she enjoyed about her haunted dreams, getting a first-hand view of more genteel eras.

The sound of the front door opening and closing pulled Sarah from the window. Walking to the entryway, she watched as Bridget greeted Mr. Borden.

"Sir, didn't think you be home so soon," she curtseyed as Mr. Borden walked past.

Sarah could sense Bridget's discomfort at her employer's unexpected return. Her stomach was still churning after she'd vomited earlier that morning.

"Got everything done I set out to do and decided to come home for a nap. Where is Mrs. Borden?" he asked.

Bridget fidgeted with the hem of her apron. "Don't know, sir. She got a note this morning and I've not seen her since."

"How odd," he said, rubbing his snowy beard. "I'm surprised she didn't leave word as to where she was going."

Bridget nodded.

"And where is Lizzie?"

"In her room."

Mr. Borden started for the sitting room. "See that I'm not disturbed, Bridget."

"Yes, sir," she replied scampering away like a frightened rabbit, her stomach cramping.

Mr. Borden reclined on the settee, leaning his head against the velvet arm and closing his eyes. Not long after, a long shadow eclipsed his slumbering frame.

Sarah braced herself for what she knew would follow. Not wanting to witness the grisly scene, she started to close her eyes but thought better of it. Perhaps she could see the person committing the crime and finally discover the truth behind the century old mystery.

Her train of thought was interrupted when a hatchet slammed into Mr. Borden's head. Sarah squeezed her eyes shut and recoiled in disgust as blood splattered against her skin. At that moment, she abandoned her goal of seeing who the killer was. When she finally opened her eyes, Lizzie was standing before her father, her eyes glazed and her lips in a thin line. A scream erupted as Lizzie ran from the room, her calls for help echoing through the house.

Sarah looked around, careful to avoid the sight of Andrew Borden's body a few feet away. Everything had happened so fast. There hadn't been time for someone else to have been there and left before Lizzie discovered her father, not to mention there was no sign of the murder weapon. Could Bridget have taken the hatchet and hidden it while Lizzie searched for help? Then again, dreams rarely happened in real time. Perhaps these were only glimpses of the things that had transpired.

A shriek from the second floor sent Sarah bolting up the

steps. Bridget stood at the foot of the bed in the guest room, horror contorting her face. A hand grabbed Sarah's shoulder, making her jump. Turning, she stared at Lizzie Borden, her face sullen as she mouthed the words, *not what it seems.*

Sarah sat up in bed, gasping for air. The room was cloaked in darkness and she realized Dallas wasn't there either. She rubbed her eyes and scanned the shadowy space. The camera light was red indicating it wasn't running. Why was there a camera in her room? Had Garrett come in, set up the camera, and taken Dallas with him? Her heart dropped. Why would he come in without waking her? Maybe he was losing interest in her.

Sarah inhaled. She swung her legs over the edge of the bed when a bloodied hand reached up from the floor, sending her scurrying backwards. Leaping from the other side of the bed, Sarah found her footing and ran for the door. She tugged on the knob but it wouldn't budge. Frantic, Sarah started banging on the door when she felt a sticky hand grip the back of her neck.

She elbowed whatever was behind her, knocking it back as she pulled on the knob. Nothing. Panic squeezed the air from her lungs as she started pounding on the door again.

"Let me out of here!" she wailed. "Garrett! Danni!"

Fingers grabbed Sarah's hair and pulled her to the floor. Glancing up, she saw Abby, her head split down the middle with blood trickling across her forehead onto her white dress. Sarah garnered all her courage and swallowed the bile burning her throat.

"What do you want?" she croaked.

"Justice," she replied.

A velvety tongue lapped at Sarah's face, stirring her from her slumber. Sarah jumped from the bed and looked around the room. Nothing was there. Of course, that's what she'd thought last time except it turned out to be another dream. Dallas let out a spirited bark and cocked his head. The door behind her opened and Garrett stepped into the room.

"What's going on?" he asked, concern veiling his face.

"Is this another dream or are you real?" she muttered, not sure what to believe.

Stepping forward, he wrapped his arms around her. "I'm real."

Her trembling frame melted against him.

He stepped back and met her gaze. "What happened?"

"I dreamed about Mr. Borden's death. Then I heard Bridget scream so I ran upstairs to see why. She'd found Mrs. Borden's body and I braced myself for the scene. I have to admit, I was surprised at how well I was able to move about and the clarity of my consciousness during the dreamscape. Anyway, I woke up, or so I thought, and noticed there was a camera in my room that wasn't running and Dallas was gone."

"And then?"

"A bloody hand reached up from the other side of the bed. I tumbled to the floor and started for the door but it wouldn't open. Then Mrs. Borden pulled me to the ground. I managed to overlook the gruesome nature of her appearance and ask what she wanted. All she said was *justice*. That's when I woke up. I've never had a dream within a dream before."

Garrett pulled her close again and kissed her cheek. "I don't suppose you saw who killed Mr. Borden."

"No."

"We need to sort through all of this. Sounds like you might be getting closer to discovering the truth behind these murders."

Sarah plunked onto the bed with Dallas snuggling beside her. "Why did I dream about Mrs. Borden in Lizzie's room?"

"Tell me more about it," Garrett said, sitting next to her.

Sarah recounted the story with as much detail as she could recall. Garrett's brows furrowed.

"None of this makes sense. Why would Lizzie be communicating with you if she was guilty? If anything, she'd want to prove her innocence. Let's face it, her presence in the house at the time of the murders suggests she did it."

"Unless the visions are wrong. Did your grandmother ever mention anything about dreamscapes being incorrect?"

"Actually, yes. Even though a dreamist can connect to the memories of the dead who seek her help, sometimes the images can distort or be influenced by the dreamists' own imagination."

"So, our abilities aren't foolproof."

"Not exactly, although they're accurate most of the time. It's rare for dreams to alter. When that happens, it's generally when the dreamist has prior experience affiliated with the situation."

"I don't have any previous knowledge of this case outside of what I've learned from the research."

"Which suggests the visions are accurate."

"I remember reading something about neighbors reporting seeing a strange man around the house on the day of the murders. I keep seeing a shadowy figure but he disappears before I can make out the details of his appearance."

Garrett's phone buzzed. Staring at the screen, he blew out a breath. "It's Val. She wants me to call her," he said, stepping out of the room.

Sarah's blood boiled at the thought of the scandalous little creature calling at this hour. And when did Garrett start calling her Val? It was getting more and more difficult to dismiss her constant interruptions. Enough was enough. Sarah was going to confront Garrett when he came back in. Except he didn't.

She waited several minutes. When he didn't return, she grabbed a change of clothes and plodded to the bathroom for a shower. All she wanted was to stand beneath a spray of steaming water to work the knots from her shoulders. What she wouldn't give for a long soak in an old tub.

Sarah closed the bathroom door, slipped out of her night-clothes, and turned the shower knob. Moments later, steam drifted from behind the shower curtain. Drawing the curtain to the side, Sarah started to step in when a disfigured form, its skull split in two stared at her from within. The horror and shock of it sent her stumbling against the toilet onto the floor with a thud. Landing on her left hip, she winced in pain. By the time she got to her feet the only thing in the shower was a misty spray and the soap dish. She wrapped the towel around her and with a shaking hand turned off the water.

Sarah lowered herself onto a stool by the sink, buried her face in her hands, and wept. Normally she could handle some of the ghastly visions and most of her frightening dreams, but Valerie's presence was complicating the situation.

Forgoing the shower, Sarah dressed, returned to her room, and flopped onto the bed. The clock glowed 5:35. It was too early to go downstairs. Instead, she stared at the ceiling trying to convince herself she was being ridiculous about Garrett. Snapshots from her dreams popped into her head making it ache. She couldn't make sense of anything right now. If only she could put her insecurities to rest so she could focus on her nocturnal visions.

After an hour of ruminating over her situation, she decided to go downstairs. She took Dallas outside before making her way to the dining room where she was surprised to find Danni with Ralph and Harry at the table sipping coffee.

"You're up already?" Sarah asked her friend.

"Haven't been to sleep yet," Danni replied, holding up a large cup of coffee. "It's like all-nighters before finals in law school."

"Where's Garrett?" Sarah asked.

"Valerie picked him up for a meeting," Harry said, not looking up from the book in his hands.

"Oh," Sarah replied, her pulse ticking up a notch. The woman had only been gone for a couple of hours, there's no way she'd gotten much sleep. What was she, a vampire? Goodness knows, she was sucking the life out of Sarah.

Danni looked at her friend and gave a quick shake of her

head. Apparently, something was amiss and Danni was letting her know this wasn't the time to address the situation. Mrs. Pearson popped in and placed a teapot and cup in front of Sarah.

"Breakfast will be ready soon," she said with a grin.

"Nothing for me, thanks," Sarah said, pouring her tea.

"Darlin', you'll waste away if you don't eat. This house can take it out of you with all its spirits and such. How about some toast?"

"No, thank you. I'm fine."

Danni stood as Mrs. Pearson left the room.

"Got a minute to help me with something?" Danni asked.

"Sure," Sarah replied, bringing her cup of tea as she followed her friend upstairs to Lizzie's room.

"Before you freak out about Garrett going to meet with Valerie, I wanted to tell you what happened."

Sarah plopped onto a chair. "What did she want, as if I didn't know."

"Stop it. This was legitimate. She needed to view some of the footage to see how things are progressing."

"Then why didn't Harry and Ralph go? They're more adept with the tech stuff."

"Because Garrett is kinda the one in charge."

Sarah snorted. "You know this group works as a team. She might want to believe he's in charge but this is more about finding an excuse to spend time *alone* with him."

Anger burned in Sarah's chest and tears threatened to fall as she thought about the blond Barbie doll who was hot for her boyfriend. At least she hoped he was still her boyfriend.

"I know what you're going through and it stinks," Danni said. "But you need to get a grip on your insecurity or you'll drive him away. You're reading too much into all of this. Trust me, neediness is a turnoff. Besides, I know Garrett, or I feel like

I do, and I don't think he's the type to get involved with someone like Valerie."

"That's what I keep telling myself and yet I'm having a hard time believing it. I've seen some of the women he dated in Edgefield and they resemble Valerie, except their body parts were natural not implanted."

"For now, you need to trust him. He's a smart guy with pretty good instincts. Let him handle this."

Sarah was shocked at Danni's words. Was she actually taking his side?

The tears finally broke free and trickled down Sarah's cheeks. "I hear what you're saying and I know it's probably true. But somehow, Garrett seems different towards me the past couple of days. More reserved."

"That's because you're thinking with your heart instead of your head. He needs to maintain a certain amount of distance on this project when the network people are around so nothing looks contrived. Hauling you along could appear like he's trying to get some free travel time for his girlfriend. And he can't reveal the real reason he brought you along, not to Valerie or even Harry and Ralph for that matter. This is a complicated endeavor for him."

"Makes sense," Sarah mumbled, wiping her eyes. "I can't believe I'm acting like such a fool."

"Welcome to the affairs of the heart. It clouds your judgment and can feel like an open wound."

"Thanks for the pep talk," Sarah huffed.

"I gave my heart to a serial killer who tried to kill us. Trust me, I know how hard this is."

"Not helping," Sarah replied. "I guess I'm just a bit tired. It's not like any of us has had a decent night's sleep since we arrived."

"Speak for yourself. Aside from staying up last night, I've been sleeping like the dead."

"Clever," Sarah snickered. "Think I'll lie down for a bit and try to get some ghost-free sleep."

"Is that possible?"

"Worth a try," she shrugged, walking to the bed with her teacup. "By the way, I saw what appeared to be Abby Borden's corpse in the shower earlier so you might want to use the bathroom on the third floor."

"What?" Danni exclaimed, her eyes the size of quarters. "Did the ghost say anything?"

"Not a word."

"What do you think it means?"

"That the house is definitely haunted," Sarah replied.

"Very funny," Danni responded, rolling her eyes. "Seriously? Do you think there was a purpose to her appearance?"

"Other than scaring me half to death and causing me to fall down which will probably leave a good size bruise on my hip, I have no idea."

"Get some rest. We can talk about this later," Danni said, giving Sarah a hug. "And try not to worry about Garrett. I know he cares about you."

"Thanks, Danni."

Danni left the room, closing the door behind her. Sarah sipped her tea, thinking about everything her friend had said. How had she let Valerie get so ingrained in her head? She'd never questioned her relationship with Garrett, until Valerie, so why all the doubt now? Placing the cup on the night table, she snuggled beneath the covers, closed her eyes, took a few deep breaths, and promptly fell asleep.

AN HOUR LATER, Sarah's eyes fluttered open. She stretched and looked around the room. She'd managed to sleep without any spirits infiltrating her dreams. The stress of everything had obviously exhausted her to a point of sound, ghostless sleep.

She heard a car door slam. Scurrying to the window, she watched Garrett and Valerie emerge from a shimmering silver Lexus. Sarah scowled at the sight. She really disliked this woman. Holding a computer and one camera, Garrett stopped to speak with the buxom blond. She smiled, resting her hand on his upper arm. He returned the smile; the same one he gave Sarah when they were together. Turning, he walked into the house. Valerie watched Garrett before glancing up at Sarah's window and smiling slyly before slipping into her car and driving away.

"Wretched little scamp," Sarah mumbled. She'd had enough. Gathering her courage, she stormed downstairs where the men stood in the kitchen talking.

"Hey Sarah," Harry said as she entered the room. "Garrett was getting ready to tell us what happened during the meeting this morning."

"Let's go sit in the dining room," he suggested.

They all followed and took their seats. Sarah purposefully sat across from Garrett. She was too upset about Valerie's behavior to speak.

"We've got a small problem," he said, exhaling.

"They aren't happy with the footage?" Ralph asked, his expression steeped in worry. "We still have a couple of nights and we're getting more each time. They need to give us a chance."

"Actually, they're pleased with what we've captured so far. Said it's good stuff. However, Valerie seems to feel we could get more if we conjured up some spirits."

"They want us to stage something?" Harry asked, his forehead wrinkling in disgust.

"Worse. She wants us to use a Ouija board and conduct a séance."

"We don't usually revert to those tactics," Harry said. "Did you agree to it?"

Garrett shook his head. "Nope. We've always prided ourselves on allowing the ghosts to make their presence known without parlor tricks and smoke screens. Regardless, we're a team and need to make the decision together."

"Is this something the network is pushing for?" Ralph asked.

"Not exactly. This is something Valerie wants. Apparently, she belongs to some sort of psychic women's group that engage in these things. Says she's a pretty good marker for spirits and can contact them readily," Garrett replied.

Sarah swallowed hard. Was he inferring Valerie was a dreamist too?

"I know I'm not part of this team but it seems like you should do what you believe in, not what some network executive tells you to do," Sarah said.

"You are part of our team," Harry responded. "You've done a lot to help us on this trip and we appreciate it. However, we wouldn't be the first group to stir the cauldron, if you will."

"Ralph?" Garrett said.

"Not sure. I'd rather try to capture spirits on film without all the hocus pocus. I feel like it discredits our integrity."

Sarah shifted in her chair. She'd always avoided Ouija boards and séances for obvious reasons. Spirits were frightening enough without the aid of portals that could allow unwanted ghosts access to haunted situations.

The three men stared at Sarah.

"What?"

"Give us your opinion," Garrett said, his emerald gaze boring through to her heart.

"I don't think it's a good idea. This is an opportunity for national exposure. If you use these means now, it will be expected in other projects. Lowering your standards will only tarnish future endeavors."

"I agree," Harry said. "The question is, will the network go along with our decision?"

"Let's hope so," Garrett replied. "What we need is something significant on tape. That should quell any requests for using artificial means to stir up the ghosts in this place."

"Then we should to get to work," Ralph said, getting up from his chair.

"But you guys haven't slept," Sarah responded.

"We'll have to muddle through. I'll make another pot of coffee," Harry offered.

"I need to take Dallas out and then we'll get to work," Garrett said.

"I'll come with you," Sarah added, following him to the door. She needed to find out what was going on between them, one way or the other. Maybe then, she could clear her head and get to the bottom of the mystery haunting her dreams.

CHAPTER 11

*D*allas romped across the yard to the far end where he started sniffing around. Garrett slipped his arm around Sarah's waist but she pulled away from him.

"What's wrong?" He dropped his hand and took a step back. "Are the dreams getting to you?"

"No more than usual," she said, trying to maintain a stalwart stance although his gaze was weakening her fortitude. She felt her resolve begin to melt as she bit her lower lip.

"Something's wrong. Please tell me what it is."

Losing her nerve, she decided to discuss the dreams instead. "My dreams are haphazard and not making any sense. Hopefully, we can figure it all out before the end of the week."

"About that...." he paused, scraping his shoe against the dirt. "Val likes what we've been able to capture so far and asked us to extend the filming. She believes we could get something significant if we have more time."

"Is everyone staying or *only* you?" Sarah snapped, regretting her sharp response as it left her lips. The pain on his face looked as if she'd slapped him.

Furrowing his brows, he spoke. "What is your problem?"

Sarah clenched her jaw. *How could he be so dense?* Surely, he could see Valerie's shameless attempts to gain his attention. The only one who didn't see it was poor Ralph who was so smitten by the woman he wouldn't flinch if she came at him with an ax.

"There's no problem with *me*," she retorted. More than ever, she wanted to blurt it all out. How Valerie was trying to seduce him and how he hadn't bothered to let her know they were dating. And how could he not realize one of his closest friends was gaga for the woman?

"Then who?" he asked, cocking his head.

"Never mind," Sarah muttered.

"This is more than the dreams. Please tell me what's going on," he said, his voice pleading as he took a step closer.

Surprised by his sudden change in demeanor, Sarah turned, too ashamed to face him as tears cascaded down her face. How could she tell him the truth? For goodness sakes, she'd faced the dead in every stage of decomposition but wasn't as frightened as she was right now. Garnering her courage, she hesitated before muttering, "It's Valerie."

Garrett's hands wrapped around her and pulled her close as he placed a kiss on her head. "I'm sorry. I didn't realize my work with Val was affecting you."

"Everything about that woman makes me...." her words trailed off. "I'm sorry if I'm being stupid about this, but her behavior towards you really gets on my nerves."

Gently, he turned her around to face him.

"It's not stupid. We've never discussed the parameters of our relationship."

Her heart froze. This was it. He was going to confess his desire to be with Tootsie.

"Oh my gosh, are you dumping me?" she squealed. "And in the back yard of all places?

Garrett's eyes grew to the size of marbles. "Of course not!" he declared. "Why would you think such a thing?"

"How could I not with *her* around? Let's face it, she's hard to dismiss." Sarah's words dissolved to a mere whisper as her gaze locked onto his.

"She's the network executive in charge of our project," he responded, his forehead wrinkling. "You can't actually believe I'm interested in her?"

His tone altered to one Sarah had never heard before, making her stomach churn.

"I don't know what to believe. Every time I turn around, she's flirting with you, no matter who's there. You even have a pet name for her, *Val.*"

"She asked me to call her that and she can flirt all she wants, I haven't reciprocated."

"Maybe not, but you also didn't make it known that we're dating!" Sarah exclaimed, finally finding her voice, the fear and confusion shifting into anger. She felt like she was on an emotional roller coaster dipping and soaring from sorrow to fear to anger with each wave of the conversation.

"Because it wasn't relevant, not to mention, it would taint the team's professionalism if the network thought we were bringing our girlfriends along." His tone was edgy, igniting Sarah's fury.

"Since we haven't discussed the terms of our relationship maybe we should do so now!" she replied, unaware they'd captured the attention of everyone inside.

"I didn't think it needed to be discussed!" he retorted.

"Why not?" she said, her hands perched on her hips.

"Because I thought it was obvious that I love you!"

Sarah's hands fell to her side as she took a small step back. Dallas was at her feet staring up at her.

"What?" she murmured.

Garrett's expression softened as he placed his hands on her upper arms. "It never occurred to me we needed to talk about this. I assumed you were aware of my feelings for you."

Fresh tears glistened in the corners of her eyes. "This relationship thing is new for me. I don't have any experience navigating them."

His eyes locked onto hers. "Then let me make it official. I love you, Sarah Holden."

Smiling, she rested her hand on his cheek, the tightness in her chest softening as his words washed away the angst that had been building up for days. "I love you, too," she whispered.

His lips met hers in a passionate kiss as applause erupted from their friends who had gathered in the kitchen doorway. Sarah and Garrett looked at Harry, Ralph, and Danni. A wave of heat flushed Sarah's cheeks as her eyes glanced at the ground. Garrett's fingers lifted her chin.

"Are we OK?" he asked, a pleading expression clouding his eyes.

Sarah nodded. "Still don't like Valerie," she grumbled.

"Let me deal with her. You focus on your dreams," he whispered, kissing her once more.

"That's enough romance for now," Harry called, from the doorway. "Come on, Dunc. We have ghosts to hunt."

Garrett offered his arm to Sarah who laced her hand through it and walked back into the house with him. Dallas followed, his tail wagging and his nose in the air as if pleased with the outcome.

Once inside, Garrett went to the dining room with the guys to discuss their next move. Sarah and Danni trudged up the stairs.

"Well, that was dramatic," Danni said, as they entered Sarah's room.

Sarah blushed. "I'm a little embarrassed about the whole thing."

"You mean the part where you let him have it about that network tramp or the part where you expressed your undying love and made out?" Danni said, placing the back of her hand against her forehead pretending to swoon.

"Not funny," Sarah replied, smacking her friend's arm. "This is unchartered territory for me. I'm still learning about this dating thing."

"You did a great job. Cornered him and then squeezed a confession from him."

"I wasn't trying to squeeze anything out of him," she said. "I only wanted to know what was going on with Valerie."

"Now you know. Feel better?"

"Much," Sarah replied, her chin tilted up.

"Since we've established what the rest of the world knew, let's talk about ghosts," Danni said, sitting on the chair.

Rolling her eyes, Sarah shook her head at Danni's abrupt change of topic.

"I'm not sure what else we can do to influence my dreams," Sarah sighed as she sat on the edge of the bed.

"Didn't you say you were able to block some of the extraneous spirits in your last set of dreams?"

"In a sense. Eliza tried to communicate with me but I was able to prevent it. Problem is, I'm not sure how I accomplished it."

"Then we need to dissect your dreams and figure it out," Danni said. "What have you dreamed recently that correlates with the evidence we have about the murders and the trial?"

"I keep dreaming about the day of the murders but with different perspectives. I've seen Lizzie, Mr. and Mrs. Borden, and Bridget. On several occasions, I've heard Lizzie scream at what I'm assuming was the discovery of her father's body. Most recently, I saw Lizzie in the guest room after Bridget discovered Mrs. Borden's body."

"These are all facts available in the records. What other information have you been able to garner?"

"Not much, I'm afraid. A few times, I've witnessed Mr.

Borden speaking with the doctor he hired to help Lizzie with her medical issues. We know she was prone to seizures during her time of the month which goes along with those scenes in my dreams. There's been a shadowy figure in the house and at the edge of the property. In one dream, I chased it but have yet to see its face. Sometimes I hear a laugh."

"Like kids?"

"More sinister than that. It gives me the creeps."

"Anything else about the murders with the family that used to live next door?"

"Like I said, I've managed to keep Eliza at bay although she's made attempts to distract me from the other visions."

Danni nodded as she got up and started pacing the room. Sarah knew this meant she was developing a theory. Hopefully, they'd make the necessary connections to help the guys as well as leading to information about what really transpired in the house on that dreadful day in August of 1892.

Halting, Danni looked at Sarah. "Wasn't there a dream where you put something in your pocket?"

"Yeah. I found a brooch hidden in the basement. I stuffed it in my pocket hoping it would be there when I woke up, but it wasn't."

"We need to investigate that further."

"How?"

Danni hesitated. "We'll need Garrett's help with this. Now that you two have survived your first official spat, I'm thinking it's a good time to brainstorm."

"What do you mean by spat?"

Pursing her lips, Danni gave her the 'I can't believe you're asking that' look. "Harry, Ralph, and I watched the two of you arguing in the back yard about Valerie. Don't try to sell this as some sort of discussion. It was a full-blown lover's spat."

"Hmph," Sarah snorted.

A sly grin curled Danni's lips. "You know I'm right. Nevertheless, we need Garrett's input to figure out the meaning behind your nightly visions."

"That's gonna be difficult with the current filming schedule."

"Well, he's going to have to make time, otherwise, this quest for answers to the Lizzie Borden murders could be for naught."

Sarah knew Danni was right. If they were going to make any progress with this mystery, they'd have to work together. Sarah was relieved she and Garrett had worked through their misunderstanding. Now they could collaborate as a team to interpret the cryptic messages from the beyond. The question was, could they find the answers to this century old mystery in the short period of time they'd been allotted without Valerie's interference?

"I'm getting on the computer," Danni said, going to her room.

"I'll get the book and join you," Sarah replied.

Sarah opened the top drawer of the dresser and removed the small brown leather tome with *Dreamist* in gilded letters on the front. Glancing in the mirror, her muscles tensed when a black swirling mist funneled across the glass. A villainous laugh swept over Sarah's skin, raising the hairs on her arms and the back of her neck.

She started to scream when a misty hand with claw-like nails emerged from the mirror, its skeletal fingers gripping her mouth silencing her. Closing her eyes, Sarah summoned Ola. The older woman's comforting presence appeared for a split second before the dark mist shadowed it.

I mean to finish you, sounded as the foul stench of decaying breath stung Sarah's nose.

Her lungs constricted as a sharp pain sliced down her sternum. The room began to spin as consciousness faded in and out.

"Sarah? You coming?" Danni called from the other room, breaking Sarah from the trance.

Doubling over, she gulped in air. When she stood and looked in the mirror, she saw only her reflection. What had happened and who was the evil spirit? Whoever it was, he'd been able to block Ola, but how?

Danni appeared in the doorway. "What's going on?" she asked.

Sarah turned to her friend, her body trembling.

"There's another spirit here and it's not a nice one."

CHAPTER 12

Fear flashed in Danni's eyes as she scanned the space. "Come in my room and tell me what happened," she muttered, motioning for Sarah to join her.

Sarah grabbed the *Dreamist* book and hurried into Danni's chambers, plunking onto the bed. She shared the horrifying vision of the dark mist with its putrid breath and ability to interact with her physically.

"Not only did he clamp down on my mouth but I think he was able to block Ola."

"This isn't good," Danni groaned. "We really need to talk to Garrett."

"I don't want to disturb him. He's busy. Let's see if we can figure this out on our own," Sarah pleaded.

"We'll try. But if we can't, we're telling him. I'm not messing around with ghosts who cross into the realm of the living."

"Deal."

"Let's go for a drive," Danni suggested.

"I thought we were going to work on my dreamist skills."

"No offense, but I'm completely weirded out right now and would rather get away from this place."

Sarah understood her friend's trepidation. Danni had stood by her through several hauntings but Sarah knew there was a limit to her spectral tolerance.

Danni grabbed her keys while Sarah placed the *Dreamist* book in the top drawer of her dresser. They headed downstairs to the kitchen.

"Hey guys," Sarah said, trying to sound chipper. "We're going for a drive."

"Where?" Garrett asked.

Sarah looked at Danni. She didn't feel like disclosing what had just happened in her room.

"We want to check out Maplecroft, maybe snap a few pictures," Danni said.

Brilliant, Sarah thought. It would also give her a chance to get a feel for the place.

Garrett smacked his forehead. "I forgot to tell you; I had Val…erie check into getting access to the house. She said the owners are out of town for three weeks."

"Bummer," Ralph said. "That would have been a great place to visit, especially if they would've let us take photos."

"We'll get some exterior shots," Danni responded.

"Thanks," Harry said with a yawn.

Garrett winked at Sarah bringing a smile to her face as she and Danni exited through the back door. She felt much better now that they'd established the parameters of their relationship.

Sarah slid into the car and buckled her seat belt. The Mercedes purred to life and they headed down the road toward Maplecroft. Daylight filtered through amber and mango hued trees as they traversed the sun dappled streets of Fall River. As they drove down French Street, the Queen Ann Victorian came into view. A squared turret towered above the sprawling mansion with its stone base and clapboard siding. Danni slowed the car in front of the house where *Maplecroft* was etched in the top stair leading to the front door.

"It's beautiful," Sarah mumbled, gawking at the structure.

"I found interior pictures online from when it was on the market. You'd lose your mind over the woodwork and mantels."

Danni parked the car at the curb and started to get out.

"What are you doing?" Sarah asked.

"Taking pictures," she replied, grabbing her phone. "Remember, the owners are out of town so there's no harm. It's not like we're looking in the windows."

Sarah watched Danni scoot across the yard and around to the back.

Getting out of the car, Sarah stood in front of the home and stared at the architectural details.

"Curious about the house?" a voice called, startling Sarah. An older woman dressed in a tweed skirt and wool jacket approached.

Crap, this woman would likely call the cops when she saw Danni was trespassing.

"I, um…." Sarah stuttered, trying to figure out what to say to prevent the lady from reporting them.

"I'm sorry, I didn't mean to frighten you. I'm Mabel Landon. I live next door."

"I'm Sarah Holden. I'm staying at the Borden House."

"Oh," she exclaimed. "You must be part of the ghost hunting crew!"

"Yes ma'am," Sarah replied, her southern manners flowing from her lips.

"Well, I don't think the owners would mind if you walked around the yard," Mabel said, smiling. "Most of the time, people take the liberty of doing so without asking. Since you're part of the filming project, I'm certain Joe and Analise would give permission. They'd be thrilled to have their house be part of the show."

"Thanks," Sarah responded. "We won't be long."

"Take your time," she said. "If you have any questions, I'll be next door."

"Thank you."

Sarah meandered across the lawn, taking in the beautiful angles and ornate details of the Victorian structure. Rounding the corner of the house, Sarah sucked in a breath. One of the rockers on the porch was swaying, yet there was no breeze. Lizzie's image formed holding a small dog in her lap. *Not as it appears* echoed in Sarah's head as the vision dissipated.

Sarah turned to see Danni holding up her phone.

"What are you doing?" she asked.

"I saw you stop and thought I'd better take a picture. Did you see something?"

Sarah nodded. "Lizzie was sitting on the porch holding a dog."

"Maybe I got lucky and something will show up in the photo."

"If you captured what I saw, the guys are going to make you a permanent part of the team," Sarah chuckled.

"I could be famous if I snapped a photo of the notorious ax murderer, Lizzie Borden!" Danni declared, her eyes twinkling.

"Hatchet, and she was acquitted," Sarah quipped.

"But not innocent," Danni replied.

"In my opinion, she didn't do it," Sarah responded. "Why would she communicate with me if she wasn't innocent?"

"Maybe she feels guilty for living a long, happy life after killing her parents," Danni said.

"She didn't do this," Sarah said, shaking her head. "I can feel it."

They finished walking around the property without any other sightings. Danni snapped a few more pictures and checked her phone.

"Anything show up?" Sarah asked, leaning over her friend's shoulder.

"Not a thing. Maybe the guys can find something."

"If there's anything to be found, Walter is the one to do it," Sarah said.

Danni rolled her eyes. "What is so special about Walter? Everyone depends upon him yet he's never here."

"According to Ralph, he's a bit of an introvert. You know, the genius type who prefers keeping his own company."

"Sounds arrogant to me," Danni mumbled.

"Don't be so negative," Sarah huffed. "Now that we've seen the outside of this place, and a bit more, let's go back to Borden House."

SARAH AND DANNI walked into the kitchen at Borden House to find Ralph scrolling through still shots from the night before.

"Hey Ralph," Sarah said. "Thought you'd be asleep."

"Too wired. Any luck at Maplecroft?" he asked without looking up.

"The neighbor gave us permission to walk around the property and take pictures," Sarah replied

Ralph spun around in the chair, his eyes glimmering. "Did you get anything?"

"You met the neighbor?" Danni asked, looking at Sarah.

"Yes. Nice lady. She said we could walk around."

Ralph cleared his throat. "Photos?"

"I took some but didn't see anything significant," Danni replied.

"I'll send them to Walter," Ralph grinned. "If anything is there, he'll be able to filter it out."

With a scowl, Danni handed Ralph her phone. He downloaded the photos and sent them to his brother.

"Anything else happen?" he asked, hope swirling in his gaze.

"Nothing to speak of," Sarah replied. She hated lying, even if it was to protect her secret.

An hour later, the group gathered in the dining room. Ralph

smiled like a cat who just caught a canary, his computer screen turned for all to see.

"What's the big announcement?" Harry asked.

"Hold on," Ralph replied. "I told Walter I'd call before the big reveal."

Sarah glanced at Danni, arching her brows. Her heart palpitated. Maybe the men caught something on film and Walter was able to edit it.

Ralph dialed Walter and placed his phone on speaker.

"Ralph," Walter said.

"Everyone's here," he replied. "Bringing the photo up now."

Ralph tapped a few keys and a picture came up on the screen.

A collective gasp rounded the table. A translucent image of a woman with a dog in her lap appeared on the computer.

"How'd you guys manage to capture this?" Walter asked. "I want to get the same kind of phone because it's obviously able to photograph spirits from the great beyond."

"Danni took it," Ralph replied.

"Ooh, I see," Walter said, sarcasm dripping from his words. "An amateur gets lucky."

Danni sneered while Sarah stared at the computer screen. This was the same image she'd seen on the porch at Maplecroft. Although the details were fuzzy, there was no doubt it was Lizzie Borden sitting in a rocker.

"Do you think this is Lizzie Borden?" Harry asked, staring at the screen.

"Hard to say," Walter replied. "Looks like a woman with a dog. The house is over one hundred years old. Could be any of the former residents."

Sarah glanced at Danni, whose eyes were as big as quarters. Apparently, no one recognized Lizzie's image. Scrutinizing the photo, Sarah realized the image was vague. The only reason she knew the identity was because she'd actually seen it.

"This is great," Garrett said. "We can add this to the final cut."

"Glad I could help," Walter replied. "Now I've got to get some real work done."

The phone went dead as the men high fived each other.

"What exactly does Walter do?" Danni asked. "Outside of manipulating video footage, I've never been sure what he does."

"He's a hacker," Ralph replied.

"A hacker?" Danni said, disdain dripping from her words. "He's a criminal?"

"No," Ralph snorted. "He does cyber security. Companies hire him to hack into their systems. If he's able to, they contract him to fix the problem. If he can't break through their firewalls, they know their systems are good."

"Interesting," Danni mumbled.

"You ladies did a great job!" Harry declared. "This photo adds a whole new element."

Garrett gave Sarah an approving nod. At least she and Danni were able to contribute something. Regardless, Danni's photo of what Sarah had seen was unnerving. Even though nothing had been mentioned about her dreamist abilities, it felt as if they were walking a fine line that could expose her secret skills. Stop being silly, she told herself. No one suspected a thing.

Daylight gave way to the muted hues of eventide, washing the interior of the inn in subdued shades of twilight. Despite Sarah's dislike of Valerie, she was thankful the deadline for the project had been extended, even if she suspected Garrett was at the core of the network exec's decision. The extension would give Sarah more time to figure out what the ghosts were trying to convey. If only they could include Ralph and Harry on the discussion, perhaps they'd be able to offer a fresh perspective on the dreams. For a brief moment, Sarah considered the idea but quickly dismissed it. Now wasn't the time, if ever, to reveal her secret.

Sarah took the *Dreamist* book from the dresser drawer and

curled up on her bed. Maybe she'd be able to garner some pertinent information to help the group decipher what the spirits were trying to communicate. Despite the year and a half she'd spent reading and rereading the century-old guide to her haunted dreams, Sarah was nowhere near interpreting most of its puzzling passages. Still, she was determined to try.

A rap on the door drew her attention from her reading.

"It's open," she called out.

Garrett's handsome face appeared, his hair damp and curling at the ends. "Is this a bad time?" he asked, entering the room with Dallas.

"Not at all," she answered.

Dallas hopped up next to Sarah while Garrett took a seat in the chair by the hearth.

"Got any advice for me?" she asked.

"Afraid not. I brought Grams's copy of the *Dreamist* book with me and skimmed through it but didn't find anything related to what you're experiencing."

"Thanks for trying. I realize each *Dreamist* book has sections specific to the owner, but it sure makes it difficult to figure things out," Sarah replied, her hopes dashed at the lack of answers. It seemed even those who had experience with dreamists had limitations.

Garrett met Sarah's gaze. "We'll figure this out."

His words soothed the disappointment brewing in her gut. Now more than ever, she needed to focus and stay calm if they were going to solve the century old mystery that had stumped lawmakers and historians for decades.

She got up and walked over to him, kissing his soft lips and reveling in his gentle nature. In all her years, she'd never imagined she'd find a man with such compassion, much less knowledge of dreamists.

"Thanks again for helping us with this. I know it's not easy," he said, his half smile tickling her stomach.

"Consider it restitution for helping me understand my gift," she replied, pride swelling in her chest.

"I need to get back downstairs," he said, kissing her once more before heading for the door. "Love you."

"Love you," she responded.

"Garrett? You upstairs?" Valerie's shrill voice sliced through the moment making the hair on Sarah's neck bristle.

"On my way," he hollered.

Valerie trotted up the stairs and sidled up beside him. Her blond hair was piled on her head in a messy bun and the dress she wore had less fabric than Sarah's pillow case. If she leaned over, they'd be exposed to parts Sarah didn't even want to consider. Poor Ralph would likely hyperventilate at the sight, thwarting any productivity from him.

"Come with me, I have something to show you," she uttered. With a sideways glance at Sarah, she gave a half-grin. "You don't mind the interruption, do you?"

Biting her lower lip to prevent the retort from emerging, Sarah forced a smile. "Not at all. I've got some research to finish."

Annoyed by Valerie's intrusion, Sarah decided to get some fresh air. Plopping her *Dreamist* book on the dresser, she passed through Garrett's room and used the back stairs, hoping to avoid any acrimonious encounters with Tootsie. Fortunately, Ralph and Harry weren't in the kitchen when Sarah entered. She heard voices coming from the front parlor and figured they were discussing the game plan for the evening's filming.

Stepping out the back door, Sarah took in the autumnal aroma of fireplace smoke. The sun was waving goodbye as the moon rose in the sky. The fresh air felt good against her flushed cheeks. Her mind drifted to the back yard scene earlier when Garrett had confessed that he loved her. How silly she'd been to doubt him. Then again, it was only natural to feel threatened by a brazen blond who flirted shamelessly whenever she was around. Sarah rolled her head a few times loosening the tension in her neck before going back inside.

She made her way upstairs, through Garrett's room, and back to her own. That's when she saw Valerie's tawdry figure.

"What are you doing in here?" Sarah demanded, her jaw set.

Valerie whirled around, her icy blue eyes locking onto Sarah's.

"What's this?" she asked, holding up the *Dreamist* book.

Sarah's throat tightened. Crap, she thought, how do I explain this?

Without thinking, Sarah marched over and snatched the book from Valerie's blood red manicured fingers. "Why are you in my room?"

A menacing smile curled Valerie's lips. "This isn't *your* room. This room is paid for by the network and thus you are merely a guest."

"With a right to privacy. Danni is an attorney and will be happy to explain it to you." Sarah squared her shoulders, proud of her quick comeback.

Valerie stepped closer, her perfume burning Sarah's throat as she glared down at her. "I have a host of attorneys at my hands who will be more than happy to explain to your friend that the network has paid for these rooms. As the executive director, I have the right to inspect any areas used for filming purposes. Now answer the question, what is that book?"

Sarah chose her words carefully, not wanting to hint at the true meaning behind the tome. "It's a book of poems. I like to read before bed. It helps me relax."

"That's more than a poetry book," Valerie scoffed. "Don't assume I'm stupid because I'm beautiful. I have a great deal of experience with the occult and know something extraordinary when I see it."

Sarah nearly choked when she referred to her bought-and-paid-for beauty but managed to crack a smile. "Think what you want, but it's just a book of poems my mother left to me."

With a roll of her eyes, Valerie tilted her chin up, turned on her heels, and started for the door. Stopping, she looked back at Sarah. "I *will* find out what that book contains. I know exactly how to get what I want from whom I want," she winked, leaving the room.

Slumping onto the bed with the book clutched to her chest, Sarah squeezed her eyes shut. How could she have been so careless to leave the book out in the open like that? What if Harry or Ralph had discovered it? They were pretty savvy about this sort of thing and wouldn't have been so easily dismissed. Then again, Valerie made it clear she wasn't going to let it go. Now more than ever, Sarah needed to speak with Garrett and warn him about Valerie's discovery. Before Sarah could act on the thought, Danni came in.

"The guys are getting ready to start filming. Wanna hang with me and Ralph until bedtime since the Barbie doll is here?"

"I'd rather hang Valerie," Sarah groused.

"Don't let her get to you. Garrett made it clear how he feels. I can't believe you're still stewing about this."

"Garrett isn't the problem, the *Dreamist* book is," Sarah replied, setting the book on the bed next to her."

"Did you find something upsetting in it?" Danni asked.

"No, but I caught Valerie snooping around my room. She found it," Sarah huffed.

"Oh my gosh! What did she say?"

"She demanded to know what it was about. I told her she had no right to be in here. She was all too happy to remind me I had no expectation of privacy when the network was footing the bill."

"Actually, there is a certain amount of privacy allotted to those staying in hotels and inns."

"I'm not worried about the legalities. I'm concerned about

the fact she found the *Dreamist* book and suspects it's something of significance. She may be a floozy, but she's not stupid."

"What did you tell her?"

"I said it was a book of poetry my mother gave me."

"That's not exactly a lie," Danni said, shirking her shoulders.

"She didn't buy my answer and said she wouldn't let it go."

Danni's posture straightened. "Was she looking through your drawers?"

Sarah felt the flush coloring her cheeks. "I left it on the dresser."

"Oh Sarah, that's not something you can leave out in the open, especially with all the people traipsing in and out of the rooms."

"Trust me, I'm upset with myself for being so careless. Regardless, I need to find a viable explanation for the book to pacify her if she pursues it. And I need to find a way to let Garrett know in case she asks him about it. I don't want him to be blindsided."

"I'll try to find a way to speak with Garrett. She won't be as suspicious of me."

"Thanks Danni. I really appreciate it."

"No problem. But find someplace to hide that book. The last thing we need is for the network to learn about dreamists."

"Agreed," Sarah replied. "Could you put it in your room? I doubt anyone would think to look in there."

With a nod, Danni took the book and disappeared into her chambers. When she re-emerged, a sly smile curled her lips. "It's well hidden. Now, would you like to join me and Ralph?"

"Why not? Might be fun to observe ghosts from the other side of the camera before I have to meet them in my dreams."

Sarah followed Danni downstairs to the kitchen where Ralph was checking the monitors. As they entered, a chill slinked down Sarah's spine and prickled across her skin. Something was brewing, she could feel it in the depth of her soul.

CHAPTER 13

*D*espite Sarah's initial unease when she joined Danni and Ralph, nothing showed up for the first couple of hours. The plan was for Sarah to go to sleep around 11:00, or earlier if she grew tired. They decided to have Sarah sleep in the sitting room again, hoping something more would materialize since they'd been able to capture the shadowy figure in her presence on a previous occasion.

Sarah couldn't explain it, but for some reason she was nervous about this evening's filming, which she attributed to Valerie's presence. She was becoming self-conscious about her sleep, knowing others would be watching her. What if she drooled or snored? She'd be mortified if those things were caught on tape. No doubt, Tootsie would want to use it as some sort of blooper reel to embarrass her. Even though Valerie was unaware of Sarah's relationship with Garrett, it was obvious she'd eliminate anyone she viewed as competition. With her arrogant nature, she probably hadn't considered Sarah in the running for his affections.

Nevertheless, Sarah needed to concentrate on her role in helping the guys secure this contract. They'd worked hard to get here and deserved to be acknowledged for their efforts. Her goal for the evening was to remain calm, communicate with the dead, and bring this excursion to a successful end.

A few minutes before 11:00, Harry poked his head in the kitchen.

"You ready?" he asked.

"Yup," Sarah responded as she followed him to the sitting room.

The green light on the camera blared through the darkness letting her know it was working. She curled up on the settee as Harry left the room.

Glancing around, Sarah took in the macabre feel of the space. A man had been viciously murdered in this room on the very spot where she now reclined. The thought sent a shiver rattling through her body. So much was riding on her ability to help identify the person responsible for one of the most notorious killings in American history.

As overwhelming as the situation was, she felt a slight sense of pride. Being able to help others, both dead and alive, was fulfilling. Despite her racing thoughts, sleep grabbed hold and led her to a land of dreams and miscommunications.

SARAH TRAIPSED through the second floor of Borden House, the air as still as death. Her skin tingled and her body shuddered with a chill despite the oppressive temperature. Why was she up here when she was sleeping in the sitting room?

She made her way down the stairs watching for any sign of movement. Nothing. As she reached the bottom step, she startled when the curtains in the front parlor began flapping wildly in the breeze. She took in a few deep breaths and continued through the house. Much to her surprise, all of the rooms were empty. No one was home. Yet something felt daunting. She stood in the kitchen, looking around when she noticed smoke puffing from the stove.

She snatched a towel from the long wooden table, grabbed the handle to the oven, and opened it. Stepping back, she coughed when smoke billowed from within, burning her throat and stinging her eyes. Inside the fiery space were scraps of calico fabric. Was this the dress Lizzie had burned? Supposedly, Lizzie had destroyed the frock because it was faded and had paint splatter on it. Knowing about 19th century living, Sarah found that particular fact odd. Victorian ladies rarely discarded old clothing. Generally, worn dresses were cut apart and reused in things like quilts or the lining of other garments. Why burn the dress instead of repurposing it? Court records also stated there were witnesses to this event so why was the kitchen devoid of people?

Footsteps echoed from the next room, alerting Sarah that someone was coming. Closing the oven door, she stepped into the sitting room where the suffocating scent of cigar smoke singed her throat, making her cough. Yet no one was in the room. Maybe Mr. Borden had returned. She didn't remember anything about him smoking cigars, then again, it wasn't exactly a relevant point regarding the murders.

Sarah continued her search through the house. Returning to the front parlor, she was relieved to find the curtains settled although summer heat had taken hold of the room. Still no signs of life. Sarah started for the front door when she heard the back door slam. Running through the house and out the kitchen door leading outside, she scanned the yard. A chill rankled her body. Something was definitely wrong. In her previous dreams, she'd seen either Mr. and Mrs. Borden, Lizzie, Bridget, the family from the neighboring house, or the mysterious figure. However, there was no sign of anyone, not even passersby on the street. It was like a ghost town.

Sarah chuckled at her choice of words. All of her dreamscapes were ghost towns. A rustling sound caught her attention. Spinning around, she searched the area but saw nothing. What was going on? This dream wasn't showing her anything. Was something blocking her ability to see things? Determination took hold, and much to her surprise, she found her words.

"I know someone is out there. If you want me to help, I need you to come forward."

"I see your little game," a voice boomed from the edge of the yard, a British accent tinting each word.

"I'm here to help, if you'll let me," she said.

Suddenly, the voice was behind her, his breath bumping across the skin at the nape of her neck.

"I'll get you when you don't expect it."

Sarah wheeled around to see the cloaked man's arm lifted above her head, a blade glinting in the sunlight. As his hand swung down, she bolted to the side, the blade breezing past her neck. Terror grabbed hold of her lungs, constricting her ability to breathe. There was no time for relaxation techniques, she needed to run.

Sprinting inside the house, she slammed the door and bolted it, locking the man outside. She ran to the front of the house to make sure it was secure too. As she reached the entryway, she let out a long breath. The door was bolted and as far as she knew, there were no other points of entry. Suddenly, the curtains in the parlor began flapping like laundry in a hurricane.

She raced into the room, slamming windows closed, her fingers trembling as she secured the locks. When everything was sealed, she plopped onto the settee to catch her breath. Rubbing her eyes, she scolded herself for being so silly. It was a ghost, he couldn't harm her, so why was she so afraid? Her goal in this dream was to catch a glimpse of the mysterious man's face so they could identify him and figure out his role in the hauntings. Instead, she'd run from him.

Taking in a deep breath, Sarah stood, her legs a bit wobbly

but her resolve strong. Marching to the back door, she was determined to face this apparition and find out who he was. However, when she reached the back door, her courage began to wane. She repeated her deep breathing and reached for the latch on the door when a hand grabbed her shoulder, squeezing out a scream.

She spun around, facing the cloaked man, his face was a blur as he slashed at her neck. She felt the blade tear at her skin. Crumpling to the ground, she grasped her throat. Blood oozed between her fingers and down her wrist. What was happening? Panic compressed her chest as she stared at her blood-stained hand. She tried taking in a deep breath but a gurgling sound resulted.

"I mean to finish you," his voice crackled.

Looking up, she watched a sly grin spread across the man's face although his features were still fuzzy. Was that his doing or the fact she was bleeding out? She tried to stand but the blood loss was making her weak. Stay calm, she told herself. You have to stay calm or he wins. Sarah closed her eyes and pictured Ola's face. I need you, she thought.

A hand rested on her shoulder. Sarah gasped as she sat upright, staring around the sitting room. Gulping down the fear forming in her throat, she tried to figure out if she was still in the dream or awake.

Breathless, Sarah leaned forward on the settee relieved as her lungs filled with air. Her limbs trembled and her stomach churned as she buried her face in her hands. Whoever was in the dream had just tried to kill her. Was that even possible? When she'd dreamed about Nora Hamilton being strangled by her husband, Sarah woke with red marks around her neck, but no damage. In Edgefield, ghosts had been able to manipulate physical objects. She remembered what Harry had said about mists, orbs, and poltergeists. Over the years, the spirits in her dreams had varied in appearance from rotting corpses to fully restored individuals. Yet, this one was mysterious and seemed to believe he could inflict harm. Was he aware of her abilities and trying to destroy her? A homicidal maniac running through the woods in the vicinity of the house where the Bordens were murdered was suspicious and warranted further investigation, no matter how terrifying.

Lost in her thoughts, Sarah jumped when Garrett crept into the room and sat next to her.

"Everything alright?" he whispered, concern glimmering in his gaze as he squeezed her hand.

"Seriously terrifying dream," she replied in a hushed tone.

"Want to step outside for a break? We can talk about it."

"OK."

They tiptoed through the kitchen where Ralph was watching several monitors and a camera. He gave a nod as they walked past. Apparently, Danni had lost interest and returned to her room on the second floor. Once outside, Sarah drew in a long breath.

"What happened?" he asked.

Sarah told him about walking through the house with not a soul around.

"When I went outside, I encountered that man again. He said something about wanting to finish me and then he tried to kill me, except this time he sliced my throat."

Garrett checked Sarah's neck. "There aren't any cuts. Did you get a good look at his face?"

"No. He was wearing a hooded cape, almost like the grim reaper and his features were blurred." Sarah shuddered at the memory. "I know what Harry said earlier about the different types of ghosts, some of which can interact physically. They can't actually hurt me, can they? Do you remember your grandmother mentioning anything about being assaulted by the visions in her dreams?"

"Not to my recollection," he replied. "I know they can gain

power in certain circumstances but I've never heard of anyone being physically harmed by them."

"That's good to know because this guy seemed adamant about stopping me from discovering his identity."

"And there's your answer. Just like fear can hinder your ability to communicate in the dreams, this entity probably knows that terror can prevent you from identifying him. Maybe he's aware you're a dreamist and was trying to block you from learning who he is, or was."

Sarah blew out a long breath. His explanation made sense, giving her a small bit of peace.

"Do you want me to go back and try again?" she asked.

"It's up to you," he replied, leaning in to kiss her when Valerie's voice pierced the night. The tall blond stood in the kitchen doorway.

"Sorry to intrude," she purred with a glint in her gaze.

Sarah bit her lower lip to prevent any unwarranted comments from escaping. If Valerie didn't know about their relationship before, she did now. Perhaps she'd back off since she'd almost caught them kissing. The urge to say something was strong but she needed to let Garrett handle this.

"What do you need, Valerie?" he asked in a professional tone.

"While I'm sure Miss Holden enjoys feeling useful, I'd like to know the reason for filming her," she scowled.

At that moment, Sarah wanted to scratch the floozy's eyes out.

"We've been filming her because the ghosts seem to be drawn to the living. For some reason, we've gotten some good footage when Sarah is in the room."

"Nonetheless, I think it's time to kick up the drama. I've been able to extend this filming endeavor but I need something substantial to keep the other execs content. I'd like to bring in some of my people to conduct a séance."

"Your people?" Garrett asked. "From the network?"

"No. These are the members from the society I spoke to you about."

"What is so special about this society?" Sarah asked, her words laced with disdain.

"The Hidden Gems is a group of individuals who not only believe in ghosts, but also conjure them. We have an impeccable record," she said with a sly smile and a tilt of her bleached head.

What a stupid name, Sarah thought, pressing her lips together.

Garrett took in a long breath. "If we use your people, then it's not our team doing the work. I thought the whole point was for *us* to capture ghosts on film."

"Of course, your team will get the credit," she replied with a simper. "You just need a little help."

"We only take credit for our own work. And we don't use séances or other tactics to conjure up ghosts."

Valerie straightened her shoulders and pursed her lips. "I'll give you two more nights of doing things your way and then my colleagues and I will step in. Please don't underestimate what we're capable of achieving if we work *together*," she said before sauntering back inside, her hips swaying like a ship on the open seas.

"That didn't go well," Sarah mumbled.

"Nope. Even worse, this society of hers is not something I'm comfortable with."

"Have you heard of them before?" Sarah asked.

"No, but anyone who uses the tactics she's talking about are opening themselves up for trouble and I won't be part of it."

"I haven't had a chance to tell you this yet, but I caught her in my room earlier with my *Dreamist* book."

"What?" he exclaimed. "How did she find it?"

Sarah's gaze shifted to the ground. "Left it on my dresser. Regardless, she had no right to be in my room."

"Sarah, I know you're still adjusting to all of this but you can't leave the book anywhere others can find it. It's imperative to keep it hidden at all times." His voice was firm but kind. All the same, Sarah's heart crumbled a bit beneath his obvious disappointment in her mistake.

"I know that now and I'm sorry."

"What did she say?"

"She asked what it was about. I told her it was a book of poetry my mother had given me."

Garrett's stare intensified. "Did she buy it?"

"Not really. I wouldn't put it past her to have another look. Just in case, it's hidden in Danni's room."

"Good idea."

"I wonder if this secret society of hers is familiar with dreamists?"

"Doubtful. I think she'd have said something if she knew," he answered. "Let's go back inside. Maybe Harry or Ralph caught something on tape while you were asleep."

"Hope so," she muttered, following him.

THE NEXT MORNING, Sarah woke with the sun, despite the long hours of filming and dreams the night before. She showered and went downstairs where she found Ralph in the dining room, drinking coffee and tapping away on his laptop.

"Morning," Sarah said, taking a seat across from him.

He grunted a response.

Mrs. Pearson entered and placed Sarah's tea before her with a smile. "Breakfast is still cooking. Would you like a granola bar or something to tide you over?"

"No, thank you. Tea is fine."

Mrs. Pearson left the room as Sarah filled her cup with the steaming brew. Raising the cup to her lips, she nearly spilled it when Ralph gasped.

"What's the matter?"

Ralph's eyes widened and his mouth gaped open. "We got something!"

Sarah rushed to his side and peered over his shoulder. Sure enough, a misty figure hovered near Sarah, except this time you could make out the outline of a cloaked man. She gulped down the scream threatening to break free at the sight. It was the same shadowy figure who'd stabbed her in her dream.

"Where are the guys?" Sarah muttered.

"Still asleep, I assume," Ralph replied, staring at the screen. "It's been an exhausting few days, so they decided to grab some shut-eye before breakfast."

"Should we wake them?" Sarah asked, desperately wanting to speak with Garrett.

"Naw, let 'em get some rest. Now that we've caught something, we've got a lot more work to do."

Sarah nodded. And now, so did she.

Much to Sarah's surprise, Danni was the next to join their breakfast club followed by Harry, Garrett, and Dallas. Sarah grinned as she watched Garrett and Harry view the tape, their eyes filled with excitement like kids on Christmas morning.

"Sarah, you're definitely our ghost magnet," Harry exclaimed. "Did you happen to see this while you were in the room?"

"Nope. Slept right through it," she replied with a sideways glance toward Garrett.

"We're going to do some more filtering before we send it to Walter," Ralph said, standing. He and Harry went to the kitchen, leaving Sarah, Danni, and Garrett at the table.

Before they could discuss anything about the previous night's haunted dreamscapes, Garrett's phone rang. Looking at the screen, he sighed.

"Don't tell me. It's *Val*," Sarah smirked.

Garrett gave a nod and kissed Sarah's forehead before walking into the hall to answer the phone.

"Can't stand that woman," Sarah grumbled.

"Don't let the bottled blond get to you. Garrett sees her for what she is," Danni said, patting Sarah's arm.

A few minutes later, Garrett walked back over to them, his disgruntled expression alerting Sarah that Valerie had requested something he didn't like.

"What did she want?"

"She's adamant we try using parlor tricks to stir up the spirits. I don't know how much longer I can hold off her requests."

"Did you tell her about what you caught on film last night?" Danni asked.

"I did. She wants to see the footage. Hopefully, it will be enough to pacify her."

"Is she coming over?" Sarah asked with a scowl.

"She's in meetings all day and asked me to email the footage to her."

"That's a relief," Sarah sighed.

"After that, I want us to brainstorm for tonight," he said with a smile.

Sarah watched him walk to the kitchen, his long stride and broad shoulders sending a flutter through her stomach. She was glad to have him in her life. If only they could identify the mysterious cloaked man and ward off the pending intrusion of the Hidden Gems with their hocus pocus approach to ghost hunting.

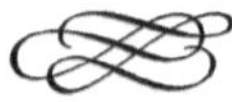

CHAPTER 14

According to the text Garrett received from Valerie after the network viewed the tape, she was thrilled with what they'd filmed. She agreed to allow them to continue with their manner of doing things, unless nothing else showed up. Then she was going to implement her own techniques to help them along. Sarah didn't know what infuriated her more, Valerie's provocative nature or her pathetic attempts to control everything.

After lunch, Garrett and Sarah were able to steal a few moments alone in her room. Garrett's lips brushed hers as he held her close.

"I'm so tired," he whispered, closing his eyes as he rested his forehead against hers.

"With any luck, you'll capture more images on tape, land the contract, and then we can go home."

"If only it was that simple," he said, plunking onto the bed. Dallas leapt up next to him with his tail wagging furiously.

"What do you mean?" she asked, sitting beside them.

"If the network signs us on, we'll have to film several episodes."

"Where?" Sarah didn't want to think about what would happen if the guys were picked up for a series.

"All over," he responded, running his hand through his hair. "We'll travel to some of the most notoriously haunted places in the country. It's what we've always wanted to do as a team, although I'm too tired to even contemplate it right now."

"How can I help?" Sarah asked.

"Let's work on keeping you composed in your dreams. Once you master that, your ability to communicate with the ghosts will be much easier."

"Where do we start?"

Dallas curled up on the pillow while Garrett went over some of the techniques his grandmother used when trying to prepare for her dreams.

"You've figured out how to contact Grams which is one way to calm yourself. The next thing is to alleviate any fear before it prevents your ability to read the situation."

"I get that," she said. "The problem is remembering to do these things when I'm actually in the dream."

Garrett smiled, sending a tingle across her skin.

"That's the problem. Once you're frightened, it's more difficult to relax. We need to train your mind to remain calm no matter what you're seeing."

"And how do I accomplish that?" Sarah asked.

"We practice while you're awake."

"Huh?"

"You need to lie down, close your eyes, and do whatever methods bring you to a state of relaxation," Garrett instructed. "Once you're relaxed, you need to think about the ghostly visions. If you start to tense up, dismiss the vision and return to the relaxation technique. Keep doing this until you're able to remain calm."

Sarah lay on her back, closed her eyes, and rested her hands on her stomach.

"Do you want me to go?" he asked.

Sarah giggled as she opened her eyes. "I can't relax with you watching me, so yes, it would be better if you left."

Leaning over, he kissed her, his lips lingering on hers before he straightened up. "I'm going to join the guys downstairs. I'll leave Dallas with you. Good luck," he said.

Sarah closed her eyes and began the breathing technique she'd been using since childhood. Taking in a deep breath, she held for a count of five, and released. Even though she was already relaxed, she could feel her muscles melting against the mattress. She started thinking about the cloaked figure from the previous night's dream. When her heart rate accelerated, she repeated the deep breathing until her body released the tension holding it captive. Sarah continued the process until her mind and body relaxed leading her to the realm of dreamland.

WALKING down the dusty street in front of Borden House, Sarah watched as a carriage swept past leaving a cloud of dust in its wake. People strolled along the road, chatting as they went. That's when Sarah noticed a gentleman in a sack coat and bowler hat approach the front door of the house, carrying what appeared to be a leather doctor's bag.

Bridget answered the door and invited him inside. Curious, Sarah jaunted to the front window and peered in. She saw Bridget escort the man down the hall. Sarah raced around the house, looking in each of the windows until she found him in the dining room where he sat across from Mr. Borden. Unfortunately, the mysterious man had his back to her. He placed a bottle on the table which Mr. Borden pushed back toward him. She couldn't hear what they were saying, but watched as Mr. Borden handed him some cash. The man counted it and shook his head.

All of a sudden, he turned slightly, revealing only a glimpse of his profile. Sarah's heart rate ratcheted up when she realized it was the man from her previous night's dream. But how could she be sure since she'd never actually seen his face? It was a question she couldn't answer, yet she knew in her soul, this was the same person. Taking a few deep breaths, she was able to calm her racing pulse.

She couldn't hear what they were saying; however, their body language suggested it was a heated exchange. Mr. Borden's face was contorted and the doctor banged his fist against the table before grabbing his bag and fleeing from the premises.

Pleased she'd been able to maintain her composure, Sarah decided to follow him. He walked several blocks to a boarding house where he entered, bolted up the stairs, and into a room at the end of the second-floor hall. The house was buzzing with activity; people chattering, a piano being played from below, and the clanging of dishes in the kitchen drifted through the space. Sarah didn't recall ever being so in-tune with her surroundings that she noticed every sound. She crept down the hall and leaned her head against the door. Stillness. That's strange, she thought. She'd watched him walk into the room and her ears were picking up every other sound in the house, yet silence emanated from his room.

Sarah decided there was only one way to identify this man and that was to face him head-on. She tensed at the idea. Taking in a deep breath, she released it slowly until her muscles relaxed. Now that she felt calmer, she rapped softly on the door and rested her ear against the wood. Still nothing.

A whoosh of air sent Sarah tumbling forward as the door flew open. A sharp blade plummeted toward her at the same time something hit her gut pushing a scream from her lips.

Sarah 's eyes popped open to see Dallas sitting on her stomach, licking her face. Danni charged into the room, her complexion pale.

"What's going on?" she asked. "I heard you scream."

Sarah leaned up, scooting Dallas to the bed.

"I fell asleep and had a dream," she replied with a scratchy voice.

"Anything notable?" Danni queried.

"I was standing outside of the house and watched a man go inside. I wasn't sure who he was at first but then realized he was the same one from my dreams last night."

"You finally saw his face?" Danni said.

"Only a glimpse of his profile, but I know it was him." Sarah replied. "Anyway, it looked like he and Mr. Borden argued and then the man ran from the house. I decided to follow him. He walked several blocks to a boarding house where he entered a room on the second floor."

"And you still didn't see his face?"

"No. The strangest part was I could hear every noise in the house but heard nothing when I leaned my ear against the door of his room."

"You had your head against the door?" Danni exclaimed.

Sarah nodded. "I don't know what prompted me to do it, but I knocked. The door flew open and a blade came straight for me."

"Then what?" Danni asked, her eyes as wide as quarters.

"Dallas jumped on top of me and woke me up."

"At least we know the ghosts can't do serious physical harm in your dreams."

"I have been choked," Sarah added.

"Nora was being strangled. Besides, you only had red marks, no serious damage," Danni said.

"Which is a physical manifestation of what I was dreaming."

"Didn't think of it that way," Danni sighed. "Still don't think the spirits can actually do any real harm outside of scaring you."

"Tell that to Brady," Sarah said.

Brady had died of a massive heart attack while confined to the hospital bed where he was under arrest. Sarah dreamed about his death on the same night it occurred. The dream showed his heart attack to be a result of the ghosts of five women he'd murdered converging on him in the hospital room.

"He had a genetic heart condition," Danni responded.

"That was triggered by the ghosts of his victims assaulting him while he was handcuffed to the hospital bed." Sarah sat straighter. "Do you think the man in my dreams knows I'm a dreamist? I mean, men can't inherit the ability so they shouldn't know about us, right?

"I thought ghosts could sense a dreamist," Danni said. "That's how they communicate with you in your dreams. They seek you out in order to enlist your help."

Sarah rubbed the chill from her upper arms as it skittered across her skin and down her back. "I don't like this. Something is off. None of the other ghosts have hidden their identities from me, even the guilty ones."

"We need to consult the book. Hopefully, we can find the answers," Danni said

"Great," Sarah rolled her eyes. "We're placing all our hope in the jumbled riddles of a *Dreamist* book. This is bound to go smoothly."

"We can do this," Danni said. "With my ability to untangle brainteasers, we should be able to figure this out. But we need to do it before you go to sleep tonight. And I really think you need to tell Garrett. We could use his help with this."

"No!" Sarah retorted. "I don't want to burden him with all of this. He's got enough going on with trying to please the network and Valerie's push to use her psychic friends. You and I were able to slog through this before him and we can do it now."

"Keeping secrets from your boyfriend isn't a good idea," Danni said her hands planted on her hips.

"I'm not keeping secrets from him," Sarah sighed. "I'll tell him when he has some spare time."

"OK, it's your decision," Danni said. "But I think you're

making a big mistake." Danni started for her room. "You comin'?"

"Where are you going?" Sarah asked.

"To get your book and my flask. I'm going to need some fuel if you expect me to unravel the mysteries of the undead."

Sarah chuckled. Danni's willingness to help her hone her abilities, despite the multitude of spirits hovering about, was a comfort.

"I'm useless when it comes to that book. No matter how hard I try, I don't get anywhere. You look through it, I'm going for a run. I've spent too much time in this place and I need some fresh air," Sarah said.

"Seriously? You're going for a run?" Danni asked.

"I need to clear my mind and running helps."

Shaking her head, Danni sighed. "You're not right. A shot of bourbon will accomplish the same thing."

"That's after the run. Maybe then I can figure out these crazy dreams and finally help the men discover who's haunting the house and be rid of the blade wielding entity trying to end my life."

CHAPTER 15

The crisp autumn air caressed Sarah's face as she jogged down the street, past a multi-story brick apartment building, suitably named for the Bordens. It had been a couple of weeks since her last run. With each footfall, Sarah felt the tension draining from her neck and back.

Although unfamiliar with the town, she'd been around enough to know which route would be the most scenic. She ran across the overpass and continued down fence lined streets with a variety of historic home styles from simple saltboxes to Victorians with wraparound porches trimmed in ornate fretwork. Without realizing it, she'd turned down French Street where Maplecroft was located. Mabel waved from her front stoop as Sarah jogged past. When she reached the front of Maplecroft, Sarah stopped, her lungs stinging with each breath of cold air.

She glanced at the window on the main floor and startled when an image appeared. The owners weren't expected back for three weeks. Sarah's insides twisted when the face turned her direction. Lizzie Borden.

Not what it seems brushed against Sarah's ear sending a shudder rattling through her core. *More to tell.*

Inhaling deeply, Sarah jaunted forward, eager to escape the image. This run was supposed to be relaxing, not expose her to more of the spirit world. If Lizzie wanted to communicate with her, she'd have to do so in her dreams. For now, Sarah needed a break to clear her head.

She continued her run, following her subconscious GPS down streets lined with more homes and a few commercial buildings. As she ran down Prospect Street, her hair bristled. A stone archway appeared with a sign that read *Oak Grove Cemetery*. Drawn forward like a dog on a leash, Sarah walked beneath the stone arch.

Gulping down the angst welling from within, she walked past a field of headstones. What was she doing? she thought. A cemetery was the last place she needed to be, yet she couldn't steer herself away.

Towering monuments, elaborately carved tombstones, along with simple grave markers studded the expanse. The air thickened making breathing difficult, as if she was trying to inhale through a wool blanket. A chill rankled her body as she surveyed the names.

Glancing down, Sarah stared at a name that was all too familiar to her. *Sarah Cornell.* That was the woman who was found hanging in the haystacks. The breeze picked up, swirling dry leaves in a mini cyclone about Sarah's feet. Not wanting to witness Miss Cornell's spirit, Sarah hurried on.

As she wondered through the graveyard, another chill bumped across Sarah's skin. A series of small stone markers caught her attention. Upon closer inspection, Sarah gazed at the name *Eliza Darling Borden*, second wife. Beside that were two more markers with the names *Baby Holder Borden*-drowned and *Eliza Ann*-drowned.

Closing her eyes, Sarah took in a deep breath and released.

Terrified she might see Eliza with the gaping wound at her throat and the two small bloated children, Sarah backed slowly away before turning to run from the cemetery.

The word *cursed* echoed in Sarah's head, making her run faster. A quick glimpse over her shoulder, to ensure nothing was following, prevented her from seeing the divot in the dirt. Her toe caught it, throwing her to the ground and knocking the wind from her lungs. Clouds gathered overhead as Sarah fought to breathe while pushing herself up. At that moment, her eyes rested on a small, arched headstone with the name *Lizbeth* on it. A myriad of small rocks and coins littered the top. Finally able to inhale, Sarah jumped up. She turned to see a monument nearby with the names *Andrew Borden* and *Abby Borden*. Another small arched stone read *Emma*.

"Good gracious," Sarah muttered, the names registering in her mind. She remembered reading somewhere that Lizzie had gone by the name Lizbeth in her later years. She was standing at the family plot of the Bordens! What were the odds the most notable of Fall River's murder victims would end up in the same cemetery?

Thunder rumbled, causing the ground to tremble beneath Sarah's feet. Lizzie's translucent image wavered, her lips forming the words, *He's in control. Not safe.*

"Who?" Sarah questioned.

Not as it seems. Beware the house.

Lizzie dissipated as the wind picked up and another roll of thunder rumbled. Drops of rain began to fall, splashing Sarah's flushed cheeks. It was the most Lizzie had said since Sarah arrived at Borden House. But what did it all mean? Lightening blazed across the steely canopy overhead, sending Sarah sprinting from the cemetery, through the stone archway, and down the street.

By the time she reached Borden House, she was soaked and shivering. Bolting through the front door, Sarah bent over, resting her hands on her knees as her hair dripped onto the entryway floor.

"You OK?" Danni called from the staircase, making Sarah jump. She came inside in such a rush; she hadn't noticed her friend coming down the steps.

"Don't scare me like that!" Sarah heaved, her hand grasping her chest.

"Didn't know I would," Danni replied. "You're soaked. Why didn't you call for a ride? I'd have picked you up."

"Didn't think about it," Sarah responded, her teeth beginning to chatter.

"Go upstairs and take a hot shower before you end up with pneumonia," Danni commanded.

"We need to talk first."

"Nonsense. Get out of those wet clothes. I'll make you a cup of tea," Danni said.

"Alright," Sarah replied, moving toward the staircase. "Is Garrett here?"

"He's with Tootsie," Danni replied with a smirk.

"I can't think about that right now. I'll fill you in on what happened after I change."

Before Danni could respond, Sarah trudged up the steps and into her room. She rummaged through the top drawer of the dresser, removing a pair of leggings and a cable knit sweater. Shivering, she went to the bathroom, turned the knobs on full force, and stepped into the steaming shower. Hot water massaged her neck and back, washing away the tension. In all her years of being haunted, the trip through Oak Grove Cemetery had been one of her most bizarre experiences. Multiple murder victims and the cryptic words from Lizzie made for a stressful run.

Sarah plodded back to her room, leaving her wet clothes hanging from the shower curtain. Much to her surprise, she found Danni waiting for her.

"Feeling better?" Danni asked.

"A little. You didn't say anything to Garrett, did you?"

"No, he's got enough to deal with. Valerie is still harping about having a séance. Tell me what happened."

Plopping onto the bed, Sarah folded her legs under her, taking the cup of tea from Danni.

"It was pretty intense," she responded, wrapping her hands around the mug and relishing its warmth. She talked about seeing Lizzie's ghost in the window of Maplecroft and then her unsuspecting route to the cemetery where the Bordens were buried. "Lizzie was more vocal there, saying something about a man being in control and the house being unsafe. It made no sense."

"Do you think she's referring to the man the guys caught on tape?" Danni queried.

"Him or her father," Sarah replied.

"Maybe we need to consult the book," Danni suggested.

"I don't mean to be a downer, but I'm tired of searching that stupid book. We only have a few days left to figure this out and I have a ghost trying to kill me! Weird stuff is happening and I need answers now," Sarah declared.

"Is there any chance a dreamist can develop new skills that haven't been recorded in the book?" Danni asked.

"I suppose it's feasible," Sarah replied. "Although it seems unlikely."

Danni leaned forward. "These books were written more than a hundred years ago. People change, as does their genetic make-up. It makes sense that dreamist skills could alter over time."

"Great, just what we need, more mystery," Sarah grumbled. "Let's review the facts about the murders and see if something connects with what I've dreamed so far." She took a sip of tea letting the steaming liquid warm her insides. "We know how and when the Bordens were murdered. We also know Lizzie was prone to brownouts affiliated with epileptic seizures that occurred approximately three to four times a year."

"We also know she was under Dr. Bowen's care for the condition. He testified on her behalf during the trial and continued treating her while she was jailed," Danni added.

"Yet in my dreams there was another physician doing business with Mr. Borden in an effort to help Lizzie with these episodes."

"Do you think the family doctor discovered this and sought revenge?" Danni asked.

"Don't know how competitive the medical profession was at the time. I suppose their regular doctor could've been upset if Mr. Borden sought the advice of another physician although killing them in such a gruesome manner does seem a bit extreme, especially for someone who took an oath to do no harm."

"Think about it," Danni said, her eyes glimmering. "Dr. Bowen would likely know their routine and how to access the house. Perhaps he was protective of Lizzie while she was on trial because he didn't want her to be convicted of a crime he committed," Danni said.

"Then why hide the identity of the other doctor?" Sarah queried.

"Hard to say," Danni sighed. "I really think we need to bring Garret in on this. He's going to be upset when he finds out you've been keeping this stuff from him."

"No. He needs to focus on his work," Sarah stated.

"At least share what you discovered at the cemetery with the gravesites. This could be another avenue for the men," Danni offered.

"Alright," Sarah breathed.

They plodded down the stairs and found the guys gathered in the kitchen sitting around the table brainstorming. Thankfully, Valerie was gone. Sarah slid onto the seat next to Garrett.

Grasping her hand in his, he smiled. "Danni said you went for a run."

"That's what I came to talk to you guys about," Sarah said. "I found Oak Grove Cemetery. Did you know the Bordens are buried there?"

Harry nodded.

"Did you also know Sarah Cornell, Eliza Darling Borden, and her children are buried there?"

"Get out!" Ralph declared.

"We should get some photos," Harry added. "It'll be great for the background scenes."

Sarah yawned and shifted in her seat, a slight ache gripping her muscles.

"Are you alright?" Garrett asked.

"Just a bit tired."

"How can you be tired after a run?" Garrett said.

"Don't know, but I feel like I ran a marathon," she sighed.

"Why don't you go upstairs and rest?" he suggested. "Take Dallas with you."

"I think I will," Sarah replied, standing. "Come on buddy," she called to Dallas.

"I need to answer some emails," Danni said, following Sarah and Dallas from the room.

"I'm going to practice the relaxation techniques while focusing on the mysterious figure," Sarah said as she and Danni climbed the steps with Dallas scurrying ahead.

Once upstairs, Danni headed for her room, stopping at the door. "Holler if you need me."

"I will," Sarah replied.

Danni shut the door behind her as Sarah rested her head on the pillow with Dallas at her side. Closing her eyes, Sarah started her breathing techniques, introducing the image of the shadowy figure into her thoughts. Inadvertently, she slipped into a land of dreams where the nameless physician eluded her sightline.

SARAH STOOD on the second-floor landing of Borden House, her senses on high alert. Would this be like the last dream where the only specter she encountered was the creepy man? She jumped when Lizzie stepped out of her room wearing a blue dress. Lizzie seemed oblivious to Sarah as she sauntered past and down the stairs. Even though she didn't acknowledge Sarah, there was a sense of tension emanating from Lizzie's body as if she was dreading something.

Sarah decided to follow her. Lizzie stopped at the bottom of the stairs and hesitated before walking into the sitting room where her father lay sprawled on the settee. A scream erupted from her lips, shattering the quietude of the moment. Sarah looked away, not wanting to witness the gruesome sight.

Knowing Mr. Borden's bloody body was only a few feet away, Sarah closed her eyes, took in a deep breath, and released. She repeated it a few more times until her heartrate steadied. When she opened her eyes, she was standing in the back yard.

Lizzie burst forth from the kitchen door, her complexion pale and her eyes blazing with fear. The words, *he's in control, not safe* fell from her lips.

Puzzled, Sarah looked around when her gaze rested on a dark mist forming behind her. Her heart started pounding like a bongo drum, reverberating through her ears. Stay calm, she thought, filling her lungs with air as she focused on Ola. Instead of relief, the scent of decay stung her nostrils. The cloaked man appeared in front of her, his face a shadowy distortion. Again, Sarah took in a deep breath and repeated Ola's name in her mind. The man held up his hand and laughed.

"She can't help you! I'm stronger than all of them. This isn't my first experience and shan't be my last!"

Gulping down the golf ball size lump lodged in her throat, Sarah conjured all of her fortitude. He was able to block Ola! Terror took hold. She was on her own. Sarah tried to form words but her mouth was bone dry and her legs were cemented to the spot.

The man raised his left hand above his head, something sharp glinting in the sunlight. Sarah gasped as the blade plunged toward her, the man's laughter stabbing at her head. Unable to move her limbs or cry out, she squeezed her eyes shut preparing for impact. Something wet and sticky coated her cheek.

Sarah's eyes fluttered open. Dallas sat dutifully at her side, licking her face. Reaching over, she pulled the little dog closer and hugged him, relieved to be free from the horrifying dreamscape.

CHAPTER 16

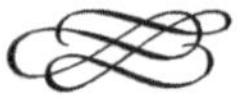

Gazing around the room, Sarah realized dusk had set in, sending shadows waltzing across the walls in an eerie dance. Her head ached.

Danni peeked through the adjoining door and grinned. "You want to get something to eat? I'm famished."

"Only if there's a pitcher of Margaritas to go along with it," Sarah said, brushing a strand of hair from her forehead.

"Did you have another dream?" she asked, stepping into the room.

"Nightmare is a better word for it."

"What happened?"

"Let's go somewhere else. I need to get away from here," Sarah huffed. "I'll fill you in over dinner."

They found a Mexican restaurant a few blocks from the house. Danni parked the car in front of a building painted a deep shade of green with *Habaneros* in bold gold lettering across the roofline. They stepped inside where they were shown to a booth by a middle-aged man with flecks of gray spotting his coal black hair. Moments later he returned and placed menus, a basket of tortilla chips, and two small bowls of salsa on the table.

"What can I get you to drink?" the waiter asked.

Danni grinned. "Pitcher of margaritas, please."

"Very good," he said, with a nod.

Shortly thereafter, the waiter approached with the pitcher and two glasses. He poured the margaritas and pulled out a notepad. The tangy sweet flavor mixed with the salt crystals on the edge of the glass, tickled Sarah's tongue. She closed her eyes, savoring the frosty elixir. It was exactly what she needed.

"Are you ready?" he asked, an accent tinting his words.

They placed their orders and chowed down on chips and salsa while waiting for their meal.

"Tell me what happened," Danni said, leaning forward.

"Things got really weird in this dream," Sarah said before taking several swallows of her drink.

"How is it any weirder than previous dreams?"

"The beginning went well. I was nervous but employed the breathing techniques until I was able to relax."

"Garrett's suggestion worked?"

"Yeah. I saw Lizzie leave her room and go downstairs where she found her father's body. Next thing I know, we're in the back yard and she said, 'he's in control' and 'not safe.'" Sarah took a long drawl from her glass. "Then *he* showed up."

Danni's eyes widened. "Did you see his face?"

"Not exactly. It was distorted. I tried to calm myself and call on Ola. That's when he blocked her and threatened me."

"Wow, that's intense. At least we're making progress."

"How so?"

"Now we know Lizzie was warning you about the mystery man," Danni said.

The waiter placed plates of enchiladas and burritos in front of them.

"Forgive my interruption, but are you discussing Lizzie Borden?" the waiter asked.

Danni straightened. "Yes. What do you know about the Bordens?"

A grin creased his coffee brown eyes. "I know there are many ghosts in the house."

"Who are they?" Sarah asked, hoping he might reveal the identity of the fearsome apparition from her dreams."

"That I do not know. I only hear people in the restaurant speaking of many ghosts haunting the house. One in particular seems to scare people more than the others."

"Which one?"

"They say it is a strange fog that disappears quickly and leaves behind an uneasy feeling."

"Does anyone know who the ghost is?" Danni asked.

"I have never heard it named, but people seem quite frightened by it."

"More so than Lizzie Borden?"

He shrugged his shoulders. "I suppose people expect to see her and the parents she killed and when this ghost appears it is unsettling."

"Thanks for the info," Danni said.

They resumed eating as the waiter walked away.

"What do we do now?" Danni asked, taking a bite of her burrito.

"Not sure, but we need to think of something fast so I can figure out who this guy is. I don't want to spend any more time with him. If he can block Ola, chances are he can interfere with what Lizzie is trying to tell me."

"When we get back, we'll talk to Garrett about it."

After finishing every bite, they placed a to-go order for the guys and headed back to the house. Sarah groaned when they saw Valerie's car parked in the drive. This night was getting worse by the minute.

They walked into the kitchen with bags of food and found the men huddled around Valerie as she watched a video, her lips pursed. Garrett and Harry watched the screen while Ralph's adoring gaze was fixed on the blond vixen.

"Interesting," she said. "Let's ramp this up a bit and see if we can capture more tonight."

"Dinner is served," Danni announced, ignoring the dirty look Valerie shot her at the interruption. "Sorry we didn't bring anything for you," Danni said to Valerie. "Didn't know you'd be here." Putting the bags on the counter, she started removing the Styrofoam containers.

"Pfft. I don't eat take-out food," Valerie replied in disgust.

"What do you mean by ramping it up?" Harry asked, seemingly unaffected by the snarky exchange and the fact their dinner had arrived.

"I think we need to conduct a séance and stir up the spirits in this place," Valerie said. "This is one of the most haunted houses in the country. You've gotten some great footage so far but I think you can get more. A little manipulation won't hurt things.

Ralph, Harry, and Garrett exchanged concerned looks.

"We don't usually engage in that sort of thing," Ralph said. "We prefer capturing spirits in a more organic way."

"This isn't a health food ad," Valerie sneered. "It's a cable network. We save the organic stuff for our sponsors."

Sarah bit her lower lip to silence the sharp retort threatening to burst forth. Danni; however, wasn't as restrained.

"It's obvious you don't believe in anything organic," Danni said with a smirk, gazing at Valerie's brassy hair and overly full lips. "These guys need to eat their dinner before it gets cold. I'm sure you want them functioning at their best."

"Whatever," Valerie replied. "This group needs something substantial, and soon." Turning toward Garrett, she smiled. "Will you see me to my car?"

With a nod, he followed her out the door, his expression grim. Sarah's heart raged even though she knew Garrett was only being polite. Now more than ever, she wanted to smack that woman.

"She's a piece of work," Harry said, grabbing a fork and opening one of the containers. Ralph followed suit; his shoulders slumped.

"She's exhausting," Garrett said, walking back in.

"I know this is aggravating, but you need to see this through, in your own way," Sarah said.

"What's so aggravating?" Ralph asked. "Valerie is a hard driven, professional. She's trying to help us do our best."

Garrett arched his brows as he grabbed his dinner and sat at the table. Leaning over, Sarah kissed his cheek and whispered in his ear. "We need to talk when you get a chance. There's been a development."

He gave her a nod and started eating. Danni and Sarah went upstairs. They needed to figure out the identity of the strange man in Sarah's dreams and prevent her from being scared to death in the process.

Twenty minutes later, Garrett joined Danni and Sarah in her room.

"What happened?" Garrett asked.

Sarah filled him in on the dream. "This guy is powerful. It's like he's pushing the others out of the way," she said, tears stinging her eyes at the memory of him.

"You're suggesting this unknown spirit is interfering with your ability to connect with Lizzie and summon Grams?"

"Exactly."

Garrett leaned back in the chair. Sarah's heart wilted at the sight of him. The odd hours and stress of trying to achieve his dreams shadowed his eyes. She felt guilty adding her problems to the list.

A sly smile spread across Danni's lips. "What if this entity knows the truth and is trying to block Lizzie from confessing? Dr. Bowen was a proponent for her innocence. Perhaps that's the identity of the ghost and he's hiding it to prevent you from discovering the truth."

"Then why block Ola and try to kill me?" Sarah responded, rubbing her forehead.

"Whatever the reason, we're not going to figure it out tonight," Garrett said, standing. "I need to get back downstairs."

"What room will I be in tonight?" Sarah asked, wringing her hands.

Garrett blew out a long breath. "Valerie wants us to film without you."

"Fine with me. Normally, I'd be furious for her intrusion; however, I could use a break."

"I'll leave Dallas with you," he said, kissing Sarah before leaving the room.

"Want me to stay too?" Danni asked.

Shaking her head, Sarah let out a long breath. "No. I need to do this on my own."

"I'll be in the next room. Holler if you need me."

"Thanks, Danni."

Sarah plunked her head on the pillow. Of all the hauntings she'd endured, this was the most frightening. If only she could dream like other people and sleep without fear of who, or what, might appear. Despite the threatening nature of the formidable physician, Sarah was determined to see this haunting through, without injury. Consciousness gave way to sleep, escorting Sarah to dreamland where ghosts were abundant and treacherous.

CHAPTER 17

Determination pulsed through Sarah's veins as she walked through the house, searching for the cloaked man. Pausing, she thought about Lizzie in her previous dream. What was it Lizzie had said? 'He's in control' and something about the house not being safe. Did she know the identity of the monstrous individual and was too afraid to tell her? Could he silence Lizzie permanently? As far as Sarah knew, ghosts couldn't be harmed since they were already dead. Then again, this specter had been able to block Ola.

For now, she needed to remain calm and find clues about what happened in the Borden House on that disastrous day in August of 1892. Perhaps if she could throw this man off, she'd have the upper hand.

Garnering all her courage, Sarah hollered, "I'm not afraid of you! I need to know why you keep trying to kill me!"

Sarah searched the upstairs rooms. Everything was quiet until she heard a shriek from downstairs. Darn it, she thought. It sounded as if Lizzie had just discovered her father's remains which meant Bridget was in her room on the third floor.

Running down the stairs, Sarah avoided the sitting room, although she caught a glimpse of Lizzie's blue dress as the young woman stood over her father. Sarah didn't want to shake her confidence by witnessing the horror of Mr. Borden's slaughtered body.

Instead, she slipped out the back door, her skin prickling as she scanned the area. He was here, she could sense it. Glancing up, Sarah glimpsed the petite housekeeper in the upstairs window, worry shrouding her expression.

"What's the matter?" Sarah mumbled.

Bridget's eyes glistened as the words, *can't say*, resonated in Sarah's head.

"Can't say what?" she asked, straightening her stature. Frustrated when no response came, Sarah tried again. "I can't help you if you don't tell me what I need to know!"

Suddenly, Bridget was standing in front of her, a hint of an Irish accent clinging to her words as she spoke. "There's no reason to risk yourself. All is done."

Sarah took a step back, surprised at the ease with which she was able to communicate. "Is Lizzie guilty?" she asked.

Bridget's eyes grew wider and she began to back away. "Tis not safe."

Sarah jumped when a hand grabbed the back of her neck, yanking her to the ground. The doctor stood over her, his cloak covering all but the wicked grin curling his lips as his fingers wrapped around her throat. She struggled to take in air but his vicelike grip prevented it.

Calm down or you'll never discover his identity.

When her vision began to blur, she visualized Ola. The old woman's image flashed through her head giving her enough confidence to speak.

"Who are you?" Sarah managed to croak.

"The last person you'll ever see," he declared, tightening his grasp.

"You're nothing more than a vision, you can't hurt me," Sarah sputtered. Her words were stronger than her nerve.

He drew closer to her, his foul breath warming her cheek. "You've no idea what I'm capable of accomplishing. I am responsible for my own fame as well as Miss Lizzie Borden's."

His fingers clenched her throat blocking the airflow and ratcheting up her terror. She reminded herself it was nothing more than a dream and no harm could come of it.

I've got to break free, she thought, her consciousness fading. At that moment, his other hand came down, slicing the side of her forearm. A squeal of pain erupted from her lips as blood trickled down her arm onto the ground. She felt herself fading when two hands yanked her away from the scene into her room at Borden House.

Blinking back tears, Sarah glanced around the room, a funnel of light streaming through the open door. Garrett sat beside her, still holding her upper arms as his emerald green stare bore through to her pounding heart.

"Are you alright?" he asked in a hushed tone.

"I think so," she mumbled, lifting her arm to inspect for the cut. Nothing. Exhaling, she dropped her chin to her chest thankful to be out of the dream. "Why are you up here?"

"I heard Dallas scratching at your door. When I walked in, you were thrashing in your sleep so I decided to wake you."

"Glad you did," she replied.

"What happened?"

"The doctor snuck up on me, pulled me to the ground, and held me down by my throat. Then he sliced my arm with something that looked like a surgical blade. I could feel the blood oozing from the wound," she said, rubbing her right arm. "Then you woke me."

Garrett reached over and lifted her arm, looking it over. He blew out a long breath. "It doesn't look like he left any marks. Did you see his face this time?"

"It was shielded by his cloak. I saw Bridget right before he appeared. At first, I thought she was trying to implicate Lizzie. But now I think she was trying to warn me about him."

"What about Grams?"

Shaking her head, Sarah murmured. "She couldn't get through."

"None of this makes any sense," Garrett exhaled.

"He was wicked. When I confronted him—"

"You confronted him?" Garrett interrupted, his brows arching.

A smile flashed across Sarah's face as a momentary wave of pride crashed through her chest. "Yeah, I did. I asked who he was and then told him he couldn't hurt me."

"How did he respond?"

"Not very well. That's when he threw me to the ground in a choke hold, slashed my arm, and inferred he could kill me. He also said he'd made himself and Lizzie Borden famous."

Garrett pondered her words for a few moments while Sarah petted Dallas.

"Sounds like he isn't aware he's dead if he believes he can kill you."

"He seems more aware than that. I get the feeling he was quite powerful when alive and has carried that perception into death. His arrogance is almost as strong as his ability to control the situation."

Garrett drew her close, stroking her hair. "Do you want to join me in the guest room? Sadly, it's not as active as your dreams."

Pulling away, her eyes met his. "No. I want to stop this man. He's dangerous and I get the feeling he's hiding something sinister."

A smile creased Garrett's cheeks as his eyes sparkled. "You're a strong woman and I love that about you."

Sarah's gaze shifted as heat rose up her neck to her cheeks. "Thank you," she breathed.

Garrett's fingers touched her chin, tilting her face toward his. He kissed her softly when Dallas snuffled his arm.

Straightening, Garrett shook his head as he tousled Dallas's fur. "You're a good dog and I love you."

Dallas replied with a resounding *bark*.

Sarah gave a half smile, thankful to have such an incredible support system.

"I need to get back to work. If you change your mind, come and sit with me," he said, standing.

"Thanks, but I have a ghost to identify."

Garrett closed the door behind him, leaving Sarah in the darkened space with Dallas at her side.

"Well little fella, looks like we have some ghosts of our own to hunt."

Sarah reclined against the pillow and glanced at the clock. 4:32 a.m. Closing her eyes, she stroked Dallas's soft fur until her mind drifted back to the realm of nightmares.

* * *

SARAH STOOD in the back yard of Borden House, her shoulders tense as she scanned the area. Looking around, she contemplated whether she should call for the violent apparition or wait to see how the dream progressed. The bushes to her right rustled.

Chewing her lower lip, she prepared for the wicked man to materialize. Instead, Eliza emerged.

"Eliza?" Sarah said, surprised to see her in the dream which meant the other spirit likely wouldn't be showing up.

"Cursed," she gurgled, the wound in her throat seeping blood as she spoke.

Sarah focused on Eliza's filmy gray eyes instead of the gash in her throat to dissuade the nausea building in her stomach. "How are you cursed?"

"Killed my children," she muttered. "Didn't want to do it. Loved them."

Compassion flooded Sarah's chest. It couldn't have been easy in the mid-19th century to give birth to three babies within a short period of time, run a household, and deal with the avalanche of hormonal changes that came with it.

"You weren't in your right mind," Sarah offered.

"Cursed," Eliza repeated. "Don't know why." Tears trickled down her sallow cheeks, blending with the blood dripping from her neck. "My mind is bad. Had to die."

"You were sick," Sarah comforted. "They didn't know about these things back then. I'm sure you didn't mean to do what you did."

Eliza's two children appeared at her side. She placed her arms around them. "Thoughts were evil. Cannot escape the pain. Couldn't stop myself."

"If you'd had medical help, perhaps…." Sarah stopped herself. How could she explain to a Victorian woman that in her era they didn't have the treatments to help a woman with post-partem depression. Granted, it didn't excuse her actions but obviously, she was tormented by her heinous act.

"Killed my children. Had to take my life."

"I'm sorry about what happened. I'm sure you loved your kids."

The ghostly form swayed at Sarah's words. "You believe me?"
Sarah nodded.

Eliza's form vacillated as the slice in her neck began to heal. Her eyes widened as her hand went to her throat.

"You removed curse?" Eliza's lips curled into a smile. She gathered her children to her side, their grayish pallor and bloated faces fading away to rosy cheeks and bright stares. Sarah watched as the three spirits vanished leaving a sense of calm in their wake. She'd actually helped them and it felt good.

"She was evil." A man's voice brushed Sarah's ear. "And the perfect pawn for you."

Sarah spun around and faced the wavering dark spirit. Clouds gathered overhead as thunder rumbled in the distance. Overpowered by the scent of rotting flesh, Sarah gagged.

"You're weak," he said, his voice booming with the thunder.

"How does helping a woman move on after being tormented by her deeds for more than a century make me weak?" Sarah shouted. Rain fell in torrents, soaking her to the bone.

"Pathetic creature," he growled. "I'll get you when you don't expect it. I will finish you."

Lightning struck the tree behind them, splintering the trunk and sending it to the ground with a thud.

"I'm not afraid of you," Sarah hollered over the roaring downpour.

"Ah, but you should be," he said with a wicked grin. His cadaverous fingers jutted from beneath his cloak, clutching Sarah's throat.

She tore at his hand in an effort to loosen his grip but only flesh came away. Repulsed, Sarah tried to wriggle free but his hold was unwavering. His eyes glowed as his face neared hers, his foul breath scraping against her skin. "You will not succeed."

"Who are you?" she managed to gasp.

"A professional with the ability to extract your secret," he replied.

Sarah's lungs felt like balloons ready to burst as she struggled to free herself. The harder she fought, the tighter his grip. He seemed to enjoy the tussle as his free hand came into view. This time Sarah saw the scalpel as it plummeted into her chest, slicing down her sternum.

"I'm saving you from yourself, wicked one," he declared.

She felt the life draining from her as a cackle exploded from his rotting lips. The sound of his laughter reverberated through her head, the pain blurring her vision.

"Ola," she whispered.

His face drew closer, his fingers pressing harder against her trachea. "She's weak too. I'll deal with her when I finish you."

"No!" she screamed, bolting upright in bed.

Glancing around the space, Sarah tried to get her bearings. She was in Lizzie's room. She was safe.

The hall light peeked below the bottom of the bedroom door sending shadows across the floor. A dark fog filtered through the light, growing in size.

"This can't be happening," Sarah whispered. "I'm awake. I'm safe."

The mist swirled into a funnel as laughter bounced off the walls.

The sound bludgeoned Sarah's skull like an ax splitting wood. Gripping her head in her hands, she rocked back and forth. The laughter increased in intensity until she was sure her head would explode.

"Stop!" she screamed, squeezing her eyes shut while pressing the heels of her hands against her temples. The bed shifted beside her. He was there. "Leave me be!"

"Sarah!" Garrett said, his hands resting on hers as she held her head.

Instantaneously, the pain subsided as small dots of light danced before her eyes.

Garrett lifted her face, his eyes searching hers. Danni appeared in the doorway, her hair sticking up where she'd been sleeping.

"What the heck?" Danni groaned. "It's 4:45 in the morning."

Sarah breathed in as her body trembled. Only fifteen minutes had passed? It felt like hours.

"What's going on?" Garrett asked.

"I...he...." she whimpered before a sob burst forth.

Danni joined them on the bed, rubbing Sarah's back as Garrett held her to his chest. Despite being awake and having Garrett and Danni with her, she couldn't stop crying. When her sobs subsided and her tears ran dry, Sarah straightened.

"Tell us what happened," Garrett said.

"I was able to help Eliza and her children," Sarah said, swiping at her cheeks. "She was so remorseful, although I question it now."

"Why?" Garrett asked.

"He used her to distract me, at least that's what he told me. I was focused on Eliza and didn't see him approach until it was too late."

Danni slipped from the room and returned moments later, handing Sarah the flask. With a quivering hand, Sarah downed a few gulps of bourbon, coughing from the sudden burn against her raw throat. Handing the flask back to her friend, Sarah continued.

"It was a full-on attack. He choked me while telling me I was weak and that he'd finish me. I tried to find out who he was but he avoided the question and stabbed me in the chest. I was able to see the weapon this time. It was definitely a scalpel."

"So, he is a doctor," Danni said.

Sarah nodded. "The question is, which one? We know there were two treating Lizzie."

"We know about Dr. Bowen. This other guy has only been in your dreams. There's no record of him so far."

"What happened next?" Garrett asked.

"I could feel myself dying. When I called on Ola, he laughed and said she was next." Tears puddled in Sarah's lids. "How does this man know about me, and Ola? I can't let anything happen to her."

"Don't worry about Grams," Garrett said, brushing strands of hair from her sweat soaked forehead. "She could handle herself in life which means she's probably doubly tough in the afterlife."

"How did you get away?" Danni asked.

"Not sure." Sarah rubbed her forehead. "I don't think this ghost will be easy to get rid of. He's not seeking help; he wants to destroy. When he laughs, it feels like my head is exploding. The pain was worse than the stab to my chest."

"How does your head feel now?" Garrett asked.

"The pain stopped as soon as you grabbed me," Sarah replied.

"Except you were awake when I came in the room."

Sarah reflected on the dream and what followed. "He was here," she moaned. "I was relieved to be awake. That's when I saw a mist seeping beneath the door."

"Let me go downstairs and help the guys wrap up. I'm staying with you tonight."

"It won't stop the dreams," Sarah mumbled. "And you need to get some sleep."

"I'm not leaving you alone until we understand what's going on."

"I can stay with her," Danni offered.

Garrett exhaled. "Alright. Tomorrow we'll figure this out. I'm not comfortable with this spirit's power."

His concern cut through Sarah's fortitude. She'd never seen Garrett this worried about a ghost before. And he'd had plenty of experience.

CHAPTER 18

It was five in the morning. Despite having Danni with her, Sarah couldn't sleep. Danni; however, slept like a corpse. Sarah lay in bed, watching splashes of autumnal sun color the floral-patterned walls of Lizzie's room. She felt as if she was in a vampire book where the heroine dreads the rising and setting of the sun.

She slipped from bed, grabbed some clothes, and went to the bathroom to shower. The hot spray pounded away at her knotted muscles as the steam soothed her sore throat. Hopefully, Garrett would have some ideas about how to deal with this aggressive spirit. Danni had been right; she should have kept him apprised of it all.

Sarah returned to the room feeling somewhat refreshed. Danni was still out. Not wanting to wake her, Sarah crept down the stairs to the dining room. Garrett, Harry, and Ralph each sat in front of a laptop, sipping coffee.

"Good morning," Sarah greeted, sitting next to Garrett. "How'd it go last night?"

"Caught the dark mist on the guest room camera," Harry replied, shadows beneath his eyes.

Sarah's skin crawled at the mention of the intimidating apparition. Garrett gave her a sideways glance. She grasped his hand under the table letting him know she was OK.

Over the past few days, the team had been filming most of the night, sleeping for a few hours, having breakfast, and catching naps in between editing and research. Since most of their excursions prior to this one had been overnight gigs, sleep hadn't been an issue. Now they looked like zombies in a B-rated movie.

"Did you get a clearer image of him?" Sarah asked. Maybe if they could identify the entity, they could find a way to be rid of him.

"Nope. Only thing we could see was his form float through the room and into the hallway."

Sarah's breath caught. "What time was that?" she asked.

"Not sure of the exact time. Probably around 4:40ish," Harry replied.

Garrett seemed to make the connection as well, squeezing her hand. This was about the time Sarah saw the misty form ooze beneath her door suggesting this spirit drifted from the guest room to hers.

After breakfast and a long discussion about the night's success, what Walter might be able to decipher from the footage, and plans for the next evening's pursuits, Garrett and Harry went to their rooms to get some sleep. Ralph went to the kitchen to work on the computer.

Sarah climbed the stairs and found Danni sitting up in bed. Her friend looked like she'd been on an all-night bender during spring break. Her hair was disheveled and her eyelids drooped.

"Just now getting up?" Sarah asked.

"Yeah," she grunted. "Why'd you let me sleep so long?"

"Because the creatures in my dreams are frightening enough without waking the monster in my bed."

Danni smirked. "I'm going to take a shower and then I need some food. I'm starving."

"We'll have to go out. Breakfast is over."

"Fine," Danni shrugged, going to her room for a change of clothes. She trudged to the bathroom for a shower as Sarah reclined on the bed, closing her eyes.

Resting her head on the pillow, she contemplated the likelihood of the spirit from her dreams slipping beneath her door shortly after showing up on the video. It had to be him. Exhaustion fluttered Sarah's eyelids and her limbs felt like lead weights. If only she could figure this out.

Danni walked into the room, her wet hair secured with a plastic clip and her gaze brighter.

"You ready?" she asked.

"Yeah," Sarah replied, sitting up, her neck stiff.

Slipping from bed, Sarah put on her shoes, and started for the door when finger nails dug into her shoulder. "Ow!" she hollered, spinning around. "What the heck…?"

Sarah gasped. It wasn't Danni. The faceless creature in the cloak hovered before her, his hand raised. Sarah saw the glint of the blade as it swooshed through the air and penetrated her shoulder.

Screaming in pain, Sarah jolted up in bed. She glanced around the room and saw Danni standing there, her complexion pale and her mouth gaping open.

"Danni, is that really you?" she squeaked.

"Who else would it be?"

Burying her head in her hands, Sarah squeezed her eyes shut. It was only a dream, she thought, trying to slow her racing pulse. That's when she realized her shoulder was throbbing.

"Sarah," Danni said, moving toward her. "Are you alright?"

"Not really," she replied, rubbing her shoulder where the blade had cut. "Let's get outta here."

Danni grabbed her keys and they started down the stairs.

"You gonna tell me what happened?" Danni asked.

"We'll talk over lunch," Sarah mumbled.

"You mean breakfast," Danni responded.

"No, I mean lunch. It's quarter to twelve."

"Ugh," Danni moaned. "I really need to start setting an alarm. This ghost hunting stuff has completely wacked out my sleep routine."

"Pfft. You drink until you fall asleep and get up when your body tells you unless you have to be in court."

"And your point?" she asked, unlocking the car.

"You don't have a sleep routine."

"Yes, I do, you just described it," she remarked with a sly smile.

With a giggle, Sarah slid onto the leather seat of the Mercedes. No matter how terrifying the circumstances, Danni's no-nonsense way of thinking could always bring a smile to her face.

AFTER LUNCH, they drove around to take in some of the sights. They'd been cooped up at Borden House for so long, they needed a break. Autumn's crispness wafted through the open windows of the car as they traversed the idyllic township of Fall River. Much of the area was adorned in Halloween accoutrements replete with ghosts, monsters, and of course, a hatchet wielding Lizzie Borden. This was the town's busy season and they were capitalizing on it.

"Who would have thought a family slaughter would bring so much attention a century later," Danni said, stopping at a cross walk to allow a group to pass by.

"Goes to show no matter how gruesome, people love the macabre."

"Too bad they couldn't spend a day in your head. Bet they'd change their minds about all this haunted stuff."

"Ha, that's the truth," Sarah replied. Once the group was safely across the street, Danni drove on.

Despite the cool temperatures, Sarah lowered the window and let the wind whip against her face blowing her hair around like the arms of an octopus. Danni found an 80s station on the radio and they belted out the lyrics to Michael Jackson's *Thriller*. Sarah could feel her mind resetting. Nothing like reliving the good ole high school days cruising around with the radio blasting. Even Danni seemed carefree, which warmed Sarah's heart. She'd been through so much since her catastrophic heartbreak in Edgefield. That was the great thing about a best friend. No matter how tough things got or how bizarre your life might become, even to the point of haunted dreams, a close friend was always there for you.

"Let's talk about your dreams," Danni said when the radio station announced a commercial break.

"Can we just cruise for a while? I need to let my brain rest."

"Not a problem."

They turned onto Prospect Street and drove past the proverbial New England style houses. Sarah remembered something from their research about this area. It had been known as 'The Hill' during Lizzie's time and had been considered an upscale place to live. Lizzie's sister Emma had resided with the Reverend Buck's five daughters in one of the homes. A shadowy glow crept across the landscape as the sun ducked behind a herd of gray clouds. Sarah shuddered at the site of a young woman clad in 1890s attire waving at her from the upstairs porch of a two-story white sided home that towered above the street. Instinctively, Sarah started to wave back but stopped when the woman's image vacillated into nothingness leaving only a rocker swaying in her wake.

After traversing the tree-lined streets, they approached a four-way stop where a brick building with arched red doors stood on a corner. The architectural details in the brick caught

Sarah's attention. She loved the craftsmanship of days gone by. Too bad they didn't do that kind of thing anymore. As they reached the cement drive in front of the structure, the arched doors flew open and a firetruck barreled toward them.

"Look out!" Sarah screamed causing Danni to slam on the breaks as the firetruck blazed past and disappeared, leaving behind a dark mist. At first, she thought it was the diesel exhaust hovering in the air until the mist wavered into the shadowy form from her dreams. She gulped down the fear stuck in her throat. How could the slasher be here? Surely, he couldn't leave the confines of Borden House.

"What the heck Sarah?" Danni hollered.

The car behind them blew the horn. Danni threw her hand up at the other driver and drove on.

"Sorry," Sarah said breathlessly, clutching her chest. "I saw a fire engine coming straight for us."

"Seriously? From the Little Theater building?"

"Is that what it was?" she asked, looking back over her shoulder.

"That's what the sign said," Danni replied, softening a bit.

"I'm really sorry. I didn't know it wasn't real until…."

Danni patted Sarah's hand. "Don't worry about it. Maybe going for a drive wasn't the best way to settle your nerves. We need to find a non-haunted excursion."

"Not likely," Sarah huffed, her stomach twisting at the idea the malevolent spirit was following her.

"What's wrong?" Danni asked with a sideways glance as she stopped at the next intersection.

Sometimes Sarah hated how Danni could read her so well. She really didn't feel like discussing this.

"I saw *him*."

"Who?"

"The ghost from my dreams," Sarah replied.

"The creepy doctor who keeps trying to slit your throat?"

"He was right behind the firetruck that was coming straight for us."

"You mean the invisible truck only you saw?"

"Yes."

Danni pulled over into an empty lot, and put the car in park. The sky darkened and a few drops splashed against the windshield.

"Are you suggesting this ghost is following you?" Her eyes were as wide as marbles.

Sarah rubbed her forehead. "It seems like it." Looking up, she met Danni's worried gaze. "I didn't see him clearly but I definitely sensed him. I got the feeling he was trying to cause an accident."

"This is insane. What kind of ghost attempts to kill you in your dreams and when he's unsuccessful follows you around town and tries other methods?"

"I don't know," Sarah replied, her voice cracking. Queasiness rolled through her stomach like a lava lamp. "I'm scared."

"Let's get back to the house. We need to find a way to repel this guy before he succeeds in his quest."

Danni pulled onto the road holding Sarah's quivering hand as they headed toward Borden House. Once they arrived, the two friends sat in the car for a moment before going inside.

"I don't care what you say, we need to tell Garrett about this," Danni commanded.

Sarah nodded. Her eyes moistened as she stared at the two-story structure that housed so many horrific memories. Exhaustion wrapped its sinewy fingers around her limbs making her feel as frail as a newly hatched baby bird. The grayness of the ashen clouds overhead mimicked her despair.

"Why is this happening? Everything was going so well. I was learning to use my abilities and ward off some of the fear I've experienced throughout my life. And then Garrett came along with all his knowledge about dreamists and I thought I'd never be afraid again. Even he's stumped. How am I supposed to deal with this entity on my own?"

"You're not alone. Garrett and I are going to help you figure this out."

"How?" Sarah muttered.

"Not sure but we haven't failed you yet and we're not about to start now."

Sarah swiped at the tear trickling down her face. "Thanks."

"We can beat this thing, trust me."

Danni's determined tone actually gave Sarah a spark of hope. She wasn't alone and knew Garrett and Danni would do everything in their power to help conquer the wicked spirit that was stalking her.

They walked inside and found Garrett, Harry, and Ralph gathered around one of the monitors with Walter on speaker phone.

"It's the best I could get. You can definitely tell it's a man and now we can see his attire more clearly," Walter's voice sounded over the cell phone.

"This is great," Harry declared, his eyes sparkling with excitement.

Ralph waved Sarah and Danni over. They gathered around and stared at the grainy figure on the screen. As soon as Sarah saw it, she shrieked and stumbled backwards, nearly knocking over the camera equipment behind her.

"What's going on?" Walter asked as Garrett steadied Sarah and Harry grabbed the camera.

"I'm so sorry," she responded, her words breathy. "I was just startled by seeing him so clearly on the screen."

"You've seen him before?" Ralph asked.

Danni's eyes grew wider as Garrett gripped Sarah's shoulder. Realizing her faux pas, she scrambled for an answer to thwart any further inquiries.

"Seeing any ghost is pretty creepy," she said, gripping her chest. "Isn't this the same man from the film the other night?"

"We think so," Harry replied, apparently pacified by her response. Thankfully, Ralph and Walter seemed to buy into it as well because no one questioned her further.

"The problem is, we don't have any idea who it might be," Ralph added.

"Don't think it's Mr. Borden. This man is too short," Harry said.

"If we can figure it out and prove there's another ghost haunting this place, it will open a lot of doors for us." Ralph smiled.

"Except we don't have time to figure it out," Harry said. "We need to focus on the Borden murders. This is probably some random ghost who may have visited the house. Chances are, there's not going to be any info on him."

"Sarah and I could look into it," Danni offered.

"That would be great," Ralph said.

"What exactly do you want us to look for?" Sarah asked.

"Any history about the house that might identify previous owners or their family members. Based on the image, the man appears to be wearing some sort of hooded cloak indicative of the nineteenth century. If we can pinpoint the time period, we may be able to figure out who it is."

"Sounds easy enough," Danni remarked.

"Ha!" Walter boomed over the phone. "Been researching the house all afternoon. The only thing I was able to find were previous owners, none of whom died in the house."

"Maybe you don't know what to look for," Danni taunted.

A sly smile crossed Ralph's lips as they listened to the exchange.

"Are you implying you're better at digging up answers than me?" Walter groused.

"It wasn't an implication," Danni replied, her brows arched as she pursed her lips.

Sarah knew that look. Danni loved a challenge, especially when someone was inferring they could do something better than she could.

"Care to prove it?" Walter asked.

"No problem," she replied, confidently. "Name the conditions."

Silence cut through the tension like a knife through butter.

"You drink?" he asked.

"Like a fish," she responded.

"First one to discover the identity of the man in the video buys the other a top shelf bottle of bourbon."

"I only drink bourbon when Sarah's around. Make mine scotch and you have a deal," she said.

"Attorneys," he sighed. "So predictable. You've got a deal."

"What if neither of us figures it out?" she asked.

"Already doubting yourself. Interesting," he crooned.

"Never. I was only trying to clarify the parameters."

Ralph interrupted, obviously attempting to halt any further taunts. "If you guys are going to help us, you need to get to work instead of hurling challenges at each other."

Danni rattled her keys. "You ready to go back out?" she asked Sarah.

"Yup."

They walked out the kitchen door toward the car when Garrett came jogging up behind them.

"What's going on?" he asked Sarah.

With a quick glance at Danni, she spoke.

"The image startled me," she huffed.

"Why?" Garrett asked, obviously not letting the topic go.

"I believe it's the same apparition from my dreams, the one who keeps trying to kill me," she said.

"The doctor?"

Sarah nodded. "I caught a glimpse of him on our way back from lunch."

"Where?"

"Side of the road about half mile away."

Garrett ran his hand through his hair. "See what you can find out about the doctor and any past residents. Maybe this guy is haunting the place because he's unhappy with what occurred at the house."

"That's not the feeling I get," Sarah said. "This entity feels angry, as if he wants to destroy anything he comes in contact with, not at all like a person dedicated to healing people."

"Considering the history of this house, it seems like a logical place for anyone with violent tendencies."

"I'll text if we find anything," Sarah said, relieved he wasn't querying further about her dreams. She didn't want to upset him by letting him know she'd been keeping things from him. But now wasn't the time to worry about it. She'd fill him in later. Until then, she and Danni had a ghost to identify before it succeeded in harming her.

CHAPTER 19

Sarah and Danni pulled into the parking lot of the historical society and went inside. Millie smiled from the front desk as they entered, her blue eyes sparkling beneath the antique chandelier.

"Hello ladies! Good to see you again," she said, stepping from behind the desk. "What can I help you with today?"

"Hey Millie," they said in unison.

"We need to do some research on the families that lived in Borden House before the Bordens," Danni said.

"Follow me."

She led them to the archives in the basement and opened one of the file cabinet drawers.

"These files contain basic information about the more notable homes in town, including the Borden House. If we don't have what you're looking for, you'll need to try the records office at town hall."

"Are there any records of the physicians in Fall River during the Borden trial?"

"The only doctor in town was Dr. Bowen. There are records

in the second drawer about his involvement with the Bordens and his assistance to Lizzie during the trial."

"What about traveling doctors?" Sarah asked.

Millie shook her head. "It was a small community. Dr. Bowen was the only physician in Fall River on record. I'm unaware of any documentation regarding traveling doctors."

"Thanks," Danni said as Millie left the room.

Danni searched the files for previous owners while Sarah skimmed the records about Dr. Bowen.

Sarah slumped back in the chair. "According to this, Dr. Bowen was an upstanding citizen and a well-respected physician."

"It was a good idea to investigate him," Danni said. "The only thing I've found is that Andrew Borden purchased the house in 1872 and had it remodeled. Prior to that it had been a two-tenant structure."

"We're not getting anywhere," Sarah sighed.

"Let's go back to the house," Danni suggested. "Maybe I can find something on the Internet. I will not lose this wager."

With a chuckle, Sarah shook her head. "We drove all the way down here for information we could have gleaned from an online data base?"

"I figured some of this stuff might not be available online." Danni replied. "Not to mention, you were freaked out about the image on the video. I thought it was best to get you outta there before the guys started asking too many questions."

"Thanks," Sarah said. "But I'm afraid this delay may have given Walter a head start."

"That may be the case but he doesn't have my secret weapon."

"What's that?"

"You."

"Me?" Sarah exclaimed. "How am I a secret weapon?"

"All you have to do is take a nap and dream so you can glean information from the ghosts."

"Humph. You don't ask for much," Sarah grumbled as they placed the files back in the cabinet. "Besides, wouldn't that be cheating?"

"You call it cheating, I call it strategizing. Either way, we won't get the answers we need unless you're asleep."

They bid adieu to Millie, hopped in the car, and headed back to the house. A foreboding feeling niggled at Sarah's nerves, as if she was about to embark on something more formidable than her previous haunted encounters.

As they walked through the back door of the kitchen, the fragrance of heavy perfume punched them in the face.

"What the heck?" Danni said, wrinkling her nose. "Smells like someone raided the cologne counter at the local drug store."

Sarah chuckled and then sneezed. The scent was powerful.

At that moment, Valerie stepped into the room, her expression souring when she saw Sarah and Danni standing there.

"Nope, eau de cheap whorehouse," she mumbled, nudging a chuckle from Sarah.

"Back from running errands?" Valerie asked coquettishly. Her shapely legs jutted from a skirt so short you'd see her goods if she leaned over. "Don't suppose you brought any coffee? I could use a kick of caffeine. Garrett's been running me ragged."

"I'll give her a kick," Danni said under her breath.

"We were out doing research," Sarah replied as kindly as she could despite the fact, she wanted to join Danni in the kick-the-bimbo-out-the-door endeavor. "Afraid you'll have to ask Mrs. Pearson for coffee."

"I think she's gone to the market. Be a dear, and fix a pot, will you?" she said with a fake smile.

"Sorry, but I don't drink the stuff and therefore don't know the first thing about making it," Sarah replied, her chin lifted.

"Of course, you don't," she sneered.

Sarah's back straightened. She held back the retort hovering at her lips. The last thing she wanted to do was take the bait and ruin any chances for the men. What was it her father always said? True wisdom is holding your tongue when you're ready to lash out? Sadly, Danni didn't get that memo.

"I would think as a network lacky, you'd know how to fix a pot of coffee," Danni said.

A wicked grin creased Valerie's contact enhanced eyes. "I'm on top of the food chain at the network, not some go-to girl," she replied.

Danni opened her mouth but Sarah gave her a stern look letting her know this wasn't the time to engage in pettiness.

Stepping closer, Valerie stared down at Sarah. "These men are going places, especially Garrett. Don't be a fool and thwart his opportunities. With looks like his, the show will top the charts."

Sarah's blood boiled as rage pulsed through her veins. Why was this woman coming after her like this? She and Garrett had been careful to hide the extent of their relationship to avoid this very scenario. Before Sarah could think of a come-back, Valerie turned and started toward the door when Ola's translucent figure materialized. Her shimmering foot extended into Valerie's path sending her tumbling to the ground, snapping her stiletto heel in the process.

Sarah's hand flew to her mouth to hide the smile spreading across her face while Danni giggled.

"Aren't you going to help me up?" Valerie barked, holding out her hand.

"Why don't you play the damsel in distress and wait for one of the men to dash to your rescue?" Danni smirked.

Valerie's milky skin turned a deep shade of crimson as she scrambled to her feet.

"At least men find me attractive," she growled, heading for the doorway.

"The mindless ones looking for Barbie dolls," Danni whispered in Sarah's ear. "One of these days all that silicone and Botox is gonna find its way south and she'll be nothing more than a sagging leather bag with fuzzy bleached hair."

Sarah muffled a laugh.

Valerie stopped and stared at them. "Did I miss something?" she asked, squinting.

"Not a thing," Sarah replied smugly.

A sneer crinkled Valerie's lips when Harry walked in.

"What's up?" he asked, making his way to the coffee pot.

"I was just getting ready to meet with Garrett," she smiled, lifting her broken shoe from the floor and slipping off the other one.

"I'm fixing a pot of coffee. You ladies want any?"

"I think Valerie could use a *kick*," Danni snickered.

Sarah elbowed her friend in the side making her wince. Harry seemed oblivious to the tension in the room. How could men be so unaware of the cattiness between women?

Harry stood at the sink filling the coffee pot, as Valerie shot Danni and Sarah a dirty look before leaving the room.

"Any luck finding information about former owners of the house?" he asked, starting the coffee maker.

"Nothing yet, but we aren't giving up," Danni replied. "In fact, we were on our way upstairs to do some more searching."

"Good luck," he said as the coffee pot sputtered and hissed.

They made their way upstairs when Sarah spoke. "I wonder where Garrett is."

"Probably hiding from the barracuda. That woman is infuriating. I don't know how you were able to keep your cool."

"I was getting ready to say something when Ola appeared."

"Seriously? What was she doing?"

"Helping out," Sarah chuckled. "She tripped Valerie."

"That's hilarious," Danni replied before her expression faded. "Ola was able to intervene physically?"

"Yeah. At least that's what I saw."

"We need to look through the *Dreamist* book before we do any more research," Danni said matter-of-factly.

Sarah swallowed hard. She'd been so distracted by Valerie's taunts she'd completely overlooked the fact Ola had physically interacted with the living which meant the man from her dreams could likely do the same.

Sarah shuddered at the thought. The entire scenario was getting more complicated by the hour.

"Let's get Garrett," Danni suggested. "He'll make this go faster."

Sarah popped from her ruminations at the sound of her friend's voice and shook her head. "We've got to do this on our own. He's got enough going on without being worried about my safety."

"OK, but if we can't figure it out, we'll ask for his help. This isn't something we can delay."

"Agreed," Sarah replied with a sigh. They went to Danni's room, got the book, and sat on the bed. After an hour of scouring the tiny print, Sarah's eyes were bleary and her back ached. She slumped back on the bed with a heavy sigh.

"Look at this," Danni exclaimed, pointing to the last stanza on the page.

"Read it to me," Sarah moaned.

Evil exists
    And will persist
    To bring you to the other side
    Where there's nowhere to hide.
    Stay on guard
    To prevent being marred
    Avoid the imposters
    For danger they foster.

In order to survive
Your skills must thrive.

"As USUAL, this makes absolutely no sense," Sarah said, sitting up.

"Actually, it does," Danni said.

"How so?"

"Think of this in respect to what's been happening in your dreams. It's saying evil exists and can harm you. In order to stay safe, you've got to use your dreamist abilities to avert the danger."

"Astounding," Sarah grumbled.

"What?"

"How you can make sense of that gibberish."

"It's pretty straightforward."

"Maybe for you, but it doesn't register for me."

Danni chuckled. "You're complicating it. Anyway, it seems you've stayed safe so far because you've been able to calm your-self and call on Ola, at least that's how I'm reading it."

Sarah contemplated what they'd just read. If they were inter-preting the passage correctly, there was potential for a ghost to cause harm.

"What's the matter?" Danni asked.

"I'm not sure I'm doing enough to stay safe."

"This man hasn't been able to hurt you yet, even though he's made several attempts."

"True. However, he's been able to block Ola and threatened to harm her. Maybe this is what's scaring Lizzie and Bridget. They almost seem intimidated by him," Sarah said.

"Pretty bad when a hatchet murderer is afraid of another entity," Danni snorted.

"She was acquitted," Sarah said with a roll of her eyes. "Do you think ghosts can be killed in the great beyond?"

"Doubtful since they're already dead."

Sarah chewed her lower lip. "I don't like this. Something tells me I'm not fully prepared for what I'm facing in my dreams. And what does the imposter line mean?" she asked. "Are there fraudulent spirits?"

"Not sure about that one," Danni said, uncertainty in her tone. "We can talk to Garrett about it later. For now, let's assume you're physically safe from menacing spirits."

Footsteps echoed from the staircase catching their attention. Garrett entered, his face drooping with exhaustion.

"How's it going down there?" Sarah asked, patting the spot beside her.

He sat down and rubbed his eyes. "I'm beat. Aside from that, we're making progress. Walter was able to do a bit more with the video of the hazy form. Now we can make out all of the ghost's features except for his face. It's strange how this spirit is a black mist, not the whitish stuff we usually see."

"If it's the same spirit haunting me, and I feel certain it is, he's definitively got a dark aura about him. Makes sense his ghostly appearance would follow suit."

"By the way, we were reading through the *Dreamist* book and found something interesting," Danni added. "There's a line that says, *avoid the imposters, for danger they foster*. Any idea what that means?"

"Yup. Grams was adamant I memorize and remember that particular line. Some dreamists have reverted to inorganic methods to communicate with the dead, specifically, Ouija boards and séances. Those things can open portals to dangerous spirits and should be avoided at all costs."

"In other words, no hocus pocus," Danni said.

"Exactly. It's one of the main reasons Harry, Ralph, and I don't use those things to conjure up spirits," Garrett responded. "Hunting ghosts may seem like fun, but it can be dangerous if you're not careful. There are things about the spirit realm we've yet to comprehend."

"And the guys were amenable to that philosophy?" Danni asked.

"Pretty much. When I explained we could stand out more by doing our own thing instead of the standard parlor tricks approach, they agreed to film ghosts in a natural manner."

"Do you think I'm doing enough to stay safe in my dreams?" Sarah queried, her chest tightening.

"I don't think you have anything to worry about. None of us are going to utilize those methods for filming."

He planted a kiss on her cheek and stood. "I'm gonna take a power nap. See you in a little bit."

Sarah watched him saunter from the room with Dallas at his heels, her heart palpitating at the sight of his broad shoulders and confident stance.

"Now what?" Danni asked.

"We keep searching," Sarah responded, more determined than ever to find the answers necessary to help the guys achieve their goals and prevent any injuries to herself.

CHAPTER 20

*E*ventide splashed vibrant shades of orange and gold across the walls of Sarah's room. Her heart thumped within her chest as a foreboding feeling niggled at her nerves. She and Danni had spent the afternoon searching for any tidbit to explain what was happening in her dreamscapes and waking hours. Unfortunately, they didn't garner much information.

"Don't know about you, but I'm hungry. Let's get something to eat," Danni said, closing her laptop and setting it on the bed.

"Already?" Sarah replied with a sideways glance.

"We ate hours ago and I didn't have breakfast, so yes, I'm ready to eat."

Sarah stood in a stretch. "The guys are probably hungry too. Let's get take-out."

"Sounds like a plan," Danni replied.

After checking with the men, they called in an order to Bob's BBQ. Danni and Sarah drove across town to pick up the food. The crisp night air nibbled at Sarah's extremities with a frosty nip. She was adjusting to the colder climate although she missed the marsh breezes and mild temperatures of home.

They pulled into the parking lot and parked in front of a red one-story building about the size of a train car. Stepping into the modest space, Sarah and Danni were greeted by the enticing aroma of smoked beef and French fries. Flames were painted on the walls and a checkerboard floor stretched out beneath square tables, several of which were occupied. All eyes looked at them as they crossed the threshold.

A waitress appeared at the checkout counter and smiled, her perfectly white teeth matching the glimmer in her eyes.

"How are you ladies this evening?" she asked with a Boston drawl.

"Well, thank you," Danni replied. "We're picking up an order for Cook."

"Just a sec," she said, turning to check the receipts on a line of to-go bags. Lifting two large plastic bags, she set them on the counter and took the money.

"This place kinda reminds me of Corner Pocket," Danni said, referring to their favorite Edgefield eatery.

"It does have that hometown hang-out feel," Sarah responded.

"You ladies visiting?" the waitress asked, handing Danni her change.

"We're from South Carolina," Sarah said.

"You with that ghost hunting group staying at the Borden House?" she questioned, her brows arching.

"Is there anyone in this town who doesn't know about that?" Danni asked.

The waitress chuckled. "No secrets around here when it comes to the Bordens."

"So, it would seem," Danni muttered, lifting the bags.

"Hope your group finds what they're looking for," she called as Sarah and Danni headed for the exit. "The residents of this town would love to know who really committed the murders."

Danni and Sarah paused. Most of the patrons had gone quiet listening to the exchange.

"I thought most people assumed it was Lizzie," Danni said, turning back.

"Depends on who you talk to," the waitress shrugged. "She was found innocent."

"Not guilty, there's a difference," Danni corrected. "Who do you think did it?"

"Not sure, but I can't fathom a tiny woman like Lizzie who was raised properly would butcher her parents. Not to mention, she was an animal lover. Most people who are kind to animals do likewise to people."

"Interesting take on it," Sarah said, pleased someone else shared her theory.

"Don't care how ladylike she was, there's no doubt she was guilty. She turned on the charm and bamboozled the jurors," an older gent said, standing behind Sarah. His pale blue eyes and scraggly salt and pepper hair gave him the appearance of a mad scientist. Dressed in a tweed jacket and tan trousers, with a yellow cravat tied about his wrinkled neck he was the picture of eccentricity.

"Why are you so adamant about her guilt?" Sarah asked him.

"What do you mean?" Danni asked.

Turning to her friend, Sarah tilted her head. "I think too many people are quick to make snap decisions based upon the rumor mill and what the press chooses to share. I'm not certain there was enough evidence to convict her. It's sad she had to live with the shame hanging over her for the rest of her life, especially if she was innocent."

Danni wrinkled her forehead. "Sarah, you're not making any sense."

"Huh?"

"You asked why I was adamant about Lizzie's guilt. I've already told you my thoughts on it."

"I wasn't talking to you; I was speaking with the...." Sarah looked back at several sets of eyes staring at her from the tables. The man was nowhere to be seen.

"Where did the old man go?" she asked.

Danni leaned toward her friend and whispered, "There was no old man."

The waitress giggled. "Mr. Pearson. He likes to challenge people regarding the Borden case."

"Is he related to Mrs. Pearson at the Borden House?" Sarah asked.

"Was related. Her father-in-law was a local attorney. He passed away several years ago."

"He's dead?" Danni gulped, her eyes bulging.

"Yes, but he loved his BBQ and still makes an appearance every now and then," she grinned. "No offense, but you look a bit stunned. You aren't going to fare well at the Borden place if you're rattled by Mr. Pearson's ghost."

"I'm with the research department," Danni said. "I leave the ghost stuff to the rest of the group."

"Good thing," she replied when the phone rang. "Have a good night, ladies," she said, answering the phone.

Danni hurried out the door with Sarah behind her.

"That was interesting," Sarah said, sliding into the car.

"What part? You talking to a ghost or all the folks staring at you like it was a common occurrence? I thought people in the South were pretty accepting of ghosts, but this place takes it to a whole new level," Danni replied, shaking her head as she turned the key.

They headed back to Borden House, Sarah's stomach rumbling at the tantalizing scent of BBQ wafting through the close quarters of the car. By the time they reached the house, she was salivating.

Stepping through the back door into the kitchen, Sarah grimaced as Valerie emerged from the basement.

"My goodness that's a lot of food," she sneered. "Can't believe you don't weigh three hundred pounds."

"The men have to eat," Sarah said, placing the bags on the center table.

Valerie's upper lip wrinkled. "Smells like meat. I never put that kind of poison in my body."

"Says the queen of implants and Botox," Danni retorted with a smug expression.

"You're not worth a response," Valerie said, sashaying toward the doorway to the sitting room.

"And yet, letting me know you wouldn't respond is a response," Danni goaded.

"You're impossible," Valerie scoffed, leaving the room.

"Good one," Sarah said, nudging her friend's shoulder.

As if lured by the delectable aroma of smoked BBQ, Harry, Ralph, and Garrett entered the kitchen one by one.

"Didn't realize I was this hungry," Ralph said, stuffing a French fry in his mouth.

Garrett kissed Sarah on the cheek. "Thanks for bringing supper."

"What am I, chopped liver?" Danni asked, shrugging her shoulders.

Garrett tousled the top of Danni's head. "Thanks for driving."

"That's better," she replied with a sheepish grin.

Everyone grabbed their dinners and convened around the dining room table. The room was quiet except for the soft whimpers of Dallas in between offerings of BBQ from Garrett.

"Are you set up for tonight?" Sarah asked, taking a bite of shredded smoked beef.

"Yup," Harry responded. "Everything's ready to roll."

Valerie walked into the room, crinkling her nose in disgust until her eyes met Garrett's. She plastered a smile on her face that turned Sarah's stomach. What a phony, she thought.

"Ready to catch some ghosts?" Valerie declared in an annoyingly high-pitched tone that could send neighborhood cats howling.

"Pretty much," Harry replied, wiping his mouth and standing.

Ralph finished his last fry, washed it down with a swig of beer, and stood. Garrett joined them.

"We'll clean up," Sarah said.

"Thanks," they all said in unison, following Valerie from the room.

"Is it wrong to want her to disappear?" Sarah asked.

"Nope. She has the same appeal as the plague," Danni responded as she gathered empty containers.

"I hope they're able to capture something significant," Sarah said with a shudder. Surprised at the sudden discomfort, Sarah glanced around the room but didn't see any sign of ghosts.

"Are you OK?" Danni asked.

"Caught a chill," she replied, her skin crawling.

Danni furrowed her brows. "Sure you're alright? You seem out of sorts."

"It's nothing. Probably just the aftermath of Tootsie's presence."

"She does leave behind a sour aura."

After clearing the table, they headed upstairs.

"Are the guys filming you again tonight?" Danni asked.

"Got another break, since Valerie has been harping on them to get some footage without me. Personally, I think she wants to weasel her way into the project with her legendary Ouija board skills and séance tactics."

"What a nutcase," Danni said, with a smirk. "It's obvious she can't stand for you to be involved."

"Doesn't matter. Whether I'm on tape or sharing snippets from my dreams, I'm rooted in this endeavor."

Danni snickered. "If only she knew how much you contribute to this little excursion, she'd flip."

"That's not a secret I'm willing to reveal to the likes of her. For now, it's just between you, me, and Garrett."

"Don't forget Dallas," Danni added.

Sarah cocked her head. "Do you think he knows?"

"The dog sees ghosts and hovers around you when spirits are close by. I'd say he's aware of your ghostly proclivities."

Sarah laughed. "Who would've thought a little dog could be so intuitive?"

"Wouldn't have believed it if you hadn't told me," Danni replied. "Then again, I didn't believe in ghosts before the revelation about your dreamist skills."

"Good to know I've enhanced your life."

Shaking her head, Danni grinned. "If being exposed to haunted houses, ghostly murder victims, and a hatchet wielding entity is enhancing my life, then I am truly enriched."

Sarah giggled. She was thankful to have such a supportive, albeit sarcastic friend.

"Since you've got the night off, let's work on the dreamist stuff."

"Sounds good," Sarah replied, following Danni up the steps.

Even though they didn't have to worry about Valerie interrupting them, her proximity to Garrett poked at Sarah's nerves. No doubt, she'd stick to him like gum on the bottom of a shoe.

As they slipped past the guest room on the second floor, Sarah noticed the glow of the camera. Although relieved to have a break from being filmed, she kinda missed being directly involved. Her feelings about being a dreamist were similar. She was happy to help the dead move on but didn't always enjoy the gruesome images that accompanied the experience.

Maybe someday she'd actually enjoy working through the clues to solve the mysteries preventing spirits from moving on.

Until that time, she'd have to keep studying and learn to tolerate some of the more frightening entities and their capers.

Right before they closed the door to Danni's room, Sarah heard Valerie's giggles from the guest room. Ugh. More than ever, she wanted to march in there and plant a kiss on Garrett's lips that would send the floozy running. Instead, Sarah thought about the incident in the kitchen when Ola's ghost tripped the little vixen, a smile spreading across her face at the memory.

"What are you so happy about?" Danni asked, pulling the *Dreamist* book from beneath her clothes in the bottom drawer of the dresser.

Sarah climbed onto the bed and leaned against the arched headboard while Danni sat cross-legged at the other end.

"Just thinking about Ola sending Valerie tumbling to the floor earlier."

"That was great," Danni replied. "Although…."

"What?"

"I'm still disturbed about her ability to cross over and interact physically. Makes me wonder about this mystery man in your dreams."

Sarah's heart sank, drawing her lips into a frown. The thought of his dark essence, his powerful presence, and his blade wielding hand anchored Sarah's enthusiasm in the depths of despair. How far could he reach from the other side? And how much longer would Sarah be able to ward off his attacks?

"Sarah?" Danni raised her voice, jolting Sarah from her ruminations.

"Huh?"

"Where'd you go? I said your name three times."

"Lost in my thoughts," she muttered, her back tensing.

"Care to share?"

Shaking her head, Sarah rolled her shoulders in an effort to loosen the tension knotting her muscles. "Let's concentrate on how to deal with the hostile doctor in my dreams. The sooner we do, the sooner I can get some slasher-free sleep."

"Eww…you make it sound like a Freddy Krueger encounter," Danni groaned.

"Freddy Krueger's got nothing on this guy. He's the epitome of terror. Imagine Freddy Krueger meets Jack the Ripper and you've got a start."

"Thanks a lot, now I'm not going to get any sleep tonight."

"What are friends for?" Sarah chortled.

After an hour of discussing the contents of chapter fifteen of the *Dreamist* book and other methods to keep her safe, Sarah's limbs were weighted by fatigue.

"I can't hold my eyes open any longer. I'm going to turn in for the night," Sarah announced, standing with a stretch. Another giggle echoed from the guest room sending a fiery rage pulsing through Sarah's veins.

Danni cocked her head. "You know she's just trying to annoy you."

"And it's working. I'm tempted to yank those blond extensions from her snooty little head."

"Wow, you are tired," Danni replied. "Ignore the bimbo and get some sleep. If you react, she wins."

Sarah trudged to the door and stopped. "Thanks for all your help this evening."

"Anything to help a friend and keep the ghosts at bay."

Pursing her lips, Sarah planted her hands on her hips. "Coward."

"Darn straight," Danni said, her brows arching. "I don't need any blade slashing, malevolent ghost chasing me around this house. Might run into guilty Lizzie with her ax."

"Hatchet, and she was acquitted."

"Doesn't mean innocent."

"You're impossible," Sarah said, shaking her head as she stepped from Danni's room into hers.

"But you love me anyway," Danni hollered as Sarah closed the door behind her.

A knock on the door to Sara's room startled her. She opened it to find Valerie standing there with a scowl.

"Could you please keep your voices down? We're trying to capture ghosts on film."

"Then you'd better stop all that giggling before you annoy the ghosts into finding a different house to haunt," Sarah retorted.

A wicked grin curled Valerie's unnaturally full lips. "Green eyes don't look good on you," she said, marching back to the guest room where Garrett was filming.

Closing the door, Sarah leaned against it, her head beginning to pound. If only she could send the creepy slasher ghost to frighten Valerie away. She walked over to the dresser and stared at her image in the mirror. Compared to Valerie, she was a bit plain. She always dressed in a t-shirt and shorts or leggings. Although her hair was pretty, it was generally in a ponytail or clip. The only make-up she wore was foundation. She leaned over the marble-topped dresser to take a closer look. Her skin was smooth but beginning to crease at the corners of her eyes and forehead.

Sarah's shoulders tensed when a mist began swirling in the reflection behind her. Gulping down the fear clogging her throat, she took in a deep breath. The last thing she needed to do was scream and bring Valerie into the room. She'd belittle her for being skittish, not to mention, it would be difficult to explain away anything she saw. With all the courage she could muster, Sarah turned to see the mist form into the silhouette of a young woman, specifically Lizzie.

Sarah took another deep breath and spoke. "What do you want to tell me?"

Lizzie's translucent visage wavered like a snowy television

screen. Her eyes held a fearful expression as she shook her head and muttered, "Beware, he's dangerous."

In the blink of an eye the apparition vanished.

Obviously, Lizzie was referring to the dark entity who kept trying to harm Sarah. She was well aware he was dangerous. Instead of stating the obvious, why couldn't Lizzie help Sarah figure out how to be rid of him?

Sarah's muscles were knotted as tight as a hangman's noose as she plunked onto her bed and buried her face in her hands. How had things gotten so out of control? She knew Garrett was committed to her but Valerie's flirtations with him and sarcastic barbs toward her were almost as stressful as the ominous figure haunting her dreams. Sarah lay back on the bed and closed her eyes when a scratching at the door caught her attention. Walking across the room, she cracked the door open allowing her favorite furry ghost alarm to scurry in. Dallas leapt onto the bed, his tongue hanging from his mottled muzzle as his tail wagged.

Sarah cupped the dog's face in her hands and kissed his snout.

"Thanks for coming to see me, buddy," she muttered as he covered her face in kisses. No doubt, the little dog had had enough of Valerie's presence and needed a place to escape. He really was intuitive to Sarah's angst, even when it concerned her heart.

"Looks like it's you, me, and the ghosts. You ready for bed?"

Yap!

Sarah changed and slipped beneath the covers as Dallas curled up on the pillow next to her. His presence always gave her a semblance of peace, something she desperately needed right now.

"Goodnight," she whispered, scratching his head.

Sarah closed her eyes and concentrated on steadying her breathing while imagining her interactions with the menacing ghost in her dreams. She was running out of time to discover the evil spirit's identity and figure out who committed the hatchet murders at the Borden residence on that fateful day in August of 1892. Now more than ever, she needed to keep her wits about her and focus on the messages from her dreamscapes.

* * *

DANKNESS ENVELOPED Sarah as she walked down a set of rickety steps to the cellar. Unease slithered across her sweaty skin and her eyes darted around searching for movement. Hesitating, Sarah waited for her sight to adjust to the extreme darkness when a scratching sound skittered through the air. The scraping increased in volume at the same time a moaning began to emanate from a stack of boxes across the room.

Moving closer, Sarah sucked in a breath when a mist began to vacillate and swirl enveloping her in a blackish fog. Pinpricks needled her skin as if she were being consumed by the misty form. The cloaked creature materialized in front of her sending panic rampaging through her body. Her heartrate ratcheted up as she employed her breathing techniques. Instead of relaxing, her nerves tightened. The wavering figure floated around her, the scent of decay burning her throat.

"You can't hurt me," she murmured.

"You're mistaken. My power grows with the help of a gifted individual," he breathed, circling her. She felt like a caged animal about to be devoured by a predator.

Sarah tried to step back but her legs refused to respond, binding her to the spot. The shadowy form was only inches from her, his arm raising as the scalpel glinted in the dimness of the cellar. Instinctively, Sarah raised her arm to block the incoming attack.

She yelped as the blade sliced her forearm, sending a trail of blood trickling to the dirt floor. Without thinking, she glanced at the crimson pool forming at her feet. The doctor pulled her into a choke hold, his decomposing breath fingering her cheek as he whispered, "I know what you are."

His cadaverous arm squeezed her trachea, increasing the terror holding her limbs captive.

"What do you want?" she whispered.

"Your life," he cackled.

"You can't kill me."

"I can do more than that," he crooned. "I can destroy you."

"I know you're a physician. You're supposed to heal people, not kill them."

"I am a doctor of death," he screeched, the noise piercing her eardrums like a screwdriver scraping against a chalkboard.

Sarah garnered all of her strength and managed to break free from his grasp. Stumbling up the stairs, she gripped the icy brass knob, and turned. A clammy hand grabbed her shoulder and spun her around. She was facing him, his eyes glowing in the darkened space. She tried to conjure Ola in her mind but nothing happened.

"I have the power to control you and there's nothing you can do to stop it," he snickered. "That old woman is no match for me."

Although Sarah couldn't make out the details of his features, his blazing stare seared into her brain. Sharp pains stabbed at her head as she struggled to sever the connection of his gaze. She was trapped in some sort of mental barricade.

Skeletal fingers wrapped around her neck as the doctor drew the scalpel across her throat. She tried to breathe but no air would enter her lungs, instead a gurgling sound emanated from the open wound.

No, she thought, fighting the drowsiness surging through her body. Somehow, she knew she needed to stay alert or this evil creature would succeed in his sinister plan. Panic drummed in her chest as her consciousness began to fade and all went dark.

Black-eyed Susans, daylilies, and lupine waved from flower beds bordering the streets of Fall River as Sarah strolled past neatly kept homes. A horse-drawn carriage clopped past, leaving a cloud of dust in its wake. Sunrays warmed her shoulders as she took in the serenity of the scene. Although bucolic, something didn't feel right about it, almost as if it had been contrived. Shrugging off her unease, she continued down the road and turned the corner where Borden House loomed before her. She stepped toward the front stoop when two hands grabbed her shoulders, pulling her backwards.

Sarah's eyes popped open as she sucked in a breath. She was lying on her back on the second-floor landing, staring up at Danni.

"What are you doing?" Sarah wheezed; her throat dry.

"I could ask you the same thing," Danni said, helping Sarah to her feet.

Sarah wavered for a moment, her head spinning. Danni wrapped her arm around her friend to steady her before leading her back to Lizzie's room.

"Sit down," Danni commanded, helping her to the side of the bed where Dallas waited.

"Why was I in the center hall?" Sarah asked, rubbing her upper arms.

"That's a great question. I heard Dallas growling and peeked in to make sure you were alright. You were walking through the bedroom door toward the stairs. I called your name but you didn't respond so I followed you. You looked like a drunken robot and started for the steps. That's when I grabbed you and pulled you back."

"I was sleepwalking?" she asked.

"Looked that way."

"I've never done that before."

Danni hurried to her room and returned with her flask. Handing the silver decanter to Sarah, she sat next to her on the bed. "Take a swig of this and then tell me what you were dreaming about."

Tipping the flask, Sarah closed her eyes letting the slow burn of the bourbon trickle down her throat. She blew out a long breath and handed the flask back to her friend.

"I was in the basement of this house when the doctor appeared," she shuddered. "He was worse this time. It was like he could read my thoughts and he blocked Ola again. He slit my throat and I started to lose consciousness. Next thing I knew, I was meandering the streets of Fall River in a peaceful state and found myself in front of Borden House. That's when you grabbed me."

"Do you think Ola removed you from the basement to keep you safe from the slasher?"

Sarah shrugged. "It's possible. I felt so serene and yet there was something unsettling about it. How could I feel relaxed and nervous at the same time?"

"Dreams can be strange that way," Danni said. "Now, give me all the details of what happened."

Sarah shared the horrifying experience with her attempt to flee, the doctor's mesmerizing stare, and his threats. "He's always coming at me with sharp objects,"

Danni hesitated before speaking.

"That answers one of our lingering questions about whether he can actually hurt a living being," Danni suggested.

"I don't understand."

"If you were injured in the dream but you're fine now, obviously he can only cause harm in the dreamscape," Danni said.

"Makes sense. Do you think the trauma of it led me to sleepwalk?"

"Perhaps," Danni replied, concern glimmering in her gaze.

Sarah rubbed her eyes. Even though he hadn't caused her

any physical harm, her shoulders and back ached from the fright.

"I know you don't want to distract Garrett, but this is getting serious. Breakfast is in a couple of hours. We need to update him. Until then, let's get some shut-eye."

Sarah massaged the back of her neck. "I'll pass on the sleep."

"Why don't you stay with me in my room," Danni sighed. "In case you sleep walk again."

Sarah knew Danni was concerned if she was inviting her to stay. Danni didn't like sharing her space, especially when the undead could be lurking nearby in her friend's dreams.

Sarah's sleep was fitful and much to her relief, uneventful. Granted, she never made it to a deep sleep due to her fear of encountering the murderous doctor again. A sliver of light peeked through the drawn curtains as Sarah slipped from bed and tiptoed to her room to change, careful not to wake her slumbering friend and the small dog curled at her feet.

After a hot shower, her muscles relaxed and she felt more alert. Trudging to the dining room, she found Garrett, Harry, and Ralph sitting at the table with steaming cups of java. Their eyes drooped and their shoulders hunched.

"You look like a pack of zombies," Sarah said, sidling over to Garrett. She leaned in to kiss his cheek and whispered, "Come see me before you take a nap."

Mischief brewed in his stare, as the right side of his mouth curled.

"Gladly," he replied.

Sarah shoved his shoulder and sat next to him.

"Good morning," Mrs. Pearson chimed as she entered the room, placing tea in front of Sarah.

"Thank you," she smiled, stirring sugar into the cup. "Mrs. Pearson, do you mind if I ask you a question?"

A broad smile crinkled her mocha-colored eyes. "Go ahead."

"What can you tell me about your father-in-law?" Sarah couldn't resist asking Mrs. Pearson about the ghost she'd seen at the BBQ place the night before.

The room fell silent as all eyes focused on Sarah.

"Hank was a great man," Mrs. Pearson replied, nostalgia warming her expression. "He came from a long line of attorneys. His father's cousin was one of the investigators on the Lizzie Borden case. Always held strong opinions about it."

Harry leaned his chin on his right hand while Garrett and Ralph stared at Mrs. Pearson.

"He thought she was guilty?" Sarah queried.

"Without a doubt. Always believed she played the jury and got away with murder, literally." Mrs. Pearson lifted the coffee pot from the buffet and refilled Harry and Ralph's mugs. "I noticed Bob's BBQ containers in the trash this morning. By any chance, did you happen upon my father-in-law while you were there?"

Sarah's jaw dropped as she plunked her cup on the table.

"Don't be shy about it," Mrs. Pearson continued. "Hank's been haunting that BBQ joint for decades. It was his favorite place. Plenty of folks have seen him. Ironically, he died of a heart attack in the parking lot after eating there."

Harry and Ralph shifted their gaze from Mrs. Pearson to Sarah. Garrett rubbed his forehead.

"You actually saw a ghost at the BBQ place last night? Why didn't you tell us?" Ralph asked, his eyes dancing to life.

Sarah's body stiffened. "I...um, wanted to get more information before discussing it," she lied, hoping to avert the conversation about seeing ghosts and leading to questions she wasn't prepared to answer. She really hadn't thought this through very well. Why hadn't she waited until she could speak with Mrs. Pearson alone?

"Most people don't recognize that he's a spirit," Mrs. Pearson said. "He was personable in life and seems to be just as charismatic in the afterlife. I'm surprised Connie didn't say anything."

"Who's Connie?"

"She's been a waitress there for almost thirty years. If you ordered take-out, chances are she rung you up."

"Bubbly personality with a Boston accent?" Sarah asked.

"That's her."

"She's the one who told me about him after my encounter," Sarah said.

"If that's all you needed to know, I'm going to finish preparing breakfast for you folks," she said, walking to the kitchen.

Once Mrs. Pearson was out of the room, Harry and Ralph leaned forward, their expressions like children standing in front of a case full of frosted donuts.

"Can't believe you actually saw a ghost!" Ralph declared. "You didn't know he was dead? Was he really that solid? Did you speak with him?"

"Well, I...," she stuttered, trying to figure out how to share without leading to further inquiries. "I did speak with him."

"What did he say?" Harry asked, eyes ablaze.

"Something about Lizzie being guilty and getting acquitted because she was a lady of good standing in the community."

"Amazing," Ralph said, shaking his head.

Before Harry or Ralph could ask any more about Hank the ghost, Sarah decided to shift the topic to the filming from the night before. "How'd it go last night?" she queried, sipping her tea.

"Active," Harry said.

"That's great," Sarah replied, sitting straighter in her chair. "Is it stuff the network would like?"

"Valerie seemed happy when she left a few hours ago," Ralph said with a sheepish grin. "The dark figure showed up."

Sarah swallowed hard, her enthusiasm for the team's success beginning to wane. "Same one from the other night?"

"We think so except he was more active this time. He actually came at one of the cameras," Harry said. "Nearly knocked me backwards it scared me so bad. And I don't scare easily."

Mrs. Pearson stepped into the room with a large tray, temporarily halting the conversation as she placed plates of eggs, bacon, and toast in front of each person.

"Enjoy," Mrs. Pearson said as she returned to the kitchen.

The men dug in to the food, momentarily blanketing the room in silence.

"Tell me more about this dark presence," Sarah said, pushing her eggs around the plate with her fork.

"Still not able to identify him. Walter's going to have a go at it this morning," Ralph said. "Hopefully, he can refine the image so we can see if it's Mr. Borden or not."

"Wow, that would be amazing if it was him," Sarah said, secretly hoping it was and not the violent doctor.

Ralph yawned resulting in a chain reaction between Garrett and Harry. They continued their breakfast, discussing ideas for better coverage when they filmed later that night.

Once their plates were emptied, Harry and Ralph left the room with a promise to talk more about their plans after they'd slept. Once they were alone, Garrett leaned his elbows on the table, his bloodshot eyes and slouched shoulders illuminating his exhaustion.

"What's up with the BBQ loving spirit?" he yawned.

"It was nothing," she shrugged. "My dreams were much scarier than seeing the ghost of an old man who believed Lizzie Borden was guilty."

Sitting up, Garrett furrowed his brows. "Tell me what happened."

She proceeded to share everything from the doctor's threats, his attempt to kill her, his ability to block Ola again, and finally her stroll through an idyllic Fall River.

"It was the strangest set of dreams I've had yet," she said, her chest tightening at the memory of it all.

Garrett grasped Sarah's hand. "This is getting more intense and I really want to investigate it further but I can barely hold my eyes open. Could we talk about it this afternoon?"

Sarah squeezed his hand. "Of course. Get some sleep. I need your mind to be sharp if we're going to solve this mystery."

"Promise me you'll stay with Danni."

"Why?"

"Just in case...." he paused. "I'll feel better knowing someone is with you until we figure this out."

Rising from the chair, he leaned in, his lips warm against hers, his mustache tickling her upper lip. "You look so comfortable. Wish I could bum out and spend the day relaxing."

Her heart palpitated from the kiss as he straightened and headed for the doorway.

Comfortable? Was that his way of saying she looked like a slob? Sarah glanced down at her leggings and oversized t-shirt. Frumpy, she thought. Valerie was always so put together and stylish, even if it was a street walker kind of look. Maybe she could dash out when Danni got up and find something a little snazzier. After all, she was here with the team and needed to make a good impression if any other network execs showed up.

Sarah sighed. Her insecurities were taking hold again. Garrett didn't care what she wore. She needed to dismiss these senseless worries and focus on the dark shadow looming in her nightly visions. Her appearance was meaningless if this entity was able to cross into a physical realm and carry out his threats.

Sarah lingered at the dining room table, sipping her tea as she contemplated her dreams and the implications for Garrett and the others. More importantly, she needed to find a way to block the menacing spirit from actually hurting her.

When her cup ran dry, she decided to go upstairs and do a bit of reading in the *Dreamist* book. The answers were there, she just needed to focus and pick apart the phrases until they made sense.

As she reached the second-floor landing, Danni emerged from the bathroom, her hair wrapped in a towel and her eyes sagging.

"Mornin,'" she grunted.

"Good morning," Sarah replied.

"You're too chipper for this time of day," Danni said, walking into her room.

"All I did was say good morning."

Danni gave her a sideways glare as she pulled the towel from her head and ran a comb through her damp locks. "Speaking to me before coffee is chipper."

Sarah smiled. Danni's morning grumpiness was a sense of routine and comfort for her.

"There's coffee downstairs and some leftovers from breakfast, although it's probably cold by now."

"I'll toss it in the microwave," Danni said.

"Where's Dallas?"

"Scooted from the room when I got up. He scratched at Garrett's door and he let him in," she said, swirling her wet hair into a plastic clip before heading for the door. When Sarah didn't move, Danni stopped.

"Aren't you coming?" she asked, puzzlement wrinkling her forehead.

"Already ate. I came to look through the *Dreamist* book."

"But you can't decipher it on your own."

"I can try again."

Shaking her head, Danni blew out a breath. "Come downstairs and sit with me while I eat. When I'm done, we'll tackle the book together."

"Alright," Sarah replied, following her friend down the steps.

In the kitchen, Danni fixed a plate of food and stuck it in the microwave, smiling at the sight of Mrs. Pearson brewing a fresh pot of coffee. She poured a cup and handed it to Danni.

"Thank you," Danni breathed, closing her eyes as she lifted the mug to her lips.

Sarah noticed her friend's demeanor begin to shift and her shoulders relax with each sip. When the microwave beeped, Danni grabbed her plate, went to the dining room, and plunked onto the chair. Sarah sat across from her.

"Anything else happen after last night's ethereal escapades?" Danni asked between bites.

"Thankfully, no," she replied. "But I need to figure this thing out before I get hurt or die of a heart attack. This man is terrifying."

"We'll get to the bottom of it, I promise."

The coffee was taking hold. Danni's alertness and confidence was almost restored. If they could work through the mystery, perhaps Sarah could relax a little. Once Danni finished eating, they went to Sarah's room.

"Have you discussed last night's dreams with Garrett?" Danni asked, sitting on the chair.

"I did."

"Including the part about the sleepwalking?"

Sarah shook her head as she sat on the edge of the bed. "Didn't get that far. He was exhausted and suggested we discuss everything when he woke up."

"This can't wait. We're dealing with things beyond our comprehension. What if this spirit is able to break through whatever divides the afterlife from the living? We can't assume he's incapable."

Sarah pondered what Danni was saying. The doctor had said

multiple times he could kill her. If he was capable, what was stopping him? Looking at her friend, Sarah's resolve melted. Danni's expression held a hint of fear unsettling the last of Sarah's fortitude. Danni wasn't a worrier.

"Fine," Sarah sighed, walking to the door dividing Garrett's room from hers. "I'll wake him up and talk to him about it."

"Make it worth his while," Danni chuckled, her carefree demeanor returning as she waggled her brows.

"You're not right," Sarah responded.

Danni went to her room leaving Sarah standing at Garrett's door. Leaning her forehead against it, she hesitated. He needed his sleep. At the same time, she was scared the sinister spirit from her dreams might find a way to break through whatever barrier kept him on the other side. Danni was right, she couldn't afford to take that risk. Garrett would understand.

She rapped softly on his door and waited. From the other side, she could hear him shift in the bed. Knocking once more, she waited until she heard his footsteps approaching. The door opened with Garrett standing there, the room behind him shadowed from the drawn curtains. His chestnut hair was disheveled and his gray t-shirt clung to the contours of his torso. He rubbed his eyes, and gave a weak smile.

"Hey," he croaked, his voice clogged with sleep. "Everything alright?"

"Not sure," she replied, a flutter tickling her stomach at the sight of him in his flannel pajama bottoms and close-fitting t-shirt.

Her concern seemed to catch his attention, bringing him to alertness.

"Come in," he said, stepping back to let her pass.

His room was cozy in the shuttered light. More than ever, she wanted to curl up in his arms and forget about evil spirits and hatchet murders. Sarah perched on the edge of his bed, gripping her hands in her lap. He sat beside her, draped his arm around her shoulders, and planted a kiss on the top of her head.

"What's wrong?" he asked.

Taking in a long breath, she tried to focus on what to say instead of the tingling sensation radiating through her body from his touch. Hopefully, he wouldn't be upset with her for not disclosing everything from the night before. As if sensing her apprehension, Dallas nuzzled his way onto her lap and sat down, his brown eyes gazing at her.

"The man in my dreams is getting more aggressive. He says he knows what I am and wants me dead."

"You already told me about this."

"There's more." Sarah talked about what happened at the end of the dream when Danni yanked her backwards before she stumbled down the stairs in a sleepwalking state.

"Why didn't you tell me earlier?"

Sarah shrugged. "You were so tired. I didn't want to worry you but Danni insisted I let you know about it now. Do you remember anything like this happening with Ola?"

Running his hand across his mouth, Garrett stared off. "I remember something about ghosts who were evil in life carrying that maliciousness into death. Otherwise, I'm at a loss."

Sarah slouched against him, the warmth of his body chasing the chill from her skin.

"I'm sorry I woke you. Danni and I weren't sure if I should be concerned or not."

"Don't ever apologize for coming to me with a problem. I'm always here for you, no matter what." He leaned in and kissed her deeply, driving all her fears to the deepest recesses of her mind. Dallas scurried from her lap as the world around her faded away. It was only the two of them until a knock at the back door of his room pulled them apart.

Breathless, Sarah smoothed her hair and patted Dallas who sat nearby. Garrett plodded across the room and cracked the door open, shielding Sarah's presence from the person on the other side. Although everyone knew they were a couple, they preferred keeping their personal time private.

Sarah's muscles stiffened at the sound of Valerie's voice.

"What are you doing here?" Garrett asked. "I thought you'd be at home asleep. It was a long night of filming."

"I was too wired so I came back. Besides, I didn't want to sleep alone and thought maybe you could use some company," she purred.

Sarah's teeth clenched as she rose from the bed, ready to slap the pretentious little tramp until Garrett spoke.

"No thanks, I've got Dallas," Garrett said.

"Oh, um, OK," Valerie stuttered.

Sarah's hands covered her mouth to stifle the laughter percolating in her chest.

"We'll see you this evening," Garrett said, closing the door before Valerie could say anything else.

Turning toward Sarah, he shook his head. "She's wearing me out," he yawned.

Sarah wrapped her arms around him, his scent of sandalwood and lavender filling her senses.

"I better let you get some sleep," she said, planting a kiss on his lips.

Pulling her closer, he returned the gesture, leaving her legs wobbly.

"When we get back to Edgefield, we need a night at Fitzgerald's," he muttered between kisses.

"You gotta date," she breathed.

Stepping back, Sarah smoothed a loose strand of hair from his forehead.

"Get some rest," she said with a grin.

"And remember, stay with Danni."

With a nod, she walked to the door as he climbed into bed and pulled the covers over his shoulders. Dallas curled up on the pillow next to him. She exited the darkened room and gently shut the door behind her. Although she hadn't garnered the information she needed, the time with him had done wonders for her nerves. She felt like melted butter on a biscuit.

Danni popped her head around the door of her room.

"Was he able to help?" she asked.

"Without a doubt," Sarah said dreamily.

"Got it," Danni replied with a knowing glance. "What about the ghost stuff?"

Sarah exhaled. "Unfortunately, he's not sure what to make of it all. Then Valerie showed up. She actually propositioned him!"

Danni's jaw dropped. "Are you kidding me?"

"Nope. She said she was too wired to sleep and came over to keep him company."

"That is one tenacious tramp."

Sarah's shoulders began to knot up again. "I know you guys don't think this spirit can actually hurt me but I still feel like he's capable of something. He's more powerful than anything written about in the *Dreamist* book."

Danni exhaled. "We need to identify this man so we can research his life. I think that's the best first step."

"We've tried and haven't found a clue. The only thing we do know is that he was the traveling doctor treating Lizzie for her brownouts," Sarah shrugged.

"Then we need to hone in on your ability to find the answers in your dreams. Maybe this guy is trying to scare you away by making you believe he can hurt you so you can't discover his secret."

"Makes sense," she replied, a tinge of relief trickling through her mind.

"Let's get to it," Danni said, going to her room to retrieve the book.

CHAPTER 22

The grandfather clock chimed from the hallway below, alerting Danni and Sarah to the noon hour.

Danni rolled her head back and forth while Sarah did some stretches to waken her senses. They'd been reading and rereading a couple of chapters in the *Dreamist* book, including the one about Sarah's specific skillset.

"My stomach is protesting its empty state," Danni said, standing.

"Let's get something to eat. I could use a break from this place," Sarah replied.

Danni got on her phone and started reading off some restaurants.

"Hey, they've got a pierogi place!"

"I love pierogies," Sarah replied.

Danni stashed the book, grabbed her keys, and they headed out. Driving a few blocks, they pulled up to a modest building about the size of a mobile home. A blue house jutted up from behind the structure along with a two-story building situated to the left, making the restaurant appear even smaller. Danni parked the car and they walked inside to the aroma of kielbasa and grilled onions wafting through the air. Sarah salivated. Even though she wasn't a fan of sausage, the scent was delectable.

Red and white checkered tables filled the space with a bar stretching across one wall. Polka music played in the background giving the restaurant an authentic feel. A lovely young lady with a broad smile and straight blond hair contained by a headband approached them.

"Hello, I'm Sandy. Two for lunch?"

"Yes," they replied in unison, following her to the table. Sandy placed menus in front of them.

"What would you ladies like to drink?"

"Pitcher of beer," Danni said before Sarah could answer.

Sarah scrunched her brow as the waitress went to the bar to fill the drink order.

"A pitcher of beer in the middle of the day?"

"Hey, you're being haunted by a fiendish slasher dude. You've earned it. Keep in mind, this trip is supposed to be a vacay for me. A pitcher of beer is what goes best with kielbasa and pierogies."

Sarah couldn't argue with her logic. Technically, Danni wasn't working on this trip, only assisting.

While they looked over the menu, the waitress returned with a pitcher and two frosted mugs.

After filling the mugs, she took out a pad and pen. "What'll you have today?" she asked.

Sarah ordered traditional pierogies with grilled onions and Danni chose the bacon wrapped kielbasa sub. They chatted about the variety of food in Fall River and some of the places they missed from home. A short time later, the waitress slid a plate of freshly prepared pierogies in front of Sarah, the smell of sautéed onions making her stomach rumble.

"Need anything else?" the waitress asked.

"More napkins, please," Danni mumbled after taking a bite of her sandwich.

Sandy returned with a stack of white paper napkins and refilled their mugs. "Is this your first time eating here?"

"Yup. We're here from South Carolina to help with the filming at Borden House," Danni said.

"Oh my gosh," she squealed. "You're working with Valerie!"

Sarah's skin crawled at the sound of Tootsie's name.

Danni's investigative attorney methods kicked in. She set the sandwich on the plate, wiped her mouth with a napkin, and grinned. "You're a friend of hers?"

"More than that, I'm part of the sisterhood."

"Sisterhood?" Danni asked.

"We're paranormal experts. We connect with spirits and speak to them."

"How?" Danni asked, leaning against the back of her chair.

"The traditional way, Ouija boards, séances, and table tappings."

"Table tappings?"

Sandy cocked her head like a confused puppy. "You know, when a group sits around a table with their hands resting on the top and the leader calls on the spirit until the table moves."

"Gotcha," Danni replied, giving Sarah a knowing glance. "And how long have you and Valerie been tapping tables?"

"It's more than just that," Sandy giggled. "I've only been part of the group for a few months. Valerie and I struck up a conversation one day when she was here. She invited me to a meeting and voila, turns out I had talent and was invited to join the group."

"Congratulations," Danni said, lifting her sandwich from the plate.

"Thanks so much. It's such an honor to work with Valerie. She has quite the reputation."

"She definitely does," Danni said with a sly grin.

"Of course, you guys already know that since you're getting to work with her on this project. You're sooo lucky." Sandy's smile was as big as the sandwich Danni was holding. "Oops, gotta get back to work," she announced, going to greet a couple who'd just entered.

Danni leaned forward once the waitress was out of earshot. "It's an honor to work with Valerie? The only truthful thing she shared was that Valerie has a *reputation*," Danni said, waggling her brows.

Sarah stared at her plate. "I've lost my appetite."

"Don't waste a perfectly good meal on the likes of that network bimbo. Besides, you need to eat to keep your strength up."

Sarah smiled. She loved Danni's ability to boost her spirits even when she was weighed down by her own insecurities.

"This sandwich is fabulous," Danni said, with a mouth full of kielbasa. "We need to come back here before we head out of town. I bet the guys would enjoy this place."

"Agreed," Sarah replied, savoring the delectable flavors of mashed potatoes, cheese, and grilled onions, thankful Danni had prodded her to keep eating.

Once the plates were cleared and the pitcher ran dry, they paid the bill and drove back to the house. It was quarter after one when they stepped through the kitchen door.

"What now?" Sarah asked.

"We work on your relaxation techniques. If this spirit is trying to scare you off, then you need to be prepared. The most important thing you've learned so far is that staying calm is key."

"Looks like an afternoon of deep breathing and muscle relaxation awaits."

They climbed the stairs to Sarah's chambers where she reclined on the bed, her head resting against a stack of pillows. She closed her eyes and began her deep breathing. Opening one eye, she looked at Danni who was standing at the foot of the bed.

"I can't do this with you watching me."

"Got it," she replied sheepishly. "Wasn't sure if I should stay in case you start sleepwalking again."

Sarah leaned up on her elbows. "I'll be fine. I'm only going to practice keeping my body and mind relaxed while introducing the image of the doctor. Hopefully, I can train my brain to stay calm when I encounter him in my dreams."

"I'll be in my room but I'm leaving the door open if you need me."

Sarah's chest warmed. Danni was incredibly supportive and she loved her for it.

"Thanks Danni," she said, lying back against the pillows.

Danni traipsed to her room as Sarah began her breathing exercises. When she introduced the image of the ominous doctor, her heartrate increased and her muscles tensed. Inhaling deeply, she held for a count of five, and released. She repeated the technique several more times until her body was free of tension.

Once again, she allowed the dark spirit's image to enter her mind. As soon as her muscles constricted, she reengaged her breathing until her body relaxed. She continued the exercise, imagining him cutting her with the blade followed by the deep breathing until her body no longer reacted to the scene. She felt as if she were floating on a cushion of pillows, peace wrapping her in a comforting embrace.

Sarah couldn't remember the last time she felt this tranquil. Pleased with her ability to calm herself, she decided to work on maintaining this state of repose. With a few more inhalations, her mind glided like a skater on ice to the different places she'd visited in Fall River, specifically the glorious brick mansion housing the historical society's museum. She could spend hours in that place exploring every nook and cranny.

The image of the sumptuously furnished house with the scent of orange oil permeating the air filled her mind as she walked down the long hall. Oddly, the house looked different. Instead of a gift shop, the front room was filled with a brocade parlor set, vibrant rugs, windows elegantly clad in silks, and oil portraits gracing the walls.

When Sarah looked down, she was wearing a deep blue bustle gown, her waist cinched with a corset. She was dreaming. Only, this wasn't one of her haunted visions, it was merely a step back to a more genteel era surrounded by the beautiful antiquities she'd spent a lifetime admiring. Most importantly, she was safe.

Sauntering across the kaleidoscope-colored rug, she relished the soft swishing of her gown as she approached the floor to ceiling pier mirror. In the 19th century, pier mirrors depicted opulence with their ornate framework and towering looking glass.

Staring at her reflection, Sarah noticed her dark brown tresses were drawn into a twist at the back of her head. Her brown eyes shone against porcelain skin and the silk dress complimented her hourglass figure. For the first time in her life, she felt beautiful. Not the kind of beauty flaunted by modern standards with full lips, bleached hair, and surgically enhanced bodies. This was a natural beauty without cosmetics or hair gel.

Sarah smoothed the bodice of the gown when she noticed movement in the mirror. A dark mist vacillated behind her. Her heartrate ticked up a notch, adrenaline pulsing through her veins and stiffening her limbs. She started her breathing technique as the form drew closer. Instead of calming, panic gripped her chest. How could he be here? Squeezing her eyes shut, she summoned Ola. Laughter erupted, rattling the pictures on the walls around her.

"She can't help you," he bellowed, his putrid breath crawling across the back of Sarah's neck. "You're a fool."

"You can't hurt me," she whimpered, the words shallow in the waves of her fear. She was shocked she'd been able to say anything at all.

"Can't I?" he whispered, his nails scraping her skin as he wrapped his bony fingers about her neck. "Your fear feeds my soul and gives me strength."

His grip tightened, strangling the scream caught in her throat. She closed her eyes and willed her pulse to slow and her muscles to release the terror holding her hostage. If she didn't calm herself, she'd not be able to glean the information she needed. "What do you want?"

"Your blood," he growled as the blade in his other hand came into view.

Sarah struggled to break free but his grasp on her neck only tightened. He held the blade against her left cheek, while his cadaver-like visage with its festering skin leaned against the right side of her face, leaving a sticky residue. Bile burned her throat and she felt her stomach recoil at the stench emanating from his rotting flesh. It was the first time she'd seen his image this clearly and now she wished she hadn't. Golden light glared from his eye sockets capturing her gaze and paralyzing her body.

This isn't happening, she told herself, it's only a dream. He can't hurt me.

"I can do more than hurt you," he mumbled. "I can destroy you."

Tears dripped across her cheeks as she fought to regain some sense of calm. Please Ola, I need you, she thought as the searing pain of the blade sliding across her throat racked her body. The room began to fold in on itself, leaving behind a bright blue sky and towering tree line.

Was she dead? Looking around, Sarah was relieved the monstrous man was nowhere in sight. She fell to the ground, heaving in the sweetly scented spring air. Flowers burst forth in velvety petals as bees buzzed their pollination song and butter-flies flitted amongst warm breezes. Standing, she noticed she was in the back yard of Borden House wearing leggings and a t-shirt. How had she gotten here? And why was it springtime?

Grass crunched beneath her feet as she walked to the back door of the kitchen and turned the knob. Locked. The parking lot was empty. How odd, she thought. Maybe the front door was open.

Walking around the side of the house, she took in her surroundings. No one was about. Even the road in front of the house was devoid of vehicles. Sarah jogged to the front door and found it was locked too. Where was everyone? And why had they locked her out? She jaunted down the front steps and noticed something moving across the street. Squinting in the sunlight, she could see a man waving her direction. Perhaps he knew what was going on and how to get inside. Sarah glanced to the right and the left before stepping onto the pavement.

Dallas barked, catching her attention. That's when she saw the car barreling down on her, panic immobilizing her limbs. An arm wrapped around her waist and hauled her to the ground. Her head smacked against the sidewalk sending stars sparkling across her vision. At the same time, a villainous laugh echoed through the air.

Sarah looked around. She was lying on the cement walkway bordering the lawn of Borden House with Garrett beneath her.

"Am I awake?" she asked, hoping this wasn't another dream-scape gone bad.

"Yes," he replied.

Sitting up, Sarah rubbed the knot forming on the back of her skull, a dull ache making its way across her forehead. Garrett untangled himself from under her and sat on the grass.

"What happened?" she moaned.

"You must have wandered out of the house toward the street. Dallas barked and when I turned around you were heading for the road. I called your name but you kept going. If I hadn't grabbed you...." Worry shadowed his expression, magnifying the dark circles under his eyes. "You were sleepwalking again."

He pulled her to him and held her close, the beat of his heart soothing the trembling in her arms and legs. Tears trickled down her cheeks. What was happening to her?

"Let's get you inside," he whispered in her ear.

Garrett stood and helped Sarah to her feet. Her legs wobbled like a newborn foal as she fought to get her bearings. Wrapping his arm around her waist, Garrett steadied her as they walked into the house to the front parlor where they settled on the settee. Dallas leapt up beside her resting his front paws and head on her lap.

"Where is everybody?" Sarah croaked.

"Ralph and Harry are still asleep."

"Why are you awake?"

"Dreamt about Grams. I woke up and couldn't get back to sleep so I decided to fix some coffee. When I came downstairs, Dallas started scratching at the front door so I figured he needed to go out. Not sure where you came from. I didn't see you until Dallas barked. I turned just as you were getting ready to step in front of that car."

"Glad you were there," she muttered, fingering the knot at the back of her head as fresh tears streamed down her cheeks. "You saw Ola in your dreams?"

Garrett nodded. "Now I understand why," he said, squeezing her hand.

"I tried to call her in my dream but she didn't appear. This monster is preventing her from helping me," Sarah sobbed, leaning her head against his chest.

Rubbing her back, Garrett gave her a minute to cry it out before speaking.

"Tell me everything that happened," he said.

Sarah sat up and wiped her cheeks with her shirt sleeves.

She talked about being at the museum house and donning a late 19th century dress. "I was looking in the mirror when the doctor's ghost materialized behind me. He held a blade to my neck and told me he'd destroy me. Then his eyes glowed bright and he cut my throat. I thought of Ola and then found myself here in the back yard. When I tried to get into the house all the doors were locked. That's when I saw a man across the street waving at me. The sun was in my eyes so I couldn't make out his features but thought maybe he knew how to get inside. Next thing I know, I was on the ground with you."

Garrett rubbed his beard. "And you still haven't discovered the ghost's identity?"

Sarah shook her head. "All I know is that he's the physician who was hired to help Lizzie. But I did see his face this time."

"What did he look like?"

"Disgusting. His flesh was rotting and he wreaked of decay. The only thing I can tell you is he's taller than me and has a powerful grip. Once he latches on, I can't break free."

"And you said Grams couldn't get through when you called her?"

"He said she wasn't strong enough to get past him," Sarah muttered. "Where's Danni?"

"Not sure."

Right on cue, Danni padded down the steps.

"There you are," she said, walking into the room. Stopping, she stared at Sarah's troubled expression and puffy eyes. "What's going on?"

"I was sleepwalking again," Sarah replied, sitting straighter.

"Oh my gosh!" Danni declared, taking a seat in the velvet parlor chair next to the settee. "I dozed off and when I woke you weren't in your room so I came looking for you. I was only out for a few minutes! I'm so sorry!"

"It's not your fault," Sarah said. "I'm beginning to think the slasher man from my dreams is driving me to it."

Danni looked around the room and then through the door at the staircase just beyond. "How did you get down the steps without falling?"

Sarah shrugged. "I have no idea. One minute I was practicing my relaxation techniques and next thing I know Garrett was pulling me to the side of the road in front of the house."

Garrett took in a deep breath. "We need to make sure you're never alone."

"I appreciate your concern but I will not have you two babysitting me," Sarah scolded.

"This is getting serious. If you won't let us help then you need to go home," Garrett said.

Sarah's back stiffened as she clenched her fists. Garrett was supposed to be her support system, not her father. She was a grown woman and had a say in what she did. The emotional turmoil of dealing with ghosts, a flirtatious bimbo hitting on her boyfriend, and an evil spirit trying to kill her was making her head spin.

"You can't send me away," she said. "I need to be rid of this entity. With his power, I can't risk having him follow me home. Besides, I'm an adult and can do as I please."

"Not in this case," he said, his voice low. "You're here as a guest of the team. I'm making an executive decision and telling you to leave."

Sarah's jaw dropped, her eyes blazing. "This is a group effort which means Ralph and Harry have to agree."

"Then we'll have to tell them about your dreamist abilities." His deadpan tone held her attention.

Sarah looked away, anger and hurt threatening to stream down her face in a waterfall of tears. She stood up and marched for the door. Stopping, she turned with her chin tilted up.

"I am not telling them my secret and I'm not leaving until I figure out what this spirit wants." Without waiting for a response, she hurried up the stairs, slammed the bedroom door behind her, and started pacing the room.

Hot tears blurred her vision. Why was he being so stubborn? And why had Danni stood by without intervening on her behalf? Swiping at her moistened cheeks, Sarah took in a deep breath. She'd spent a lifetime running from her haunted visions. She had the opportunity to face this apparition and be free of him except the person who was supposed to be helping was trying to send her away. Didn't he understand her need to bring this nightmare to a close?

Sarah contemplated her next steps. She'd never felt so bold before. The adrenaline rush was mesmerizing. Now she under-stood the high Danni got during her protests in high school or when she confronted people in the courtroom.

A knock interrupted her thoughts. Garrett cracked the door open and peered inside. "May I come in?"

"Do what you want, you're in *charge*," she snapped.

He stepped inside, closing the door behind him. His sympa-thetic gaze locked onto Sarah's heart and squeezed.

"I'm sorry if I upset you. I'm only trying to keep you safe."

"I understand your concern but I'm perfectly capable of taking care of myself."

"Are you?"

He stepped closer and gently turned her toward the mirror. He stood behind her as she gazed at her reflection. Shadows eclipsed her eyes and the deathly pallor of her skin was disturb-ing. She looked like a heavy smoker on a three-day bender. The bump on the back of her head was throbbing.

"Look at yourself," he said. "You need to leave this place. I don't know what's happening but I won't stand by and let this spirit destroy you."

Swallowing her pride, Sarah stepped closer to the mirror. She was a wreck. But she couldn't leave now, not without knowing why this ghost was trying to kill her and if he could follow her. So far, he'd shown up in different places around town which meant he might be able to haunt her anywhere she went. Would relocating sever the connection?

"I'm not sure leaving will keep me safe," she said, her voice cracking.

"I don't understand."

"Think about it. I dreamt about being at the museum and he was there. I saw him when Danni and I were cruising around town. He blocks Ola and I'm pretty sure the other ghosts fear him. Lizzie and Bridget always seem inhibited when he's around. Up until now, the ghosts in my dreams have only appeared in areas affiliated with their death. If he's been able to manipulate his way into my dreams regardless of the location, who's to say he couldn't find his way into my dreamscapes elsewhere? The only way to truly be rid of him is to see this haunting to the end."

Garrett blew out a long breath. "If you stay, I'm going to insist Danni or I be with you at all times. I won't be able to concentrate if I'm worried about you."

His eyes met hers, pleading for her to agree.

"Alright, I'll let you and Danni keep watch. But we have to keep trying to figure out this ghost's purpose." Sarah's gut churned. The idea of being watched like a helpless child was annoying. Despite the aggravation of having a body guard, she understood their concern and appreciated having people who cared deeply for her welfare.

A soft rap at the door interrupted the conversation. Danni stepped inside.

"Have you two made up?" she asked.

"It wasn't a fight, more of an intense discussion," Sarah replied.

"Call it what you will," Danni chortled. "Just wanted to know if it was safe to join you."

"We've come to an agreement," Garrett said.

Sarah crossed her arms over her chest and pursed her lips.

"And?" Danni queried.

"One of us will stay with Sarah at all times," Garrett responded. "This entity has shown itself to be pretty powerful. Until we understand how to stop it, we need to stay vigilant."

Sarah plunked on the bed. "This is exactly what I didn't want to happen. We're supposed to be looking for the truth behind the Borden murders, not babysitting me."

"Let the guys worry about the Borden case. Chances are Lizzie is guilty, otherwise she would have led you to the truth by now," Danni said. "You and I can concentrate on identifying Dr. Death."

Sarah shuddered. "That's what he called himself in one of my dreams, a doctor of death." Rubbing the back of her neck, Sarah scooted her legs beneath her. "And I still don't believe Lizzie killed her parents. Her demeanor in my dreams is gentle. It's the doctor who's bent on butchering people."

"Hold on," Danni declared, sitting next to Sarah on the bed. "What if the man in your dreams *is* Dr. Bowen?"

"I don't see how it could be," Sarah replied. "My dreams have revealed this other doctor was hired to help Lizzie with her seizures and brownouts because Dr. Bowen was unable to."

"You keep saying this spirit is powerful which means he may be distracting you from the truth. Think about it. What if Dr. Bowen is hiding his identity and making up a story about another doctor to throw you off."

"It's possible," Sarah muttered. "He did say he knows what I am."

"Exactly, which gives him reason to interfere if he's trying to hide the truth."

"Which is?" Sarah asked.

"Dr. Bowen was the family's physician. He treated Lizzie throughout her childhood, during the trial, and after. He was a staunch supporter of her innocence and testified on her behalf.

He would look incompetent if anyone discovered he defended a hatchet wielding murderess."

"Still doesn't make sense. It's more than a century later. Who cares if he was covering for Lizzie? It's not like he could be charged with perjury. He's dead," Sarah stated.

Garrett ran his tongue across his teeth. "Wait a minute, this is plausible. Dr. Bowen prescribed morphine to Lizzie while she was in prison. He claimed her confusion about the facts when testifying could have been a result of the drug. If the doctor was aware of Lizzie's violent proclivities and covered them up, he would want to protect his reputation even in the afterlife, especially if he was an arrogant man in his living years."

"He'd also want to prevent Lizzie from disclosing the truth," Danni added. "Thus, the reason why he's preventing her from communicating with you."

For the first time since they arrived, things were beginning to make sense. Sarah mulled over everything trying to connect her nocturnal visions to this new theory.

"While I agree that what you're proposing is possible, we still don't know how this ghost is able to keep the other spirits at bay and control me in the dreamscapes," Sarah said.

"Then we need to find a way to defeat him," Garrett suggested. "Before he succeeds in silencing you permanently."

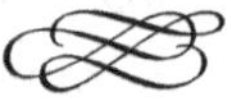

CHAPTER 23

"This could actually work in your favor," Danni said to Garrett.

"What?"

"You guys came here to film Lizzie Borden, something countless other groups have done. Many visitors have reported seeing the dark mist in some of the rooms without knowing who it was. We know," Danni said with a sly grin.

"Are you suggesting they focus on the doctor instead of Lizzie?" Sarah asked.

"Exactly. If they can prove the identity of the misty apparition in the house, it could garner as much attention as Lizzie."

"It's not a bad idea," Sarah replied.

"First thing we need to do is get Ola back in Sarah's dreams," Garrett said. "The fact we've had someone with you and you were still able to sleepwalk down the stairs and into the street tells me we need help from the other side."

"I'd love nothing better, but what if he hurts her? He's gone to great lengths to prevent her from reaching me," Sarah replied.

"Not sure you can hurt a ghost," Garrett added.

"I would have agreed with you before now, but I can tell Lizzie and Bridget fear him. If he's harmless then why are they afraid?"

"Maybe they're afraid of him because they knew him in life. Has he ever been mean to them in your dreams?"

Sarah thought for a moment. "Not that I can recall. The only time I've seen him angry was with Mr. Borden when he was dismissed for not helping Lizzie."

"Loss of income is a pretty good reason to be upset," Garrett said. "Andrew Borden was a well-known and influential man in this community. He could easily ruin a person's reputation."

"For some, reputation is everything," Danni added.

"You're suggesting the doctor's need to maintain his status in town drove him to abandon his oath to heal in order to seek revenge?

"Explains why he's so vindictive in your dreams and why the ghosts of Lizzie and Bridget might be fearful of him," Danni said. "Not to mention, it would be a good reason for Dr. Bowen to hide his identity from you. If he went to these lengths to protect his reputation when alive then he's probably just as determined in death."

Sarah shook her head. "This is a stretch."

"Have you seen Dr. Bowen in your dreams?" Danni asked.

"No."

"So, it's possible this traveling doctor is a false identity to prevent you, a dreamist, from discovering the truth about Lizzie Borden."

Garrett shifted, his eyes dancing as he leaned toward Sarah. "It's not that farfetched. What if he threatened Lizzie and Bridget while he was alive and therefore the ghosts are aware he's dangerous? Grams always said, evil in life, even more evil in the afterlife."

"Well, this guy is definitely malevolent so there's no question he was wicked when he was alive."

"Which leads me to finding a way to get Ola back in your dreams. She has so much experience and will be able to help you. If I didn't know better, I'd swear she's your spirit guide."

"That's exactly what it feels like," Sarah declared. "She's always there to lead me or calm me so I can think clearly." Sarah rolled the stiffness from her shoulders. "Which is why I don't want to take any chances. If this ghost has the power to cause harm, I'd never forgive myself if something happened to Ola."

"I knew Grams pretty well and there was very little she'd shy away from. Give her a chance, she's stronger than you think."

"I'll gladly do so as soon as we remove whatever is blocking her. Any idea where to start?"

"Unfortunately, no." Garrett exhaled.

"While I can't stand to have Valerie around, I'm glad she was able to get an extension for a few days," Sarah said, clutching his hand. "Gives us a bit more time to figure this out."

"It's rare to get this much time to capture ghosts. If we can link the doctor's identity to the misty form on tape, we'd have something substantial to take to the network."

"Sounds promising," Sarah said, part of her hoping for their success while another part hoped they could return to South Carolina and escape the violent entity and Valerie's flirtations.

Garrett leaned over, his lips brushing against Sarah's in a soft kiss.

"Regardless of what happens, I need some time alone with you. Can't wait to go dancing at Fitzgerald's like we talked about.

"Sounds wonderful," she replied, her heart still palpitating from his kiss.

"Excuse me," Danni protested. "I'm still here."

Garrett glanced at his watch. "I need to meet with Harry and

Ralph to plan camera placement for this evening." He walked to the door and turned. "Danni, you're on watch."

Sarah exhaled, her shoulders slumping. "I'm wide awake. I don't think I'm in any danger."

"Not taking any chances. Text if you need me," Garrett said, giving Sarah a knowing look as he walked out.

"What shall we do to entertain ourselves?" Danni asked.

"What can we do? We've read through that blasted *Dreamist* book a dozen times and still don't have any answers. Apparently, I'm confined to quarters with a babysitter in case I fall asleep. It seems our options are limited," Sarah huffed, flopping back on her bed.

"I realize this is frustrating but the situation is unusual. You know it's complicated when Garrett insists someone stay with you. He's had a lot of experience with this and I trust his judgement."

Danni's words weighted Sarah in guilt. Deep down she knew she was in danger with this particular spirit. There was a darkness about him she'd never experienced before. The idea he'd been a physician responsible for healing people made it even more disturbing.

"I can't just sit here," Sarah said. "I'll go mad if I don't try to figure this thing out."

"Then I suggest we find a way to solve this mystery."

"My mind is too frazzled to think about it anymore," Sarah sighed.

"Let's see what the guys are up to," Danni suggested.

Sarah shrugged a shoulder and followed her friend downstairs. As they reached the bottom of the steps, they heard Valerie's shrill voice.

Sarah tugged Danni's sleeve. "Never mind," she said. "I don't feel like dealing with Tootsie. I'm going for a walk."

"Not without me," Danni retorted. "And I don't walk."

"Well, I'm going with or without you," Sarah said, heading for the front door.

Danni blew out a long breath. "The things you'll do to get me to exercise," she replied. "I'll go this time, but you're gonna owe me."

CHAPTER 24

An hour later, after a brisk walk through the neighborhood, Danni and Sarah stepped into the warm embrace of the kitchen. The house was eerily quiet. Sarah glanced around at the monitors, cords, transistor radios, and empty coffee mugs. The guys must be working somewhere in the house since the truck was parked out back. Much to her relief, Valerie's car was gone.

Danni and Sarah walked into the sitting room as rain began pelting the window panes in a rhythmic tapping. A chill ran down Sarah's spine as if someone had dropped an ice cube down the back of her shirt. Something was off.

"You OK?" Danni asked as they made their way to the staircase.

"Yeah, I'm fine. Rain always adds a layer of spookiness to a place, especially this one."

With each step, the air grew colder, shrouding Sarah in unease as she made her way to the second floor. When she reached the top, she felt lightheaded. Pausing, she blinked a few times until her equilibrium was restored.

"You can't escape me," an ominous voice whispered at the same time Dallas's barking echoed from Garrett's room.

"Sarah?"

She could hear her friend's voice but her vision was beginning to blur. She felt Danni's hands grab her at the same time her knees buckled.

"Sarah, get up," Danni pleaded.

The doctor's distorted image flashed in her mind, his flaking lips letting out a howl of laughter. "You cannot escape me! I will finish you before you learn the truth!"

Sharp pains ricocheted through her head as if someone were doing target practice inside her skull. Danni's voice faded as Sarah gripped her head and rocked in an effort to dull the agony.

"Make it stop," she groaned.

In the distance, she heard a door open and footsteps. Had the ghost pulled her into a dream? The pain intensified like an ax splitting her skull. Consciousness began to waver as the pain intensified.

"Sarah!" Garrett shouted. He placed his hands on either side of her head, tilting her face towards his.

Blinking, Sarah opened her eyes, the torment subsiding at his touch. Garrett kneeled before her, his hair disheveled and his chest heaving as if he'd been running a marathon.

"Are you OK?" he asked in a scratchy voice, a sleepy expression blanketing his face.

"I don't know," Sarah gasped. "I could hear Danni calling but it sounded like it was coming from a faraway place. I couldn't respond. The worst part was the pain," she breathed. "When he laughs it feels as if my skull is shattering. As soon as you touched my head the pain stopped."

"Garrett must have the magic touch, because nothing happened when I tried to help." Panic flushed Danni's cheeks, something Sarah had never witnessed in her friend.

"What did you see?" he queried.

"The doctor was here. He said he'd kill me before I discovered the truth," Sarah whimpered. "Were you asleep?"

The desperation in her voice seemed to shove Garrett into wakefulness.

"Just taking a power nap."

He helped Sarah up from the floor of the upstairs landing and led her through Lizzie's room to his with Danni trailing behind. The curtains were drawn adding an extra layer of darkness to the space making it feel like the inside of a crypt. Dallas jumped onto the bed, his ears pricked and his nose sniffing the air. Garrett wrapped his arms around Sarah and held her close. Danni sat in the chair by the dresser.

"Tell me everything that happened," he breathed into her hair.

The warmth of his body against her cheek and the faint scent of lavender chased the chill from her core. Sarah shared the relaxing walk around the neighborhood and the horrid encounter with the doctor when they returned.

"Let's go through the book again," Garrett said.

Sarah grabbed his arm. "We've been through that stupid book a dozen times since we got here. We're not missing anything," she growled, tears cresting in her eyelids. "We need to figure this out before I lose my mind."

"Which leads us back to our current conundrum. How do we get this ghost away from you while keeping you safe?" Garrett said.

"How many times has the doctor caused these headaches?" Danni asked.

"Twice now," Sarah replied.

"And what stopped the pain?" Danni quirked an eyebrow as she asked the question letting Sarah know she had a theory.

Hesitating, Sarah thought about it. "Garrett."

"What do you mean?" he asked.

"On both occasions, the pain stopped when you put your hands on my head."

"That's interesting," he mumbled. "Looks like I need to stay with you at all times."

"Until we figure this out, I think that's a good idea since you seem to have the ability to break through this spirit's hold," Danni said.

Silence blanketed the room as each of them ruminated on how to handle the situation.

"Except you need to be filming," Sarah said.

"Then, you'll have to stay with me while I film. Dallas can alert us if anything mysterious arrives."

Sarah shifted. "What about Valerie? Didn't she discourage you from filming with me in the room?"

"Don't care at this point. This is about you, not a network gig."

"Harry and Ralph might have a different perspective on that," Sarah said.

Garrett leaned forward. "They care about you. They'd never sacrifice someone's safety for a film clip."

"But will they understand the seriousness of the situation?" Sarah queried, slouching. "Maybe I need to tell them about my abilities."

"Only if you're comfortable with it," he replied, rubbing her shoulder.

Sarah massaged her temples. "I don't know what to do. I want to be rid of this spirit but I don't know if I'm ready to disclose my secret yet."

"Take some time to consider it," Danni said.

Garrett yawned.

"Why don't you go back to sleep?" Sarah suggested.

"I need to make sure you're safe," he responded.

"I can lay down with you," she said.

"I'll do some more digging online and see if I can find anything about this traveling doctor. If he did exist, there has to be a record of him somewhere," Danni offered.

Once Danni was gone, Garrett and Sarah curled up together with Dallas at their feet. Closing her eyes, Sarah inhaled deeply and released. Her limbs loosened as her body melted into Garrett's and the room faded away.

SARAH GLANCED AROUND, her back and shoulders as tight as guitar strings. Lizzie skittered through the door of her room and turned the lock. Her breathing was labored as if she'd run up the stairs and her cheeks were flushed. What had her in such a state?

Lizzie pressed her right ear against the door for a few seconds before hurrying to her bed. She perched on the edge, wringing her hands like a dish cloth. Footsteps echoed from the staircase bringing Lizzie to her feet. Fear washed over her porcelain features as she looked around the room. She rushed to the bureau where a silver dresser set was sprawled across the marble top. Grabbing the nail file, Lizzie watched the doorknob rotate slowly one way and then the other. Her petite hand shook as she stood ramrod straight watching the door.

"You can't escape me," bellowed from the other side of the door making Sarah's muscles constrict. He was here, the man who wanted to destroy her. Sarah watched as Lizzie started backing towards her. With a few deep breaths, Sarah managed to find her voice.

"Lizzie, who are you afraid of?"

Lizzie spun around and looked at Sarah, shaking her head as she pressed her forefinger to her rose petal lips.

"You have to tell me," Sarah pleaded.

"Let me in!" he yelled, making Sarah jump.

Lizzie's body shook as she looked back at the door.

Determination coursed through Sarah's body. Surprised at her gumption, she grabbed the nail file from Lizzie's hand and started for the door. She was tired of being frightened and cowering in the shadows wasn't going to help her identify this specter and get her life back. Besides, Garrett was nearby and he and Dallas wouldn't let anything happen to her, or so she hoped.

She felt like one of the heroines in those slasher movies when they've had enough of the terrorism and take matters into their own hands. Blood pulsed through her veins so hard it buzzed in her ears. Reaching for the bolt on the door, she slid the lever and grasped the knob. Before she could open it, a blackish mist seeped through the cracks between the door and its frame, filling the area. Instinctively, Sarah took a step back. When she glanced over her shoulder, Lizzie was gone.

The mist swirled like a cyclone, growing bigger and darker with each twist until the cloaked doctor stood in front of her.

His eyes glowed gold as his stare fixed onto hers.

"You've underestimated me and now you will see what I am capable of accomplishing," he cackled, his bony fingers reaching her direction.

There was no time to think, if she didn't act now, he'd kill her. Sarah lunged at the spirit, stabbing at his chest with the file. A hand wrapped around her wrist, shattering the moment and tossing her from dreamscape to reality.

Garrett's back was against the wall, his eyes wide as his chest heaved for breath. He held her right hand in a vicelike grip, the nail file shimmering in the light seeping between the drawn curtains.

Sarah dropped the nail file to the carpeted floor.

"Are you alright?" she whispered. "What happened?"

"Is it you, Sarah?" he asked. "Or are you the monster trying to trick me into letting down my guard.

"Of course, it's me. Why would you ask such a thing?"

With his eyes locked on her, he knelt down and retrieved the file. "You really don't remember what happened?" he asked, standing.

Sarah shook her head.

"I got up to use the bathroom. You were sound asleep, didn't even stir. When I came back in the room you were standing right here. Your expression was fixed like you were sleepwalking again. When I reached out to guide you back to the bed, you raised your hand and stabbed at me with this file. I caught your arm and for a brief moment your face altered into a man's. His skin was gray and tattered."

Sarah's legs began to wobble and her stomach churned. What was happening to her? The doctor said he would destroy her. Is this what he meant? Turning her into a sleepwalking killer? She sat on the bed, her hand resting on her chest. Instantly, Garrett was by her side, his arm around her shoulders while Dallas licked her hand.

"I don't understand any of this," she whispered, meeting his gaze.

"Me either. This apparition is powerful and able to manipulate the living."

"Why do you think he's doing this?"

"Not sure. This is going to require more guidance than what the *Dreamist* book can offer," he sighed. "Don't suppose Grams showed up."

"Sadly, no. But Lizzie was there."

"Did she say anything?"

"Nothing. She did seem afraid of this ghost. She'd locked herself in her room and when he tried to get in, she grabbed the nail file and acted as if she'd use it to defend herself."

"How did you get it?" he asked.

"The doctor's dark mist seeped through the seams of the

doorjamb. I grabbed the file from Lizzie and decided to confront him. Don't know where the bravado came from, but I was determined to be rid of him."

"Except you tried to stab me instead."

Tears hovered behind her eyes at the thought she'd tried to hurt Garrett.

"Where did I get the file?"

"I assume from the dresser set on the bureau."

"I'm sorry. It wasn't you I was stabbing at; it was the ghost.

Sarah rested her head against Garrett's chest as he squeezed her shoulders.

"I'm not upset, only startled. I've seen some pretty frightening things in my time but nothing like that."

"Did you get a good look at him?" Sarah asked.

"Only a quick flash. He was definitely in a state of decay."

"Maybe Danni had some luck finding information about the doctor."

"If not, we can always ask Walter to give it a try."

Sarah raised her brows. "Might not be a great idea to involve him right now. Danni and Walter are doing battle over that wager to see who can identify the mystery ghost in the videos," Sarah grinned.

"That's much better," Garrett said.

"What?"

"Seeing you smile." He leaned in to kiss her when a knock on the door split them apart.

Garrett opened the door and Danni scooted in.

"I got something," Danni declared.

Sarah's heart leapt. Finally, some good news. Danni sat on the other side of Sarah and pulled out her phone.

"I found an old newspaper clipping mentioning a physician passing through Fall River with promises of remedies to cure everything from baldness to lady problems."

"Did it give a name?"

"Dr. Howard Webster was all. No address or background information. It did mention he specialized in hypnosis and disappeared right after the murders."

"This has to be the same man." Sarah exclaimed.

"If it is the right guy, I'll win the bet with Walter, if we can find a way to prove it."

Sarah chewed her lower lip. "If the doctor was angry about being fired and left town, why is he coming after me?"

Danni sat up straighter. "What if the doctor didn't leave town? What if he was murdered too?"

"By whom?"

"Lizzie," Danni replied.

"I know Lizzie didn't do this, she's not violent," Sarah stated.

"She was in your dream," Garrett responded. "You said she was going to stab the doctor if he got into her room."

"Wanna fill me in?" Danni asked.

Sarah shared the dreamscape and her attempt to stab Garrett.

"Oh my gosh! This guy is a maniac!"

"Which could explain why he's haunting you," Garrett suggested. "Maybe he needs help resolving the circumstances surrounding his death."

"Are you two actually suggesting that a petite Lizzie Borden hatcheted her parents to death and then killed the doctor with a nail file and disposed of his body?"

"Maybe she had help," Danni said. "It would explain why the murder weapon was never found. The doctor may have been her accomplice in killing her parents. He hid the murder weapon while she cleaned up. Then she killed him to cover it up."

"That is seriously farfetched," Sarah replied. "And if the doctor wants my help, why not ask for it instead of trying to harm me or make me hurt someone else?"

Garrett smoothed his beard. "If this Dr. Webster was angry

enough to kill two people over being let go while enlisting their daughter's help, then he was probably a self-absorbed, arrogant man. He might not be the type to ask for assistance, instead forcing those around him to do his bidding."

"But Lizzie seemed genuinely terrified of him. She bolted the door so he couldn't enter her room. I don't think she's the driving force here."

"Unless, she's trying to protect her reputation," Danni offered. "She obviously knows you're a dreamist and can expose the truth."

"This is the weirdest haunted house I've ever encountered," Garrett said.

"I'm beginning to think this place is cursed, not haunted."

"I'm inclined to agree," Sarah said. "Now what do we do?"

"Don't know about you two but I'm hungry," Danni said.

"Unbelievable," Sarah laughed. "Your appetite never takes a break."

"Actually, I could use something to eat too," Garrett said. "That adrenaline rush took a lot out of me."

"Let's get pizza," Danni suggested. "It's an easy way to feed the team."

Sarah got up and started to follow her friend from the room. Danni's expression sagged.

"What's the matter?" Sarah asked.

"Not sure I want to be around you. What if you try to kill me too?"

"You'll be fine," Sarah said with an eye roll. "Hopefully, it won't happen again."

"*Hopefully?* Don't think so. We might need to handcuff you to a chair or something. I'm not taking any chances with a ghost who can manipulate the living and may have helped Lizzie ax her parents to death."

"Hatchet, and she was acquitted," Sarah retorted.

"Sarah," Garrett said gently. "I think you need to stay here with me."

Danni nodded. "I'm siding with him on this one. I can handle grabbing a couple of pizzas on my own."

279

CHAPTER 25

Garrett and Sarah found Harry and Ralph downstairs in the kitchen working on one of the cameras.

"Hey you two," Harry greeted. "We were reconfiguring the camera for the EVP, the new amplification device Walter overnighted."

"EVP?" Sarah queried.

"Electronic Voice Phenomenon. It's the ability to record spirit voices amongst static or background noise. This one is state of the art."

"And it records conversations?" Sarah asked.

"Not quite. We usually only get a word or a phrase but it can be very telling," Harry said. "Since the ghost seems attracted to you, would you be willing to wear a mic so we could tape anything it might say? I assure you it's perfectly safe to use."

Before Sarah could respond, Garrett spoke. "I appreciate your enthusiasm but my girlfriend is not some sort of experimental specter device."

Sarah's heart thumped harder when he said 'my girlfriend.' Having people appreciate her ghost magnetism was an extra bonus. Instead of viewing her as some sort of freak, they were excited about her gifts, even if they didn't know the full measure of them.

"I don't mind helping out," she said. "And you're sure Valerie will be OK with me being filmed this evening?"

"Don't see why not," Ralph replied. "The best footage we've captured has been with you in the room. She wants us to be successful."

"Since you're using Sarah for this, I'd like to man the camera where she's going to be."

"No problem, Dunc," Harry replied. Looking at Sarah, he spoke. "Let me show you how this works."

Harry explained how the mechanism functioned. Garrett shot her an affectionate glance, obviously thankful for her willingness to help the team out, especially given the circumstances of her recent encounters with the doctor's menacing spirit.

The back door opened, and Valerie stepped inside. "How's my favorite ghost hunting group this evening," she crooned, giving Sarah a sharp look.

"Getting ready for this evening's shoot," Ralph answered, his eyes twinkling. "So glad you've decided to join us."

Sarah rolled her eyes at Ralph's infatuation for the network bimbo.

Ignoring Ralph, Valerie looked at Garrett. "Can I speak with you in private?" she asked, giving him a wink.

"Sure," Garrett responded, following her to the dining room.

"I'm going upstairs to grab the adapter," Harry said, hurrying from the room.

Ralph started for the basement stairs.

"Where are you going?" Sarah asked.

"Need to find the modem and add this booster," he replied. "Sometimes, the EVP drains the Wi-Fi connection."

Sarah's heart froze. She wasn't supposed to be on her own. And while she didn't feel she needed to be guarded, she also knew Danni and Garrett would chew her out if she didn't abide by their agreement. *Ugh.* She hated having to deal with this but knew it would be easier to go along with their wishes than to cross them. Especially, if something did happen while she was alone. "OK, if I come with you?"

"If you want."

The air grew more frigid as they descended the steps to the basement. Sarah scanned the space with its stone walls and dank odor. A single bulb illuminated the room, casting shadows in the corners giving an eerie feel to the place.

"Do you know where the modem is?" she asked.

"Mrs. Pearson said it was on top of a stack of boxes in the far corner."

Sarah followed Ralph while keeping watch for any unexpected guests.

"Don't see it," Ralph said, looking around. "Maybe it fell behind the boxes."

Sarah helped Ralph move the cardboard containers in search of the missing modem.

"Here it is," he called over his shoulder. "Hey, what's this?"

Sarah leaned over to see his discovery when a sharp pain shot through her head, blinding her. Suppressing a scream, she doubled over, clutching her head in her hands as the doctor's laughter echoed through her mind.

"What on earth?" Sarah heard Ralph declare but she couldn't respond for the pain clawing at her skull. "Sarah!" Ralph exclaimed, resting his hand on her back. "What's wrong?"

Squinting, Sarah whispered. "Get Garrett."

"Garrett!" Ralph yelled. "We need you down here!"

You cannot escape me, a voice breathed in her ear, ratcheting up the pain.

The sound of footsteps pounding down the stairs kept beat with the pounding in her skull. As soon as Garrett's hands touched her head, the pain subsided.

"Are you alright?" he whispered.

"I think so," she groaned, straightening.

"What the heck is that?" Garrett growled.

Sarah looked at Ralph who held a Ouija board.

"Found it behind the stack of boxes where the modem was located."

Garrett's eyes blazed and his complexion reddened. He grabbed the board and broke it across his knee. Tossing the board to the floor, he grasped Sarah's arm. "We need to get you upstairs."

They started for the staircase when Valerie appeared, a sneer wrinkling her upper lip as she watched Garrett helping Sarah, until she saw the Ouija board on the floor. A scream pierced the air as Valerie dashed across the room and cradled the broken board in her arms.

"Who did this?" she growled, spittle flying from her puffy lips.

Garrett let go of Sarah and walked over to her.

"I did," he replied. "What is that thing doing down here?" His voice was firm and his stare fixed.

Valerie lifted her chin. "I was helping you guys out. You should be thanking me instead of destroying my property. Your footage improved after I summoned the spirits with this."

Sarah watched as his shoulders tensed and he took a step closer. Through gritted teeth, he spoke. "And I told you we wanted nothing to do with this thing."

"Didn't give you the right to break it!" she squalled.

Sarah exhaled. "We'll go to the store tomorrow and buy you a new one."

Valerie stormed toward Sarah, tears welling in her spidery lashes as she gripped the broken pieces to her chest. "You can't get this in any store. This was a special board made specifically for me by Madame Clarice."

"I don't care if it was blessed by the Pope," Garrett retorted. "You had no right to bring it here."

Valerie's demeanor shifted, a cold glare in her eyes. "Perhaps if Sarah hadn't been so secretive about that *Dreamist* book, I wouldn't have had to revert to such tactics."

"How is this my fault?" Sarah asked, her brows furrowing.

Looking at Garrett, Valerie played the victim card. "I asked Sarah about a book I found in her room that I have no doubt is of great significance. A spiritualist of my caliber knows these things. She refused to tell me about it."

"What does that have to do with the Ouija board?" Garrett asked.

"I brought it down here and asked it to reveal the meaning of a dreamist."

"When did you do that?" Garrett said.

"Couple of days ago."

Sarah gasped. That was when the doctor started attacking her. No wonder he was so powerful. Valerie had inadvertently given him access to her dreams. Now she understood the significance behind the phrases in the book and Ola's warning to Garrett about using artificial means to communicate with the spirit world.

Tension radiated in the air as they all looked at each other.

"What is a dreamist?" Ralph asked, cutting through the silence.

Garrett looked at Sarah, his expression sorrowful.

"Yes, please share," Valerie chided. "We're all supposed to be working as a team, not keeping secrets."

"Pizza's here!" Danni called from the kitchen at the top of the stairs.

"Well?" Valerie said, her jaw clenched.

"Time for dinner," Sarah replied, thankful for the interruption. "Care to join us?"

"Of course not!"

Without another word, Ralph climbed the stairs and joined

the others. Sarah followed, stopping at the top step to listen to what the bimbo said to Garrett.

Valerie's tone softened to that of a disappointed child.

"I'm so sorry I lost my temper like that," she crooned. "I know you're upset with me but I'm more than willing to make it up to you."

Sarah's pulse raced. The nerve of that tramp.

"I'm not interested in anything from you, Valerie."

"You and I make a great team. Don't be foolish and throw it all away."

"I'm already part of a team and in a committed relationship with Sarah."

Pride washed away the tension in Sarah's shoulders at his declaration. If only she could see the look on Tootsie's face but she dared not let them know she was eavesdropping.

"Ha! With that mousey little thing?" Valerie mocked. "I can do so much more for you," she purred, "including making you a star."

"I'll take my chances with Harry and Ralph. We have a few more days and I feel confident we'll get something worthwhile on tape."

"Oh my," Valerie responded. "In all of the commotion I forgot to tell you the bad news. The network can't extend your stay after all. They need the tapes by tomorrow at noon."

Sarah heard Garrett sigh. "Fine, we'll send you what we've got."

"It's not too late to change your mind," she said. "I promise, you won't regret it."

"I'll pass."

"Fool!" she yelled. The clicking of Valerie's heels across the basement floor sent Sarah scurrying to the dining room, sliding into her seat at the table where everyone else was eating. The kitchen door slammed, shaking the house.

Garrett walked into the room without Valerie.

"You don't look so good," Harry said.

"Got some bad news," he said, plunking onto the chair next to Sarah. "The network has moved the deadline back up to tomorrow. We have to submit by noon."

Harry dropped his pizza onto the plate. "What the heck happened?"

"Valerie had a Ouija board hidden in the basement. Ralph found it and I smashed it. She got angry and changed the deadline. Sorry guys."

Ralph looked at Garrett and then at Sarah. "What about the dreamist thing?" he asked.

"Who's the dreamist?" Harry queried, leaning forward.

Swallowing hard, Sarah glanced at Garrett and Danni, panic gripping her chest as she pondered how to respond.

Harry looked from Sarah to Garrett, his brows arched. "Well?"

"Are you familiar with the term?" Garrett asked.

Harry leaned back, folding his arms. "I might be."

Garrett blew out a breath, his head dropping to his chest. "Tara told you."

"Obviously, she shared it with you too."

"Why didn't you say something?" Garrett asked, looking at his friend.

"She swore me to secrecy. It's not something that's supposed to be common knowledge."

"Exactly," Garrett replied, his forehead wrinkling. "So, why did she tell you?"

"Because I have a lot of experience with ghosts. She thought I might be able to help her out," Harry replied, tipping his chin up. "Why'd she tell you?"

Garrett ran his hand through his hair as Sarah's stomach churned at the exchange. Would she be able to keep her secret from Harry or would he figure out that she was a dreamist too?

"We were good friends," Garrett replied.

"Not buying it." Harry looked back at Sarah. "You're a dreamist, aren't you?"

Her heart seized. This was it. Should she admit her dreamist abilities or deny it? All eyes stared at her. If she denied it, would they believe her? There was only one way out of this. Sarah chewed her lower lip before answering. "I am."

"Wow," Harry declared, throwing his hands in the air. "I'd never heard of this dreamist thing before Tara and now I meet a second one. Although I can't say I'm surprised. Every time we filmed, the ghosts were always more active with you in the room."

"Does someone want to fill me in?" Ralph exclaimed.

Sarah blew out a long breath. Now that her secret was exposed, she didn't have to worry about them inadvertently discovering her abilities.

Resting her elbows on the table, she proceeded to explain the intricacies of being a dreamist. "Please understand, I never meant for so many people to know about this. Promise you won't tell anyone."

"Of course not," Harry said. "I knew about Tara long before she was murdered. And I never told anyone even after she was dead."

"Who am I gonna tell?" Ralph shrugged.

Sarah glanced at Danni who smiled, letting her know she was behind her on the decision to share her secret.

"Now what?" Ralph asked.

Sarah looked at Garrett who gave her a nod. "Things have been pretty intense over the past few nights in my dreams." She told them about the doctor's menacing spirit and his attempts to kill her along with him blocking her ability to communicate with Lizzie. "The timeline of when Valerie brought the Ouija board into the house seems to correlate with an increase in activity from the spirit who we now believe is Dr. Webster based on Danni's research."

"So, you're suggesting the Ouija board gave the ghost in your dreams power over you?"

Sarah shrugged. "Looks that way."

"The book mentioned something about avoiding artificial means to conjure spirits as well," Garrett added.

"Tell me more about this book," Ralph said.

"It's a guidebook for dreamists," Sarah responded. "There are chapters with general instructions and others with directions for skills specific to each family line of dreamists."

"Fascinating," Ralph muttered, his eyes glimmering.

"Until you try to read it," Danni snorted. "It's written in brainteasing riddles."

"I love a good brainteaser," Ralph declared.

"You're welcome to look through it," Sarah offered. "We'll take any help we can get with interpretation."

As the discussion ensued, Sarah began to relax. She felt as if she had a team of professionals to help with her haunted life. Even better, she trusted them. If only she could share this special gift with her parents. But she knew better. Her mother would never accept her belief in ghosts more or less that she had a genetic ability to communicate with them in her dreams.

The conversation shifted to camera placement for the evening in conjunction with Sarah's location. Garrett insisted on staying wherever Sarah would be to which the team agreed.

Excitement sparked the air with electricity. Ralph continued peppering her with questions about the book and the extent of her skills.

"It's getting late and this is our last night to film," Garrett said. "We can talk about the dreamist stuff tomorrow."

Despite Valerie's reneging on the extension, the team seemed optimistic knowing about Sarah's ability to help them. Still, Sarah wondered if the doctor's ghost would be as powerful now that the Ouija board had been removed. Only sleep would tell.

Garrett and Sarah went to the guest room while Danni stayed with Ralph in the kitchen. Harry took the sitting room. Once the camera was set up in the guest room, Garrett hooked up the EVP microphone on Sarah's shirt.

"Are you ready?" he asked.

"I think so. Do you think the doctor will be weaker since the board is gone from the house?"

"Hard to say."

Sarah slouched. "If only Ola could get past that monster. I'd feel so much better if she were with me."

"It's a shame we can't strengthen her," he replied. "Wait a minute…." Garrett ran from the room.

Moments later, he returned with Ola's *Dreamist* book. "Take this," he said, handing it to Sarah.

"You want me to read it now?"

"Keep it with you. Maybe it will create a stronger connection between you two."

"Like a talisman?" Sarah asked.

"Exactly."

While Garrett fiddled with the camera, Sarah paged through the tome, imagining Ola reading the yellowed pages. Halfway through, a piece of paper tumbled from within.

"What's that?" Garrett asked, walking over to the bed where Sarah perched.

"A note," she said, unfurling the parchment as if it were the most delicate of butterfly wings and began reading.

Follow your heart right from the start,
 Don't make the error of succumbing to terror,
 They're only strong if you lead them along
 And ignore the ways of bygone days.

· · ·

"IT'S HANDWRITTEN. I guess Ola left this in the book," Sarah said, handing the paper to Garrett.

"It's definitely Grams' handwriting but I know there wasn't anything between the pages. I've read through the book several times since her death," Garrett said, his eyes meeting Sarah's.

"Are you suggesting Ola put it there recently?"

"If she wasn't able to help you in your dreams, maybe she found another way to communicate with you."

"That is cool and creepy at the same time," Sarah replied. "I'm not afraid of Ola but the idea of a ghost being able to cross the physical realm to leave a note takes this stuff to a whole new level of spooky."

"Count on Grams to find a way, even from the afterlife. She never was one to give up easily."

"At least we know the doctor hasn't been able to block her completely. This might be the gap we've been looking for to thwart the spirit's ability to control me."

"It also confirms what we've known all along that staying calm allows you to communicate better in your dreams." Garrett refolded the note. "At what point did you lose the ability to connect with her while dreaming?"

"Couple days ago. The same time the doctor started getting more aggressive which was supposedly when Valerie started using the Ouija board in the basement."

"Darn Valerie and her antics," he growled. "She could've gotten you killed. Now I understand why Grams was so adamant against the use of those things."

"The question remains, will the doctor still have power in my dreams tonight?" Sarah said.

Garrett squeezed her hand. We're about to find out but don't worry, between me and Dallas, we've got you covered."

Dallas let out a spirited *yap*! Sarah scratched the little dog's head as he sat beside her.

Ralph's voice crackled over the walkie-talkie. "You guys ready to get started?"

"It's a go," Garrett replied.

He turned out the lights as Sarah reclined on the bed slipping Ola's *Dreamist* book under the pillow.

"Good luck," he whispered, as the camera light glowed green.

Sarah smiled, comforted by his presence and the idea that perhaps the doctor's ability to harm her had been thwarted. She continued ruminating on staying calm and blocking the malevolent spirit as consciousness slid to the realm of the dreams.

CHAPTER 26

Sarah stood in the kitchen of Borden House. The tension congealed like blood clotting on an open wound. The calendar on the wall showed August of 1892. But what day? The morbid feel made her believe it was the day of the murders. The air was tinged with a coppery taste of blood and the scent of decay. The tomblike atmosphere made Sarah's heart pound as she walked through the house. Swallowing hard, she took a few deep breaths in an effort to slow her racing pulse, but to no avail. Despite the trepidation gripping her, she had to see this through or she'd never be free from the doctor's destructive spirit.

Voices echoed from the dining room. Sarah headed that way, her heart rate accelerating. *Stop it, you have to stay calm or he'll gain control.* Pausing outside the dining room door, she took in a deep breath, closed her eyes, and summoned Ola. She sighed when she opened her eyes and nothing appeared. Even though she couldn't see her, she felt oddly at ease, as if Ola's spirit were somewhere close by.

Leaning toward the door, Sarah peered through the opening

where the hinges connected it to the wall. Her breath caught when she saw Mr. Borden speaking with the doctor.

"We no longer require your services, Dr. Webster," Mr. Borden said.

Sarah exhaled. Finally, she had confirmation of the man's identity who'd been trying to kill her in her dreams.

"What do you mean you no longer need my services?" the doctor growled. "Your daughter is improving with my treatments."

"If you consider sleepwalking an improvement then I question your training," Mr. Borden replied.

"A mild side-effect, I assure you. Has she been taking the herbal compound I prescribed?"

"As far as I know. Still, I've not seen much change except she's more isolated. I fear her social interactions have waned. Lizzie has societal obligations and she's running out of time to find a good match. Your remedies appear to be impairing that aspect of her life and thus I have no choice but to dismiss you."

"What basis do you have for these accusations?" the doctor snapped.

"My own observations. I've spent entirely too much money on you already. Here is the remainder of the monies we agreed upon. You'll not get another penny from me, I assure you," Mr. Borden said, his tone resolute.

"As a medical professional I do not abandon patients who've only received partial treatment. It could be detrimental to her, and your family," he replied with a sneer.

"What are you inferring?" Mr. Borden demanded, nearly knocking his chair against the wall as he stood.

The doctor got to his feet, a wicked smile curling his lips.

"I'm not *inferring* anything, Mr. Borden. I am stating plainly that dismissing me prematurely will lead to unpleasant circumstances."

Mr. Borden slammed his fist onto the table making Sarah jump.

"Leave this house! And while you're at it, pack your snake oil trickery and leave town! I'm a man of good standing in this community. One word from me and no one will invest in any more of your schemes!"

"As you wish," he said with a slight bow. "But rest assured, you will regret it."

Dr. Webster placed his bowler hat upon his head, lifted his leather doctor's bag, and started to leave. Turning his gaze toward the space where Sarah hid, he paused. Her blood turned to ice as his blazing stare met hers. *Not rid of me yet*, he mouthed. With a wink, he left.

Sarah's heart raced with the speed of a gazelle fleeing its predator. He'd seen her hiding but hadn't tried to kill her. He obviously knew she was there so why not attack as he had in previous dreamscapes?

Sarah contemplated everything she'd heard in the conversation. They'd discussed Lizzie's sleepwalking. Was it truly a side-effect of the medication or had the doctor done something to cause it? And if so, what exactly had he done to control her like that? The clues were beginning to align, letting Sarah know the extent of this man's evil ways. Immersed in her thoughts, she didn't hear anyone approaching. The door swung closed revealing Sarah's hiding spot. She started to scream until she realized it was Lizzie and Bridget standing in front of her.

Grasping her chest, Sarah inhaled. Once her breathing steadied, she looked at the two women. "What do you want to tell me?"

"We know what he's done," Lizzie replied, her voice shaking as her eyes darted around the space.

"Tell me," Sarah said. "Maybe I can help you."

"He's too powerful," Bridget muttered, Irish highlighting her words. "Tis not safe for us or you. He means to do us harm if we don't follow his commands."

"Help me understand," Sarah said. "You're already dead. How can he hurt you?"

Tears crested in Lizzie's eyes. "Not all is as it seems."

"What does that mean?" Sarah was beginning to lose patience. The doctor could return at any moment and she needed to find out his secrets before he reappeared. "You need to speak to me plainly or I can't help you."

Bridget puffed out her chest and squared her shoulders. "Miss Lizzie did not harm her parents," she blurted.

Sarah sucked in a breath. Was she hearing this correctly? Lizzie Borden really was innocent.

"If it wasn't Lizzie then who did it?"

Lizzie shrugged her shoulders. "Not sure but I suspect *he* had something to do with it. What I didn't know at the time was that he was in control of me. Made me do things I'd never have done in a conscious state."

"What are you saying?" Sarah asked, shocked she was still able to speak considering her blood was pulsing through her veins like white water rapids.

"I stole items from my parents," Lizzie said. "I bought poison and did other horrible things."

"Weren't those your brownouts?" Sarah asked.

Lizzie shook her head. "These things occurred after he began hypnosis with me. He made me do it."

"Then why not implicate him when you were accused?" Sarah asked.

Lizzie and Bridget exchanged glances. Bridget gave a nod as if imploring Lizzie to reveal everything.

"He made it clear he'd end us if we spoke about his remedies or his threats to our family."

"You knew about the threats?"

Lizzie nodded. "I was standing where you are now and overheard the conversation between Dr. Webster and my father."

Sarah's mind buzzed with nervous energy. Dr. Webster may have murdered the Bordens. "Is there any evidence regarding his involvement with their deaths?"

"Not a thing," Lizzie whispered.

"Do you have any idea how he was able to kill your parents while you were both in the house?"

"I was washing the windows when Mrs. Borden was killed. Wasn't feelin' well after I finished the task and Lizzie offered me some of the tonic from the doctor. Said it helped her relax and I should try some." A tear trickled down Bridget's cheek. "I went to my room and dozed off. Slept like I never slept before."

"What about you?" Sarah asked Lizzie.

"I was in the barn when my stepmother was killed," she replied. "My stomach had been in knots since I'd heard Dr. Webster's threats. He'd never been cruel but something about him didn't settle well with me. I didn't want to share my suspicions with Father. I hadn't any proof of wrongdoing by the doctor, and Father wouldn't accept a woman's intuition as a reason to discontinue a treatment in which he'd invested heavily. I locked the door to my room, took some of the tonic to relieve my nervous stomach, and fell asleep."

"You're suggesting Dr. Webster had been giving you something that rendered you unconscious?"

"Yes."

"If you didn't trust him, why take the tonic?"

"It gave me such peace. I'd sleep for hours without any lingering effects. It was a most pleasant feeling."

"Were you having problems sleeping?" Sarah inquired.

"At times. As I said, the medication was for my episodes but once I discovered how relaxing it could be, I took it during periods of distress," Lizzie said, her eyes glancing at the floor. "I have no doubt the doctor is responsible for the death of my parents. I saw him in the street earlier in the morning, only it wasn't his scheduled day to visit. That's when —"

"Shhh!" Bridget hissed, holding her finger to her lips.

An icy chill rankled Sarah's frame. Something sinister lurked nearby, she could sense it. Shocked she'd been able to remain calm for so long and speak with Lizzie and Bridget openly, Sarah tried to settle her nerves. How she'd accomplished so much in this dream was a mystery she'd think about later. For now, she needed to get away before Dr. Webster was able to harm her. She scanned the space but saw nothing. When she turned back around, Lizzie and Bridget were gone. This wasn't a good sign.

"You think you've beaten me but I will prevail! The old woman can't hold me off forever," a voice grumbled as a dark form materialized before her.

Sarah looked for Ola but saw only the doctor. How was he still able to block her? The Ouija board had been destroyed and Ola's *Dreamist* book was under the pillow where she slept. At that moment, a hand gripped her shoulder. Squeezing her eyes shut, Sarah willed herself to remain calm while trying to take in a breath.

When she opened her eyes, fog misted around her feet as she traipsed along cobblestone streets. Moonbeams cut through the haze like a scalpel through flesh. Alleyways snaked between two- and three-story buildings in various stages of dilapidation. The stench of mildew and defecation stung Sarah's nose. She couldn't identify her location although something about it was familiar.

No one was about even though the shadows seemed to have souls and the fog crept across her flesh like a swarm of beetles. Sarah's heart seized as a cat scurried across the path into the murky darkness of night. Grasping her chest, she took a few deep breaths before regaining her composure. This was definitely not Fall River. Relief washed over her. If it wasn't Fall

River, then it was probably a regular dream, not something affiliated with her dreamist abilities which meant no evil doctor.

She continued along the gas lit street toward what appeared to be a wharf. Water sloshed against pilings and the silhouette of boats bobbed on the water. Wherever she was, it wasn't present day. The scene reminded her of a Charles Dickens novel. Perhaps Ola removed her from the doctor's presence and placed her in one of her favorite literary scenes. She half expected to see Mr. Peggotty emerge from a boat at the dock.

Her fear subsided as she meandered down a slender path toward the pier when a clammy hand wrapped around her neck and pulled her into an alley. Her heart thundered against her ribcage as her captor whispered in her ear.

"You can't escape me now," he growled, clutching her throat.

Terror choked back her words as Sarah struggled to calm her racing pulse. She recognized that voice. It was *him*.

"Why do you want to harm me?" she muttered, astounded she was able to speak in her current state of panic.

The foul stench of his breath brushed her cheek as he leaned closer.

"I know what you are! Your power is great but I will destroy it," he said, his words slithering from his lips like a snake through the grass.

Stall him, she thought. If she could get answers then perhaps, she could escape the dream and the evil clutching her.

"Where am I?"

"On my turf. You haven't a chance of escape here. No one to help you or wake you from the nightmare that awaits."

"You're powerless. This is only a dream. Your ability to cause harm is limited." A wave of courage flushed through her veins surprising her. Maybe she was progressing with her abilities.

"Don't underestimate me, my dominance is implacable once unleashed. I will not allow the likes of the weaker gender to sever my ties to the living. I've haunted for more than a century and won't stop," he said, a cackle punctuating his words. Except this time his laughter didn't pierce her skull with stabbing pains.

"You're a ghost, nothing more," she replied, more assuredly than she felt. "You can't destroy me."

"I can and I will. There's no one here to stop me," he snarled. "The realm of protection on which you rely is of no use here. Once the portal was opened it allowed me access to this dimension, and you."

He turned her around to face him. Glimmering eyes glowed in the darkness, cutting through to her soul.

"What portal?" she slurred, her consciousness beginning to fade.

"The board," he hissed.

"That's not possible," she muttered, her eyelids drooping beneath his stare. "It was removed from the house."

"Stupid girl! It will take more than the destruction of a parlor game to cage me now!"

Numbness ran from Sarah's fingertips to her shoulders and her legs began to buckle. His gaze was intoxicating. Something deep within screamed for her to look away but her eyes were glued to the shimmering orbs.

"Once you're dead," he taunted, "I'll keep you with me and use you like I do the others. This is the stuff of which nightmares are made." Laughter erupted from his thin dry lips as zombie-like figures emerged from the mist. Sarah's head lolled as she glimpsed several women in various stages of decomposition come into view. Yellowed teeth jutted from black lips as they chanted, *no escape now.*

Sarah's heartrate increased as her body began to sway. The doctor gripped her upper arms holding her upright as her head bobbed. Panic thrummed through her frame. *Wake up,* reverberated through her muddled mind. The sound of Garrett's voice rang out in the distance, yet she couldn't rouse herself from this state of mental paralysis. She was trapped in the dream with a maniacal killer and ghastly undead creatures with no obvious means of escape.

Her lungs felt heavy, as if an ocean was swirling through them. Something cold pressed against her throat followed by a warm sensation trickling down her neck.

This was it; she was actually going to die and there was nothing she could do to stop it. Murder by dreamscape. She seemed to be in a state of suspension, everything moving in slow motion. Apparently, removing the Ouija board didn't sever the doctor's ability to commit his heinous acts. The worst part was, no one would ever know what happened. Would they find her lifeless body and conclude it was heart failure? Would Garrett and Danni know the truth? Even so, they couldn't tell people she was murdered by a ghost. No one would believe it. Tears crested in her eyes but refused to fall. Is this what death felt like? She sensed her body lifting into a void when something strong grasped her arms and pulled her forward.

Sarah's eyes shot open, her heart beating at the speed of hummingbird wings. Garrett sat before her, his grip on her upper arms firm.

"Are you OK?" he whispered.

Looking around, Sarah tried to get her bearings as Dallas licked her quivering hand. "Am I really awake?"

"Yes," Garrett said, pulling her to him.

She folded into his body, relieved to be out of the dreamscape.

"What happened?" he asked.

Sarah sat back, and swiped the tear trickling down her flushed cheek.

"It was different this time," she sniffled. "Lizzie and Bridget were able to communicate. Bridget confirmed that Lizzie didn't murder her parents."

"Did she say who did?"

"No, but Lizzie inferred it was Dr. Webster. Supposedly, the herbal remedy he prescribed knocked her out for brief periods. She gave some to Bridget the same day as the killings before taking some herself. Neither of them were in the house for Mrs. Borden's murder and they were unconscious during Mr. Borden's death. It explains why they didn't hear anything."

"And you were able to confirm the mystery man is actually Dr. Webster?"

Sarah nodded.

"What else?" he asked, excitement dripping from his words.

"He wasn't as powerful at first but then the dream shifted and I was somewhere else."

"Where?"

"It looked like England. I thought maybe Ola took me there as a safe haven to escape the doctor. I had brief episodes of calm. Even though I couldn't see Ola, it felt as if she was close by. Nevertheless, the doctor showed up along with zombie-like creatures."

"Zombies? That's a new one."

"Somehow the doctor seemed to regain his strength because he was able to subdue me again. His stare was intoxicating and rendered me in a strange state of paralysis. I thought I was actually dying." A sob escaped her lips as she leaned her head against Garrett's shoulder.

Wrapping his arms around her, he continued his questioning. "Do you think it was hypnosis? Wasn't that what he was doing with Lizzie in addition to the herbal tincture?"

Sarah sat back and nodded. "Hadn't thought about that. I remember his eyes glowing in some of my other dreams which seemed to prevent me from fighting back." Sarah cuddled Dallas, kissing his head. "Were you able to capture anything on tape?"

"Actually, yes. I saw the dark mist in the same corner where Abby Borden's body was found."

"Do you think it was her or the doctor?"

Garrett shrugged. "Won't know until we play it back. If it's too grainy we'll let Walter have a crack at it."

"Do I need to go back to sleep?" Sarah muttered.

Garrett leaned over and kissed her. "Only if you want to. I think we've got enough info to supplement what we've filmed."

Leaning her forehead against his, she smiled. "Thank you."

Sarah sat next to Garrett until Ralph's voice came over the radio suggesting they call it a night. Relieved it was over, Sarah was still concerned the doctor's spirit would continue to torment her. She'd not been able to sever the tie with him which meant things weren't finished for her yet.

Everyone gathered in the kitchen to discuss the evening's progress. Ralph was grinning like a child who just saw Santa Claus.

Once the group was seated, Ralph clapped his hands together.

"It's been a hugely successful night," he announced.

"How so?" Harry asked with a yawn.

Ralph turned one of the monitors around and hit replay. The grainy images from the guest room camera flashed across the screen. The dark mist vacillated from the corner where Abby Borden's body had been discovered to the bed where it hovered over Sarah. Then, it moved from side to side as if it couldn't make contact with her slumbering form. The book, she thought. He couldn't get close because of Ola's *Dreamist* book. Yet he'd still been able to intervene and transport Sarah elsewhere. It was all so confusing.

"It's the dark figure!" Harry declared, his sleepy demeanor awakening.

"It's Dr. Webster. I got confirmation in my dream tonight," Sarah said.

"This is incredible," Ralph exclaimed. "It's like having close captioning but for the dead."

"The problem is, you can't tell anyone how you know this," Sarah said, apologetically. "My gift can't be exposed."

"Not a problem," he replied. "We'll find a way to use the information without divulging your role."

Sarah gave a half-smile. She knew the men would keep her secret no matter what happened.

"Were you able to record anything with the EVP?" Sarah asked.

"Actually, that's the best part," Ralph said with an artful look. He tapped a few more keys until the sound of static filled the air.

Sarah's skin prickled when the words, "You can't escape me now," echoed from the computer.

Gulping down the fear rising in her throat, Sarah started fidgeting with her hands. She could still feel his icy breath on her cheek and the nauseating stench of decay as he spoke the words.

"You know who said it?" Harry asked Sarah.

She nodded. "The doctor said it after he transported me to a different location."

"I don't understand," Harry said. "Where did he transport you?"

Sarah shared the gory account starting with Mr. Borden and Dr. Webster's argument, the discussion with Lizzie and Bridget, and then finding herself in an unfamiliar place that resembled the setting of a Dickens' novel.

"Astounding," Ralph said, drawing the word out.

Sarah exhaled. While she appreciated Ralph's enthusiasm, it was difficult to see her situation as anything besides horrifying.

"The worst part were the zombies."

"Zombies?" Harry screeched. "There's no such thing as zombies."

"Apparently, you've never been to night court," Danni chortled.

Ralph furrowed his brows. "I realize believing in ghosts is a stretch for some, but zombies?"

"I don't know that they were zombies in the sense of what you see on TV," Sarah explained. "They looked like the walking dead with decomposing flesh and slash marks all over their bodies. Granted, it was dark and hard to see."

Danni shuddered. "Eww."

"What do we do now?" Sarah asked with a yawn.

"We send the videos to Walter and let him work his magic," Ralph said. "And then we turn in. We've done all we can for now."

Garrett grasped Sarah's shoulder as she stood in a stretch. "Your room or mine?" he asked.

"Yours," she replied.

Once the equipment was put away and the lights turned off, everyone retired to their quarters. Sarah grabbed her night-clothes and changed in the private bath in Garrett's room. He was already in bed with Dallas sitting at his side.

"Dallas has been waiting patiently for you," he smiled.

As soon as Sarah sidled beneath the covers, Dallas curled in a ball between them.

"Looks like my dog wins again," Garrett chuckled. "I don't even get to snuggle with you."

"I can move him," Sarah said.

"Not likely," Garrett replied. "Once he makes up his mind where he wants to sleep, that's it. I've woken up with muscle cramps because he settled where he wanted and wouldn't move during the night. My sleep patterns are often akin to a contortionist."

Sarah laughed as she leaned over to kiss him. Right before her lips met Garrett's, Dallas's snout nudged between them, his tongue licking her nose.

"Not even a goodnight kiss?" Garrett said to his dog.

Dallas shook his head, flapping his ears like a bongo.

Sarah leaned up on one elbow and across the little dog, planting a kiss on Garrett's lips.

"Goodnight," she said.

"G'night," he yawned.

Sarah felt a sense of comfort with Garrett and Dallas at her side. A few deep breaths later, she drifted off to a dreamland of horrors.

$\mathcal{A}$ sweltering breeze rustled through the trees behind Borden House. Sweat glistened across Sarah's forehead and trickled down her back. Obviously, it was summer in Fall River. Roses bloomed, perfuming the air as birds darted about in song. Clouds gathered overhead, shielding the sun and cooling the temperature. A foul odor chased away the fragrant scent of roses and the birds went silent. A shiver replaced the sweat, chilling Sarah to the bone as an eerie sensation rankled her nerves. Something sinister lurked, she could feel it.

She took in a deep breath and scanned the yard for whatever awaited. Nothing.

"I know you're here!" she hollered. "Whatever you think you can do, come on and do it!"

Her boldness was driven by the knowledge that Garrett was close by. Thunder rumbled, shaking the ground. She started to walk toward the house when something wrapped around her ankle sending her plummeting to the ground. Her head smacked against the dirt, a display of stars sprawling across her line of sight. Looking toward her foot, she saw a vine winding around her ankle, inching up her leg. The doctor's wicked laugh harmonized with the thunder booming overhead.

Sarah tugged at the vine snaking toward her thigh as Dr. Webster approached. His eyes glowed and his gaunt face stared down at her.

"I told you I'm the stuff of which nightmares are made!" he laughed. "I may not be able to harm you with my hands, but I can certainly stop your heart from beating!"

Sarah hadn't contemplated being scared to death. The idea heightened her terror, her heart thrashing against her ribcage. Her breath came in short puffs as she waited for his next move. He kneeled at her side, his fetid breath and thin black lips close to her cheek.

"I will finish you," he grinned. "You've severed my connection to control you; however, that doesn't stop me from getting in your head. I know what terrifies you. Once you're frightened, I gain more power. Good luck calming yourself now!"

His knowledge of how she functioned as a dreamist was disturbing, especially since he was using it against her. What he didn't know was that Garrett and Dallas were close by. One sound and they'd wake her from this nocturnal torment.

"He can't help you either," he muttered in her ear.

Panic seized her chest. How did he know what she'd been thinking? Another vine inched up her other leg, holding her in place.

His skeletal hand scraped her cheek. "An early grave while still breathing won't be pleasant. Although I can no longer hypnotize you, your terror allows me control over the situation. There's little you can do."

Sarah felt blood trickling down her cheek as his nails dug into her skin. Vines scrambled up her torso to her neck where they wrapped around her throat and squeezed ever so slowly. Shaking her head, she struggled to shift her weight away from the suffocating tendrils but to no avail. She tried to speak but the words wouldn't come.

A decaying hand popped from the earth in front of her followed by another beside it sending her heart racing. Several more, each in various stages of rot, sprouted from the soil. Like a field of deathly flowers, the hands grew from the dirt, revealing forearms, heads, and shoulders until the corpses were completely out of the ground. Their faces were scraps of flesh with black veins bulging beneath their gray skin as they started crawling toward her.

It was like watching a horror movie except this was real. Sarah struggled to breathe as the vine crushed her trachea and fear squeezed her lungs. These are only ghosts, she told herself, they can't hurt you. Stay calm or he wins.

Lightning sliced through the clouds, illuminating the gruesome creatures as their putrefying bodies moved closer, the stench of the grave suffocating what little breath Sarah was able to draw in.

"No," she managed to croak. "I'm a dreamist and can help you move on. I'm not the enemy."

"Ha!" the doctor hollered. "These are creatures of my design. You have no power over them, try as you may." He moved away. "Only I can stop them!" Another flash of lightning shot across the sky, reflecting in his glowing eyes. "Terror is an excruciating way to die. Will you suffocate from being pulled beneath the earth or will your heart give out from the torture these ladies will inflict?"

Sarah struggled to breathe. Maybe this was part of his plan. Lying to her about her ability to escape and playing on her fears. Nevertheless, she had to find a way to escape.

"You don't have to do this," she choked as the tendrils tightened around her neck and the earth below her began to shift. "I really can save you."

The corpse closest to her, cocked her head, her glassy gaze

fixed on Sarah. Something had happened. With every shred of strength Sarah had left she forced the words from her mouth.

"Please, let me help you."

The creatures halted, their cloudy white eyes staring at her. One of them moved closer, a bony finger with a razor-sharp nail reaching for Sarah's throat.

This is it, she thought, I'm actually going to die. Her heart beat with the force of a freight train barreling down a mountain. Closing her eyes, she thought of Ola. If only she could help. An icy fingernail scraped Sarah's neck, cutting through the vine releasing the tendril from her throat. Sarah coughed as air filled her lungs.

"You will not disobey me!" the doctor squalled as the corpses rose to their feet. "I destroyed you in life, I can do so in the afterlife!"

Instead of stopping, the undead women shuffled toward him. With each of their steps, the vines restraining Sarah's body receded. Scrambling to her knees, she turned to see the women circling the doctor.

"You cannot harm me, wenches! I will enact revenge!" he blustered, his eyes glowing. When they didn't relent, he pulled the scalpel from his cloak and began slashing at their moldering bodies. Still, they pushed forward. "This is not the end," he screeched as his form swirled into a dark mist and dissipated.

Sarah struggled to her feet, her legs trembling when an image appeared near the group of women. Ola.

"You're here!" Sarah breathed, relieved to see her bene-factress.

"By way of your ingenuity," she smiled. "How did you know that appealing to his victims would break his hold on them?"

"I don't understand," Sarah said, her voice scratchy and her lungs tight.

"When you offered to help, it resonated with them. Their humanity took hold, allowing them to push the doctor away."

"Didn't realize that's what I was doing."

Glancing at the women, Sarah watched as their decaying faces and lifeless eyes morphed into their original state while tattered frocks clung to their restored bodies.

"You can move on now," Ola said to the women, a smile creasing her eyes.

The veil of torment faded from their expressions as if they'd been freed from some sort of terrible nightmare. A tear trickled down the cheek of the one who'd cut the vine clinging to Sarah's throat. With a nod, the woman mouthed the words *thank you* before vacillating and fading with the others until only Ola and Sarah remained.

"What about Lizzie and Bridget?" Sarah queried.

"You know the truth. They too can rest."

"I still don't understand how you were able to get here," Sarah said.

"Once the Ouija board was removed, it severed the doctor's potential to not only control the situation but siphon power from our dreamist abilities."

"Then why weren't you in my dream earlier tonight?"

"Because it took some time to regain my strength," she replied. "Thank goodness my grandson was there to help."

"He's been very supportive."

Ola chuckled. "My dear, he's done more than that. Although he's not a dreamist, he has my blood running through his veins. That's why he was able to pull you away from the doctor. When he touched you, it made a connection between me and you."

"Are you saying he's like a conduit?" Sarah asked.

"In a sense, yes. Let him know when he connects with you, he forms a link between us which can strengthen your ability when in a dream state."

"I'll let him know," Sarah replied.

"Tell him I love him and I'm proud of him. I knew this would be the perfect match," she said as her image faded from view.

Dallas nudged Sarah from the dream. Sitting up, she rubbed her eyes and glanced around the room. Garrett was sound asleep and daylight peeked through the edge of the curtains. Although pleased she'd been able to reconnect with Ola and help the doctor's victims move on, there was a lingering ache over not being able to confirm whether he actually killed the Bordens. And who were the women from her dream? Were they victims of his poor medical practices or did he kill them outright? It seemed that information would stay buried. Garrett stirred, and rolled over on his side.

"Mornin,'" he mumbled.

"Good morning," Sarah responded, leaning over to kiss him.

"Any interesting dreams?" he asked.

"You have no idea," she replied. "Should we wait until we're all together to share?"

Garrett nodded as he sat up and ran a hand through his hair. "Yeah. Let me hop in the shower and then we'll go downstairs. Did you get any answers?"

"Yup, although they may not be the ones we were hoping for."

Thirty minutes later, the group gathered around the dining room table, bleary-eyed but enthusiastic as they chattered about their prospects with the network. Mrs. Pearson entered the room, placing plates of pancakes, eggs, and bacon on the table.

"Valerie called last night and told me you'd be heading out later today. I've enjoyed having you here and hope things work out with your ghost hunting endeavors."

For a moment, no one spoke. The official announcement that Valerie had halted further filming seemed to suffocate the group's fervor like a wet blanket on a hot summer day.

"Thank you, Mrs. Pearson," Garrett said. "We appreciate all you've done for us while we were here."

With a smile she went back to the kitchen, leaving the team shrouded in silence.

"We're going to do well," Harry said. "We don't need any extra time. The footage we've caught in addition to the information gleaned from the research will win the confidence of the network execs. Valerie isn't the only deciding factor in this."

"Agreed," Garrett replied.

Ralph stared at his plate. "I can't believe Valerie could be so spiteful."

"For goodness sakes," Danni declared. "The woman is a vindictive floozy. I don't mean to hurt your feelings, Ralph, but she's not worth the heartache."

Ralph looked at his colleagues, his shoulders slumped. "I know you're right but I'm a sucker for a pretty face."

"Don't you mean a fake face?" Danni added.

"It was only a mild infatuation. I'll get over it soon enough," Ralph replied, taking a forkful of eggs, apparently trying to convince himself.

Everyone followed suit, eating breakfast in silence. When the dishes were cleared and coffee mugs refilled, they started discussing Sarah's dreams from the previous night.

"It's probably the most terrifying experience I've had yet," Sarah said, taking a sip of her tea. "Before I start, I was wondering how you're going to use this information without exposing my secret?"

"I've already sent the footage to Walter," Ralph said. "If we can find documentation to support what you learned in your dreams, then we can put it together with whatever he finds on the videos. At least we'll have a lead on what to research."

"Guess this makes you an official part of our team," Harry declared. "Now we can call ourselves the Dream Team."

A round of laughter erupted. Sarah started to share the details of her dreams when Garrett's phone rang. Looking at the screen, his smile faded.

"It's Valerie," he sighed. "Hello."

Everyone watched as Garrett held the phone to his ear,

saying nothing for several minutes while Valerie apparently carried on.

"I'm sorry, but that's not acceptable...yes, I know it's a team decision...they're here if you want me to put you on speaker."

Garrett pressed the button and set the phone on the table. "Go ahead."

"First I want to congratulate this group on their hard work," she spouted. "Once I get the video from last night, I'll share it with the network. However, I'm prepared to recommend the contract regardless of last night's footage. You guys are passionate about what you do and I feel strongly it will make for a successful show."

"Thanks," Harry replied, high-fiving Ralph. The two men beamed like a couple of football fans whose team just won the Superbowl.

"Here's my proposal. Garrett and I will cohost the show. Ralph and Harry will handle the behind-the-scenes film editing and technical stuff."

Silence.

"Hello? Can you hear me?" Valerie asked.

"We heard you," Harry replied. "We've always worked together, equally."

"You'll have to trust my expertise in television. Garrett and I will make a great duo on screen while you use your skills behind the cameras. With our outgoing personalities and your talents, the show will be a hit."

The men exchanged glances.

"What do you want to do, guys?" Garrett asked in a hushed tone. "I already declined but I'll go along with whatever you decide."

"I'm with you, Dunc," Harry said.

Ralph nodded in agreement.

"Thanks for the offer, Valerie, but we've decided against it.

We've always worked as a team and prefer to keep it that way," Garrett answered.

"You're making a huge mistake," Valerie retorted. "Garrett and I can make you stars. This is not the time to allow egos to influence your decisions!"

Sarah looked at Danni who was biting her lip obviously trying to prevent a snide remark from escaping.

"You have our decision. Do you still want us to send the footage over?" Garrett asked.

"Yes," she snapped. "This was a contest and the other executives will need to see this through."

"We'll have them to you by noon, per your request from yesterday."

The phone went dead.

"Sorry about that," Garrett said, sliding his phone back in his pocket.

"Whatever we filmed belongs to us. We'll pitch it to other networks. Worst case scenario, we put it up on YouTube," Harry replied.

"We came so close," Ralph said, slumping in his chair. "This really stinks,"

No one said a word until Harry came back with a positive spin. "We may have lost the contract but we gained a dreamist."

"I suppose that's a good way to look at it," Ralph said. Taking a sip of his coffee, he looked at Sarah. "Why don't you finish telling us about your dreams."

Sarah resumed her story about the living vine traveling up her body, to the undead women, the doctor's threats, and Ola's surprise appearance at the end. She didn't tell them about her discussion with Ola, that was something she'd share with Garrett in private.

"That is incredible," Harry said, shaking his head. "I can't imagine being attacked by a vine with walking corpses coming for me."

"The doctor said he was using my fears to scare me to death, literally."

"You mentioned he had a British accent?" Ralph asked, furrowing his brows.

"Uh huh."

"And one of your dreams was set in England?"

"Looked like it."

"How many women?" Ralph queried.

Sarah thought for a moment. "Five."

"Where are you going with this?" Danni asked.

"I have a theory, but we need to discuss it with Walter," Ralph said, his expression serious.

"We can't tell him about my abilities," Sarah pleaded.

"Walter is the poster child for discretion. I promise he won't tell a soul. Since we're the only ones he talks to, your secret is safe. Trust me. We need his expertise on this one."

Sarah exhaled. She was already uncomfortable having shared her dreamist abilities with so many people. Now they wanted to include Walter?

She glanced at Garrett who gave her a nod. "Walter can be trusted."

"Alright," she replied.

Ralph phoned Walter and put it on speaker.

"Yeah," a gruff voice answered.

"Hey, Walter, I've got you on speaker phone," Ralph said.

"Why?"

"Because Sarah is here and has something she needs to tell you. The information is related to the footage we sent."

"Go on," Walter prompted.

"What I'm about to say is confidential," she said. Her heart palpitated as she explained her special skillset to Walter and asked that he not reveal it to anyone.

"Certainly didn't see that coming," Walter declared. "This officially surpasses the zombies interbreeding with vampires' conspiracy in unbelievability. To answer your question, I'll not tell another living soul."

Sarah released the breath she didn't realize she was holding, relieved at Walter's willingness to keep her secret. She went on to disclose everything that had happened in her dreams the previous night. Walter followed up with several questions about previous dreamscapes.

"Interesting," he mused when she'd finished. "Ralph, I assume you called me in on this because of my expertise on the topic?"

"Yup."

"What are you an expert in?" Sarah asked.

"Jack the Ripper."

Silence blanketed the room.

"Are you saying Jack the Ripper came all the way to Fall River to murder the Bordens?" Danni blurted. "That's the most preposterous thing I've ever heard. By the way, I unearthed the doctor's name a couple days ago which means I won the bet."

"Care to hear my argument before declaring victory, Miss Cook?" Walter said sarcastically.

"Please, enlighten me," she replied with a roll of her eyes.

"I've been researching Jack the Ripper since childhood," he began.

"Of course, you have," Danni quipped.

Sarah glared at Danni and put her finger to her lips.

"Jack the Ripper committed his crimes between August and November of 1888. The only thing the police could ascertain was that he was most likely a doctor with surgical skills. Then he disappeared. Theorists have speculated the reason Jack was never found in England was because he left the country. Some suggested he came to America. I found a couple of doctors listed on a steamer from England to Massachusetts in 1888.

"That's a far cry from ending up in Fall River nearly four years later and butchering two people," Danni added.

"Are you always this impatient, Miss Cook? Or are you upset because I'm going to win this wager?"

Danni slumped back in her chair with her arms crossed.

"Evidence of another serial killer in Chicago arose when two women went missing in 1893. It was believed Dr. Holmes, as he was then known, murdered the two women along with several others over the years, some in the same fashion as Jack the Ripper."

Goosebumps skittered across Sarah's arms.

"In recent years, a handwriting analysis was conducted showing Jack the Ripper and Dr. Holmes were one in the same."

Sarah swallowed hard. This was almost too much to process. Was it possible Jack the Ripper was the one who'd stalked her dreams?

"Still doesn't prove he had any connection to the Bordens," Danni said.

"The Bordens were massacred in August of 1892. With the hypnotic skills revealed in Sarah's dreams it would make sense he was able to disable his victims by placing them in a catatonic state in order to commit his heinous acts. Furthermore, Sarah said the doctor was a sinister man who'd apparently made use of his skills to dupe people out of their money. Mr. Borden discovered this fraud and not only stopped payments but threatened to expose him. Even Lizzie and Bridget pointed the finger at him. Apparently, his tincture rendered Lizzie and Bridget in a deep state of sleep while he murdered Mr. and Mrs. Borden."

"It would explain the lack of physical evidence on Lizzie and why she and Bridget didn't hear anything," Sarah said.

Walter continued. "The description of the injuries of the five undead women in your dreams correlates with the wounds made by the Ripper. Dr. Holmes used many techniques to kill his victims. His fraudulent activity was also a prominent aspect of his crimes. If you consider the possibility that Jack the

Ripper and Dr. Holmes were the same person, then killing the Bordens with an ax wouldn't be inconsistent with his repertoire."

"Hatchet," Danni called out.

"Excuse me?"

"They were killed with a hatchet, not an ax."

Sarah closed her eyes and shook her head. Danni was not going to let Walter off easily.

"So, you're saying the sinister spirit in my dreams who tried to butcher me, scare me to death, and caused me to sleepwalk is the ghost of Jack the Ripper who was possibly the same man as Dr. Holmes?" Sarah asked, not sure she really wanted to know the answer.

"That is what I'm proposing," he said. "Didn't you say he stabbed and sliced your sternum in one of the dreams?"

Sarah shuddered at the memory. "Yes," she whispered.

"I rest my case."

"But he killed the Borden's with a hatchet, he didn't slice them open," Danni retorted. "And his name was Dr. Howard Webster which I discovered and Sarah confirmed."

An audible sigh came from the phone. "Obviously, the doctor didn't want to be linked to his previous crimes and changed tactics. Besides, if he was trying to frame Lizzie for the murders, he'd have to use a different method. No one would've believed she could perform medical type procedures; however, a hatchet would have been something readily available. Even in Chicago, there was no correlation until a woman was found in the same condition as the Ripper's victims. That's when speculation began." Walter paused. "Regarding his name, Dr. Holmes was believed to be Herman Webster Mudgett using the aliases Dr. Henry Howard Holmes or the more commonly known Dr. H.H. Holmes. One doesn't need a law degree to make the connection."

Sarah mulled over everything Walter had shared while

Danni scowled. Now that she thought about it, his theory wasn't implausible. However, it was a far stretch for the imagination.

"What now?" Sarah asked. "Even if this could be proven, we can't share the source of the information."

"Then you'll have to settle for being content with the knowledge and not the glory of revealing the truth to the world," Walter said.

Sarah rubbed her forehead when a chill rankled her body. Cautiously, she glanced toward the doorway leading to the hallway. Lizzie's shimmering image hovered, a smile crossing her face as she gave Sarah an approving nod. My gosh, she thought. Was Walter's theory actually correct? Some things were truly more bizarre than fiction. Sarah returned the smile as Lizzie dissipated.

Now that the century old mystery had been revealed to this group, Sarah wondered if Lizzie would continue to haunt the house. Then again, the haunting was most likely the doctor's spirit wreaking havoc on guests and those who'd inhabited Borden House over the years. Hopefully, Sarah's discovery would put a stop to his menacing escapades.

For the first time since arriving in Fall River, a sense of calm washed over Sarah. She did it. Glancing around the table, she grinned, her heart full. She'd made it through one of the most horrifying hauntings of her life with the wonderful group sitting with her at the table. While she hoped never to experience anything as gruesome again, she was comforted knowing she had intelligent and knowledgeable people to help her through it.

"I need to get back to work if you want this stuff by noon," Walter announced. "Miss Cook, I believe this constitutes my winning the bet. I'll take a bottle of Eagle Rare 10-Year-Old Bourbon."

Danni sulked. "Fine," she mumbled.

"Talk to you soon," Ralph said.

A round of 'thanks' echoed through the room before Ralph hit the red button on his phone.

"We should start packing up the equipment," Garrett said, standing.

"What about the stuff that belongs to the network?" Harry asked.

Garrett gave a sly grin. "I'll text Valerie and let her know she can come by and pick it up."

Chuckles erupted as each person went to pack. Sarah followed Garrett up the back stairs to fill him in on the rest of her dream. Once in his room, Garrett wrapped his arms around her and smiled. "How are you feeling about all this?"

"Much better," she replied, punctuating it with a kiss.

Pulling her closer, he deepened the kiss, leaving her knees trembling. It felt good to be in his arms and past this haunting.

When she looked up, she could see the love radiating in his stare. "I have more to tell you," she grinned.

"Wasn't this morning's reveal enough?" he asked, walking across the room to get his suitcase. Sarah plopped onto his bed as he started packing.

"This is about Ola."

He stopped what he was doing and sat beside her. Eagerness radiated in his eyes.

"As you know, she made it into my last dream," Sarah said. "According to her, the doctor's power came from the presence of the Ouija board. While it opened me up to his control, it also allowed him to drain Ola's strength."

"Are you saying he siphoned her power to increase his?"

"That's the way I took it which explains why he was able to do as much as he did. He was getting access to us through the board while draining our strength," Sarah replied. "That's why she couldn't help me. She was too weak to get past his interference."

Garrett shook his head as she continued.

"She attributed my safety to your presence."

"How?" he asked.

"It seems you act as a conduit between your grandmother and me. She said although you aren't a dreamist, you do have it in your DNA which enables you to strengthen me when I'm in a dream state."

Running his hand through his hair, Garrett blew out a long breath. "Incredible," he muttered.

Sarah reached for his hand. "She went on to say that she loves you."

Tears crested in his eyes as his head dropped. Sarah pulled him close and whispered in his ear. "She also told me she knew we were the perfect match."

He leaned back, a twinkle reflecting from his stare. Touching Sarah's chin, he smiled. "Already knew that."

CHAPTER 28

Suitcases cluttered the entryway as the team gathered in the front parlor.

"Any word from the network yet?" Danni asked.

Garrett shook his head. "Doubt we'll get a positive response. Considering Valerie's influence and her disgruntled nature the last time we spoke, the odds of us landing a contract are slim."

"As I said earlier, we can always post our footage on YouTube and hope for an offer," Harry said.

"Like the *Ghost Hunting Guys* except legit," Ralph declared. "They posted a video of what was obviously a sheet being dangled outside the window of an abandoned house on YouTube and became an overnight sensation. A major network actually picked them up. Still can't believe people watch their stuff. It's so hokey."

"Sorry about all this," Sarah said. "Maybe you'll get another opportunity soon."

Ralph shifted on his feet. "Speaking of opportunities, I got a phone call from my friend, Joey, in Virginia about a ghost hunting opportunity. His wife's college campus is in ruins. Place closed a few years ago and the property isn't being maintained.

Alumni are hoping to raise awareness to the plight of the campus in an effort to save the buildings. According, to Joey's wife, Laura, and her college buddies, Paula and Sid, the place is a haven for hauntings, specifically a ghost by the name of Vera. Joey thought we might want to stop on our way home and film there. He's hoping we can generate some interest to aid their endeavors. After all, ghosts sell."

"Sounds like a great opportunity," Harry replied.

"I'm in," Garrett said, looking at Sarah. "You and Danni want to join us?"

Arching her brows, Sarah looked at her friend.

"Why not," Danni shrugged. "I don't have any trial dates scheduled."

"Where is the campus located?" Garrett asked.

"Bristol," Ralph replied.

"It's not Virginia Intermont, is it?" Sarah queried.

"That's the place. You know it?"

"My mother graduated from there back in the 60s."

"Cool! I wonder if she knows anything about the ghosts," Ralph said, excitement glimmering in his eyes.

"Doubtful. She's not exactly a believer," Sarah huffed.

"Could you ask her?"

"I'll call her later. I need to catch her before she and Dad leave for the Mediterranean," Sarah replied. "Don't get your hopes up. As I said, she doesn't believe in ghosts so I doubt I'll get anything from her."

"Looks like we're heading to the haunted campus of the former Virginia Intermont College," Harry announced, clapping his hands together. "Let's get on the road."

Sarah smiled at Garrett. At least this would be an easy stop. The dorms had been empty for several years. The only ghosts residing there were probably those of failed tests and drunken escapades.

Dallas and the guys got into Garrett's truck as Danni and

Sarah slipped into the Mercedes. The truck pulled out first with Danni and Sarah following. As they drove down the drive, Sarah closed her eyes, thankful to be leaving Borden House. There was nothing she'd miss about this place except Mrs. Pearson having a pot of tea waiting for her in the mornings. Sarah was eager to get on the highway toward Virginia and onto milder hauntings. Unbeknownst to her, a dark mist swirled behind the car before dissipating into the cold October air.

A shiver rattled Sarah's body catching Danni's attention.

"You, OK?" Danni asked. "I can turn up the heat if you're cold."

"I'm good. Probably just a goodbye shiver from the ghosts in this place," she said, taking in a deep breath.

Sarah's phone rang giving her a start. "It's my mom. What are the odds she'd call after we were just talking about her?" she said, pressing the green button. "Hey Mom."

"Are you on your way home?" she asked, her voice chipper.

"Actually, we're making a stop on the way back to a place you'll remember well."

"Where's that?"

"Virginia Intermont," Sarah replied, bracing for her mother's response. She'd want to know why they were going and probably wouldn't react well when she learned it was to search for ghosts.

"Why? The school closed years ago."

"The guys wanted to do a little ghost hunting," she replied.

"Are they looking for Vera?"

Sarah sucked in a breath. Her mother actually called a spirit by name? The same woman who dismissed any notion of spectral activity and considered it nonsensical?

"You know about the ghost?" Sarah asked.

"Everyone knew about Vera. The story was legendary."

"I'm surprised you never mentioned it," Sarah said, still

stunned she was having this conversation with her non-believing mother.

"No need to mention things that don't exist," her mom responded curtly. "How did the group learn about this?"

Sarah filled her in on the alumni's efforts to salvage the campus before it was damaged beyond repair.

"It sounds like a noble endeavor. If Vera's ghost can help save the campus, I suppose it's a good thing."

Her mom's cheerful tone had returned. For the first time, and probably the only time in her life, Sarah had her mother's blessing to seek out the otherworldly.

"Do you have any stories to share?" Sarah asked.

"Not right now," she replied. "I need to get to town for a meeting with the historical foundation. Please be careful. Love you."

"Love you too, Mom."

Sarah hung up and looked at Danni.

"That sounded bizarre," Danni said. "I thought your mom didn't believe in the spirit world."

"Generally, she doesn't, yet she called the ghost by name. When I asked her to share any memories about it, she hurried off the phone. I got the feeling she didn't want to talk about it."

"Makes sense if she doesn't believe," Danni replied. "At least you won't have to deal with any haunted dreams since we'll be staying at a hotel."

"Let's hope," Sarah replied, resting her head against the seat. After the week in Fall River, she was certain nothing could ever be as terrifying as the doctor's ghost. Within minutes, she was floating through dreamland with visions of antiquated buildings on a college campus in Virginia with spirits of its own.

The Lizzie Borden case has fascinated people for generations. My interest was piqued after watching a documentary several years ago about Lizzie Borden's house and its gruesome history. The program shared a story I'd never heard before about a tragedy on the neighboring property. Forty plus years before the infamous murders of Andrew and Abby Borden, Eliza Darling Borden drowned two of her three children in the cistern in the basement before slitting her own throat. Postpartum depression was unheard of at that time but is the current theory applied to the crime. This story got my writer mind going. What if the land on which the houses sat was cursed? What if Lizzie was driven to kill her parents by some unseen evil force affiliated with the property? At that moment, I knew the Lizzie Borden house would be the setting for one of the books in the Dreamist series.

Once I started researching both crimes and realized they'd occurred forty years apart, I knew I'd have to take a different avenue to make the story work. Thus entered Jack the Ripper, another mysterious crime that has captivated the world for more than a century. With a little digging, I discovered the timelines for the Ripper's crimes and the murders of the Bordens lined up. Many people over the years believed the Ripper left England to evade capture and settled in the United States. I was also able to locate passenger logs for ships with doctors on board sailing from England to Massachusetts during this time.

Then I learned about Dr. Holmes, a serial killer in Chicago. One of his crimes mimicked the Ripper's leading some to speculate the Ripper had come to America and started a new crime spree. I took some artistic liberties with the timelines of Dr. Holmes's killing spree since some of his murders overlapped with the date of the Borden's deaths. This is the beauty of fiction; you can manipulate the facts to fit the storyline. A handwriting analysis had been done showing the Ripper and Dr. Holmes to be the same person. Whether true or not, it lends for imaginative storytelling.

Additionally, I studied the Borden house's layout, as well as garnering information about the mansion housing the Fall River Historical Society, Maplecroft (Lizzie's home after the trial), and Oak Grove Cemetery. The Fall River Historical Society is a wealth of knowledge regarding the town and Lizzie Borden. Historic elements of Lizzie's life, health, and trial were obtained from books and websites. After reading *A Private Disgrace; Lizzie Borden by Daylight* by Victoria Lincoln, I was even more conflicted regarding Lizzie's guilt or innocence.

Information about Jack the Ripper and Dr. Holmes was found through online research. Many of the phrases used by Dr. Webster's ghost in this book were taken from actual letters the Ripper wrote to police. Some of the quotes included:

Excerpt from letter dated September 17, 1888 from Jack the Ripper to police.

"I love my work."

Excerpt adapted from letter dated September 27, 1888 from Jack the Ripper to police.

"How can they catch me now?" (altered in the book to: "Catch me if you can.").

Excerpts from a letter dated October 6, 1888 from Jack the Ripper to police.

"I have you when you don't expect it." (altered in the book to: I'll get you when you don't expect it).

"I see your little game."

"I mean to finish you."

I chose the name, Dr. Webster for the traveling doctor and sinister ghost as an adaptation of Herman Webster Mudgett, otherwise known as Dr. Henry Howard Homes or Dr. H.H. Holmes, serial killer in Chicago in the late 19th century.

Generally, I followed the facts of the murder investigation and the trial for Lizzie Borden. However, I took some artistic liberties with Lizzie's health records and certain events on the day of the murders to make the story flow. Lizzie did suffer from brownouts where she was known to steal. I added the hypnosis portion with Dr. Webster to coincide with these brownouts. Lizzie also testified about being in the barn the day of the murders reportedly searching for lead sinkers for an upcoming fishing trip. While she hid jewelry in the basement in this story, it was actually pills that were found in the original investigation.

The records of the arrest and trial of Lizzie Borden are fascinating. Fall River Historical Society is a wealth of knowledge and should be a destination for all who visit Fall River whether searching for Lizzie Borden facts or local history.

We'll never know who Jack the Ripper was or who actually murdered Andrew and Abby Borden. No doubt, conspiracy theorists, writers, and the general public will continue to speculate about the identity of Jack the Ripper and Lizzie Borden's innocence for centuries to come. Until then, the imaginations of writers and storytellers will continue to speculate and weave tales about the horrifying events in London, England and Fall River, Massachusetts.

ACKNOWLEDGMENTS

To my husband, Darryl, thank you for your love, support, never-ending patience as I write these stories, and for listening to them! I love you!

To my mom, Karen Oates, thanks for reading, proofing, editing, and supporting my work! Love you!

To my writing coach, Charlotte Rains-Dixon, thank you for guiding and helping me be a better writer. You are the best coach ever!

To my cover designer, Rena Violet, thank you for creating the most amazing covers for my books! You are truly a gifted artist!

To my 'other mother', Millie Boyce, thanks for always being there and encouraging me! Love you!

To Mindy Lucas, thanks for helping me understand hashtags, teaching me to use Canva, and tolerating my impulsivity when learning new things on the computer! You are an amazing friend and instructor!

To the businesses who carry my books, Nevermore Books, Beaufort Bookstore, MacIntosh Books, The Lowcountry Store,

Grayco, Lowcountry Living Room, and Main Street Reads-thank you for your support!

To my friends and family who cheer me on, Joan Jones, Gina McNeill, Darlene Stokes, Lynn Bristow, Diane Morrison, Michelle Dufour, Mary Beth Klinar, Kay Keeler, Richard Norris, Jo and Ralph Beaver, Teresa Partin, Charlie Frost, Peggy Callahan, Janell McClure, Sarah Hetzler, Kelly Taylor, Bernie Ladd, Jonathon Haupt, and Janet McCauley -thank you for all that you do! Love you all!

To all my readers- I appreciate all of you and thank you for reading my books! Your kind words and continued support mean so much!

A special thanks to the Fall River Historic Society for their assistance with the research for this book!

Most importantly, thanks be to God! With Him all things are possible!

In Memorial:

Thanks to all those who supported me over the years but have gone on to Heaven. Harvey and Catherine Oates, Michael Wiegel, David Clark, Sam Poovey, Rachell Poovey Navratil, Mark Navratil, Tom Boyce, John Keith, Phyllis Sooy, Cathy Benson, and Becky Baldwin. Love you always!

ABOUT THE AUTHOR

Kim Poovey is a storyteller and author of historical fiction and hauntings. She has traveled the Southeast for more than 20 years presenting on 19th century fashion, mourning practices, and other Victorian era topics. Kim has also been a presenter for the OLLI program at USCB and a guest speaker for the past two years at Camp Conroy, a summer writing camp for kids sponsored by the Pat Conroy Literary Center in Beaufort, SC.

In 2011 she portrayed Mrs. Stanton, wife of Secretary of War Stanton (Kevin Kline), in the Robert Redford film, *The Conspirator*. Additional film projects include portraying the wife of a villainous husband in the Vook version of Jude Devereaux' novella *Promises,* the Fireball Run fundraising series 2012 *Southern Excursion* at Frampton Plantation, and the documentary Beyond the Oaks, Lowcountry Plantations.

Her published works include *Truer Words, Through Button Eyes: Memoirs of an Edwardian Teddy Bear* (out of print), *Dickens' Mice: The Tails Behind the Tale, The Haunting of Monroe Manse* (book 1 in the Dreamist series), *The Haunting of Edgefield Manor* (Book 2 in the Dreamist series), *The Haunting of Borden House* (book 3 in the Dreamist series), and *Shadows of the Moss* (first in the trilogy). Kim has also written for several magazines to include Beaufort Lifestyles, Bluffton Breeze, Citizen's Companion, and the Civil War Times.

Kim lives in a haunted 1890s Victorian cottage in the SC Lowcountry with her husband, Darryl, and their furry children.

ALSO BY KIM POOVEY

Truer Words

Through Button Eyes: Memoirs of an Edwardian Teddy Bear (out of print)

Dickens' Mice: The Tails Behind the Tale

<u>Dreamist series</u>

The Haunting of Monroe Manse

The Haunting of Edgefield Manor

The Haunting of Borden House

<u>Shadows trilogy</u>

Shadows of the Moss